MORTAL IMAGES

MORTAL IMAGES

Dennis P. O'Neill

Rev. date: 03/18/2016

To order additional copies of this book, contact:
Xlibris
1-888-795-4274
www.Xlibris.com
Orders@Xlibris.com
725938

To **Him** Who Inspires Us All:

Dominus illuminatio mea et salus mea, quem timebo?

Acknowledgments

I wish to express my appreciation to Sheila Kedski and her invaluable services in helping me with the editing and preparation of this novel.

The writing of this novel has been a truly inspirational experience for me. The support and encouragement that I received from my family during its creation greatly assisted me in this endeavor. My love for writing has grown stronger with each new novel.

For My Father and Mother

Raymond K. O'Neil Sr.
(1924–1991)

Irene T. O'Neil
(1928---2011)

PROLOGUE

The antique clock hanging decoratively on the wall of Helen's new office chimed twelve times before she finally looked over in its direction. It announced proudly to everyone around it that another day had ended and that a new one had just begun. She took off her thin-rimmed spectacles, and with her long fingers, she began to gently massage her tired eyes and the tense muscles of her beautiful face. The clock's unexpected interruption had made her now more keenly aware of how exhausted she really was. Whenever she found herself working on something very important, she seemed to lose all track of time and the people around her. She loved her research and all that it would mean someday to the whole world. At that particular moment, however, her body's fatigue was telling her that it was time to call it quits for another day.

Helen lazily shoved her research notes back into her briefcase and then securely locked it. She slipped into her gray pin-striped blazer and switched off the office's overhead lights. She carefully closed and locked the outer door of her private office on the mezzanine floor. Quietly, she turned and walked toward the building's main escalator. From the deafening silence that filled the building's lobby, she surmised that she was all alone in the new office tower. As she rode the escalator down to the lobby, her thoughts were still focused on her day's earlier workload. The Sanford Building was one of Boston's better classes of research office towers, and she was glad that she had decided to move all of her research operations into it a few months earlier. She proudly glanced around at the ostentatious lobby that spread out impressively in front of her. She noticed that Brad, the building's night security officer, wasn't sitting behind his desk in the lobby. She assumed that he was probably off making his rounds of the building's lower two floors, a tour he made once every hour each night.

The force of the high-caliber bullet sent Helen's body reeling sideways over the escalator railing and crashing down onto the hard marble floor located six feet below her. With her arms outstretched openly in front of her, she had managed to shield most of her head from striking hard against the unyielding surface of the floor. The searing pain and the shock of what had just happened to her sent her body's adrenaline level skyrocketing. She looked down at her throbbing left leg and saw a bloody wound of torn flesh and shattered bone protruding from her dress pants. The terrifying sight suddenly made her feel nauseous.

Lying motionless on the hard lobby floor, she struggled to overcome an overwhelming urge to lapse into unconsciousness. She focused her thoughts on her leg wound and soon managed to regain some control over her senses. After what felt like an eternity, she instinctively began to drag herself across the cold marble floor in an attempt to reach the relative safety of the building's elevators. From there, she knew that she could make her way down to the executive garage, which was located just below the main lobby. Thinking about how she had just been shot, her mind quickly concluded that the sniper would not be able to see what she was now attempting to do. Her will to survive and to flee from the area was growing stronger with each passing second, stronger than even the throbbing pain that was radiating outward from the massive wound on her left leg. Once inside the open elevator, she frantically tried to reach up for the elevator's garage button. She eventually managed to slide her bloody fingers across the thermal button, and the doors slowly closed behind her. With the closed doors protecting her, she once again felt safe. She quickly unfastened and pulled the thin belt from her dress slacks. Slowly, she began to tighten it around her upper leg in order to slow down the flow of blood, which was escaping from her open leg wound. Her actions seemed to cause the pain in her leg to worsen, but she soon observed that the flow of blood oozing from her massive wound had appeared to stop. A few seconds later, the elevator doors opened again but now onto the floor of the underground parking garage. A wave of terror once again seemed to envelop her.

With the aid of the elevator's interior railings, she painfully dragged herself up onto her uninjured right leg and peered out into the lighted garage. It appeared to be deserted. She could clearly see that her car and Brad's were the only two remaining vehicles still parked inside the garage. Utilizing the garage's outer wall for support, she slowly and painfully made her way across the garage to her car, which was parked about twenty feet from the elevators. She had to force herself to walk because every step was becoming increasingly more painful. Somehow, she managed to find the inner strength and willpower to drag herself over and up into her car.

Holding her keys in her trembling hands, she eventually managed to start the engine.

Driving her car soon proved to be no easier a task than had her walking been a few minutes earlier. Slowly, she drove her car over to the underground garage's rear exit where she carefully typed in her security access code onto the door's control pad. As soon as the outer security grid had opened up just high enough for her car's roof to clear, she recklessly accelerated her vehicle forward. It just managed to clear the moving grid. She then made a sharp right-hand turn out onto the main boulevard. Her mind kept trying to decide where she could safely go for medical treatment. She was unable to focus her mind clearly on where the nearest hospital was located in the city, and so she instinctively headed out of the city toward her mother's home. She carefully kept a watchful eye on her rearview mirror for any signs that she was being followed. Six months earlier, Dr. Mathews had inherited her mother's home in the suburbs after she had suddenly passed away. From there, Helen decided she would be able to contact the local police for medical help and protection.

She soon arrived at her mother's small home. She attempted to pull herself up and out of her car seat, but an intense wave of searing pain shot up from her leg. She moaned out loud in agony. As her tear-filled eyes glanced around her car's interior, she suddenly remembered that she had left her cellular phone in the car's glove compartment earlier that morning. Her trembling fingers fumbled with the small latch until it finally flipped open. Grasping the small phone in her blood-covered hands, she carefully dialed 911 for help. When the emergency operator finally came on the line, she shakily volunteered her present location to her. She then informed her that she had been shot and needed immediate medical assistance. Having now summoned help, she exhaustedly dropped the phone down onto the passenger seat beside her.

A set of bright headlights suddenly appeared in her rearview mirror. A sickening feeling of fear once again engulfed her as they slowly approached her location. She crouched down in her seat as the car slowly drove up alongside her vehicle, but it didn't stop. It continued slowly on its way down the deserted street.

Now realizing just how vulnerable she really was while she sat alone in her parked car, she decided to once again try to force herself out of her vehicle. She swung her body sideways out through the open car door and down onto the cold asphalt driveway. With her right leg partially clear, she pushed the rest of her body away from the car. Her injured left leg fell out of the car and down onto the pavement, making a hard thump. A second wave of excruciating pain rushed up from her wound to her brain. She fought hard to keep herself from fainting into unconsciousness. Slowly, she began to drag herself over to the base of the front porch's steps. She remembered how, as a young girl, she had playfully hidden from her friends under these same stairs when they were playing hide-and-seek together. Knowing that she would not be able to climb up the six steps to the front porch, she decided to hide herself under them once again until help arrived.

A faint smile formed on her lips when she observed that the small opening in the latticework that she had crawled through as a small child was still there. Her father had never gotten around to repairing it before he had died. The amount of blood that she had lost from her gunshot wound had now become quite serious, and she knew that she had to find a safe hiding place until help arrived. With each passing minute, the pain in her leg was becoming more and more unbearable. Helen carefully squeezed her bleeding body through the narrow opening. After a few minutes, she had managed to hide herself completely under the dark porch. Her left leg had once again started to bleed profusely. Her current efforts to reduce the flow of blood escaping from her burning wound were proving to be far less effective. Who had been waiting for her outside her office, and why had they tried to kill her? She kept asking herself. Her mind kept trying to figure out why anyone could possibly want her dead! Had she hurt someone in the past that she had forgotten about? Or did it have something to do with what she was currently working on? Her mind wandered back over the events of the last ten years of her life, but still, she couldn't remember having wronged anyone in such a way that they would now want to see her dead. *They must've made a mistake!* she thought to herself. *They were probably after someone else!* Over and over, in her mind, she tried in vain to convince herself of this fact. But then her thoughts moved on to the other obvious possibility: What if she was their intended target? They might've targeted her because of her current research. She tearfully convinced herself that it had to be the latter possibility.

She carefully moved her exhausted body up against the foundation wall for more support. Her injured left leg was slowly beginning to grow numb. With her left hand, she roughly tore off a piece of her soiled blouse and then firmly pressed the piece of cloth directly into her bleeding wound. Her fingers could feel several pieces of shattered bone protruding precariously from the open wound. She knew that she had to stop the bleeding if she wanted to live. The searing pain that resulted from her actions caused her to scream out loud in agony. In the still of the night air, the sounds of her agonizing screams resonated loudly out into the darkness of the deserted neighborhood.

Once again, she bravely forced her mind to overcome her body's pain. She knew all too well that her 911 phone call may've been overheard by her attackers. A few minutes later, her greatest fears turned into a reality when she saw a small van pulling up silently behind her car. From her vantage point under the stairs, she could clearly make out two men exiting the van. They both appeared to be holding a weapon and wearing masks. After they had looked inside her car, one of the men made his way over toward the rear of her house, while the other man quietly climbed the steps to her front door. She thought that she heard the sound of glass shattering somewhere around the back of her house. A few seconds later, she heard her front door being opened and the footsteps of the other stranger on her porch entering her house. She could hear their footsteps scurrying around the inside of her house as they looked for her. A few minutes later, she heard their footsteps descending the front steps again. The muffled sounds of their voices seemed to be coming from somewhere out near her car. She had to remain perfectly still under the porch so that they wouldn't be able to find her.

As she rested up against the cool foundation wall, she drifted off into unconsciousness. How long she was out, she didn't know. The sounds of the sirens that she heard in the distance made her feel safe. Just as she thought that everything was going to be okay, the latticework on the side of the front porch was suddenly torn away. One of the two men stuck his head in under the stairs. She found herself frozen in complete terror in the darkness, unable to even scream for help. He slowly pulled off his ski mask and looked directly into her eyes. His dimly lit face was only a couple of feet away from her.

"It's you!" she shrieked at him in disbelief.

"Yes, it's me! I told you what would happen to you if you continued with your research, but you wouldn't listen! Now you will pay the ultimate price!"

Gathering all her remaining strength, she let out a faint last-second cry. "Oh, John, what have I done to us?"

The force of the gun's bullet tore into the soft flesh of her neck, severing both her carotid artery and her windpipe. She reached up toward her neck, grasping at her now open throat. Choking in her own blood and pain, she could feel herself slowly dying. The gunmen continued to stare at her until her hands slowly fell away from her neck. The two men quietly walked back to their van and then slowly drove away from the scene. They had completed their sinister job all too well that night. The sound of their gun's powerful discharge was not heard in the quiet neighborhood because the assassin used a silencer to muffle the noise. The two men easily fled the area before the police and ambulances arrived . . .

CHAPTER 1

The first police cruiser arrived at the murder scene at approximately one thirty in the morning, and the two officers inside it were completely caught off guard when they came upon the body of the young woman sitting upright under the front porch. Officer John Winston ran back to his cruiser to inform their dispatcher that the area had now become a murder scene. While responding to the call, they had only been told by their radio dispatcher that a female shooting victim had called in for emergency medical assistance. The gravity of the crime was not lost on either of the two law enforcement officers as they immediately began to secure the crime scene area. During the course of their long careers as policemen, both officers had responded in the past to many murder scenes before. This murder scene, however, had a very disturbing effect on the two officers. It was a combination of how she had been fatally shot and where they had found her hiding that seemed to bother the two men the most. From what they had been able to quickly surmise, she appeared to have been a very beautiful young woman who had been savagely executed in cold blood by someone only minutes before they had arrived.

With their guns drawn, the two young officers carefully made their way over to the back of the darkened house. They were being particularly careful in their movements because they did not want to stumble upon or disturb any of the possible pieces of evidence that they might find in the dark. They knew all too well that their detectives would need all the help that they could get in order to solve this heinous crime. While they were near the back of the house, a couple of additional police cruisers arrived on location. Officer Hank Gallo kept a watchful eye on the back of the house, while his partner, John, ran back to the cruisers to get some of the other officers to secure the front and other side of the house. Sergeant William

Braxton walked up to Officer Winston and asked him to bring him up to date on what they had learned so far.

After getting some of the other police officers to back up his partner and to secure all of the sides of the house, he informed his sergeant about what they had discovered so far. The sergeant then immediately took charge of the crime scene and ordered his men to carefully enter and secure the interior of the house. He knew that it was very important for them to determine whether or not there were any other victims inside the house. He also had to make sure that whoever had just killed their young victim wasn't still hiding inside the house.

In the bright illumination of the cruisers' headlights, a blood trail could now be easily seen leading from their victim's car over toward the front porch. Once the interior of the house had been safely secured by the police officers, some of the patrolmen began to string out a yellow crime scene tape around the area to prevent all unauthorized persons from entering their crime scene. This would ensure that any evidence or clues in the area would not be disturbed. They strung the yellow tape out from the railing on the right side of the front porch over to their victim's alleged vehicle and then over to the fence bordering the left side of the driveway. Having now secured the entire crime scene area, everyone waited impatiently for the detectives and medical examiner to arrive. A small group of concerned neighbors began to gather across the street from the house. The sergeant ordered some of his men to move them all further back from their police lines.

Detectives Sean Murphy and Peter Savanovitch arrived at the crime scene with the other members of their investigative team about ten minutes later. The sergeant summarized to them everything that he had learned about the crime scene from his men and what he had ordered his men to do prior to the detectives' arrival on scene.

"Sergeant, I want a complete list of the names of everyone who has entered this house tonight. I also want a full report on my desk by tomorrow morning that summarizes everything about this investigation up until now," Detective Murphy said to the patrol sergeant. "We'll be taking over the rest of the investigation from now on. Please have some of your men remain here to help us secure the area until we're finished up here," he added with authority.

"Okay, Sean, it's all yours!"

The two detectives looked into their victim's alleged car through its open driver's side window and observed its blood-covered interior. They also observed a blood-covered cellular phone lying open on the passenger seat. It was an all-too-familiar scene that they had witnessed so many times in the past since becoming detectives on the force. The two men carefully wrote down notes on what they saw as they continued to inspect the car and the surrounding areas for evidence and clues.

"From what we can see, there appears to be a large amount of blood pooled inside the car. I would have to say that our victim must've been bleeding for quite some time from her wound(s)," Peter announced to his partner.

"It seems to appear that way. She was probably shot at some other location and then somehow managed to drive herself out to this location. She probably used the cell phone on the passenger seat to make her call to the emergency 911 operator for help. It appears to be covered with our victim's blood also."

"It looks as though she exited the car right here and then crawled over to the front of the house. I can see a definite blood trail on the asphalt and grass. By the looks of it, she was bleeding quite a lot out here also! She didn't even try to stand up," Peter concluded as he stood up from his squatting position over the illuminated blood trail.

"Let's continue to follow the blood trail over to our victim. If we're lucky, her assailant(s) may've left behind some clues for us," Sean said as he walked over toward the front porch.

Lying conspicuously on the ground and off to one side of the blood trail was a large section of wooden latticework. It appeared to have been pulled away from the left side of the front porch. The two detectives bent down next to the stairs and illuminated the area under the front porch with their bright flashlights. It was a truly gruesome site to behold as they focused their eyes onto the bloody body of the young woman.

"This looks really bad, Sean! She's still wearing a makeshift belt tourniquet around her upper left leg, which seems to support our earlier hypothesis that she had been shot at a different location earlier tonight. Somehow, she was able to drive herself out to this lonely location and to call for help. Whoever shot her earlier tonight must've followed her out here and then finished her off under here. From the obvious powder burns showing on her neck, she was shot at very close range. It appears as though she was executed! She must've been really terrified when the SOB found her hiding under the porch. He must've put his gun almost right up against her neck before he shot her. Sean, we have to really get this bastard!" Peter declared emotionally to his partner.

"I couldn't agree more! This guy is really a cold-blooded animal!"

A van carrying the rest of their team of special investigators pulled up alongside of one of the police barriers. They slowly exited the van and made their way over to where the two detectives were now standing. The team's leader checked in with them and tiredly announced that they were ready to begin processing the crime scene.

"What do you want us to do first?" Jefferson, the team's commander, asked the two detectives.

"I want you and your team to photograph everything around here very carefully. Gloves are to be worn by everyone inside our crime scene. I don't want to see anyone inside our crime scene who hasn't been specifically authorized by Peter or myself. Does everyone understand?"

"Perfectly!" they all answered back.

"Okay! Now I want photographs taken of the interior of the car, the blood trail, the torn-off piece of wooden latticework from the porch, the interior and exterior of the house, and the front and rear entrances of the house. When the ME's finished with our victim's body, I want a complete set of pictures taken of it from all angles under the porch! Fingerprint the car's exterior and then seal it and have it impounded. We'll process it later for evidence back at the station. Jefferson, make sure your people fingerprint the latticework very carefully. I believe our shooter pulled it off the porch in order to get to our victim. Also check out the front and rear doors for possible fingerprints . . . and don't forget the front railings! We'll discuss the interior of the house later. For now, just get everyone started! We have a lot of work to do out here tonight!"

"We're on it, boss!" Jefferson answered back as they all walked away.

The medical examiner arrived a few minutes later and carefully began his examination of their victim's body under the porch. He then officially pronounced her dead at the scene. He listed the preliminary cause of her death to be murder by a close-range gunshot wound to the neck. He informed the two detectives that the bullet had inflicted a massive amount of trauma to the bone and soft tissue of their victim's neck. He explained to them that their victim probably died rather quickly after being shot in the neck due to a massive loss of blood and suffocation. Before he allowed their victim's body to be taken away, he made sure that the entire area under the porch had been carefully photographed.

"Okay, boys! You can move the body now!" the medical examiner said to his men.

Peter and his team discovered two bloody fingerprints on the side of one of the porch's floor joists, which they surmised may've been left behind by their victim's killer. The investigators photographed their location on the porch and then tried to collect them from the scene. The wooden latticework also showed signs that their victim had probably squeezed through a small opening in the grid to hide under the porch. They collected blood and cloth fibers from the surface of the wooden latticework also.

The interior of the house contained numerous fingerprints. Most of them, however, they theorized were probably from their victim and other members of her family.

"Do we know for sure who she was?" Detective Savanovitch asked his partner after he had returned from questioning some of the neighbors in the crowd.

"I believe so. From a general description given to us by one of the next-door neighbors, I believe her name was Dr. Helen Mathews. She had just inherited this place from her mother who had died of natural causes about six months ago. The neighbors said that she stayed here now and then when she was in the area. They said that she was quite successful and worked in Boston at the Sanford Office Building. When we get back to the station, I'll put a call in to the Boston police to see if they know anything else about her."

It was almost 9:00 AM before the investigators finally finished processing the crime scene and sealed up the house.

In the city of Boston, another team of skilled detectives was carefully studying a blood trail inside the lobby of the Sanford Office Building. Detective Carol Bates carefully followed the blood trail from the escalator, up over the railing, and down onto the marble floor below. From there, she followed the trail of smeared blood across the lobby floor and into one of the garage's two elevators. From the elevator, the blood trail led her down into the parking garage and out about twenty feet into the parking area itself, where it then ended abruptly. Her partner, Detective Bolten, also discovered some bloody fingerprints on the keypad mechanism of the parking garage's outer door control.

After the two detectives had finished walking the entire crime scene area, they allowed their crime scene processors to take their photographs and to collect blood and fingerprint samples from the involved areas. The two detectives then turned their attention back to Brad, the building's security guard, who had been on duty that night.

"So let me see if we have your statement correct. You said that you returned to your station in the lobby right after having made your evening rounds . . . and that it was at that time that you discovered the trail of blood and the briefcase. You then called us right away?" Detective Bates asked him.

"Yes! I didn't know what else to do! It was terrible! I saw blood everywhere! I could only guess that someone had to have been hurt really bad! When I checked the building's night log, I discovered that Dr. Mathews appeared to be still inside the building. I tried to contact her office, but no one answered. She must've been hurt really bad when she fell off the escalator," he tearfully explained to the two detectives. "I checked the garage's exit security camera and saw that she drove out of the garage alone after she had been hurt!"

"We will need to see that security tape also. Please give it to one of my field investigators when they arrive," Detective Bolten informed him.

"Of course!"

"Now we believe that she was not hurt so much from the fall over the escalator railing as she was from being shot," Detective Bates explained to him.

"Shot! By whom? You guys have to find her! If only I had been here to help her!" he chastised himself out loud in front of them.

"Be glad that you weren't here. You could've been shot just like her or even worse!"

He sat back down in his chair, thinking about what Detective Bates had just said to him. He still felt bad for Dr. Mathews and wished that he could've helped her. Detective James Bolten moved around the lobby slowly while he carefully looked up at the numerous tall plate glass windows for a possible bullet hole in one of them.

"Carol, I think I found it! There appears to be hole in one of the lobby's tall glass plate windows about fifteen feet above the lobby floor!" Detective Bolten shouted over to her.

Detective Bates scurried up the steps of the stopped escalator to a location where she assumed their victim had been standing when she had been shot. She positioned her head down next to the blood splatters on the side of the escalator and looked up in the direction of the hole in the lobby's exterior glass plate window. She quickly made a rough determination of the bullet's suspected trajectory. Her eyes focused in on a window of the building located across the street. The window was on the fourth floor of the building, second from the right.

"Jim, I have a possible location for our shooter! Let's check it out!" she yelled down to him.

The two detectives rushed out of the building and made their way across the street to check out their new lead. They rang the doorbell of the building's superintendent's office to gain entrance into the locked building. A few minutes later, the night superintendent arrived and opened the outer door of the lobby when he saw their badges.

"Who occupies the offices on the fourth floor, right front side of the building?" detective Bates asked him as they made their way over to the working central elevator.

"I . . . I believe that office is vacant right now," he answered back a little, unsure of his answer.

"Do you have a key to that office on you now?" she asked him as the elevator doors opened in front of them.

"Yes, but I'll have to go up with you. I'm not supposed to give the master keys out to anyone."

"We're not just anyone, sir, and for your own personal safety, we want you to wait near the elevator when it stops on the fourth floor. Do you understand what I'm saying?" she asked him. He nodded his head in agreement.

The doors of the elevator opened noisily onto the fourth floor, and the two detectives peered down the partially illuminated hallway in the direction of the front right side of the building. Earlier that night, as they were making their way across the street, they had observed that most of the building's offices had appeared dark and unoccupied. Detective Bates, however, had called in to their dispatcher for some additional officers for backup, just in case. They were informed that their backup would be on scene in less than three minutes.

"Go downstairs to the lobby and wait for my men to arrive and then bring them up here," she whispered over to the building's superintendent.

"Carol, do you really think our shooter is still in there?" her partner asked her.

"No, but we still have to play it safe."

A few minutes later, their backup arrived in the elevator. The two men were brought up to date by the detectives as to why they were requested. They took up defensive positions in the doorways of the adjoining offices in the event that the detectives needed help.

With his glove-covered hand, Detective Bolten quietly slid the master key into the door lock and turned it until it stopped. Using the same glove-covered hand, he swung open the door widely. With their bright flashlights held in one hand and their guns aimed forward in their other one, they burst into the office. With a strong sigh of relief, they found the offices empty. They switched on the overhead lights and looked around the two rooms for any visible clues of their shooter.

The two patrolmen moved slowly into the room behind the detectives. Having secured the two rooms, the detectives thanked the two officers for their assistance and said that they were free to go.

From their new vantage point across the street, Detective Bates made a call over her radio to Andrew, whom she could see had already arrived at the Sanford Building's crime scene with the rest of his team. His team was already actively processing the lobby for evidence and clues.

"Andrew, I need you to send over a couple of your people to process a couple of empty offices that might've been used by our shooter. We're located across the street on the fourth floor of the office building. We'll wait here until your people arrive. The two lab techs completed their work in the two rooms in less than an hour. They found no additional clues from their processing of the two rooms. The two detectives did observe, however, a faint discoloration on one of the two windowsills that could be opened manually from the inside. So just in case, she had the lab people take a scrapping of the sill and test it for gunpowder residue. Having finished their work in the two offices, they thanked the superintendent for his cooperation and exited the building.

After another brief discussion with Brad, the night security guard, Detective Bates advised him that it would be a good idea for him to put a call into his building's maintenance people to be ready to come in right away to clean up the lobby, the elevator, and the garage area after her people had completed their work. She told him that it would be much better for everyone concerned if the bloody areas were cleaned up well before the other tenants in the building began to arrive for work in a few hours. He agreed with her completely and immediately contacted them for the cleanup.

A short while later, the two detectives and their lab team left the office tower and returned to their station to write up their reports and to process the evidence that they had collected. An all-points bulletin (APB) was put out by Detective Bates for Dr. Helen Mathews's location. They initiated a thorough search for her at all of the hospitals in the area, but no one with a gunshot wound and fitting her general description had checked in anywhere for medical treatment that night. The detectives knew that they were in for another long night of waiting.

CHAPTER 2

The telephone on Detective Bates's desk rang out loudly in the smoke-filled squad room of the Downtown Boston police station. The tranquility of the room was shattered by the numerous conversations all going on at the same time. The persistence of the telephone's annoying ringing finally paid off when Detective Bates suddenly interrupted her paperwork to answer it.

"Detective Bates, Downtown Precinct. Can I help you?"

"I believe so. This is Detective Sean Murphy from the Newton Police Department. I just returned to my office and found an APB report that was sent out by you earlier this morning. I think we may have located your missing person . . . a Dr. Helen Mathews," he informed her over the telephone.

"Is she okay? We have good reason to believe that she had been shot early this morning in the lobby of her office building and that she left the area in her car before she could receive any medical assistance."

"I'm sorry to have to inform you like this, but her body was found by a few of my men around one thirty this morning. She had been murdered. We found her body outside of her deceased mother's house in Newton. From what we have been able to ascertain so far from the evidence that we gathered at the crime scene, she appears to have been shot at least twice. First in her left leg and then sometime later in her neck at very close range," he announced to her.

Detective Bates leaned back slowly in her chair. The news of Dr. Mathews's murder had caught her off guard. After a few seconds of silence, she spoke into the telephone again.

"Detective, I think we should meet to discuss this case ASAP. Since we've both been up for most of the night, maybe we can get together later in the day," she said to him.

"That sounds good to me. I'll have some copies of our crime scene photos made up for you by then. I'd appreciate it if you can also get me some copies of whatever evidence you may've been able to find at your end of this case also. We're going to have to work together very closely on this one. It's not going to be an easy case to solve, but we have to bring those responsible for this woman's death to justice. I'm looking forward to meeting with you and your people in your office . . . let's say around six o'clock this evening," he politely declared as he ended their phone call.

"Jim! The Dr. Mathews case has just been officially changed from a missing persons report to a homicide. She was found murdered out in Newton around 1:30 AM. I've set up a meeting with Detective Sean Murphy in our office this evening around six o'clock to go over some of the details of the case. You should probably try to attend this meeting also. We're both going to be working very closely with his team to solve this one."

"There never seems to be any rest for the weary. Is there Carol? I'll be there too."

"Well, I'm exhausted, and I'm going home right now for a few hours of sleep. I suggest that you do the same. From what I was just told about this case, we're both going to have to be at our best to catch this bastard," she tiredly said to him.

Detective Bolten watched Carol as she packed up her personal possessions and headed over toward the elevators. He couldn't imagine why she was divorced. She was still very attractive, and she kept herself in really great shape. Many rumors had circulated around the station as to why her marriage had failed. The only one that he really believed was the one that said that she always took her work home with her every night. He remembered how she had confided in him one day about her messed-up life. It occurred just after her husband had filed for divorce. She told him how her husband had lost his temper one night and had told her that he had had enough of her wild mood swings and her late-night shifts at work. She told him that her husband wanted a divorce so that he could meet someone who wanted to be a real wife and a mother to the family that he so desperately wanted to start. He remembered how she was always complaining to him about why anyone would want to bring a child into such a screwed-up world. He shook his head in frustration and mumbled the words of "what a waste" to himself. He followed her lead a half hour later and left for his own apartment to get some much-needed sleep also.

Detectives Sean Murphy and Peter Savanovitch arrived at the downtown headquarters of the Boston Police Department a few minutes before 6:00 PM. The desk sergeant directed them upstairs to the third floor, where the detectives were stationed. He told them to just follow the signs after they exited the elevator. When they walked into the third floor squad room, Carol walked over to them and cordially introduced herself to them.

"I assume you must be Detective Sean Murphy?"

"A good guess . . . and this is my partner, Detective Peter Savanovitch."

"It's a pleasure to meet with the two of you. I only wish that we were meeting under better circumstances than this. This is my partner, Detective James Bolten. Since we will all be working very closely together on this case, I think it might be better that we start calling each other by our first names. It might help us to move this case along much faster. If that's okay with everyone?" she asked.

"That will be fine for us." Detective Murphy answered back.

"Good. Now I assume that since the capital crime occurred in your jurisdiction, you'll be handling the primary investigation. Am I correct in my assumption?" she asked them.

"That's correct. Now during the course of this murder investigation, your people are free to pursue all possible leads that you uncover at your end of the investigation. I only ask that you keep me or Peter apprised and up to date on everything that you uncover. Our office will also keep you up to date on our progress at the other end of the investigation. If we keep our communication lines open on this and meet as often as necessary, we'll all get along just fine." Detective Murphy announced to everyone.

That sounds great. Now here's a complete copy of the file of what my team has learned so far from the original shooting scene that occurred downtown in the Sanford Office Building. We still have a couple of lab reports that are still being worked on. I'll make sure that you get a copy of them also as soon as they are completed. What about your end of the investigation? What did you mean when you told me that she appeared to have been executed in cold blood?" she asked him curiously.

"I brought along some copies of the crime scene photos for your files and a copy of our preliminary investigation reports up until now. A number of the reports and tests are still being worked on as we speak. When they're complete, I'll also make sure that your office gets a copy of them too." Detective Murphy handed the file over to Carol and her partner.

"Wow! You weren't exaggerating. The powder burns on her neck can be seen quite clearly in the photographs, thus indicating the close proximity of the weapon during discharge. This really does appear to be like a cold-blooded execution-style murder or one made by someone who really hated her. Whoever they were, they certainly didn't have any reservations about getting in real close to make sure that they killed her. This type of a shooter is really cold, maybe a professional killer who appears to really enjoy his work. Your preliminary report states that you found her hiding under the front porch and that they may've torn off a piece of the wooden latticework around the porch to get to her. She never really stood a chance of escaping, did she? We're definitely going to have to pool all of our resources on this one to bring this animal or animals to justice," Detective Bolten announced to the group as he stared at the photos of the victim.

"I agree. We don't get that many murder cases in our city, and so we're going to need one another and all of our combined resources to solve this one. We would like to visit the Sanford Office Building, where you said the initial shooting took place, if it wouldn't be too much trouble," he politely asked them.

"No problem at all. Let me get a car so that we can all go over there right now."

"We have one of our cars parked outside right now. Why don't we all use that?" Detective Savanovitch suggested to her.

"That's great! I hate driving in the city anyway!" She smiled back at him.

The two Boston detectives went over all of the details of the crime scene very carefully with the Newton detectives. Detective Bates used the photos of the original crime scene to help support their earlier conclusions about the crime. Brad was not on duty that night, and so they were unable to ask him any additional questions.

When they were satisfied with seeing the two building locations, Detectives Murphy and Savanovitch drove everyone back to the main headquarters of the Boston Police Department. After a friendly exchange of business cards, the two Newton detectives headed back out to Newton.

"Well, they seemed to be quite friendly. I just hope that between the four of us, we can track down the bastards that killed that poor woman. I keep seeing her eyes looking up at me from the photographs," Jim said emotionally to Carol back in their office.

Inside the station house, they continued to work on some of their other cases and to look over the files that the Newton detectives had just turned over to them. The next day, they would both be back on day shift where their investigative work would really begin in earnest. They knew that they would have to make a personal visit out to Dr. Mathews's lab and to start interviewing all of her coworkers for some possible leads. Any new leads in the case might eventually help them to uncover a possible motive behind her murder and even lead them to a suspect.

CHAPTER 3

The overall mood of the employees in the research laboratory the next morning was quite somber and depressing to say the least. All of the senior technicians who had known and worked very closely with Dr. Mathews for many years were completely devastated when they first heard the terrible news. As each of them had arrived for work that morning, the building's security staff informed them that Dr. Mathews had been murdered the night before on her way home from work. The tragic news seemed to affect Nina more than everyone else because she had been the last one in the office to have seen her alive. Throughout the morning, she kept berating herself for not having stayed a little later with Helen that evening. If she had, she guiltily thought to herself, her best friend might still be alive right now. *Who could've done such a terrible thing to someone so caring and loving as Helen?* she thought to herself. Those who had been lucky enough to have really gotten to know her knew that she didn't have a bad bone in her entire body. She loved everyone openly and unconditionally. All of her closest friends had warned her repeatedly to be more suspicious of people. They had told her to be less trusting, but she continued to ignore their warnings and politely told them that it was her nature to be friendly to everyone. Secretly, many of them believed that she was setting herself up for a hard fall someday.

None of her friends, however, truly believed in their hearts that she would've ever come to such a terrible end. Throughout the morning, many of her friends could be seen and heard breaking down into moments of uncontrollable grief. With Helen's untimely death, the future of the laboratory was now placed in jeopardy. At that particular moment, however, none of her friends were thinking about their careers but more about how they would be able to cope with the loss of someone so dear to all of them. John buried himself even deeper into his research in the hope that the day's long hours would pass faster. Time, however, had all but stopped for him that day. He tried not to think about Helen and how she had been so suddenly taken away from him forever. At first, their love for each other had begun as nothing more than a subtle flirtation, but it soon blossomed into something much bigger. Gradually, their friendship had evolved into a heated romance. It was based on a mutual need and a desire hidden deep within each of them. Their love for each other was totally unconditional, unselfish. When they were together, they felt as though they had become a single being. In their love for each other, they had become soul mates. He felt that his love for her had become the one and only accomplishment in his whole tragic life. Now in less than the blink of an eye, she had been ripped away from him forever. What would he possibly do without her by his side? John had been secretly involved with Helen for almost a year now. He had been planning on asking her to marry him that very weekend. Now his life had once again become meaningless to him, almost not worth living. Oh, how his heart screamed out in silence for her not to be dead!

A few of Helen's friends had their suspicions that she had become romantically involved with someone special because she had been showing obvious signs of being in love. On a few occasions, when Carol and Nina had broached the sensitive subject with her, she cleverly managed to shift the subject of their conversation away from her. Her sudden actions, however, did not dampen their opinions that she had fallen deeply in love with someone. They were both extremely happy for her, and they knew that in time they would be told who the mysterious new stranger in her life was. Now they were saddened to think that they would probably never really learn who he was. For now, they could only hope that his identity would become known to them through the ongoing criminal investigation into her death.

Dr. David Stern, Helen's partner in the laboratory, made a decision to shut down the lab at 1:00 PM that day until further notice. He felt that everyone was making too many mistakes and that the quality of the work in the lab might be dangerously compromised.

Most of the people in the laboratory agreed with his decision, but the news did not sit too well with John. He felt that by burying himself deeper into his research, he would be able to better cope with the loss of his precious Helen. David's decision to close the laboratory was final, and so at 1:00 PM, the lab was closed until further notice.

Everyone was informed that they would be contacted by telephone when the laboratory would reopen again and when Dr. Mathews would be waked at a local funeral parlor. John's earlier insistence that he be allowed to continue working seemed to bother some of his coworkers very much.

Eventually, most of them could see that he was showing signs of denial that Helen was really dead and that his research work was helping him to deal with the terrible tragedy. David asked everyone to remain close to their homes for the next few days in case the police wanted to question any of them about Dr. Mathews.

On Monday, Detectives Bates and Bolten spent the entire day interviewing everyone who worked in the new laboratory. They were intrigued to learn from two of Dr. Mathews's closest friends that she may've been romantically involved with someone. Neither of them, however, was able to shed much light on who her mysterious new lover was, but at least they had something to follow up on. The rest of their interviews with the other coworkers in the laboratory proved to be even less enlightening. As seasoned investigators, they both knew that most crimes were either solved within the first forty-eight hours after the start of the investigation or left unsolved for months or even years. After the initial time period, evidence and witnesses tended to disappear. Memories and details about the crime itself seemed to fade rapidly from all but the most obvious sources. In general, all crime investigations tended to be a race against time. After the initial period of an investigation was over, most future leads seemed to come out of the forensic laboratory reports or their own aggressive field investigations.

With the conclusion of the last of the interviews with Dr. Mathews's coworkers, the two detectives soon came to realize just how much more difficult their case was going to be to solve. Pondering out loud over all of the details of their case, Detective Bates tried to tie together everything that they had learned so far about their case.

"There seems to be one underlining fact that appears to be present in all of our interviews. Everyone seems to have cared very deeply for our victim. She was genuinely loved and highly respected by all of her friends and peers. I can't figure out who the hell hated her so much! The fact that they had tried to kill her twice meant that they really wanted her dead. After having critically wounded her in the Sanford Building, they even pursued her all the way out of the city until they eventually found her at her mother's house. Then they executed her in cold blood. Her killer or killers had to have been driven by something very personal that she must've done to them. But what was it? On the other hand, if this scenario is wrong, then she had to have been murdered by a professional killer. Maybe because of what she knew or was working on at work." She shook her head in frustration

Detective Bates and her partner soon arrived back at their headquarters where they once again reviewed their notes for any possible leads that they might've overlooked. They found nothing that even remotely looked suspicious.

"I think I'm going to call our friends over at the Newton Police Department. Hopefully, they might've uncovered some new leads on this case!" she said to Jim. "So far, our entire investigation has led us to nothing more than a bunch of dead ends. Did we get the lab report back yet on the empty offices across the street from the Sanford Office Building?" she asked him curiously.

"Yes, I found it lying on my desk when we returned from our interviews. I glanced through it rather quickly, but I did learn that our people found no fingerprints on the doors and window areas of the offices. On some of the walls, however, they did manage to lift a few partial prints, but the entire office had just been freshly painted and cleaned. They believe that these prints are probably from some of the painters or cleaning people. A list of their names and addresses is being put together by the staff of the building's maintenance department. As you suspected, the dark stain on one of the windowsills tested positive for gunpowder residue. Putting together that evidence, the hole in the lobby window of the Sanford Building and the probable location of our victim standing on the escalator, we appear to have our shooting scenario figured out. I have asked our lab people to put together a 3D animation of the shooting scene," he explained to her.

"Good work, Jim! I believe it's time for me to call our friends in Newton."

"Detective Sean Murphy, please! This is Detective Carol Bates calling from the Boston police," she announced to the operator. She waited patiently as her call was transferred over to Detective Murphy's desk.

"Yes, Detective, or should I say Carol? It's a pleasure to talk to you again so soon. What can I do for you?" he politely asked her.

"We just finished interviewing the last of Dr. Mathews's coworkers, but there appears to be nothing definite to report at this time. We did learn, however, that she was secretly involved with someone romantically for quite some time. Some of her closest friends all seem to think that she was quite in love with him. Nobody, however, seems to know who this mystery man is. Other than that, everyone else appears to have nothing but great things to say about our victim. So far, we haven't found anyone that had even the slightest motive to kill her. We seem to be hitting all dead ends at our end of the investigation. Our lab people found gunpowder residue on one of the windowsills in the vacant offices across the street from the Sanford Building. This, in conjunction with all of the other evidence found in the lobby, appears to confirm our shooting scenario. Our people are putting together a complete report on the shooting, including the bullets trajectory through the lobby glass to our victim's leg as she stood on the escalator. I'll have the report in your hands by tomorrow."

"That's great."

"Jim and I were curious to know whether you may have heard anything new from the ME's office about our victim's body," she asked him. "I've asked him to listen in on the speaker phone in the other office and to take down some notes. He will not be able to speak to either of us from out there during this call."

"Well, I just received the ME's preliminary report about two hours ago, and it seems to confirm most of our earlier suspicions about what may have occurred that night outside her mother's house. The medical examiner has determined that the second gunshot made to her neck was the one that killed her. He stated that the trajectory and force of the weapon's bullet inflicted a massive amount of trauma to the tracheal area and the major blood vessels on the right side of her neck. He confirmed the presence of substantial amounts of powder burns and residue in the area also. This all confirms our own observations that she was shot at very close range. The medical examiner also stated in his report that she would've died within ten to twelve seconds, after having received the second gunshot. He summarized his report with the sentence that she probably drowned choking in her own blood before she passed out and died."

"What a nightmarish way to die!" she unconsciously interrupted him to say.

"I couldn't agree with you more on that statement! He also stated that during his autopsy on the doctor's body, he had discovered that she had lost a great deal of her blood from the initial gunshot wound to her left leg even before she had made it to the area under the porch. He believes that from the amount of blood that he discovered in and around her body and inside her vehicle, she had to have been drifting in and out of consciousness. Her efforts to stop her leg from bleeding with the simple belt tourniquet were only partially successful. From his tests taken on her body at the scene, he was able to say that she was killed only minutes before my men had arrived at the house. Her 911 call came in at 12:58 AM, and my men arrived at 1:30 AM sharp. He believes that she was shot about ten to thirteen minutes after her 911 call. He based his conclusions on his observations and tests, which he conducted on her body at the scene. These included lack of body rigidity, temperature drop, blood loss in the area, and blood coagulation. In his medical opinion, he stated that she probably died at approximately 1:20 AM. I will be receiving his final report within a few days, but I felt that you might want a copy of this information as soon as possible. I'm faxing it over to you as we speak!"

"I really appreciate that, Sean. I'll be in touch with you if we learn anything else." She politely thanked him for keeping them up to date on the ME's findings.

Detective Bolten had been taking down some notes in the other office about the ME's preliminary report. Hearing the information firsthand eliminated the chance of any errors being made. He made his way down the hall to their department's fax machine to pick up the copy of the ME's completed report. As he walked back over to his desk, he flipped through the gory details and diagrams of Dr. Mathews's terrible death.

Chapter 4

Over the next couple of days, Detective Bates's team of special investigators painstakingly pursued every new lead in their murder case, but all of their efforts failed to turn up any new clues. Investigating every new lead demanded a lot of extra time and energy from everyone involved. All of their efforts just seemed to lead them to one dead end after another. The city's two leading newspapers found out about the Dr. Mathews's murder case early on in their investigation. Their editorial pages soon began to relentlessly press the police for additional details on the case and a timeline for when the public could expect an arrest to be made in the heinous murder. Gradually, the barrage of critical editorials began to turn public opinion against the police for their ineffective handling of the murder investigation. Even the mayor's office was beginning to feel the heat from their scathing articles. After a while, he too started to pressure the police chief and his detectives into making more progress in the case. Every day Carol and the rest of the detectives in her department had to wade through a crowd of newspaper reporters, all demanding to know the latest details about the ongoing investigation. Detectives Bates and Bolten managed to politely brush aside most of their questions by saying that they could not comment any further on their ongoing investigation. They both knew, however, that this delay tactic would only work for a short while longer.

Their first real break in the case came a few days later in the form of a telephone call from Detective Murphy. His phone call came into their precinct around 2:00 PM.

"Detective Bates, please! This is Detective Murphy calling."

The operator immediately forwarded his call upstairs to her desk. "Detective Bates speaking! Can I help you?" she asked without knowing who was on the other end of the call.

"Detective Bates, this is Sean calling from out in Newton. I believe we may've finally received our first major break in the Dr. Mathews murder case," he said to her.

"That has to be the best news that I've heard all day! What is it Sean?" she patiently asked him while trying to contain her own excitement.

"Do you remember reading somewhere in my field notes about some bloody fingerprints that we found out at the Newton crime scene? They were found on one of the front porch's floor joists."

"Yes, but I thought that you wrote in your notes that they weren't too clear and that you probably wouldn't be able to identify them!"

"We weren't able to at first, but then we got lucky. Some of our bright techs down in Washington at the bureau managed to come up with a match for them a couple of hours ago. They identified them from an old gun permit application that they still had on file," he excitedly told her. "I think we may have just found our killer!"

"What's our suspect's name?"

"You won't believe this, but he was one of the people whom you and your partner interviewed the other day! His name is John Haggerty. He's one of the researchers who works in Dr. Mathews's laboratory," he eagerly volunteered.

"What do you want us to do about him right now? Do you want us to bring him in for further questioning . . . or do you want us to just put a tail on him for now?" she asked him politely because he was still in charge of their overall investigation.

"We don't want to make him suspect that he's a person of interest to us right now, but I do think we should be keeping a much closer eye on him. It's just in case he begins to suspect that we're on to him and he then decides to make a run for it. If he starts to act suspicious in any way, then we'll have no choice but to bring him in for further questioning. I'm putting together a request for a search warrant for both his car and his house right now," he informed her. "I'll call you back as soon as we get the warrants in our hands." Detective Murphy had to cut their conversation short because he had just been informed that he had another very important phone call waiting on his other line.

Carol hung up her telephone. She then began to hurriedly flip through a couple of stacks of field notes that she had made during their many long hours of interviews with Dr. Mathews's coworkers. Eventually, she came across her notes on their interview with Mr. Haggerty. During the course of every one of their interviews, Detective Bates had been very careful to record in her notes a written description of each of Dr. Matthews' coworkers. Her notes thoroughly described their demeanor and emotional state regarding their victim's sudden death. She was somewhat surprised to read in her notes that she had observed Mr. Haggerty's demeanor throughout the long interview to be not one of fear and evasiveness but one of full cooperation and a genuine sadness. She had also written down in her notes that Dr. Mathews's sudden death seemed to have greatly affected him emotionally. During their interview, he had volunteered the statement, "I hope you get the ones that are responsible for doing this evil deed and you put a bullet between their eyes!"

As she sat at her desk carefully reading over her interview notes several times, she became more and more convinced that Mr. Haggerty was not their murderer. The circumstantial evidence, however, was slowly starting to build a solid case against him. The next day, Detective Murphy called her to let her know that he had just received his search warrants. He asked that she and her partner meet him over at Mr. Haggerty's house in Arlington. He wanted to personally serve his search warrants on their suspect while she took Mr. Haggerty into custody for further questioning.

Detective Bates made a call out to one of the two detectives who were keeping Mr. Haggerty under close surveillance. Upon confirming that their suspect was still at home, she relayed the information back over to the detectives in Newton. All arrangements had been set in motion for a 1:00 PM surprise raid on their murder suspect's home.

John sat alone in his living room, silently staring at a picture of Helen and him. It had been taken by a waitress one night in a good restaurant where they had gone out on one of their first romantic dinner dates together. He took another long drink from the can of beer that he was holding in his right hand. He then threw the empty can back onto the table in front of him. He gave into the wave of sadness that he had been feeling all day and began to sob uncontrollably. The loud sound of a telephone ringing just a few feet away from him startled him for a brief moment. It forced him to bring his emotions back under control again. His left hand shakily reached for the telephone and brought it up to his ear.

"Is this John Haggerty?" a strange-sounding voice on the telephone asked him.

"Yes, I'm John Haggerty. Who's this?"

"Who I am is not important. I know who killed your girlfriend, Helen, and that your own life is now in real danger also! Pack a small travel bag for a couple of days and then meet me at the airport. Come to the Continental Airlines Terminal at Logan Airport. You'll have to purchase a one-way ticket to Los Angeles in order to meet me at gate 10. I have a package of documents to give you that will list everyone that had anything to do with her murder. This package of evidence will help the police bring all of these people to justice for their crime. You have just forty minutes to get here. I will be wearing a brown overcoat and a light brown dress hat. If you're late, you will never hear from me again! Do you understand? Forty minutes from now!" The stranger's voice emphasized the forty minutes strongly over the telephone again.

John looked down at his watch and saw that it was 11:37 AM exactly. "I understand, but who are you, and how do I know that you're telling me the truth?" he pleaded to him in vain over the telephone.

"Thirty-nine minutes!" the stranger impatiently answered back to him in response as the line went dead.

John's mind questioned himself as to whether or not he should believe the stranger. It could be a trap or even an ambush. After all, he thought to himself, he did say that his own life was now in real danger also. But what if the stranger was telling him the truth! He thought to himself. Then this could be his only chance to find out who really killed Helen. He knew that he had to take the chance. The loss of this man's evidence was too great a risk even for him to take. He hurriedly packed a few personal items into a small travel bag and then ran out of his house. He jumped into his car. As he sped away from his house, he didn't even notice the unmarked police car that was following him from a safe distance.

The detectives following Mr. Haggerty's car contacted Detective Bates by radio that their suspect had just left his residence in a hurry and that he appeared to be carrying a small travel bag. They also said to her that he appeared to be heading out to the airport. As they kept his vehicle in sight, they continued to update Detective Bates as to their exact location every few minutes.

John took a number of shortcuts through the streets of Medford, Somerville, and Revere in order to reach the airport on time. After he had parked his vehicle inside the terminal's main garage, he made his way up to the ticket counter to purchase a ticket. He then quickly walked over to the passenger's security check in location, where he had to show them his ticket to gain access to the gates beyond. He and his carry-on bag were scanned by the agents on duty and cleared for access down to the gates. He looked down at his watch and saw that he still had seven minutes to spare as he arrived at gate 10. As he quickly glanced around the area for a stranger dressed in a brown overcoat and wearing a light brown dress hat, he realized that the mysterious stranger wasn't there. He walked over to gate 12 and once again quickly glanced around the passenger waiting areas. He still didn't see anyone that matched the stranger's description. A wave of fear suddenly came over him as he realized that the stranger may've already left or, even worse, that he had never intended to meet him there at all. The entire meeting was nothing more than a ruse or a setup, he thought to himself. He turned around slowly when he heard some heavy footsteps coming up behind him in a hurry.

"Mr. Haggerty, we are detectives from the Boston police, and we are here to take you into custody." They informed him as they pushed him up against a wall and placed handcuffs on him. While they read him his rights, they patted him down for any hidden weapons. One of them picked up his small travel bag. In handcuffs, he was then led away from the area by the two detectives. As they were taking him away, he glanced back over his shoulder to see a man who appeared to resemble the stranger that he was supposed to meet. He was stepping out from behind a barrier and looking in his direction.

"You don't understand!" he shouted at them. "I'm supposed to meet someone here who told me that he knew who killed Helen! I think I recognize him over there now! Please, we have to go back!" he kept shouting as they forcefully pulled him along a long corridor toward a now-waiting police van that was parked in front of the main terminal. The entire area had become a flurry of curious onlookers. He could hear some of the people around him whispering, "He must be the one that the police were looking for. He killed that poor woman scientist a week ago!" John could now plainly see how he had been setup by Helen's killer to take the fall for her murder. What a fool he had been! He thought to himself.

From the back of the police van in which John was being transported to the Downtown Boston police station, one of the police officers overheard him saying quietly to himself, "Oh, Helen, what have I done to myself now?"

The police van made a sharp right-hand turn onto a busy street that passed directly in front of the Downtown Boston police station. It then made another sharp right-hand turn into the entrance of the underground police garage. It came to a complete stop in front of the building's elevators. A couple of uniformed police officers walked over to the police van and unlocked its two rear doors. They stepped up into the van and released Mr. Haggerty from his seat restraints. They then helped him up to his feet and carefully out of the van. He was then escorted into the booking area of the station by the two arresting detectives.

As John sat secured to a bench in the holding area of the station, he saw his whole life passing in front of him again. He felt completely alone and without any hope of ever being believed. Detectives Bates and Bolten exited the elevator at the far end of the hallway and started walking toward the booking area. From his location on the bench, he could just barely see the two men that had arrested him earlier and the detectives talking. He could only assume that they were all talking about him and his stupid trip out to the airport. At that very moment, he knew that he had to get some really good legal help if he was ever going to be able to prove that he didn't murder Helen.

When Detectives Murphy and Savanovitch arrived at the residence of Mr. Haggerty, they received word over their radios that their suspect had been apprehended at the airport while attempting to escape. It was great news for Sean and Peter to hear. It meant that they had been right in their earlier suspicions that he was, in fact, their murderer. As they pulled up in front of their suspect's home, they assigned two police officers from the town of Arlington to stand watch in front of the house. Knocking loudly on the front door, they received no response back. They then forced open the front door and then carefully entered the house.

Once they had secured the interior of the house, Detective Murphy and his team of investigators began a careful search of the premises for evidence. They were careful to wear gloves at all times and to adhere to all of the procedures required for the gathering and documenting of evidence. They seized everything in the house that even remotely looked suspicious.

"I want everything in here photographed and dusted for prints," Detective Murphy said to his men. "If it looks suspicious, document it, bag it, and then take it with us. I don't want to hear in court any legal problems about how we gathered our evidence in here today. Jefferson, don't forget to check out the attic also." Sean then directed one of the two patrolmen standing guard in front of the house to move the growing crowd of curiosity seekers further back. Over the next two hours, the detectives and their crime scene investigators searched Mr. Haggerty's home for evidence. When they were finished with their evidence gathering, the house's front door was resecured and then sealed.

Since their suspect's car had been seized and impounded at the airport by Detective Bates's people, he decided to allow her lab people to conduct a thorough search of it for additional evidence.

Detectives Bates and Bolten exited the small office located off to the left of the main booking area and walked directly over to where Mr. Haggerty was sitting. Jim released him from the securing pin that kept him close to the bench.

"Why are you doing this to me?" John protested. "I never hurt Helen! I told both of you that before!"

"Everything will be all right. If you did nothing wrong, you will have nothing to worry about," Detective Bates said to him reassuringly.

"I don't know why everyone's doing this to me!" John said to the two detectives as they loosened his handcuffs a little. "I could never hurt poor Helen like that!"

"What do you mean by that statement, Mr. Haggerty?" Detective Bolten asked him curiously.

"I don't want to say anything else until I have a lawyer present."

"Okay, Mr. Haggerty. You have that right. You can contact an attorney after we finish checking you in." They then led him into a special area where he contacted one of Boston's larger law firms in the hope of getting a good attorney to represent him. When he mentioned to the operator the subject of his phone call, he was immediately transferred over to Atty. Paul Tucker. Paul was one of the firm's senior criminal defense attorneys.

"Mr. Haggerty, this is Atty. Paul Tucker. I will be there within thirty minutes. Do not answer or volunteer to answer any more questions from anyone until I get there. Do you understand what I've just said?"

"Yes, I do!"

"Now don't worry. I'll take care of everything!"

"Thank you, Mr. Tucker, for agreeing to help me!" John added before he hung up the telephone.

After he had finished talking to his new attorney, he was taken to a holding cell to wait for his lawyer to arrive. The cell area looked clean, but it still smelled of urine and vomit. The officers had taken away his wallet, belt, and watch before they had placed him in the cell. His heart was pounding away rapidly in his chest as the minutes slowly passed by. He grew nervous and fearful about what was going to happen to him next. He kept looking up at the clock in the hall outside his cell to see if the thirty minutes was up yet. He kept hoping that he was dreaming and that he would wake up any second from this terrible nightmare. He hoped that he would find everything just as it had been a week earlier. He knew in his heart, however, that everything that was happening around him was not a dream but a real life nightmare!

"The phone on Detective Bates's desk rang a few times before she made an effort to pick it up. It was Detective Murphy again, and he informed her about what that had discovered in Mr. Haggerty's house. After hearing what he had to say, she quietly hung up the telephone again. Jim watched her in silence, impatiently waiting for her to speak.

"Well! Who was that?" he impatiently asked her, unable to contain his own curiosity any longer.

"That was Detective Murphy again. He said that they seized a pair of our suspect's shoes from his closet and a shirt from his hamper for further testing. He said that they both appear to have visible traces of dried human blood on them.

While Carol and Jim were discussing the particulars of the Mathews murder case, the phone on Carol's desk rang once again. She picked it up and listened very carefully to someone on the line who informed her that they had just found a few empty shell casings and bullets inside their suspect's impounded automobile. She was then told that they appeared to be of the same caliber as the one that was used to kill Dr. Mathews. They told her also that they did not find any weapons inside the vehicle. Carol thanked him for the quick report and then informed Jim about what their lab people had discovered.

"Well, that does it! We've got the bastard cold! The chief will be real happy to hear this great news!" he shouted back at Carol. "It's certainly great to know that this monster won't be walking our streets anymore!"

"Yes, it's great. Really great news!" she said quietly to herself. Until that call, she had been almost completely convinced of John Haggerty's innocence. Now she didn't know what to think about him anymore.

CHAPTER 5

The holding cell at the police station in which John was being detained suddenly felt very cold to him. It was as though someone had opened a window, and the cold outside air had suddenly been allowed to rush into his cell. It was a deep wrenching type of cold, the type that most often accompanies a deep sense of fear. His entire body shuddered suddenly in order to shake off the new sensation that was suddenly overwhelming him.

He was feeling completely alone, and any sense of hope that he may've been trying to hold on to seemed to abandon him at that very moment. He felt like a caged animal, trapped and without any hope of ever being freed. It was a feeling of utter hopelessness and sheer isolation. He had no one left in his life in which he could turn to for emotional support. It was a feeling that he had felt only once before when he was a small child. It was on the night that both of his parents had been killed in a terrible motor vehicle accident. His grandparents had taken him in gladly after that tragic accident. They had raised him with all the love and guidance which they could possibly give. Now even they were gone, and his isolation from the real world was complete. When Helen had come into his life some six months earlier, she had saved him from this deep sense of isolation from the world. Her love for him had become a beacon of warmth and desire; it had offered him a strong sense of security in an ocean of uncertainty. By falling in love with him, she had saved him from himself. In time, she was able to slowly strip away his mind's deep emotional scars. He soon found himself falling madly in love with her as well. He remembered how on one occasion she had described their relationship as that of two lovers who had fallen off a ship into a vast turbulent ocean. Their love was like two life preservers tied tightly together so as to resist the ocean's cruel fury. She had told him on several occasions how their love had become her most important reason for living also. In a strange wonderful sort of way, she had told him that they had somehow become soul mates forever. Now that she was gone, there was nothing left for him to live or hope for. He was filled with a deep sense of emptiness and a drive to help find the people who had murdered her.

Being held as a prisoner in a small prison cell didn't seem to bother him too much, but the very thought of being alone again without Helen in his life terrified him. Knowing that some people might be thinking that he was responsible for killing her infuriated him. He vowed to himself that no matter what the cost might be, he would somehow uncover the truth behind her death. He owed it to himself and to Helen's memory so that she could rest in peace.

As he looked up from the soiled floor of the main holding cell, his eyes slowly glanced around the cell at his fellow prisoners. He wondered what sort of crimes or innocent accidents had brought them all to such a terrible place. From their general appearances, he tried to imagine what had happened to each of them. Three of his five roommates appeared to be there for no other crime than for being drunk and somewhat bloodied from their public brawling. A fourth man appeared to genuinely happy in the surroundings of his cell. He had probably been arrested so many times in the past that the cell was beginning to feel a lot like home to him. The fifth individual was scary. His eyes looked as though they were pure evil. He appeared to be strung out on drugs and that the slightest provocation might set him off into a violent and uncontrollable rage. John quickly looked away from him so that he wouldn't become that fuse. Even though John was surrounded by a cell full of people, he still couldn't shake the feeling of being completely alone in the world.

At thirty-one years of age and still single, John had finally found someone who had come to understand him completely. From their very first date together, Helen had been attracted to something in him that she had found missing in her own life. In time, however, it didn't matter what the original catalyst may've been that brought them together. For now, the only thing that mattered to the two of them was that they loved each other. Now through a combination of fate and pure evil, she had been torn from his heart forever. They had stolen from him her life and their glorious future together.

He looked up again at the clock in the hallway and saw that he had been waiting for almost forty minutes for his lawyer to arrive. He assumed that his attorney would be there any minute now. As his mind continued to relive his last memories of Helen and himself together, he heard the sound of a door at the far end of the jail being unlocked. As the door swung open widely, he could hear the sounds of multiple footsteps approaching his cell. He heard one of the guards loudly calling out his name from down the hall.

"John Haggerty! Your lawyer's here to see you!"

John struggled to see what his lawyer looked like as the two men slowly approached his cell. To his surprise, he could see that he appeared to be a young man not too much older than himself. He was clean shaven and carried a thick briefcase by his side. He was about five feet nine inches tall with a medium build. His hair was light brown and slightly wavy. He seemed to project an air of confidence about himself as he walked. His demeanor seemed to instill in John an instant feeling of confidence in his ability to defend him.

"Mr. Haggerty?" the young attorney inquired in front of the holding cell.

"I'm John Haggerty . . . Are you Mr. Tucker?" he asked him.

"Yes, I am."

"Thank you for coming! I didn't know who else to call!"

"Well, I can say to you that you made a very wise decision in calling our firm. As I told you earlier, my name is Atty. Paul Tucker. Even though we talked only briefly over the telephone, I can assure you that I can help you in this matter." He turned his attention back to the police officer who had just let John out of the holding cell. "Officer, I will need a private room in which to confer with my client before we meet with your detectives," he announced to him.

"There's a private room down the hall that is monitored only visually. In there you can talk freely with your client without any fear of being overheard. However, both of you will still be under visual observation by at least one police officer at all times for security reasons. It's department policy."

"That will be okay, Officer."

The officer asked them to follow him down the hall to the other conference room. After they had both entered the room, he informed them that the detectives assigned to the case were waiting to question Mr. Haggerty as soon as possible. He then closed and locked the door behind them. He then made a call upstairs to Detective Bates to tell her that Mr. Haggerty was now meeting with his attorney.

"Well, Mr. Haggerty, did you follow my instructions exactly and not talk to anyone else about this case until I got here?" he asked him curiously.

"I did exactly as you said and kept my mouth shut!"

"Good! Then let's get down to business. We have a lot of things to discuss. You can call me Paul from now on. It'll make things go a hell of a lot smoother between us. I will call you John, if that's okay. Now do you know why the police have detained you in here today?"

"I thought that they had arrested and charged me with murdering my fiancée, Dr. Helen Mathews!" he answered back.

"Well, you are only partially correct in what you've just stated. As of right now, they have not officially charged you with Dr. Mathews's murder. You are being held at this time only for questioning, but that could change quite quickly.

"Now everything that we discuss in here and in the future comes under the protection of an attorney/client privilege rule. I cannot reveal or discuss our conversations with anyone outside of your defense team without your consent. Now I have a legal contract here for you to sign that will make me your attorney of record. Please read it over and then sign it. It allows me and the members of my firm to represent you fully in this matter. Our fee is purposely left open, and we will deal with that matter at a later date. For now, it is only important for us to get down to the facts of this case. Now John . . . did you kill Dr. Mathews or have anything whatsoever to do with causing her death?"

"No! No! I could never hurt Helen! She was my life, and I loved her very much. In fact, we were planning on getting married in a few months!" he pleaded back to him.

"Good! Now I want you to tell me everything about your relationship with Dr. Mathews and what events led up to your being detained in here today."

John slowly elaborated on all of the details of his relationship with his fiancée and everything that had occurred over the last week between them. He made sure that he left out nothing from his attorney. His attorney carefully recorded his statement on a small tape recorder and also took down notes on items that he felt were important. He explained to John that all of this would help him to defend him much better in the event that he was charged with Dr. Mathews's murder.

"Well, John"—there was a short pause in his words—"from what you've just told me, I think we can now meet with the police detectives. Now during their questioning of you, I may advise you not to answer certain questions. And if I do, please don't volunteer any answers, no matter how much you want to! Do you understand?" he asked him firmly.

"I understand completely!"

Paul stood up and walked over to the door to get the guard's attention. When the guard heard him knocking on the door, he rose up from his chair at the far end of the hall and walked over to unlock the conference room door.

"We're ready to meet with your detectives now," Paul informed him.

"I'll make a call upstairs to let them know that you're ready to meet with them."

"Thank you."

Paul Tucker once again took his seat at the table next to his client. While he was looking over his notes, John began to tell him one more important fact.

"There's one more thing that I haven't told you about yet!" he said to him uneasily. "I did see Helen on the night that she was murdered, but I swear to you that I had nothing to do with her death!" he said emotionally to him.

"Why didn't you tell me about this earlier?" he asked him, a little concerned that he had held something as important as this back from him.

"I was ashamed! I panicked when I arrived at her mother's house and found her lying dead under the front porch. I knew that she was dead when I felt her bloody wrist. Her neck had been blown away. Seeing her like that completely overwhelmed me! I was overcome with fear. I began to even fear for my own life and of being discovered there! I quickly drove away from the place. I knew that there was nothing else that I could've done for her. She was gone!" He then broke down emotionally in front of his attorney.

While Paul quietly tried to console him, John informed him that, out of shame, he had denied seeing Helen that night when the detectives had asked him questions earlier about her death.

"I wish that you had told me this earlier before I had told the guard that we were ready to meet with the detectives. But don't worry! We'll get through this thing together!" he added confidently.

John was still feeling emotionally distraught when there was a loud knock on the conference room door. Detective Bates opened the door and informed them that they would be going into another room for their interrogation. John followed his attorney down the hall through a couple of locked gates to another similarly sized room with a large mirror mounted conspicuously on one of its walls. Having seen many police shows on television before, John immediately assumed that the mirror was a piece of one-way glass.

Everyone took a seat at the table in the center of the room. Atty. Paul Tucker sat on John's left, while Detective Bates sat directly across from John. Detective Bolten sat directly across from Mr. Tucker at first, but he soon began to pace around the room. His actions seemed to make John very nervous. He began to tremble more and more as his nerves began to unravel.

"Well, here we go again Mr. Haggerty! I told you at our last meeting that we would continue to investigate this case and that we'd get to the truth eventually. Do you recall me telling you that at our last meeting?" he asked him intimidatingly.

"I recall everything that was discussed at our last meeting," John answered back nervously.

"Good, then let's get down to business! Now you have been informed of your rights earlier by some of my men, and your attorney, Mr. Tucker, is now present to legally advise you during our questioning. Now as my partner and I asked you before, did you kill Dr. Mathews or have anything whatsoever to do with her murder?"

"No! I did not kill her! I loved her with all my heart!" he responded back emphatically.

"Well, that certainly doesn't seem to fit in with all of the evidence in this case. Why were you at the airport today? And where were you planning on going?"

"I wasn't planning on going anywhere. I went to the airport to meet with someone who had said over the phone that he knew who was responsible for killing Helen. He said that he had documented evidence that would put all of them behind bars for the rest of their lives!" he explained to them.

"That's so noble of you, Mr. Haggerty! What are you trying to do, play us for a couple of fools! Just as we were about to bring you in for further questioning, some of my men observed you bolting out of your house with a travel bag in hand. They then followed you as you raced out to the airport. After arriving at the terminal, you were seen purchasing a one-way ticket to LA. All of this took place after having been told by us earlier not to leave the area! Why don't you just admit to us all right now that you panicked and were trying to flee the state in order to avoid being arrested! How did you learn that we were about to pick you up? Who told you?" he shouted at him.

"Nobody informed me that I was about to be arrested or brought in for further questioning. I received a telephone call at my house from a stranger who said that he knew who had killed my girlfriend and that he wanted to give the evidence to me in person before he left town. He said that if I was late, I would never hear from him again. Don't you understand? I had to go there! When some of your men were busy arresting me, I thought I saw a man who fit his description down by the barrier of the last gate. But I couldn't get them to listen to me! They just frisked and handcuffed me and then dragged me away. Now I will never know who that man was and what evidence he may've had for me!" he answered back in frustration.

"Then what about the one-way ticket to LA that we found on you?" Detective Bolten threw back at him loudly.

"He told me that I had to purchase a ticket in order to get through security to the gates beyond!"

"Another convenient excuse!" Detective Bolten answered back unbelievingly.

Detective Bates interrupted her partner's questioning of their suspect. "How were you going to recognize this man from the other travelers in the departure area?" she asked him curiously.

"He said that he would be dressed in a brown overcoat and wearing a light brown dress hat," he answered back quickly.

"And did you see anyone who matched that description down there by the gates?" she inquired further.

"Not at first, but as I was being placed in handcuffs by your men, I thought I saw him! He appeared to step out from behind a barrier next to the last gate. He was looking straight at me! It must've been him!" he declared back to her anxiously. "But now we will never know for sure! Will we, Detectives?"

"You don't believe this guy, do you, Carol?" Detective Bolten asked her in disbelief as he resumed his nervous pacing around the small room again.

"Well, let's just suppose for argument's sake that what you just told us is true, and I might add that I don't believe a single word of it, even for a second. Then how do you explain our finding of some of Dr. Mathews's blood on some of your clothes and shoes found inside your house?" Detective Bolten screamed back at him.

"Please, Detective! My client is cooperating with you completely. He's answering every question that you've asked him. So let's try to keep this entire questioning at a civil level!" Mr. Tucker interjected into the interrogation.

There was a brief moment of silence in the room as everyone took a few seconds to compose themselves again.

"Mr. Haggerty, please tell us again where you were on the night that Dr. Mathews was murdered," Detective Bates asked him.

"I was at home relaxing. I had a very strenuous morning in the research lab that day, and so I left work a few hours earlier than usual to get some rest at home. I had a terrible headache. It was around ten o'clock in the evening when I called Helen at the lab to tell her that I still wasn't feeling that good and that I might just stay home and rest. We were supposed to get together for a late-night supper around midnight. She was supposed to call me back just before she left the office that evening, but she didn't. Earlier in the day, we had made plans to meet either at her mother's house in Newton or at her apartment in Cambridge. She said that she wanted to make sure that her mother's house was okay. So when I called her office around midnight and received no answer, I assumed that she must've left for the evening. Since I didn't know where she had gone, I merely assumed that she must've driven over to her mother's house in Newton. So I decided to surprise her out there," he slowly reiterated to them.

"Well, you certainly did surprise her, didn't you, Mr. Haggerty?" Detective Bolten loudly volunteered.

"I didn't kill her! You have to believe me! I loved her! I worshipped the very ground that she walked on!" he pleaded back to everyone.

Detective Bates continued to take down notes on what John was telling them. She was also carefully studying all of his actions during their interrogation, trying to ascertain whether he was lying to them. She couldn't detect any noticeable signs from his demeanor or tone of voice that he was lying, but she couldn't rule it out either.

"So what happened next?" she asked him.

"Well, I believe I arrived at her mother's house around 1:20 AM. I saw her car parked out on the street in front of the house. I couldn't understand why she had parked out there when she had always used the driveway. She felt that it was safer. I didn't see any lights on inside the house when I first drove up. As I exited my car and looked around the area, I saw that some of the wooden latticework had been pulled away from the side of the front porch. I went over to investigate it. When I arrived at the porch, I strained my eyes to look in under the porch itself. The streetlight located directly in front of the house partially illuminated the area under the porch. The entire area had an eerie, almost-surreal look to it. That was when I saw her sitting there!" John once again started to become very emotional during his interrogation. Detective Bates offered him a glass of water to drink, and after a minute, he was able to continue.

"What happened next?" Detective Bolten impatiently asked him.

"I was in shock at what I was seeing, but it was still Helen sitting under there up against the foundation. So I bent down and went in under the porch to see if I could help her. She was so badly hurt that I knew that she was probably already dead or very close to it. Part of her neck was actually missing, and blood was everywhere! I didn't even know how to check her bloody wrist for a pulse! I heard the sound of police cars or ambulance vehicles somewhere off in the distance, and I panicked. I knew that no one would believe me, and so I pulled myself back out from under the porch and drove away from the area as fast as I could. I drove around aimlessly for most of the night before I finally went home. I didn't know what else to do. She was gone!" he said to them emotionally. He then broke down in front of them again in a flood of tears.

Detective Bates signaled to her partner to follow her out of the room. In the adjoining room, there were two other detectives waiting. Both of them had just witnessed the interrogation of Mr. Haggerty from behind the one-way glass mirror.

"Well, what do you guys think?" she asked them.

Jim was the first to answer. "I think he's as guilty as hell and that he's trying to make us all believe that he's the innocent victim here!" he proclaimed staunchly to everyone in the small observation room.

"Well, what about you two? What do you think? Do you believe his story or not?"

"I honestly don't know! He was trying to get our attention back at the airport about something, but we weren't listening to him when maybe we should've been." His partner nodded his head in agreement. "It's up to you, Carol! It's your call!" he added.

"Well, I can't take a chance on letting him go. He may or may not be our guy. In either case, I'm going to have to keep him here until I talk to the DA's office tomorrow. Let's let the DA make the final decision on this one."

Carol and Jim quietly walked back into the interrogation room. "Mr. Haggerty, you'll be remaining in here with us for at least tonight and until we decide what to do with you by tomorrow. In the meantime, you will be escorted down the hall by one of the guards and placed in a private cell for the night. There you will be our guest for the next twenty-four hours until we can check out some of the details of your story. Do you understand?" she asked him politely.

"Does that mean that you are arresting me for killing Helen?"

"No. Not at this time. We are merely holding you in here for further questioning."

"Everything will be okay, John. Try to get some rest tonight. I'll be back tomorrow to see you again," his attorney told him as a guard led him away down the hall.

"Detectives, my client is completely innocent of his fiancée's murder, and all of you know it. He's just another victim in this terrible crime. They were planning on getting married, not going to a funeral. He's cooperating fully with you. He's completely devastated by her death and quite obviously still emotionally in shock!"

"Your client, Mr. Tucker, may or may not be innocent of this crime! In the meantime, we still have to check out some of the details of his story. Then we will have to go over everything with the DA's office," Detective Bolten responded back.

"Okay, Detectives, I guess we'll have to leave it at that. I'll check back with you sometime tomorrow afternoon. If you find out anything new, please give my office a call right away." He handed the two detectives a couple of his business cards. He then left the room.

CHAPTER 6

"Sir, they arrested him a few minutes ago!" a mysterious-looking stranger whispered into the public telephone located off to the side of the small crowded airport lounge. "Shall I leave the area tonight or stick around for a few more days to see if there are any more new developments in the case?" he quietly spoke into the receiver so that nobody could overhear what he was saying.

"Stay up in Boston for another day or two, but contact me immediately if you hear about any new details precipitating from his arrest," a raspy voice on the other end of the call said to him. The phone line went dead a few seconds later. The stranger carefully wiped down the entire phone before placing it back onto its cradle. He then inconspicuously walked out of the crowded airport lounge and headed over to his car parked in the main garage.

* * * * *

It didn't take the Boston newspapers very long to learn about the Boston police's apprehension and detention of a possible suspect in the Dr. Mathews murder case. The main switchboard at the DA's office was soon inundated with phone calls from curious reporters and concerned citizens only minutes after the morning newspapers hit the streets. Early the next morning, as the assistant DA from the Middlesex County's Office drove his bright blue sport sedan into the private parking lot for court officials, he could clearly see the small crowd of anxious reporters and spectators already waiting for him outside the main entrance to his building.

He reached for his briefcase and quietly exited his vehicle, hoping that his slow movements wouldn't attract the attention of anyone in the small crowd. As he made his way slowly over to the crowd, he saw that there were a lot more of them packed around the building's main entrance than he had originally thought. "Oh hell, there are even more of them here than there were at my home! They're like rats, always underfoot and looking to be fed a story!" he mumbled to himself softly. "I'll never get past them without being swamped with questions about the Dr. Mathews murder case."

When the crowd caught sight of him approaching the building, they quickly moved in his direction. He soon found himself surrounded with dozens of microphones and reporters all shouting out questions to him about the Dr. Mathews murder case.

"Everyone, please, please be patient! Let me do my job in this investigation. There is nothing new to report to you beyond my early morning press release. We are presently holding someone for questioning and nothing more! We will let you all know later on today if there are any further developments in this case!" he announced to them as he pushed his way through the crowd toward the building's main entrance.

When he walked into his office a few minutes later, he found the mayor waiting patiently inside for him to arrive. "Good morning, Mr. Mayor. What brings you in here so early this beautiful morning, as if I didn't already know?" he said to him in greeting. "I'd offer you a cup of coffee, but I can see that my beautiful secretary has already taken good care of you."

"Tom, this is serious! What did you find out from the detectives downtown? Is he our man or not?" he anxiously asked him. "There's an enormous amount of pressure being put on all of us to quickly solve this murder case!"

"Well, some of our investigators are not completely convinced that we have the right suspect in custody. First of all, they can place him at the Newton murder scene around the time that Dr. Mathews was murdered. Hell, he even admits to being there and that he fled the area after having discovered her dead body. Some of his personal belongings, which were seized by the police in his house in Arlington, are still being tested for traces of our victim's blood on them. We should be receiving a preliminary answer to these tests sometime later on today. We found his bloody fingerprints at the crime scene and some empty shell casings in his car. The casings are of the same caliber as the bullet that was used to kill Dr. Mathews. To make matters even more damning to him, we picked up this guy yesterday at the airport, trying to flee the state."

"That's absolutely fantastic! In fact, it sounds like we have this guy guilty without even a shadow of doubt!" the mayor said to him now, feeling a lot better that the troublesome case had finally been solved.

"But I'm still a little bit concerned as to whether or not we really have the right guy in custody yet!" the DA announced to him as he paced around his office.

"Are you out of your bleeping mind, or are you just plain teasing me, Tom? You have everything that you need to put this animal away for good!" the mayor shouted back at him in disbelief.

"Yes, everything but a plausible motive!"

In a major city like Boston, it didn't take the local newspapers and news stations too long to hear that the police were holding a suspect in the Dr. Mathews murder investigation. The story first broke as an instant news bulletin on all of the late-night newscasts and then on page 1 of the newspapers the following morning. New leads in the murder case began to slowly come into the police station shortly after the first papers had hit the streets. At first, the detectives began to receive their usual amount of crank phone calls from people who claimed that they had seen their suspect kill Dr. Mathews. These nuts were only trying to make themselves feel important in the eyes of other people. With every major case, these same types of nuts seemed to come out of the woodwork. The case also got its fair share of crazies who confessed that they had killed Dr. Mathews and that the police had arrested the wrong man. None of these people, however, could even describe what their victim was wearing on the night of her murder. Most of these callers were quickly weeded out by the detectives but a few of them had to be followed up by many valuable hours of wasted police work.

The detectives received a real break in the case when they received a phone call from a waitress who said that she had waited on a man and their victim in a small restaurant a few days before she was found murdered. She told the detectives that she had seen and heard them arguing over something during dinner. She said that she was not sure what they were arguing about, but she did recall that it had something to do with their work. She said that she recognized the woman from her picture in the newspaper and that she had called the man with her John. She was able to describe John Haggerty perfectly over the telephone to them.

With this new information now in hand they contacted the assistant DA, Thomas Parker, who was assigned the case. He was now able to put together a possible motive for the murder. The police had speculated to him that she may've been dissatisfied in some way with his work performance. They further speculated that she may've threatened to cut back his funding or, even worse, fire him. Upon hearing this, they asserted that he might've become enraged with her, which led him to murder her a few days later.

It was enough for the DA to hold and charge him with the first-degree premeditative murder of Dr. Helen Mathews. Detective Bolten answered Carol's phone and took down the DA's message.

"I think you guys made the right decision, Tom. This guy is as guilty as hell and the evidence proves it. I've never seen so much physical evidence pointing to a suspect's guilt as we have in this case. I'll take care of the arrest booking personally, and I'll let Detective Bates know about your decision."

* * * * *

John had just finished eating his lunch at 1:00 PM when he received a phone call from his attorney. Mr. Tucker informed him that the DA's office had just informed him that they had made a decision to charge him with the first-degree premeditative murder of Dr. Helen Mathews. In a state of shock, he quietly listened to his attorney's attempt at trying to reassure him that they would beat the murder charge together. Paul told him to remain calm and to not become too depressed. After John hung up the telephone, the guard escorted him back to his cell. When he was alone in his cell, he quietly broke down in a flood of tears.

Not much time had passed before he again heard the sound of some of the guards returning to his cell. They took him downstairs to the central booking area. There he was fingerprinted, photographed, and officially charged with Dr. Helen Mathews' murder. Throughout the entire ordeal, he remained calm and in a surrealistic state of shock. It was the worst nightmare that he could have ever imagined happening to him. Knowing that he was innocent and that Helen's real killer was outside walking around free made him feel much worse.

Early the next morning, he was once again placed in handcuffs and then escorted over to the courthouse for his arraignment on the first degree murder charge. With his attorney by his side, he entered a plea of not guilty on his own behalf. The next issue that was brought up before the judge was that of his bail.

"Your Honor, the state is asking that there be no bail allowed in this capital case. The defendant was arrested at the airport by the police in an apparent attempt to flee the state. He had been previously warned by the detectives not to attempt to leave the area. A one-way ticket to LA was found in his possession at the time of his arrest. We feel that the defendant in this case presents a high risk of flight in order to avoid prosecution. We strongly urge the court to deny bail in this case," the district attorney argued adamantly before the court.

"Your Honor, my client was not attempting to flee the state as the DA has so clearly pointed out. When he was apprehended at the airport by the police, he tried to explain to them that he was meeting someone at one of the departure gates. That person had told him that he had information about his fiancée's murder. In order to gain access into the gate areas, he had to purchase and show a valid ticket to the gate security people. Furthermore, my client does not have any prior record of violence or crime. He owns property in the area, and he has resided in the community for most of his adult life. Therefore, I ask that the court allow a reasonable bail to be set in the case before it," his own attorney argued back in John's defense.

"The court understands the severity of the criminal matter before it today, and it can plainly understand the concerns of the DA's office in this matter. But I am going to allow bail in this matter before the court. The court orders that a cash bail of five hundred thousand dollars be set in this case. This case shall be bound over for trial . . . in four weeks . . . on April 20. Next case!"

John collapsed down into his seat again when he heard the judge's exorbitant bail order. He knew that he would never be able to post such a high bail in order to get released from jail until his case came up for trial. As he sat there in disbelief, the two detectives who had escorted him earlier from his cell over to the courthouse walked up to where he was sitting. They informed him that they had to take him back to his cell again. He nodded his head in agreement and stood up. They took hold of his arms and carefully led him out through the back door of the courtroom. His attorney said a few words of encouragement to him as they led him away.

"Now, John, don't worry! We are going to beat this thing together because we both know that you're innocent! I will be in touch with you in a couple of days. Try to hang in there until then!" Paul said to him with a confident smile showing on his face.

His air of confidence seemed to lift John's spirits as the two detectives led him away in handcuffs. On their way back to the police station, he was informed that he was going to be transferred later that day to the new Middlesex County Jail, where he would remain until his trial.

CHAPTER 7

Atty. Paul Tucker and his law firm had earned a solid reputation of being one of the city's finest law practices. They had earned this solid reputation as a result of their aggressive style of uncompromising work on behalf of their clients. Their courtroom skills helped earn them a high percentage of wins while defending against a wide spectrum of criminal complaints against their clients. Murder cases, however, had unexpectedly become a major percentage of their firm's criminal caseload. More often than not, many excellent DAs had fallen victim to their very thorough field investigations and skillful courtroom maneuvers. Many seemingly rock-solid cases for a prosecutor had become shredded with holes of doubt by their relentless skillful attacks. They had become known as a law firm that never refused or ceded a case because the odds of winning it were too low. Most of the time, they either managed to get their clients acquitted of all charges or at least moved into a very favorable plea-bargaining position. Whenever the DA's office saw their law firm's name listed as the opposing counsel on the court docket, it usually sent waves of apprehension running throughout their office.

As soon as John's court arraignment was over, Paul Tucker returned to his office in order to make a personal phone call to his firm's chief private investigator, Harold Parks. Their conversation lasted for almost an hour, as he carefully filled him in on the state's case against their client. Harold had a knack for sniffing out new evidence in many cases that the police had inadvertently missed in their haste. Whenever Paul's law firm assigned a new case to him, he relentlessly persisted in his efforts to uncover new leads or pieces of evidence in the case.

"Well, did he do it or not?" Harold inquired of his friend as their conversation was slowly drawing to a close.

"Well, he says that he's innocent, and I tend to believe him! So it's up to you to find me something out there that will clear his name and point a finger at the real murderers!" he pleaded back at him. "Harold, I've never lied to you before, and I believe that this case is going to be a real tough one for us to win. I'm going to be relying on your special skills a lot more for this one!"

"Paul, as you already know, I'll do my very best to not let you down on this one either! How much time do we have before our case comes up for trial?"

"I've checked with the court and found out that Judge Zimmer has been assigned our case and that it has been marked up for trial on April 20. With all of the judges in this great big liberal city, how the hell do we keep getting one of its toughest judges?" he said to him in disbelief.

"I believe they call it the luck of the draw, Paul. Since I have to work fast on this one, you will have to get me access into both our client's house and our victim's. I will probably need to check out their places of employment also. I promise I won't let anything get by me on this one!" he said to him confidently.

"I'll make all of the necessary arrangements for you by tomorrow. Detective Carol Bates of the Boston PD and Detective Sean Murphy of the Newton PD are in control of the two crime scenes, and I will have to notify them that you need to get into both of those locations. I'll send over to you later this afternoon a copy of the DA's filed charges, a list of all of the evidence gathered so far by the police against our client, and a copy of our client's official statement also."

"That's great! I'll let you know how I make out real soon, Paul."

Harold Parks was an ex-cop. He had served with honors on the Boston Police Department for over twenty years. He had voluntarily retired from the police force three years earlier after he had been responsible for the accidentally shooting a young boy in a drug bust gone bad. The IA investigators had ruled that the shooting had been a tragic accident, and they had cleared him completely of all wrongdoing in the matter. When the internal affairs people had completed their investigation, he was given permission to return to work again. The terrible guilt that he felt after the shooting, however, prevented him from performing his police duties to the best of his abilities. Each night after he closed his eyes to sleep, he kept seeing the poor little kid's face looking up at him in fear as he slowly died in his arms. He was determined to never be responsible for the shooting of another young kid again. He knew that the drug scene in the city was out of control and that a lot of young armed kids were still out there dealing in drugs. He didn't want to ever be placed in a similar position like that again.

As a PI, or a private investigator, he was well-respected by the men and women on the police force, and he still had access to a lot of people on the force that owed him favors. He had been a good detective all those years, and he was finally cashing in on his hard-earned skills as an investigator. His close partnership with Paul's law firm kept him very busy. He liked being a PI, and he was less likely to ever shoot anyone again.

The next day, Harold began his own investigation of all of the evidence gathered by the police so far in their case. He knew that Paul had a very tough case ahead of him because so much of it pointed the finger of guilt directly at their client. It was cases like this, however, that seemed to set off an alarm inside Harold's head. It was telling him that there were just too many clues out there all pointing to Mr. Haggerty as the killer. He began his own investigation at Mr. Haggerty's house in Arlington. He spent almost two hours looking around his place for new evidence. From what he was able to discover inside the house, he was soon able to piece together a rough idea about their client's life. When he was satisfied with his inspection of the house, he snapped pictures of all of the rooms. He took with him some personal letters and pictures from their client's bedroom. He made notes as to where he had found each of these items in the house before he left.

* * * * *

A couple of days later, Harold and Paul sat down together in his small office to review some of the evidence that he had collected from the two houses. Paul wanted to meet with him away from his own office in order to avoid being constantly interrupted.

"Well, what have you uncovered so far?" Paul asked him curiously.

"Now it's still quite early in my investigation, but I have managed to come up with some pretty interesting information." He handed over to him some of the pictures of John Haggerty and Dr. Mathews posing happily together. Along with these pictures, he gave him a stack of personal letters that they had written back and forth to each other. Some of them had been mailed just one week prior to her death.

"Now after having read all of the letters, did you find anything in them that I should be made aware of right now?" Paul asked him.

"Well, from what I was able to deduce from reading them, these two people were deeply in love. I didn't find even a hint of bad feelings between them. Up until three days before her murder, she was eagerly looking forward to marrying our guy. His murdering of her doesn't make any sense to me. I can't seem to put my finger on this case yet, but I will!"

Nobody is that good! Every murderer seems to leave behind one or more unexplained or overlooked clues, and I'm going to find one of them. I can promise you that!"

"I sincerely hope so! I feel real bad for this poor guy right now. Not only did he lose the one person in this whole world that he really loved, but he's being framed for her murder also. Don't let up on this one Harold. We both need you!"

"I know that. Tell him to hang in there. If there's something out there to be found, I'm the one who will find it!"

"Call me immediately when you discover anything important," Paul said to him as he exited his friend's office.

"I will."

* * * * *

The short drive to the new jail in Boston was taking Paul much longer than he had expected. The Big Dig highway construction project was having a very disruptive effect on all of the surrounding roadways. As he waited patiently in the slow-moving traffic, his mind reflected back over the contents of Dr. Mathews' love letters written to John. He had always found talking to someone about their most intimate romantic feelings a little bit uncomfortable, but he knew that he had to pursue this line of inquiry a little further with him. It was an area that he knew the DA would definitely try to exploit to his own advantage. After what felt like hours in the slow-moving traffic, he finally drove his car up into the jail's private parking lot. He parked his vehicle in one of the spaces reserved exclusively for attorneys. He waved hello to one of the parking attendants that recognized him.

"I'm Atty. Paul Tucker, and I'm here to meet with my client, John Haggerty," he said to one of the guards on duty inside the jail.

He was directed through a metal detector by one of the guards, while another one physically inspected his briefcase for weapons. His cellular telephone was taken away from him until he exited the jail again. He thought to himself how foolish that prison rule really was; it didn't make any sense to him. What could a prisoner do with a cell phone except make unmonitored phone calls to his lawyer and friends?

As Paul waited in the visiting area for John to be brought down, he quickly read over some of Dr. Mathews' letters that she had sent to John. Her written words held the true emotions of her heart in each of them. He felt deeply saddened in knowing that all of her hopes and desires had been stolen away from her by some cold-blooded animal.

John entered the holding area a few minutes later. He looked lazily over at Paul as he was escorted into the small room. The guard turned and exited the room, leaving the two of them alone together. John looked tired and distraught from his incarceration in the new jail. Paul could only imagine what was going on inside his mind every day as he continued to live out this unending nightmare.

"I put one of our best PIs onto your case, and he told me not to worry. He said that if there's anything out there to be found, he will find it! So try to be patient, John. In time, this entire nightmare will be over."

"When it is, I will still have to live the rest of my life remembering what Helen looked like on that terrible night! I honestly don't know whether I can handle living my life without her by my side!" he said hopelessly to him.

"Now don't start talking like that! I know Helen wouldn't want to hear you talking like that!"

"And how would you or anyone else know how she would feel?" he snapped back at him.

"Because of these! She loved you and believed in you more than life itself. You owe it to her and yourself to survive this nightmare. And most importantly, we have to find out who did this terrible thing to her! These letters are a living testimony of her love for you. They show a bond of love that the DA and the whole court system can never destroy. We will make these letters the foundation to our defense and strike out at the evidence as it is presented against you by the DA. The truth will be our weapon against the DA's charges. Right now, however, I have to talk to you some more about your relationship with Dr. Mathews. Do you feel up to it, John?"

"I guess so. Maybe my talking to you about her might help make some of my nightmares go away."

"Good! Then let's give it a try."

The two men talked for almost two hours that afternoon before they finally agreed to end their meeting. John thanked him for being there for him and for listening to him as he talked about his deep feelings for Helen. John had bottled up inside of himself the feelings of anger and a deep frustration. Their intimate conversation helped him to release some of these pent-up feelings. On several occasions during their long talk, John became very emotional. Paul also observed that a faint smile would sometimes form on John's red face when he was discussing a happy memory that he and Helen had shared together.

"Before I go, I want to ask you one more time if you can think of anyone who might've wanted to harm Dr. Mathews in any way? Did she have any problems at work that she may've been very concerned about?

Or was there anything in her past that she might've mentioned to you, something or someone that she was afraid of?"

"I don't think so, but I'll give the matter some more thought. She didn't talk to me too much about her past."

"Okay, I think we've done enough for today. Try to get some rest. You look tired, John."

"I know, but that's all that I can do in here. I'm beginning to go stir crazy. I only wish that I had enough money to post my bail. Then I'd get out of here and try to prove my innocence."

"Don't worry about that right now! We will find the key to this entire puzzle and get you acquitted soon enough. I promise!"

* * * * *

Time seemed to be standing still for John as he shut his eyes each night to sleep. The days slowly turned into weeks and still he had not received any new hope back from Paul that they had uncovered any new leads in his case.

There were still five more days remaining before his trial was scheduled to start. He was becoming scared for the first time in all of his days of incarceration. He couldn't imagine living the rest of his life in a cage, a prison cell that he didn't deserve to be in because he was innocent. Every night, his mind screamed out loud in silence to the world that he was innocent, but his screams went unheard.

"Oh, God, please help them uncover the truth!" he prayed silently in his cell.

Rest finally came to him around 1:00 AM. He let his mind drift back to a place and a time where he and Helen had first met. He felt at peace there once again. He could see and hear her talking to him, and he dreamed that he could even smell her intoxicating perfume in the air around them.

The next morning, as everyone was walking out to the exercise yard to play basketball and to use some of the jail's other pieces of exercise equipment, he felt a sudden sharp burning pain in his back. As he turned to face his attacker, he felt a heavy blow striking him on the back of his head. In panic, he grabbed for the fence and held onto it for support. All of the other prisoners in the line continued to walk past him, leaving him hanging onto the cold wire fence. He felt his legs slowly starting to buckle out from under him. He fell down onto his back. He thought that he could hear the guards rushing over to him and shouting out that he had been stabbed. He could feel them picking him up and rushing him down the hall to the medical area for treatment. He found himself drifting in and out of unconsciousness. How long he remained unconscious, he didn't know. As he groggily looked around the room and at his body, he found himself in a hospital all hooked up to an IV drip. His back was hurting painfully from some emergency medical procedure that must've been performed on him. Unable to move, he attempted to call out to someone for help.

"Nurse, I need some help in here! Is there anyone around here that can hear me?" he shouted out even louder.

The door to his room swung open, and a police officer looked inside at him. He waved at him and then said that he would get his nurse for him. A few seconds later, a nurse hurried into his room to offer him some help.

"What happened to me? Where am I? And how the hell did I get here?" he asked her now more calmly but still quite confused. He found out that any effort on his part to speak seemed to hurt him a lot more.

"You must remain quite still while your body heals. You're in Massachusetts General Hospital. You were brought in here yesterday with a deep stab wound in your back. It punctured your left lung. You almost died on the operating table! You lost a great deal of blood, and you're really lucky that you survived the operation."

"I didn't even know that I had been stabbed!" he whispered up to her.

"A police officer has been assigned to guard you while you're in here. I've just given you a little more medication for your pain. It will help you to sleep. Please try to get some rest. You'll feel a heck of a lot better in the morning." She smiled back at him as she turned and exited his room.

He felt his mind growing sleepier as he slowly drifted off into unconsciousness.

Two doctors and his nurse walked into his room around seven thirty the following morning. As he listened to them, they looked over his chart and discussed his condition out loud.

"Well, Mr. Haggerty, welcome back to the land of the living! For a while, we didn't know whether you'd make it or not! How do you feel today?" the older doctor asked him as he listened to his heart and lungs.

"I don't seem to be hurting as much right now. The nurse said that I had been stabbed in the back. Is that true?"

"I'm afraid so. The knife or whatever it was that they used punctured your left lung and collapsed it. We had a terrible time trying to control the bleeding, but you seem to be no worse off right now. Just try to take it easy while you're in here, and you should recover completely in a few more days."

"That's great. Thank you, Doctors!"

"You're welcome. Now just relax and let your nurses take good care of you. We'll check in on you later this afternoon." They then both quietly exited his room to check on some of their other patients on the same floor.

A short while later, his door opened again, and his lawyer and a prison guard walked in to see him.

"How are you feeling today, John?" Paul asked him.

"Much better, I think."

"This is William Pointer. He wants to ask you a few questions about what happened to you back at the jail. What can you tell us about it?"

"Nothing really! We were all walking out toward the exercise yard when I was bumped and then probably stabbed by someone. When I turned around to see who had bumped into me, I felt a heavy blow to the back of my head, and I began to lose consciousness. I can only say that I think he was tall. I only saw a blurred image of him as he quickly walked by me."

"Did you have any arguments with anyone in the jail since you arrived?" Mr. Pointer asked him.

"No . . . never. I tried to keep to myself as much as possible. I was ashamed of being in there, and so I purposely avoided talking to anyone unless I absolutely had to. Someone in there went out of their way to kill me and for no apparent reason, as far as I know!"

"Maybe and then maybe not! You might've been attacked by someone who wants this entire case to just go away. We might be stirring up the water a little too much, and they don't like that at all!" Paul surmised to the two of them.

"Now don't start jumping to any unfounded conclusions quite yet. We're still checking with the other prisoners to see if any of them saw something," Mr. Pointer added.

"You know very well that nothing positive will come out of that line of investigation. Mr. Pointer, I want my client to receive around-the-clock protection. Something is not right about this case, and I'm going to find out what it is. I'm holding you personally responsible for this man's safety. If you think that your department isn't capable of protecting him, then just say so! I will then provide my own armed guards to do the job."

"We can handle his security without any outside help from you. He's still under arrest, you know!"

"Yes, but he's still innocent until proven guilty in a court of law. So let's get my client into that courtroom before there are any more attempts made on his life."

"I agree. We'll take good care of him until then. I promise!"

"Thank you, Mr. Pointer. I know you will."

The detective from the jail turned away from them and left the hospital room. John found himself once again alone in his hospital room with Paul.

"Do you really think that someone tried to have me killed yesterday so that Helen's murder investigation would've been closed down for good? I guess that with my death, everyone would've logically assumed that I was her killer and that justice had been served by my death. Isn't that what the DA's office would've done with the case?"

"I don't know for sure, but that's what Harold told me when we first heard the news about your stabbing. He said that nothing in this case seems to add up. All of the evidence against you is just too overwhelming. It's just too perfect! You have to understand that almost all murderers make mistakes, but not like the ones that the police have discovered in your case. It's as though everything was methodically planted by someone to convict you."

"Then they must think that Helen told me something very important before she was murdered, something that I might remember someday. It might even lead the police back to them. I wonder what it is. If only I could recall what she may've mentioned to me."

"If you think of anything, anything that might help us, please give me a call right away. I had the telephone turned on in here for you. Here's my mobile number. There has to be something out there that we've all missed, but what? John, you still look very tired, so I want you to try to get some rest. Your trial is still scheduled to begin in a couple of days, and I want you to look sharp and well-rested for it."

"Thanks, Paul, for being on my side and believing in me also!"

"I told you on the first day that we met that I believed you were innocent. We are going to find out who killed your fiancée," Paul reiterated again to him as he exited his hospital room.

* * * * *

"He's still alive, sir! Our man blew a perfect opportunity in which to kill him. He should've died from that wound, but he didn't. We're going to have to wait for another opportunity to take him out!"

"I want this guy out of the picture once and for all! Now do you understand what I mean by that?" A deep raspy voice on the other end of the telephone call shouted back at him.

"I do, sir!"

"Good! Now I'm relying on you to do it. We can't afford to allow him take the witness stand in court and to deny that he killed his fiancée. His testimony would cause a lot of people to start asking questions. It would be a major mistake on our part to allow him to cast even the slightest bit of doubt on any of the evidence that the police have gathered so far during their investigation. The longer that this case and trial remain open, there is an ever increasing possibility that someone might discover some new evidence that we might've overlooked. Have I made myself clear on this point?"

"You have, sir!"

"If you need more help up there, just tell me! Otherwise, I'm relying confidently on your word as a professional that the problem will be taken care of by you both quickly and permanently!"

"It will be done as you said, sir!"

CHAPTER 8

As the first day of John's trial rapidly approached, his troubled mind watched in awe as the entire event soon began to take on a life of its own. It had even become the main topic of conversation among the inmates and guards in his jail. His own active imagination also seemed to be adding to his deep feelings of paranoia and anxiety. When the first day of his trial finally arrived, he was able to observe firsthand how the newspapers had turned his public trial into a media circus. When he arrived at the courthouse early in the morning, he saw a large crowd of spectators already lined up in front of the building. Many of the people in the crowd shouted insults at him as the van drove past them to the secured back entrance of the courthouse. Once inside the building, the two detectives who were accompanying him took him downstairs to a secured holding area. There they all waited until the clerk's office summoned them upstairs to the main courtroom. They didn't have very long to wait before they received a call from the clerk's office to bring him upstairs.

The two detectives carefully removed John's handcuffs before they escorted him upstairs to the crowded courtroom. Atty. Paul Tucker was already waiting for him at the defense table on the left front side of the courtroom. He greeted him cordially and motioned him to take a seat on his left side at the table. A deep sense of foreboding suddenly enveloped John's entire body, causing his adrenaline level to skyrocket. John's heart was pounding away so wildly in his chest that he began to imagine that everyone could hear its loud throbbing beats. Paul could sense John's deep sense of anxiety, and so he attempted to calm him down.

"Try not to worry so much! The first day of trial is always reserved for legal motions and opening arguments by the two sides in front of the judge. You won't have to do anything today but just sit there and listen to everything that's being said. We will get our chance to present a formidable defense after Mr. Parker, from the DA's office, has presented the state's case against you. We will have ample opportunity to cross examine every one of their witnesses and to challenge any and all of their evidence before it is placed into the record. The entire trial could last several weeks. It all depends upon how long the DA takes to present their case against you. So I want you to try to be patient," he quietly explained to John.

"I'm trying to be, but it's not very easy! Whatever possessed you into becoming a criminal defense attorney? To me, I see your job as a living, breathing, twenty-four-hour nightmare filled with unbelievable amounts of stress. It's a perfect heart attack just waiting to happen."

"I guess I chose it because of people like you. You know, there are all kinds of victims out there in this world. A victim doesn't always have to be someone who was an object of a violent criminal act. Some people just happen to be in the wrong place at the wrong time. Some people, like you for instance, become victims when they're accused and arrested for something that they didn't do. Don't forget evidence gathered at a crime scene can be interpreted sometimes in many different ways. Most of it is purely circumstantial. It can place a person at a crime scene, but not always at the right time. In some of the criminal cases that I've worked on in the past, I've come across evidence that has been carefully planted at a crime scene in order to incriminate an innocent person. I'll admit that this may be rare, but nevertheless, it does happen sometimes. It's my job to investigate all of the facts in a case and to point out to the jury any inconsistencies in the time line and the impossibility of the accused to have been there. It's a rather complex legal game, but the outcome of it is something never to be taken lightly. The outcome of my actions can mean the difference between freedom or prison for most of my clients. In some states, it can even mean their very lives. So I have to be alert and prepared to defend my client's rights at all times to the best of my ability no matter whether I believe that he or she is guilty or innocent of the crime. In this country, everyone is entitled to the best possible defense available," he explained to him proudly.

The first few days of the trial before Judge Zimmer were filled with legal motions and legal challenges to prospective jurors from the jury pool by both the district attorney and his own lawyer. John could easily see how Paul had become such a good defense attorney by the type of questions that he proposed to each of the prospective jurors. Through probing inoffensive questions, he was able to carefully discover how some of the jurors had been greatly prejudiced by the news media's coverage of their case. In some instances, he even discovered that some of them had been victims of a past violent crime themselves. When he was able to eventually weed out these people, they were excused by the judge from serving on the jury. After three days of careful jury selection, the two sides were finally able to agree on a satisfactory jury panel with six backup alternates.

The final makeup of the jury was like a cross section of American society. It was composed of four African Americans, seven Caucasians, and one Native American. Some of them were professionals, but most of them were just average everyday working people. Three of them were housewives. Paul wanted his jury to be made up of average people. He wanted people who would be both fair and open to his interpretation of the facts. He wanted them to see the real John Haggerty, another tragic victim of this very violent crime. He wanted them to see through the implausible motive of the prosecutor's case. He wanted them to identify with his client and to see how he had been set up by the real murderers of Dr. Helen Mathews.

The first full day of trial began promptly at 10:00 AM four days later. It was a day that John had been trying very hard not to think about. As he glimpsed into the stoic faces of each of the jurors, he suddenly felt terrified. The very idea that his fate, his freedom, and his very future was solely in each of their hands terrified him. He covered his face with his two hands and slowly rubbed his forehead nervously in disbelief. He felt completely powerless and without hope.

The district attorney slowly rose from his seat and began to address the jury in a soft, deliberate manner. He meticulously chose his every word and paused every so often to allow the jurors to think about what he had just said and to glance over at the defendant. John could hear Mr. Parker's words describing him as an animal, a cold-blooded murderer. He could almost sense a growing hatred rising against him in the courtroom as the DA continued to outline the case that he said that he would prove to them during the course of the trial. John wanted to stand up and shout out his innocence to the world, but he knew that he had to remain silent.

After a long forty-minute opening statement, the prosecutor returned to his seat at his table. Paul was not in a rush to jump up and to quickly attack the DA's opening statement in a flurry of emotional statements. Instead, he rose to his feet in a carefully orchestrated motion and then slowly made his way over to where the jurors were waiting patiently in anticipation for him to speak.

"My colleague, Mr. Parker, has laid out before you a heinous crime. And that's exactly what it was: a cold-blooded murder! The murder of a beautiful young woman whom you will hear had no enemies that we know about so far. She wasn't just killed by someone accidentally or in a moment of sudden rage or passion. She was, in fact, methodically stalked! She was terrorized! Then, without even the slightest bit of mercy or remorse, she was slaughtered in cold-blood by someone! She was seen by her killer, or killers, as a valueless object. Someone void of feelings, without even a soul. Someone, that for whatever unknown reason, had to be murdered!

"The prosecutor has said to you that the person who did this violent act is my client, but that is not true. He said to you that he will prove that it was a crime of emotional rage. He will not prove this to you either because it is not true. The person that committed this heinous crime was a monster! Whoever was responsible for murdering Dr. Helen Mathews saw her as nothing more than a gnat, a nuisance to be done away with. She was seen as less than nothing in their eyes. We contend that she was murdered by a professional killer. To this person, she was only a mark, a job, someone whose life meant nothing to them. There was no intense hatred here for her but only a cold, impersonal evil. I will show how my client was deeply in love with Dr. Helen Mathews. In fact, they were planning on getting married within the next two months. The prosecutor's theory is completely without merit, and we shall prove it to be just that. The police have not found another suspect in this case because they had stopped looking for one almost from the very beginning of their investigation. They were handed all of the evidence that they needed to implicate my client. But I say to you, the members of this jury, that the evidence of this crime shouts—no let me rephrase that—it screams out loud to us from our victim's grave that my client is completely innocent of the murder of Dr. Helen Mathews, his loving fiancée!" he concluded and then slowly walked back to his seat next to John at the table.

"The prosecutor shall call his first witness," Judge Zimmer announced loudly to the open courtroom.

"Thank you, Your Honor. The state calls Detective Carol Bates to the stand."

After being sworn in by the clerk magistrate, she took her seat on the witness stand to the left of Judge Zimmer.

"Please state your full name and occupation for the record," the DA said to her.

"My name is Detective Carol Bates. I am presently working for the Boston Police Department. I'm assigned full-time to the Downtown Precinct Station, where I have been working as a detective for the last ten years as one of its criminal investigators."

"Now, Detective, can you please tell the court what events led up to you first getting involved in the Dr. Mathews murder case," the DA asked her.

"My office received a phone call at approximately 12:28 AM on Friday, April 10, from a security guard who was working at the Sanford Office Building in Boston. He informed me that there appeared to have been some sort of a bloody accident or crime committed in the lobby of his building. He explained to me that he had just finished making his last security round of the building. As he was returning to his station in the lobby once again, he came upon what he described as a bloody crime scene in the lobby. I advised him to keep everyone away from the area in question and that we would be there within ten minutes. Upon arriving at the Sanford Office Building, my partner and I soon determined that there had been a shooting in the lobby. From the evidence that we observed at the scene, we surmised that the alleged shooting victim had managed to leave the area under her own power before anyone could provide her with any emergency medical assistance."

"What evidence first led you and your partner to assume that there might've been a shooting in the building's lobby?"

"Well, after we had arrived at the building, we observed a large quantity of blood pooled and smeared on the marble floor just below the lobby escalator. We also observed and followed a smeared blood trail over to and into one of the lobby's elevators. It eventually led us down into the secured executive parking garage, which was located directly below the lobby level. We observed bloody fingerprints on both the elevator control panel and on the garage's inside outer door control panel. We also followed a trail of blood droplets out from the elevator to a specific location in the garage itself. We assumed that our victim's car had been parked at this location the day before. Upon returning to the lobby, we were then able to determine from the evidence that we observed at the scene that our victim appeared to have been shot in her left leg. This occurred while she was riding the escalator down to the lobby from her office on the mezzanine floor. We discovered blood splatters on the left side of the escalator and on the railing directly above it. We surmised that the force of the bullet striking her leg drove her sideways over this railing and down onto the marble floor below. As we continued our inspection of the lobby, we discovered a hole high up in one of the lobby's large pane windows. Our crime scene investigators later determined that the bullet had entered the lobby of the Sanford Office Building through this opening."

"Your Honor, may I approach the witness?"

"You may Mr. Parker."

"Now, Detective, are these the photographs that your investigators took on the night of your visit to the Sanford Office Building's crime scene?"

"Yes, they are," she answered back after she had carefully looked at each of them.

"Your Honor, the state wishes to place into evidence at this time these photographs marked as state exhibits numbers 1 through 12. These photographs accurately represent the lobby of the Sanford Office Building and the crime scene therein."

"Without objection, Your Honor," John's lawyer declared to the court.

"So ordered," the judge answered back.

"Now, Detective, you stated earlier that you found a bullet hole in one of the glass windows of the lobby. Upon further investigation, what were you able to conclude from this?"

"By positioning our eyes in the approximate center of the blood splatter pattern on the left side panel of the escalator, we were able to follow the bullet's suspected trajectory up through the hole in the lobby window to a fourth-floor corner window in the building located across the street. We obtained access right away into this locked building by means of its night superintendent. We learned from this individual that the offices in question were unoccupied. Hurrying upstairs to a location just outside this vacant office area, we waited for additional backup personnel before moving into the suspected shooter's location. When it arrived, we then proceeded to enter and search the two rooms for suspects and evidence. We found the offices to be empty. I made a call down to our CSIs in the Sanford Building to get them to send up an investigator to this new location to examine the two offices for additional evidence."

"Did the members of your CSI team write up reports on the two locations?"

"Yes, they did. My people determined that there were no clear prints in the newly painted offices except for those made by the cleaning people. Upon further field investigations and interviews, these individuals were completely ruled out as suspects in the shooting. We did, however, discover some traces of gunpowder residue on one of the windowsills in the office. My lab people were then able to reconstruct a highly probable shooting scenario by aiming a special laser beam pointer from this windowsill down through the hole in the Sanford Office Building's lobby window. It was clearly demonstrated that if a weapon was fired from this location, the bullet would've hit our victim's leg exactly where she stood on the moving escalator."

"Did your men perform any lab tests on the blood samples that they collected from the crime scene?"

"Yes, they did. They were able to confirm that they matched our victim's blood type exactly!"

"Your Honor, the state wishes to enter into evidence at this time, these two photographs marked as exhibits number 13 and 14. They show the fourth-floor office area across the street from the Sanford Office Building and a view looking down from this office into the lobby of the Sanford Office Building, respectfully. I would also like to enter into evidence at this time the police lab reports. These reports summarize the police lab's testing results that were done on the blood samples found in the Sanford Building, the fingerprints found in the lobby elevator, the windowsill's gun powder residue test, and the lab investigators' conclusions."

"Without objection, Your Honor," Paul declared to the judge again.

"So ordered," the judge responded back.

"I have no further questions for this witness, Your Honor," the prosecutor announced.

"The defense has no questions for this witness at this time, Your Honor, but it wants to reserve its right to recall her at a later time."

"You can step down now detective. You're excused. Mr. Parker, you may call your next witness."

"The state wishes to call Detective Sean Murphy to the stand at this time."

After he had been duly sworn in by the clerk magistrate, he took his seat on the witness stand.

"Detective, please state your full name and occupation for the record."

"My name is Detective Sean Patrick Murphy. I am a detective with the Newton Police Department. I have been working at this position for the last eighteen years."

"Detective, during your career on the Newton police force, have you been involved in many murder case investigations?"

"I have been involved in over thirty cases. The degree of violence that each of them contains continues to surprise me even to this day! Just when you think that you've seen it all, something even worse seems to come along."

"Are you referring to the Dr. Mathews murder case in your last statement?"

"Yes, I am!"

"What events caused you to become involved in this murder case?"

"On April 10, at approximately 1:05 AM, our police dispatcher received a telephone call from a 911 emergency operator stating that a woman had been shot and that she needed medical assistance. We were told by the operator that the victim had been shot in the leg by someone at a different location and that she had driven herself out to a location in Newton. The 911 operator gave us the caller's present location. At that very moment, all of our police units were busy responding to other calls in the city, but we still managed to clear two of our units within a few minutes to respond to her location for assistance. These two supervisory units had to cross the city in order to reach her location. Our dispatcher also informed our two responding units that an ambulance had already been requested by the emergency operator and that it was en route to her location.

"Our two police cruisers arrived at the victim's location at approximately 1:30 AM. In a follow-up meeting with these two responding officers, I was able to confirm that our dispatcher had only informed them that a woman had been shot in the leg at a different location and that she had only requested emergency medical assistance. They were told to respond to this location ASAP and to render all necessary assistance to the victim and the ER personnel en route or already on scene. Upon arriving at the caller's location, they quickly discovered that the injured woman had now become an apparent murder victim. The senior officer on the scene contacted our dispatcher immediately to say that their location had now become a murder scene and that the detectives should be notified.

"Additional units arrived on the scene a short while later, and the entire perimeter was taped off and secured. When Sgt. Braxton arrived at the crime scene, he was quickly brought up to date by one of the officers already on scene. He assumed charge of the crime scene and ordered his men to carefully enter the house in order to determine whether the assailant or assailants were still on scene. He also wanted to check the interior of the house for any additional victims. Everyone was warned not to move or touch anything that they found inside the house before we arrived.

"My partner and I arrived at the crime scene a few minutes later and took over the entire investigation. We interviewed everyone at the scene and procured written statements from all of the police personnel who were involved before we arrived. After the interior of the house had been safely secured, the sergeant directed some of his men to string a police barrier around the property in order to keep all of the curious neighbors and spectators away from the crime scene.

"My partner and I carefully looked over the victim's bloody car, which was parked in front of the house. We observed what we believe was the victim's blood-covered cellular phone lying open on the passenger seat of the car. We then observed and followed a heavy trail of blood on the ground that led us over to the front porch area. The light provided by a street lamp located across the street enabled us to see the victim's body leaning up against the foundation wall under the porch. A large piece of the wooden latticework that had been attached previously to the left side of the porch had been torn off by someone. We observed what we thought were blood smears and cloth fibers around a smaller opening near the base of this latticework. This smaller opening appeared to have been made sometime in the past.

"While shinning our flashlights onto our victim's body, we observed a makeshift belt tourniquet still tightly wrapped around our victim's upper left leg. From what we observed at the scene, we were able to deduce that she had been shot earlier in this leg and that she had managed to drive herself out to this Newton location. This possible scenario would explain the large amounts of blood that we discovered in her car and on the ground leading over to the porch. In addition to this possible scenario, we surmised that our victim, out of fear, had probably crawled over to and through the existing opening in the latticework. She probably did this in order to hide herself under the front porch away from her assailant. When her assailant found her hiding under the front porch, he summarily executed her with a gun fired from very close range," he explained to the jury in a very methodical manner.

"What do you mean by the word "executed," Detective?"

"Well, from what we observed on our victim's body, she had been shot from a very close range and with a very powerful handgun. There were powder burns clearly visible on her neck tissue and clothing. Whoever shot her was really pissed off at her and hated her a whole lot. The manner in which she was shot was very cold and impersonal. Her killer had to have been looking right into her eyes when he shot her. There was no way that she could've survived that type of a wound!"

Paul thought about objecting to the detective's medical conclusion, but he decided to allow it to pass without objection.

"Did you and your crime team find any other evidence at the scene that you deemed to be very important to your investigation?"

"Yes, we did, but we didn't know if we would ever be able to identify it," he answered.

"What was that?" the prosecutor eagerly asked him in anticipation.

"On the side of one of the front porch's floor joists, we found two partially smudged bloody fingerprints. Since none of my men had touched the body, they could only have come from either the victim or her killer."

"I object, Your Honor. The detective is drawing a conclusion about the source of the smudged fingerprints!" Paul complained loudly to the court.

"Sustained," the judge responded back. "Just stick to the facts, Detective, as you observed them."

"Detective Murphy, can you please explain to the court what action you took regarding these smudged bloody fingerprints that you found on the joist under the front porch?" the prosecutor asked him again.

"Well, we were able to successfully lift the prints from the wooden joist. We then sent them out to the FBI lab in Washington for further analysis. We got really lucky down there! They were able to identify them as belonging to the defendant, John Haggerty."

"And is the defendant John Haggerty sitting in the courtroom today?"

"Yes, he is."

"Can you please point him out to the jury?"

"He's sitting at the defense table, next to his attorney, Mr. Tucker," he said as he pointed at the defendant.

"Let the record show that the witness has pointed to the defendant, Mr. John Haggerty. Now, Detective, what events transpired next at the crime scene?"

"The ME arrived on the scene a few minutes later and officially pronounced Dr. Mathews dead at the scene. He took over the actual investigation of her body at that time. My partner and I made sure that all of our men carefully documented everything that they found at the crime scene. We didn't want to make any mistakes."

During the lengthy course of the detective's questioning, the prosecution offered into evidence several photographs taken of the victim's body as it was found under the front porch. Along with these photographs, he also offered into evidence photographs of the interior of their victim's car, her bloody cell phone, and a photograph of the blood trail leading over to the front porch. Two pictures of the torn-off wooden latticework were also identified by the detective and offered into evidence as well. A piece of the actual wooden floor joist that contained the bloody fingerprints found under the porch was identified by the detective and also placed into evidence.

Paul Tucker once again did not object to the placing into evidence of any of the crime scene photographs because he wanted to show the real viciousness of the crime to the jury.

"Thank you, Detective. I have no more questions for this witness at this time, Your Honor, but I will be recalling him at a later time."

"Your witness, Mr. Tucker," the judge announced to him.

"Detective, you told the court earlier that in your opinion, the victim had been executed. You said that she had been shot from such close range, that her killer had to have been looking right into her eyes when he fired the gun! Isn't that what you just testified to in court?"

"I believe that's what I said."

"That would have to be a really cold-blooded act for anyone to do, wouldn't you agree?"

"Absolutely! In my opinion, I deduced that the shooter had to be in a state of uncontrollable rage, so filled with hatred for the victim that he wanted to watch her die from up close," he explained to him.

"That seems rather unusual. After all, anger and rage both tend to cool off as time passes, but this murderer seems to have purposely stalked his victim. After having allegedly shot her earlier in Boston, this killer then pursued her all the way out to her mother's house in Newton. Then in an ultimate act of cold-blooded apathy, he murders her. Have you ever seen such a degree of viciousness like this in any other murder case that you've investigated before, Detective?"

"No, this one has to be one of the worse that I've ever seen!"

"Detective, I believe you said it best earlier! You said that our victim was executed. She was killed by someone who had no remorse about killing someone. Who could do something like that, a professional assassin? A crime of passion, on the other hand, is just what it implies. It's an act committed in a state of intense anger or emotional rage. This murder, however, appears to be something much more heinous, doesn't it? This killer wanted to make sure that his victim saw him as she died. After having blown his victim's neck apart with a large caliber handgun fired from very close range, this monster quietly left the scene. I say to you and to all of the members of this jury that what we are dealing with here is not a crime of angry passion, as the DA wants us all to believe, but a crime of a cold-blooded execution."

"I object, Your Honor! Counsel has not allowed the witness to answer any of his questions. He has instead been making a long oration of his own opinionated conclusions!" the DA complained loudly to the court.

"Sustained. Now Mr. Tucker, you know better than that. Please allow the witness ample time to answer your questions. No more long speeches," the judge warned him.

"Yes, Your Honor. I have no further questions for this witness at this time, but I will need to recall him at a later time also."

"The witness is hereby excused. You may step down from the witness stand, Detective."

"Since it's already twelve forty-five, we will take our afternoon lunch break at this time. The court will reconvene at two o'clock. Court adjourned!" the judge announced to the courtroom with his wooden gavel striking loudly against the strike plate on his bench top.

"All rise!" the court officer shouted as the judge left the courtroom.

"Well, I don't know what to say!" John said to his attorney.

"There's nothing to really say about what just happened in here so far. Today, the prosecution has been simply placing before the jury the facts of their case. It is a case that shows the real viciousness of our killer. I want them to show how cold-blooded and detached the murderer really was from his victim. After that, we will then show the jury how that person could never have been you. Now go have some lunch, and I'll see you back here in a little while."

"Okay, Paul. I'm really glad that you're on my side."

The detectives escorted him from the courtroom to a small holding area, where they once again placed handcuffs back on his wrists. They then took him back to the police station to get some lunch. On his way back to the jail, he and his two guards remained very quiet. They made the entire trip in silence. Even he was deeply aware of what the prosecution's photographs had shown. He couldn't help but think about Helen and how she had been so savagely murdered.

The afternoon session began promptly at two o'clock, and the prosecutor wasted no time in calling his next witness to the stand, the 911 emergency operator who had responded to the phone call from their victim. After she had been sworn in, she took her seat on the witness stand. She identified herself to the court as Ms. Jackie Thompson, who was employed by the state as a 911 emergency operator.

"Now, Ms. Thompson, how long have you been a 911 emergency operator?"

"I have been employed in this position for the last nine years."

"That's a long time, Ms. Thompson. Now during that time, you have probably handled all sorts of emergencies, haven't you?"

"Yes, I have."

"Wouldn't it be safe for me and the court to assume that you've probably become quite an expert in quickly determining over the telephone what a caller's emergency situation is? You have to make a rather fast decision as to whether the caller's emergency is one that requires you to send out a police response or a medical emergency that could require EMTs and an ambulance being sent out to their location or even both."

"I would have to answer yes to your question. Every day we receive quite a lot of 911 calls. Some of them are real emergencies, and some of them are not. I have to listen to each caller very carefully, obtain their location if they are not calling from a hard line, evaluate their situation, and talk to them calmly and reassuringly. While I'm doing this, I'm also notifying the proper emergency personnel to be dispatched out to their location. It could be police units, EMTs, or even both."

"Now, on April 10, you were on duty early in the morning when Dr. Helen Mathews called in on your 911 line, were you not?"

"Yes, I was," she answered nervously.

"Will you please describe to the court what information the victim acknowledged to you over the telephone regarding her emergency?"

"Our equipment is able to instantly identify a caller's location if they are calling from a hard line number. In Dr. Mathews' case, she was calling from her cell phone, and so I had to get her to tell me where she was. She communicated this vital information to me early on during our conversation. I learned from talking to her that she had been shot in her left leg and that she needed medical assistance. Through a series of follow-up questions, I learned that she had been shot at a different location and that she had driven herself out to her present location. I entered a request for an ambulance and paramedics to be dispatched immediately to her location!"

"What about the threat of her shooter?" the DA asked her.

"I had determined that the shooter was no longer a threat to her safety at her new location! After all, she had told me that she had been shot earlier at another location. My immediate and only real concern was for her health, the medical treatment of her gunshot wound. I was also becoming very concerned about the amount of blood that she may've lost from her leg wound. In listening to her vocal responses to my questions, I had determined that she was growing weaker from her loss of blood and about to possibly lose consciousness. Her speech was becoming much more labored and sluggish. I surmised that she was slowly drifting in and out of consciousness."

"Did you inform the police about your medical concerns about this gunshot victim?"

"No, I didn't! I just notified their dispatcher to send over some officers ASAP to her location to offer some additional assistance to the gunshot victim and the paramedics when they arrived! I did, however, contact the EMTs about the seriousness of our caller's gunshot wound and severe blood loss!"

"I am now going to ask you and the jury to listen to the 911 phone recordings taken between you and Dr. Mathews on the early morning of April 10."

"Okay."

The jury and all of the spectators in the courtroom listened very intently to the phone recording made between the 911 operator and Dr. Mathews. It was an awful moment for John to sit through. In his mind, he could see Helen sitting in her car, bleeding and in a state of terrible pain. He covered his eyes as he listened to the final words that he would ever hear her say. He could feel his eyes filling with tears as she ended the call after a few minutes. Paul had seen how the tape had emotionally affected his client, and he patted him supportably on the shoulder.

"Now, Ms. Thompson, after having heard the tape of your conversation between Dr. Mathews and yourself made in the early hours of April 10, do you wish to add anything else to your testimony?"

"I stand by what I have said earlier to the court, but I now add sadly that I wish I had pressed the police more strongly into rushing to her location! I never would have guessed that her assailant had followed her home in order to finish killing her! In a way, I feel somewhat responsible for letting that poor woman down!" she announced very emotionally and tearfully to the jury.

"Your Honor, the state wishes to place into evidence at this time the recording of the 911 phone call made by the victim," he announced to the judge as he handed the tape over to the clerk. "I have marked the tape as the state's exhibit number 24."

Hearing no objection from the defense counsel, the judge ordered the clerk to enter it into the record as such.

"The prosecution has no further questions for this witness, Your Honor."

"The defense has no further questions for this witness either," Paul added briefly.

"Thank you, Ms. Thompson. You may step down from the witness stand. You are excused," the judge informed her. "Mr. Parker, approximately how much time will you need for your next witness to testify?"

"Your Honor, I believe that my questioning of my next witness will take several hours to complete," the DA responded back.

"Then in light of that information, Mr. Parker, I am going to adjourn the trial a little bit earlier than usual because it's already late in the afternoon. We shall reconvene again tomorrow morning at ten o'clock. The members of the jury are instructed to not discuss this case with anyone or even amongst themselves. You are further instructed to avoid reading, listening, or watching any of the media's coverage of this case. Court is now adjourned!"

"All rise!" the court officer announced to the courtroom as Judge Zimmer rose up from his bench and left the courtroom.

The courtroom emptied out rather quickly after the judge had adjourned the trial for the day. Paul leaned in close to his client to inform him that he wasn't going to be able to meet with him later on that day. He explained to him that he had an important meeting scheduled that night with Mr. Parks, their firm's private investigator. After that meeting, he said that he would be too busy catching up on a lot of paperwork needed before their trial resumed the next day. He told him to get a good night's sleep because their next day of trial was going to be a long one. He informed John that the district attorney was going to call the medical examiner to the stand as his next witness. He said to him that the ME's testimony would most likely be very graphic and quite painful for him to listen to.

CHAPTER 9

The block of new jail cells was unusually quiet that evening as John lay awake in his bunk, thinking about the terrible changes that had taken place in his life. He allowed his mind to recall the many wonderful and precious memories that he and Helen had shared together over the last six months. Thinking about Helen and how she had been happily planning the details of their future marriage, he suddenly began to feel sorry for himself. He still couldn't believe that she was really gone and that he had been accused of murdering her. How could so much have gone so wrong so quickly in his life? He kept asking himself. As he lay there quietly thinking, he couldn't help but wonder if her killer had been sitting in the courtroom for the last four days, watching his growing uneasiness. He wondered if he was laughing at him as his noose of growing evidence slowly tightened around his neck. The very idea of him gloating over his handiwork infuriated him. Somehow, he had to get revenge on him, but how? He didn't even know why he had murdered Helen. Eventually, he closed his eyes and drifted off into a light restless sleep.

The sound of the jail's main lights being switched back on again awakened him abruptly from his shallow sleep. It was early, and his body still felt exhausted. He could hear the loud shouts of the guards telling the prisoners to get up and get ready for breakfast. Getting up quickly in the morning had always made him feel nauseous. It was a nervous condition that had plagued him for most of his adult life. It usually left him within a few minutes, but it often left him feeling a little dizzy. As soon as the moment had passed, he carefully splashed some hot water on his face and began to shave. He couldn't help but think about what Paul had said to him the day before. He tried to imagine what sort of appalling details the medical examiner would present to the court when he began his testimony that day. It was a day that John had hoped would never come but one that he knew was inevitable. Paul had told him that he would have to sit quietly through the ME's many long hours of testimony. He said that the medical examiner would painstakingly describe the crime scene, and then he would move on to Helen's autopsy report. It had taken John a long time to get over seeing Helen's bloodied body sitting under the porch, and now he would be forced to endure that painful memory all over again. He knew that the prosecutor would not miss a single opportunity of carefully pointing his accusing fingers toward him during the medical examiner's testimony.

After he had finished washing up and shaving, the guards led him and the rest of the prisoners on his floor down to the cafeteria for breakfast. Overall, John had found the food that they served in the jail to be quite good. In fact, he thought to himself, much too good for some of the hardened criminals who were being held in the new jail facility with him.

After a quick breakfast, all of the prisoners were once again taken back to their cells. When John returned to his cell, he found his dress suit, shirt, tie, and shoes all waiting there for him to change into. A guard told him to change into his suit right away so that they could bring him over early to the courthouse. Paul had brought the suit over from his house a few days earlier for him to wear during the trial. As he changed into it again, he recalled sadly how Helen had helped him pick it out in the store.

John and his escort of two police detectives arrived at the courthouse around 9:30 AM. Judge Zimmer had earned a reputation for demanding punctuality in his courtroom. Neither of the two officers wanted to incur his wrath by being late in delivering their prisoner over to his courtroom. When he had announced to everyone the day before that the trial would resume at 10:00 AM the next day, he meant promptly at 10:00 AM. After the judge had entered the courtroom, the prosecutor and John's attorney approached the judge's bench in order to discuss with him some upcoming legal procedures. Their private conference with the judge lasted for over ten full minutes before all of the attorneys returned to their respective tables. The judge then asked the bailiff to bring the jury back into the courtroom.

"Mr. Parker, you may now call your first witness," the judge said to the district attorney.

"Your Honor, the state wishes to call to the stand Dr. James Witherspoon."

Dr. Witherspoon slowly made his way up from the back of the courtroom toward the witness stand. He was only forty-eight years old, but he moved like he was much older. His dark suit appeared to be somewhat ruffled, almost like he had slept in it the night before. He also appeared to be a little preoccupied in his thoughts. After he had been sworn in by the clerk magistrate, he was told to take his seat on the witness stand.

"Now, Doctor, can you please state your full name and current occupation to the court?"

"My name is Dr. James Andrew Witherspoon. I am the chief medical examiner for the Middlesex County area of Massachusetts."

"Now, Doctor, can you please describe to the court your current qualifications, board certifications, licenses, and other special organizations of which you are presently a member of?"

The doctor's education and list of credentials was quite impressive. It seemed to take forever for him to list all of them for the record. Paul could see that the key to winning his client's freedom would only come if he was able to punch some holes in this expert's testimony.

"Thank you, Doctor. Now can you please describe to the court what events took place on the morning of April 10 that brought you out to the Newton crime scene: the scene of Dr. Mathews's ghastly murder?"

"I received an early morning phone call from the Newton Police dispatcher to come out to an alleged murder scene. Upon my arrival at the crime scene, I discovered the victim's body sitting under the front porch. She was leaning up against the foundation wall. I went over to the victim's body, and after a quick inspection for vital signs, I pronounced her officially dead at that time. During my initial examination of the body, I discovered that the victim appeared to have been shot at least two times. I found that she had been shot at least once in her left leg and at least once or twice in the neck. The victim's upper left leg was encircled tightly by a thin dress belt. I assumed that she had tightened it around her left thigh in an effort to stop the bleeding coming from her lower leg wound. Through a more thorough examination of the body, I was able to calculate and determine with a high degree of medical certainty the approximate time of the victim's death. I was able to place the time of her death at sometime between 1:15 AM and 1:25 AM. We use a number of different techniques to arrive at a victim's approximate time of death. I was able to accurately record her body's temperature drop and to observe that there was a definite lack of rigor mortis. I also observed a large quantity of blood pooled near her body and inside her car. By carefully observing the degree of clotting, which I observed around her wounds, I was better able to fix the victim's approximate time of death. I had also been informed earlier by the detectives that the first two officers had arrived on the scene at 1:30 AM and that they had discovered her body a few minutes later. Taking all of these facts into consideration, along with our victim's own call into the 911 operator at 1:05 AM, I was able to narrow the time of her death down to within a few minutes with a high degree of medical certainty."

"Your Honor, may I approach the witness?" the DA asked the judge.

"You may, Mr. Parker."

"Are these the photographs that you took of our victim when you discovered her body sitting under the front porch of the house?" Mr. Parker asked him as he handed the pictures over to the medical examiner.

"They are," he answered back after he had flipped through them carefully.

"The state wishes to place these seven photographs taken by the medical examiner at the crime scene into evidence at this time."

"Without objection, Your Honor," Paul responded.

"These photographs shall be marked as the state's exhibit numbers 25 to 31," the Clerk announced to the court.

"Now, Doctor, can you please tell the court how you would go about securing a crime scene in order to prevent the possible loss or contamination of evidence at a murder scene?" the prosecutor asked him.

"The most important rule for protecting evidence at a crime scene is to prevent everyone who isn't authorized from entering the area. Secondly, nobody should be touching any of the evidence without the proper training. This rule has to be rigidly adhered to by all of the investigating officers and CSIs at the scene. To ensure the integrity of a suspected crime scene, the officers in charge should immediately tape off the area to keep out all unauthorized people and foot traffic from the area. When I arrived at the Newton crime scene, I found that the area in question had already been taped off by the police. I then asked the senior officers and detectives on the scene to bring me up to date as to what they had found in the area. After that was done, I entered the actual area of the body to confirm that our victim was indeed dead. I took precautions not to disturb any of the evidence that might be in the area until the body and the areas close to it had been carefully photographed. After this was done, I proceeded to then examine the body more closely. I carefully observed and took blood samples from around the body for further testing. I then carefully examined the victim's wounds and took down notes on what I found. As I said earlier, I also recorded her body temperature, the outside air temperature, and other personal observations in my field notes for future reference. I took particular interest in the degree of coagulation of the blood on the body and in the surrounding areas."

"After you had finished examining the victim's body and taking notes on the surrounding areas, did you render a preliminary opinion as to when and how she had died?"

"I did!"

"And what was your preliminary professional opinion as to how our victim had died?" the district attorney asked him.

"I believe I said to Detective Murphy that she had died between 1:15 and 1:25 AM. I told him that she had died from a powerful gunshot delivered at close range to her neck that caused her to die choking on her own blood."

"I object, Your Honor!" Paul interrupted loudly. "The ME has already testified that in his earlier preliminary examination of the body that there was a great deal of blood on and in the proximity of Dr. Mathews's body. The defense contends that the victim probably died as a result of the gunshot made to the victim's neck, but there has been no evidence presented to the court to support the ME's last statement."

"Sustained!" the judge answered as he glanced over at the DA.

"Okay, Dr. Witherspoon, did you later perform an autopsy on Dr. Mathews's body?"

"Yes. I performed an autopsy on her body the following day."

"Is this the official autopsy report that you prepared after examining Dr. Mathews's body back in your lab?" the district attorney asked him.

"Yes, it is! In a detailed examination of our victim's body, I learned that she had almost completely bled out. The bullet that had struck her in her lower left leg had nicked an arteriole as it shattered and lodged in her tibia bone. She had been losing a great deal of blood from this initial gunshot wound. Her attempts to stop the bleeding were only partially successful. She was probably floating in and out of consciousness."

"The neck wound, however, was altogether different. As I testified earlier, this wound was inflicted as a result of the killer placing his weapon in close proximity to our victim's neck at approximately a thirty-degree upward angle, like this. When the gun was discharged, it tore into the soft skin, muscle tissue, and bone located in the center and right side of her neck. The power of the weapon was so great that it quite easily severed all of the major arteries and veins in her neck. Our victim would've died within a few seconds after being shot. My statement to Detective Murphy at the scene that she had died choking in her own blood wasn't too far off the mark!"

"The amount of powder burns that I found on her neck and jacket confirmed the close proximity of the shooter's weapon to her body when it was fired. The gun used was a nine-millimeter pistol. I was able to determine this fact by following the bullet's suspected trajectory. It passed upward through our victim's neck and out of her body. It ricocheted off the concrete foundation wall and then embedded itself inside a wooden support beam. I removed the bullet fragment from the beam and placed it in an evidence bag at the scene."

"Doctor, is this the bullet fragment that you recovered from the wooden support beam under the porch?"

"Yes, it is."

"The state wishes to place this bullet fragment into evidence at this time," he said as he handed the evidence bag containing the lead slug over to the clerk for labeling.

"Without objection, Your Honor," Mr. Tucker added.

The medical examiner spent the next hour going over his notes and explaining to the jury how he was able to fix the time of death so accurately. His testimony on the rate of blood coagulation and body temperature drop were quite fascinating to the jury at first, but they soon all appeared to be getting quite bored with so much technical information. The ME then went into a detailed explanation for the jury's benefit of how his autopsy was able to show how the victim's body had bled out almost completely from the two gunshot wounds."

"The state wishes to place the ME's autopsy report into evidence at this time, Your Honor."

"Without objection," Paul added almost simultaneously.

"I have no further questions for this witness, Your Honor," the DA said to the judge.

"I'm going to stop the trial for our afternoon lunch break. Court will reconvene again at one thirty. The members of the jury are once again instructed to avoid reading, watching, or listening to any of the media's coverage of this trial. You are again warned not to discuss this case with anyone or each other until you are told to do so by me. Case adjourned!"

"All rise!" the bailiff shouted out loud as the judge rose up from the bench and left the courtroom.

Instead of going all the way back to the jail for lunch, the two detectives ordered some sandwiches from the corner deli for John and them to eat. While they were all eating their lunches, John asked the two detectives whether they believed that he was innocent.

Frank, the older of the two men, said that it wasn't up to them to make a call regarding his guilt or innocence. John continued to press him for his opinion.

"Based solely on the evidence just presented in the case so far, I'd have to say that you killed that poor woman in cold blood," he said to him coldly.

"What about you, Tom? Do you think I'm guilty also?"

"I'm not completely convinced of that yet, but there's a heck of a lot of hard evidence that says that you did murder her! I'm keeping an open mind until I hear all of the evidence."

"Well, I didn't kill her, and if I could just get out of jail, I'd find a way to prove my innocence! I really loved Helen. We were planning on getting married in a couple of months. There's no reason in the world for me to want to hurt her! If it's the last thing I ever do, I will prove that I'm innocent. Somebody out there knows that I'm innocent because they killed her! I'm being framed by someone, and I don't even have a single clue as to who they are! Last night, while I was resting in my cell, I began to suspect that they could even be in the courtroom, watching and gloating over their handiwork. Do me a favor when we go back in there. Take a good long look at all of the spectators to see if any of them look suspicious. I swear to you both, I'm innocent!"

* * * * *

"All rise! The courtroom is now back in session with the Honorable Judge Zimmer presiding. Please be seated," the court officer announced to the packed courtroom.

Dr. Witherspoon, the county's chief medical examiner, took the witness stand again.

"Now, Doctor, I must remind you that you are still under oath," the judge said to him.

"I understand, Your Honor."

Paul Tucker stood up from his seat at the defense table and walked over to the speaker's podium located between the two tables. He carefully opened up his notes and began to address the medical examiner.

"Dr. Witherspoon, I was quite impressed with your long list of credentials that you presented earlier to the court. Looking back over your long distinguished career as a medical examiner, you must've seen and investigated quite a few homicide cases. Is that true?"

"I have been involved in the investigation of quite a few homicide cases over those years. I was involved either directly in my capacity as the chief medical examiner for this county or as a consultant who was called in by other law enforcement agencies outside my jurisdiction to offer some assistance."

"Now, Doctor, you testified before this court that our victim in this case was shot by someone at very close range."

"Yes, I did say that."

"Now based upon your field experiences observed over your long career as a medical examiner, isn't this type of a shooting somewhat unusual?"

"I guess I would have to answer yes to your question. Over the years, I have found that most victims of a shooting crime are shot from a distance.

It is relatively rare to find a victim who has been shot at such a close distance. In almost all of these rare cases where a victim had been shot at such a close range, it usually came as a result of an accidental discharge or during a physical struggle where the gun suddenly went off. There is, however, another category that does not fit into either of these categories and that is an execution-style shooting. This type of a shooting is almost always done by a professional killer, up close and usually to the victim's head. This method of execution, however, is not always the only method used by these people."

"Have you ever worked on that type of a murder investigation?"

"Oh yes, numerous times."

"Does the shooting in this case have any similarities to the type of cases that you've just referred to?"

"I suppose it does in a certain way. All of the victims in the cases that you just referred to were shot in the head and at close range. Our victim was also shot at close range and in the neck/head area."

"Why do you suppose these killers always choose to shoot their victims in the head or neck area?"

"I can only speculate that the shooters wanted to make sure that their victims died almost instantly from this type of a shooting. A head shot to the back of the head or to the neck area would more than likely inflict massive amounts of damage to the body. The victim would have little or no chance of being medically saved."

"Looking back over your years as a medical examiner, have you ever seen this type of a shooting used by a partner in a domestic dispute?"

"Yes, but only once. In the case that I'm referring to, there was a long history of severe domestic abuse between both of the partners. The relationship eventually ended in a final highly emotional, hate-filled climax . . . a cold-blooded execution-style shooting. In my opinion, this type of an up close shooting between two emotionally involved people occurs only during a highly charged argument or disagreement where one of the two people gets access to a gun. It's very rare, indeed. In the case that I'm thinking about, one of the two people involved used the gun in a threat, but the other person didn't believe that she would really shoot him. He called her bluff, and she shot him in the head!" he volunteered in response to Paul's question.

"You have to understand that some domestic abuse cases do become so violent that they may eventually lead to the murder of one or both of the parties involved. When a gun is used during one of these highly charged struggles, it sometimes ends in an accidental discharge of the weapon in a close struggle or in a violent shooting from a safe distance. But even in these violent altercations, it is extremely rare to see this type of an up close execution-style shooting of the victim, like we have in the case before us today."

"Thank you, Doctor. I have no further questions for this witness, Your Honor."

The district attorney stood up at his desk and once again pushed home his argument to the jury with a follow-up question for the medical examiner.

"Dr. Witherspoon, isn't it true, though, that this type of a cold-blooded up close shooting does, nevertheless, occur now and then between domestic partners?"

"Yes, it does, but as I said, not too often."

"Thank you, Doctor. The state has no further questions for this witness."

"Doctor, you may step down from the stand. You are excused," the judge said to him.

After looking over his notes for a few brief seconds, the district attorney recalled Detective Sean Murphy to the stand once again. Detective Murphy was summoned from the hall outside the courtroom by the bailiff. A few seconds later, he came through the doors and made his way up to the witness stand again.

"Now, Detective, I must remind you that you are still under oath."

"I understand, Your Honor."

"I understand that your people have been working very closely with Detective Bates of the Boston Police Department on this case. Am I correct?" the DA asked him.

"Yes, that's true. We have been sharing information and leads on this case from the very beginning of the murder investigation. My office took the lead in the investigation because the murder took place in our jurisdiction."

"What event or fact led you to first believe that Mr. Haggerty was involved in Dr. Mathews's murder?"

"At first, we all dismissed him as a possible suspect in Dr. Mathews's murder. Detective Bates and her partner had handled the initial questioning of all of the victim's coworkers a few days after murder had taken place. Later, however, we found a critical piece of new evidence that made him our primary suspect in her murder. As I stated earlier in my testimony, my men recovered a partial set of smudged bloody fingerprints at the crime scene. They were located on one of the front porch's floor joists. At first, I didn't think that we would be able to identify them, but some smart guys down at the FBI labs in Washington came up with a match. They were able to match them to an old firearm's permit application that they still had on file down there. In their report, they positively matched them to the defendant, Mr. Haggerty."

"I guess you could say that this information broke the case wide open for you!"

"Yes, it was our first major break in the case!"

"Now after you had learned about Mr. Haggerty's involvement in this case, why didn't you immediately arrest him?"

"Detective Bates and I were not completely ready to arrest him just on the strength of this new evidence alone. We wanted to get more on him, and so we decided to place him under twenty-four-hour surveillance. We applied for search warrants for both his Arlington residence and his vehicle."

"While your men kept the defendant under surveillance, did he do anything suspicious that alarmed you in any way?"

"Yes, he did! While we were waiting for our search warrants to be granted, the defendant suddenly bolted out of his house one afternoon while carrying a small travel bag. Our men followed his vehicle out to Logan Airport. They were told not to apprehend him unless he attempted to board an airplane."

"And did the defendant try to board an airplane at the airport?"

"Yes! Our men intercepted him at one of the departure gates at the Continental Airlines terminal. A flight to California had just started to board."

"Was the defendant arrested by your men at that time? And did your men also advise him of his legal rights after they had arrested him?"

"Yes, they did. After they had patted him down for weapons, they found in his possession a one-way ticket to LA. It was currently boarding at that very gate."

"Detective, it appears as though your men intercepted the defendant just before he was able to board that flight to LA."

"I believe so!" the detective answered back proudly.

"Where did your men take the defendant after they had apprehended him at the airport?"

"He was placed in a police van and taken back to the Downtown Boston Police Station for further questioning. His vehicle was impounded at the airport garage and towed back to their secured police yard for further examination and safekeeping. We were only detaining him at the station for questioning and until your office made a final decision as to whether to charge him with Dr. Mathews's murder. While he was being held at the station, my men and I were carrying out the terms of our search warrants for his house and motor vehicle."

"Did you and your men discover any new evidence during the search of his house?"

"Yes, we did."

"And what was that new evidence?" the DA asked him eagerly.

"We found in his closet a suspicious-looking pair of shoes and a soiled dress shirt rolled up inside his bathroom hamper. Both of these items appeared to have dried blood stains smeared on them. We bagged both of these items and sent them out to the State Police Crime Lab for further testing."

"And what did the State Police Crime Lab learn after testing the two items?" the DA inquired further.

"Their tests confirmed that the stains seen on the shoes and shirt were dried human blood. Upon learning this new information, your office ordered DNA screening tests to be done on the blood stains and compared to samples of Dr. Mathews's blood. We just received the results back from the lab yesterday. They confirmed that the blood traces found on the defendant's shoes and shirt matched Dr. Mathews's blood exactly!"

A soft murmur of muffled voices could be heard coming from the spectators sitting in the courtroom. The judge tapped his gavel lightly against his strike plate to restore order in the crowded courtroom.

"The state would like to place into evidence at this time the defendant's shirt and shoes. We would like to also place into evidence the State Police Crime Lab reports summarizing their tests done on these two items. The DNA blood screening tests were done at an independent DNA testing lab in Boston, and their report is also being submitted at this time, Your Honor."

"Without objection, Your Honor," Paul responded quietly.

The clerk assigned exhibit numbers to all of the state's new pieces of evidence and recorded them into the official court record. The DA then announced to the judge that he had finished questioning the witness.

Paul walked over to the podium again with his notes and carefully began to question the detective in detail about his client's arrest at the airport.

"Now, Detective, you testified earlier in this courtroom that my client was apprehended at the airport terminal by your men when they believed that he was about to flee the state. In fact, that wasn't the case at all, was it, Detective?"

"He was arrested at gate 10, where a flight to LA was just starting to board. In the process of searching him for weapons, the detectives found on him a one-way ticket to LA. Now if that's not getting ready to flee the state, then I have no idea what is!"

A quiet laugh could be heard again in the courtroom from the spectators.

"Detective, what was my client doing when he was apprehended by your men near gate 10? Was he checking in with the agents for a seat assignment on the flight, or was he roaming the hall looking for someone?" Paul asked him a little more forcefully.

"I don't know. My men reported that he was just standing around the area between the gates when they approached him. He might've been waiting there purposely until the very last minute. For all we know, he may've been planning on making a last-minute dash toward the plane just before the doors closed."

"Now, Detective, let's be accurate about this. Didn't your men report to you that my client had told them that he had gone to the airport in order to meet with a man who had called him at his house? Didn't he also tell your men that the stranger on the phone had informed him that he had some very important evidence for him that could lead to the arrest and conviction of those who had murdered his fiancée? And didn't he . . ."

"Your Honor! I object! Defense counsel hasn't allowed the witness to answer any of his questions. Instead, we are all being subjected to a tirade of the counselor's unsubstantiated statements!" the district attorney pleaded.

"Sustained! Now, Mr. Tucker, I've warned you before to ask your questions and to allow the witness ample time to respond to them."

"I'm sorry, Your Honor. I'll try to be a little bit more accommodating in my line of questioning."

"Now, Detective, didn't my client tell your men that the stranger had told him that he was about to leave the area for good and that this would be his only opportunity to get the incriminating evidence from him?"

"My men said that he was mumbling something about a man that he was supposed to meet out there, but he wasn't very clear about who the man was. So they dismissed his loud ramblings as nothing more than the venting of his frustration in being caught by them."

"So in their haste to apprehend my client, the real murderer, or information about who that person was, was dismissed by them without even a second thought. Your men could've at least looked around the gate areas for this stranger. After all, my client wasn't going anywhere. They already had a description of the stranger as given to them by my client when he was being placed in handcuffs. Instead, they just handcuffed him and carted my client away. I would have to say that a serious injustice was done to my client at that time by your two men."

Paul pressed this information home quite loudly to the jury. He shook his head in disgust to show the jury that the detectives had closed their ears to his client's pleas for help.

"My men did a great job in apprehending a man whom they had good reason to believe was a fleeing murderer! Why else did he have a small travel bag of clothes with him and a one-way ticket to LA?" the detective shouted back at Paul.

"Did either of your men ever ask my client those questions at the time? No, they didn't! My client would've told them that he needed a valid ticket on him in order to gain access into the gate areas. That's why my client had to purchase the ticket and for no other reason! He took the small travel bag with him just in case he had to jump onto the plane to follow the stranger if he arrived at the airport too late for their meeting! Do you see how easily your facts fall apart when they are looked at from another angle?"

"Your Honor, I object! The defense counsel is once again trying to volunteer unsubstantiated answers on behalf of the defendant. If he wants to explain away his client's actions, then let him put him on the stand!" the DA protested.

"Sustained! Now Mr. Tucker I've warned you before that you are not to press your opinions into evidence as facts like that again. The jury is instructed to totally disregard what Mr. Tucker has just volunteered in the way of unsubstantiated statements of facts. There has been no testimony given to support any of his conclusions."

"I'm sorry, Your Honor," Paul said to the judge again, but he was still glad that the jury had heard his explanations.

"My men did their duty, and they did it well. They apprehended your client before he entered the plane. It was a field judgment call, something which they have been trained to make every day. It is based on protecting the safety of the other people on board the plane and in the gate waiting areas. I don't buy your client's explanations. You may think that your explanation of the facts works here, but it doesn't! It stretches the truth just a little too far!"

"That's your opinion, Detective, but your job is to gather evidence and to trace down all possible leads, not to dismiss them without even a second thought. I'm sorry, but your men blew their chance at finding the real murderer that day!"

"I have no further questions for this witness, Your Honor," Paul concluded.

"You're excused, Detective," the judge said to him.

The judge decided to stop the trial after the detective left the witness stand. It had been a long hectic few days of trial for both sides. Judge Zimmer warned the jury once again not to listen to any of the media's coverage concerning the case and to not discuss the case with anyone or each other until told to do so by him. It was Friday, and so the case was adjourned for the weekend and not scheduled to reconvene again until Monday at 10:00 AM.

"I think everything went a little better for us today, John! We managed to show the jury how rare this type of a domestic murder is and how the police made a few major errors in their pursuit of the truth in this case. They did manage, however, to score some pretty powerful points in the evidence that they seized at your house. We'll take care of that one later. All in all, we didn't do too badly today! I have a lot of work to do this weekend on putting together our defense. So I'll see you again on Monday in court."

Paul's positive assessment of the day's events made John feel a lot better as he was led out of the courtroom by the two detectives. He knew that he would be able to sleep a lot better that night.

CHAPTER 10

The smoke from his cigarette appeared to hang stationary in the air in front of him for a long time. It was a vaguely familiar image that he hadn't thought about for quite a long time. He tried to remember why the image seemed to bother him so much, but he couldn't. He took another long drag from his cigarette and then once again slowly exhaled it into the cool night air. After a few minutes, his mind began to recall a similar image from his distant past. It was an image that had happened so long ago that he had all but forgotten about it. It had taken place in a small isolated village in Central Siberia. He had been quite young back then: a mere teenager trying to survive on his own. He remembered how cold and deathly still the Arctic night air had been. It was a time in his life in which he seemed to be always hungry and cold. Whenever he exhaled his warm breath into the cold Arctic night air, he watched in awe as it floated only a few feet away from him before it stopped abruptly. Even back then, he remembered how much the image had bothered him. His mind had told him that it should've dissipated into nothingness, but instead, it had simply formed a moisture cloud directly in front of him. He remembered asking a few of the older villagers why their breaths had just hung in the air in front of them whenever they exhaled, but their only explanation to him was that it was called the living fog. It sounded strange to him at the time, but he had accepted their explanation without question. They told him that it was a common phenomenon seen in all of the villages in Northern Siberia during the cold Arctic winters. It was a sign that something living had recently passed by.

As he now looked out across the well-lit square in the center of the financial district of Boston, he could see that he was almost alone. He observed a few lonely souls scurrying by to get home or to a late Friday night rendezvous of some sort. He could still see the silhouette of Mr. Paul

81

Tucker sitting behind the darkened glass panes of the old lounge. He would be an easy target for him to hit, but he knew that his death would serve no purpose for them. He silently moved his body back into the shadows of the darkened doorway across the street from the old restaurant. He continued his lonely surveillance. The air was colder than usual that night, and so he pulled his collar up tighter around his neck for some additional warmth.

It was almost nine thirty in the evening when Mr. Parks eventually walked into the old restaurant/pub near Post Office Square in Boston. It was becoming a regular meeting place for him and Paul Tucker. Irene, the owner's wife, recognized him immediately and warmly directed him over to where Paul was sitting alone in a booth in the far corner of the small restaurant. He could see that Paul was deeply engrossed in his work of carefully plotting out his ever=changing strategy for the defense of their client, Mr. Haggerty.

"Ah, Harold, I was wondering where you were. Would you like to order something to eat? Jim doesn't shut down the kitchen in here until after ten o'clock," he politely asked him.

"No, thanks, Paul, I ate dinner a couple of hours ago. I'm still trying to lose a few of those extra pounds that I managed to put on over the last twenty-two years while on the police force. I could use a strong drink, though. It's a little raw outside tonight."

Irene had sent a young waiter over to their booth after he had been seated, and he now quietly stepped forward to take his order.

"I think I'll have a double scotch please . . . and something else for you, Paul?"

Paul hesitated for a brief moment before he answered, "Yes, I think I'll try another drink . . . Ah, Peter, bring me an Irish coffee this time. I'm in a rather nervous mood and maybe a little whiskey with my coffee might help settle down my nerves a little bit!"

The waiter nodded his head and headed off toward the bar. Jim's Pub was located just inside the business district of the city, and it offered its patrons a limited selection of great meals. Jim's kitchen was small, but what he made in there was very much appreciated by everyone. The lounge was a great place in which to get a quick drink, a great no-frills dinner, or simply to catch up with some old friends again. During the week, it was quite busy all day long. It stayed open until eleven o'clock every night, but its crowd thinned out rather quickly after nine o'clock. James Doherty, the restaurant's lone owner, didn't mind the fact that his place got much quieter at night. It was the perfect time in which he got to meet and talk to many of his regular customers. Paul Tucker had become one of Jim's favorite customers over the last six years. During that time, Paul had been able to help his friend successfully get out of a number of legal problems, which he had been having with the city's licensing board. Over the years, Paul had come to see his friend's place like a second home. Back at his law office, his secretary always knew where to get in touch with Paul whenever he wanted to be alone. Jim's Pub had also become a favorite meeting spot for many of the city's other lawyers: a place to hang out in for a few drinks after a long trying day at work.

"How did we do in court today?" Harold asked him curiously because Paul was still busy tapping away on his notebook computer. It was an all too familiar sign that Harold had come to recognize in his friend's actions whenever he was deeply worried.

"Not too bad, but it could've been better. The DA has a very strong case against John, but I'm trying my best every day to poke as many holes in it as I can. It's the hard evidence, such as the blood-covered shirt and shoes found in his house, that are going to be almost impossible to explain away without putting John on the stand. Today, they focused most of their case on their apprehension of him at the airport. I think I may've planted a few seeds of doubt in the minds of some of the jurors. Everything in this case seems to be so pat . . . so set up that I can't seem to put my fingers on what this whole case revolves around!"

"What about you? Did you manage to find out anything more about our victim's past?" he asked him curiously as Peter, their waiter, returned to their table with their two drinks.

"No, nothing yet, but I still have a few more friends out there trying to dig up something on her past. So don't worry so much! I'll turn up something new in a few days. For some reason, there seems to be something about this case that bothers me a lot also. I've had a strong hunch from the very beginning that this case is a hell of a lot bigger than either one of us could ever imagine!"

"Well, I certainly hope that you can turn up something solid and real soon. I hate to admit it, but we're running on empty on this one, and it's slowly starting to fray my nerves."

"Did they put any of my old detective friends up on the stand today?"

"They put Detective Sean Murphy from the city of Newton up on the stand today. Under my cross examination, I let him know that his two Boston detectives did a very poor job at the airport when they didn't even attempt to check out our client's explanation for being there. After that statement, I may have to avoid driving through Newton and Boston for the next two months."

"Na! If he's anything like me when I was on the force, he won't hold a grudge against you for any longer than two weeks," he answered back with a smile now showing on his face.

"Thanks, that's very reassuring to know."

"I'm trying to track down some of Dr. Mathews's old college friends and colleagues this weekend. They might be able to shed some light on what and with whom she was working with for the last three years. I figure it's worth a try at least," he announced to Paul as he swallowed down the last of his scotch.

"Well, if you happen to find out anything important, let me know right away!"

"I will do that partner. Is there anything else that you want me to check out more closely for you this weekend?"

"No, nothing right now. I'm still kind of groping around in the dark. I still don't know which way to move yet."

"Okay . . . then I'll give you a call later on this weekend. Thanks for the drink, and try not to knock yourself out. I'll turn up something on this one to help you. I always do, you know!"

"Let's hope so . . . especially for John's sake!"

"Take care, Paul," he said as he stood up and walked away from the table.

Paul took another long sip from his mug of hot Irish coffee. It had been a long day for him, and he was letting the case get to him personally. He knew better than to allow that to happen to himself, but this was a case whose facts were just too pat. If his client was innocent, which he now strongly believed, how could there be so much irrefutable evidence showing up against his client? There had to be a bigger point to this case, and he was determined to find it.

Harold waved good-bye to his friend Jim, who was still standing quietly behind the bar, filling new orders for some of his other customers. Jim nodded his head in Harold's direction. Harold carefully made his way around a few people who were standing together having a loud conversation near the center of the bar. He then slowly made his way through the thinning crowd toward the exit of the cozy old pub. He too had come to know Jim quite well over the last two years ever since he had first started working for Paul's law firm. As he pushed open the restaurant's heavy exterior door, he could feel a cold blast of the outside night air rushing in to meet him. It sent a chill running up his spine. He buttoned up another button on his long coat and then hurried down the empty sidewalk toward his car. Having spent a lifetime of working and living in the city, he was always keenly aware of everything that was happening around him. The distant footsteps of someone walking across the street made him hesitate in his stride for a brief second in order to take a look back in its direction, but there was nobody there. He shrugged his tired shoulders and dismissed it as nothing more than an echo bouncing off one of the city's many tall buildings in the area.

Harold had been a good detective on the Boston Police Department for many years. He had received a lot of special commendations from the city for those many years of faithful service. As he made his way toward his home in South Boston, he had a strange feeling that he was being followed. He had become a real pro at picking up a tail from his years of undercover work in vice and homicide. He kept his eyes focused on the car that appeared to be following him. Whoever was following him was good. It was not an obvious tail but one that he knew was there. He wasn't too far from where he lived, and so he made an awkward turn onto G Street to see if the vehicle would continue to follow him up the hill. As he slowly made his way up the hill, he could see the headlights from the strange car as it also turned onto G Street. As soon as Harold's vehicle made its way over the top of the hill, he pulled his car over to the side of the narrow street. He switched off his headlights and waited there with his engine still idling. He waited patiently for a full five minutes, but the vehicle never came up over the hill. Whoever had been following him had probably seen through his ploy and had turned off onto another side street instead. Harold had at least managed to partially make out the type of vehicle that had been following him. It looked like a dark late-model two-door Ford.

He pulled his car back out into the middle of the street and continued on his way home. He did not see the strange vehicle again that night as he pulled into a parking space in front of his building. The entire incident was starting to make him feel a little bit more uncomfortable. Now he knew that he would have to be a lot more careful wherever he went.

Harold sat alone in his small kitchen, staring patiently at his automatic coffee maker. He never liked to use the machine during the week because he enjoyed the company of his old friends down at the local coffee shop instead. On Saturdays, however, he preferred to stay home and enjoy his coffee alone in his kitchen. It was the hassle of dealing with the weekend crowds that seemed to bother him the most down there.

He glanced down at his morning newspaper. After a few minutes, he began to think about what he had to do later that morning. He looked over at his rather plain-looking wall clock and observed that it was now 9:45 AM. Karen had told him to come by her security office on the MIT campus at around 11:00 AM. On Friday, she had informed him over the telephone that she would not be able to gather all of the information that he needed before then. From the very first moment that he had met Karen, he knew that he was attracted to her. Their fifteen-year age difference didn't seem to bother either of them. They had dated a few times after their initial meeting, but he didn't feel comfortable dating her again after he had learned that she had just separated from her husband. He never liked being in the middle of a complicated relationship, and so their relationship gradually moved in another direction. Over the last twelve years, they had become very close friends.

They had first met on a case in which he was investigating the death of a young MIT student. The young man had been found murdered one night in an alley in Boston. She had helped him track down some information on who his friends were at the university. Karen and Harold had worked so well together on that case that they had remained close friends ever since.

When he had met with Karen earlier in the week, he had asked her to dig up some of the university's old personnel records from around the time when Dr. Mathews had worked at the university under Dr. Tinkoi. He had informed her that he was particularly interested in finding out the names of some of her closest friends and colleagues from that time. He had also asked her to try to learn about what kind of research projects she had been working on back then. She had told him to call her back on Friday after she had done some of her preliminary detective work.

The coffee machine had finally finished brewing his coffee, and so he carefully poured himself a full cup. He then settled down in his favorite chair to enjoy his coffee with his morning newspaper. Glancing momentarily up at the wall clock, he could see that he still had plenty of time to spare before he would have to shave and dress for his important meeting with Karen.

CHAPTER 11

Karen poured herself another cup of hot coffee from the steaming fresh pot that she had just finished brewing in her office. She stirred in a couple of teaspoons of sugar and then added a small amount of cream to soften its rich flavor.

"Are you sure I can't get you another cup, Harry?" she politely asked him again.

"No, thanks. I've already had one too many cups since early this morning."

"It's been a long time since you and I have worked together on a case. Hasn't it?"

"I guess it has been at that!" Harold answered back with a smile showing on his face.

"When we bumped into each other the other day, I was really glad to see you again. I had been wondering what the heck had happened to you since we last saw each other. You look really good! I think retirement seems to be agreeing with you. So what have you been doing with yourself for the last two years since you retired from the police force?"

"Well, I tried to stay retired, but after a while, I found myself with much too much free time on my hands. The walls of my small apartment started to close in on me. There just weren't enough things out there to keep my mind occupied. I soon found myself missing the company of my old friends and all the excitement that my job as a detective had provided me. I eventually had enough of it and took on a job as a private investigator for one of Boston's most prestigious law firms. It's a job that really keeps me on my toes every day. I like my independence and the feeling of being able to decide when and where I want to go without some department head continuously looking over my shoulder every minute. I still manage to keep in touch with most of my old friends on the force. In a way, I guess I would have to say that I'm really enjoying my retirement from the department. I've also found out that being an ex-cop gives me a definite advantage. It still opens a lot of doors for me that would be closed ordinarily to most other private eyes."

Karen quietly shut her office door so that they could talk in private without the fear of being overheard by any of her staff. As she walked back over toward her desk, she caught a quick glimpse of Harold unconsciously checking her out. When he saw that she had caught him looking at her body, he nervously tried to look away. She was glad to see that he still found her very attractive. His actions suddenly made her feel young once again. At forty-five years of age, she had managed to keep herself in great shape. She worked out hard every morning for at least an hour at a gym down the street from her apartment. Her efforts had managed to keep her figure slim and her muscles taut. It was an exhausting daily routine to adhere to, but it kept her from falling apart like most of the other guards whom she worked with every day.

"I suppose it would. Now what exactly is your involvement in the Dr. Helen Mathews murder case?"

"Well, the alleged suspect in the murder case is being represented by the law firm that I work for. Our client, Mr. Haggerty, swears up and down that he's completely innocent, and frankly, most of us believe him. Did you read that he and Dr. Mathews were engaged? They were planning on getting married in a couple of months. The DA's case has no real motive behind it. The thing that bothers me the most about this case, however, is that there is so much incriminating evidence stacked up against him. Only a complete fool could have left behind so many damaging clues. It just doesn't make any sense! In all of my years as a police detective, I have never seen so much incriminating evidence collected against a suspect as I have in this case!"

"Well, are you really that sure that he's innocent?"

"I'm almost positive that he is! In fact, none of us at the law firm have been able to find even the slightest hint of a plausible motive for him to have killed her! They were totally in love!"

"So why are you bothering to look into Dr. Mathews's past?" she asked him curiously.

"I have a hunch that this case is a whole lot bigger than any of us could ever imagine! I believe that the key to solving her murder lies somewhere in her past. Where exactly is a question that I don't seem to have the slightest idea about where to look yet."

"So that's why you wanted me to dig up as much information as I could on Dr. Mathews's past when she was doing some of her research work over here at MIT?"

"That's right! It might be our only way of tracing down her murderer. What did you manage to find out about her?" he eagerly inquired.

"Now you know that everything that we are about to discuss in here is unofficial. All of the information that I have collected so far can be obtained anytime by the police in the files at the school's archives department. The trick is in knowing where to look for it. I was quite surprised to learn that some of her research was being sponsored by the U.S. Government. I discovered that a large number of files concerning her research work have been either misplaced or removed completely from the archives by someone."

"What do you mean by misplaced?"

"Just what I said. Most of the files relating to her research, her grants, and her personal notes and files have all disappeared. They had to have been removed or stolen from the department by someone. I didn't see anything in the department's official records for that time period that would have authorized such a purging or appropriation of these files."

"This case seems to be getting even more bizarre with every new clue that's supposed to turn up but doesn't!"

"It is certainly starting to look that way right now, especially since we now know that some of her research was being funded directly by someone in our government. And who could've absconded so cleanly with all of these records and files better than someone in our own government? We may've unknowingly stumbled upon something that might eventually become very critical to your investigation!"

"I think so! In the records that you did manage to find, did you happen to come across the names of some of the people who might've known or worked with Dr. Mathews when she was around here?" he asked her hopefully.

"I think so! It took me a hell of a lot longer to read through some of those old files than I had originally planned, but I did manage to come across the names of a couple of researchers. One of them worked in Dr. Mathews's lab for only a couple of months before he took sick and dropped out of school. He returned about a year later in order to complete his doctoral studies in electrical engineering and computer science. The second individual only showed up when I began to search through some of the records of another laboratory that was located directly across the hall from the labs that were under Dr. Tinkoi's direct control. This researcher was hurt in a small explosion and fire that occurred one night in the labs across the hall. I found a number of references in this other lab's records that seemed to suggest that the two labs sometimes worked together. I discovered numerous invoices in their lab files that suggested that they were sharing a lot of chemicals and specially designed pieces of electrical testing equipment between them."

"What was the name of the first person . . . the one who was working with Dr. Mathews until he dropped out of school?"

"His name was Philip J. Stevens. He's a PhD now. He might be working somewhere now as either a professor or a researcher in his own field of electrical engineering."

"And what was the name of the second person who was hurt in the fire?"

"The second name that I came across in the files was a . . . Toni Grey."

"Is that a man or a woman?" he asked her, somewhat confused.

"Well, from the way that the name was spelled in the records, I can only assume that this Toni was a young woman."

"Were you able to find out what may've happened to this Ms. Grey after she was hurt in the lab fire?"

"No, not really. The entire record of what Ms. Grey had been working on in her labalong with all of her personnel records have all been mysteriously removed from the school's archives also. It was only through a few accidental cross-references that I was able to get even these small tidbits of information. All of the school's main computer records have also been conveniently altered or purged. They only mention vaguely that Dr. Mathews was doing some research work at the school for a couple of years under Dr. Tinkoi's supervision. I wasn't even able to locate any of the payroll records or equipment requests on our main frame computer for that time period. Whoever doctored our computer records did a very thorough job of it!"

Upon hearing everything that Karen had been able to uncover so far, Harold's facial expression gradually changed from one of curiosity to one of frustration. His mind began to put together a new twist to the Dr. Mathews murder case. It was quite obvious to him now that the government was somehow behind her research and possibly even her murder. It was not going to be easy for him to uncover much more about Dr. Mathews's past, especially since most of the relevant information had been thoroughly purged from the school's records years earlier. He sat back in his chair and silently began to ponder over his remaining options. Karen watched him closely as his mind began to work out a possible way to track down the two people whose names she had been lucky enough to uncover in the old files.

"Karen? Whatever happened to this Dr. Tinkoi? Does he still work at MIT?" he asked her hopefully.

"No, he doesn't. He's dead. Don't you remember hearing about a crazy accident that took place down by the waterfront about three years ago? It involved an accidental shooting between a security guard and Dr. Tinkoi. The guard thought that he was attempting to break into one of the government's few remaining naval storage depots in Boston. The guard accidentally shot and killed him when he thought he saw him reaching for a gun. The shooting was investigated thoroughly by the FBI and the military police. They concluded that the entire incident was nothing more than a tragic accidental shooting. They ascertained that Dr. Tinkoi had parked his vehicle down by the pier and was preparing to do some night fishing. It had been his fishing reel that had reflected back at the guard and not a handgun. There had been a couple of attempted break-ins at the depot that week, and so all of the guards were a little bit edgy that night. Now I'm starting to wonder if his shooting death wasn't part of another governmental cover-up," she said to him.

"His death might've been the successive elimination of another loose end in this case!"

"What else do you want me to do for you?"

"Your work on this case is over for now. I don't want you to get into any trouble over what you just uncovered. I'll let you know if I find out anything else about these two people. Karen, I really appreciate what you just did for me. I owe you a first-class night out on the town for this!" he said to her.

"I'm going to hold you to that!" she smiled sensuously back at him.

"I hope you will!" he answered back with his own face now slightly flush.

"Don't wait so long this time to give me a call again. We still have a lot of unfinished things to catch up on!" she mischievously added.

He could hear and see in the tone of her words and subtle actions that she still liked him a lot also. He could feel his body's own mutual attraction for her urging him to take her in his arms. He was eagerly looking forward to rekindling their romance again now that she was divorced. He slowly got up from his chair and walked over toward the door of her office. She followed his actions and quickly moved in the same direction. At her office door, she moved in close to him and gave him a soft lingering kiss on his lips. Then without saying anything else, she slowly opened her office door, allowing him to leave. As he made his way through the lobby of the small security office, a smile formed on his face as his senses continued to detect the inviting scent of her perfume and the taste of her sensuous lips. His car was parked directly in front of the campus security building. As he lowered his body down onto the driver's seat, his mind flashed back over everything that he had just learned about Dr. Mathews's past. He was slowly beginning to realize that the more he searched for clues, the more unanswered questions he would probably find. He knew that he still had to uncover the real truth behind her murder, but where? As his mind quickly recalled and sifted through all of the intricate details of the bewildering case for answers, he couldn't stop himself from thinking about Karen's sensuous kiss upon his lips . . .

* * * * *

"They couldn't have found out anything that was important from the university's official records, sir. Everything at the university concerning her research records, her friends, and her colleagues at the school have been completely purged from the official record. We were very thorough in what we did over there. We left behind only a few basic facts that confirm that she did some research work in the science building. We left absolutely nothing else behind that could lead them to us. I promise you sir that anyone who looks at the school's official records will only discover that she did some research work over there and nothing more!"

"Let's hope so! Again, keep me posted on anything new that develops in this case. I do not want it to get out of hand."

"I will, sir!"

CHAPTER 12

Paul looked down nervously at his watch again. He knew that he was going to be late for his 11:00 AM appointment with Harry, and there was nothing that he could do about it. As his eyes scanned down the long row of cars stuck in traffic in front of him, he could sense his body becoming more restless. He hated to be late for anything in his life. He felt very strongly that being on time for everything was a true measure of a man's professionalism and respect for other people's feelings.

"Damn it! Doesn't anyone in this state stay home on Sunday mornings anymore?" he shouted inside his car to himself.

The driver in the car next to him glanced over in his direction when he heard Paul's loud shout. He then just as quickly turned away from him again in order to keep a watchful eye on the cars stopped in front of his own vehicle.

Paul allowed his eyes to wander away from the road and upward into the clear blue sky. It was a perfect day to have spent at home with his loving family, but the urgency of John's case had demanded that he go to his office that Sunday morning to meet with Harry. The damning evidence against his client was beginning to shake even his strong belief in his client's innocence. He inwardly hoped that Harry would be able to stem this rising feeling of doubt about John's innocence.

His eyes focused in on a few isolated wispy white clouds that seemed to be just floating high above the city in the clear blue sky. Without the wind, they appeared to be stuck in one place in the sky. As he continued to stare up at them, he could sense their gentle therapeutic effect acting upon his strained nerves. Gradually, he became more relaxed as his eyes continued to stare up at them.

The loud sound of a horn blasting from one of the cars stuck behind him in the traffic startled him back to reality. He felt his entire body lurch slightly forward from the loud sound. As he quickly glanced around, he could see that the long row of cars in front of him had already moved forward. He waived his left hand in acknowledgment of his lapse in attention and slowly allowed his vehicle to catch up to the now slow-moving traffic ahead of him.

As he made his way into the city, he looked out upon the vast amount of highway construction that the state had undertaken in the Big Dig Project. Everywhere he looked, he could see construction workers and their massive machines busy at work even on a Sunday. For a brief moment, he wished that he too had chosen a less nerve-racking occupation than that of a criminal defense attorney. As he reflected on some of the alternative occupations that he saw around him, he soon dismissed them all because none of them paid enough money. The hard physical exertions, which most of them demanded every day, was something that he had never really been very good at doing. At that moment, he knew that he had made the right decision in becoming a trial lawyer. It was a decision that had made him both popular and very wealthy. His reputation as a successful defense attorney was something that he had become very proud of.

The parking lot at his office building was almost empty when he drove his car into it at eleven twenty that morning. He could see that Harry's car was already parked in the corner of their main lot. He felt guilty once again for being late. He quickly hurried up the steps to the main lobby of his office building. He signed in at the security desk and then hurried over to one of the two main elevators, which were kept working on Sunday. As he opened his office door, he observed Harry reclining on a long office sofa patiently waiting for him to arrive.

"I'm sorry, Harry, for being so late. I'm usually very good at keeping my appointments. It was that damn traffic on the Southeast Expressway and all the new construction taking place down there that's responsible for making me late today."

"Don't worry about it, Paul. You are only a few minutes late anyways," he said to his nervous friend.

As he poured himself a strong black coffee, he began to ask Harry a few questions. "How did your meeting at the university go yesterday? Were you able to find out anything new that might help us in our case?" he inquired of his friend.

"Yes and no! In a manner of speaking, the evidence or general lack of it over there seems to suggest that there's a major conspiracy afoot! Everywhere that Karen and I seemed to look, we discovered more and more missing files. It's as though someone had deliberately emptied the main frame computers at the university of everything that even remotely referred to the fact that Dr. Mathews had worked there in the past! Someone did a real thorough job to make her and any information about her research completely disappear!"

"Do you have any ideas as to who those people might have been?"

"No, not yet, but there still might be a way to find out who's behind this conspiracy. Karen's still trying to locate some of the school's old hard copy files that might still be around. From what we have been able to learn about them so far, they were extremely thorough in what they were able to accomplish over there."

"What do you mean by that?"

"I believe that we are dealing with someone or even a group of people in our own government. For some unknown reason, I believe they're behind this entire cover-up and murder!"

"What makes you think that they're from our own government?"

"Who else could've gotten away with such a surgical purging of all of the university's computers? They managed to purge every single record about Dr. Mathews. They also managed to purge every document that even remotely mentioned anything about her research, its funding, and any of the people who were involved in it. We did learn, however, that some of her research was funded by the government. They were really good at covering their tracks over there. They left behind almost nothing for us to follow up on. And besides that, both of us have never worked on a murder case that has provided us with so much incriminating evidence as this one has!"

"I couldn't agree more with your last statement. And if you're right about our own government being involved in this cover-up and murder, then where do you suggest we go from here?" Paul asked his old friend.

"Well, that's precisely why I wanted to meet with you today to discuss a future strategy."

Paul got up from his desk and walked over to the large picture window in his office that looked out over the city of Boston. He stared out at the picturesque silhouette of the city beyond; its uniquely styled buildings were illuminated in the late-morning sun. After a few minutes, he turned around to face his friend again. He had a strange expression showing on his face. It was an expression that Harry had not seen on his face before; it was an expression of fear.

"If you and Karen are right in what you have surmised about this case, then all of us could be putting ourselves in real danger. If Dr. Mathews was involved in some sort of a secret government-sponsored research project, then she may have been killed because of what she knew. Whoever ordered her death will not stand around idly while we attempt to uncover the real truth behind her death. There has to be a reason as to why she was murdered, and we have to find out what that reason was. Our problems in this murder case have now increased twofold."

Most importantly, I will have to continue to put up a good defense against the DA's case. I cannot allow them to convict an innocent man under any circumstances. While I continue to do my best in the courtroom, you will have to keep digging away at Dr. Mathews's past. There has to be someone out there who knows a lot more about her past than what we've been able to uncover so far. Harry, I'm really counting on you now more than ever. You may, however, be placing your own life in real danger when you start making inquiries about Dr. Mathews's past. Please be careful out there and watch your back at all times. If you need more help, I will gladly pay for it! I kind of got used to having you around here these last two years. Promise me that you'll be careful out there on the streets!" Paul said to him very concerned.

"Believe me when I say to you that I understand the risks. I haven't lasted twenty-four years on the streets as a detective and a PI by being sloppy and careless!" he answered back confidently and reassuringly to Paul.

* * * * *

When ten o'clock eventually rolled around on Monday morning, Paul found himself sitting at the defense table busily scribbling down a few last-minute changes in his notes. The sound of the bailiff's voice momentarily interrupted his concentration.

"All rise! The Honorable Judge Zimmer is now entering the court!" the bailiff's voice shouted loudly to the courtroom full of spectators. As soon as the judge had taken his seat behind the bench, everyone in the courtroom once again sat down in their seats. Because the media's coverage of the murder trial had become so intense, there was a high demand for the limited number of spectator seats available in the courtroom every day. In an effort to be fair, the court officers drew lots out of a jar every morning for those who had come early enough to register for a chance to get one of the highly sought-after seats. The judge hit his gavel against the striker plate on his desk to call the court proceeding to order. He then directed the bailiff to bring the jury back into the courtroom so that the trial could get under way again.

"Mr. Parker, you may call your next witness."

"Thank you, Your Honor. The state, at this time, wishes to call to the stand, Mr. Andrew Gold."

One of the court officers went out into the hall of the courthouse to summon Mr. Gold into the courtroom. After a brief delay, the officer returned to the courtroom with Mr. Gold. The bailiff directed him over toward the witness stand. He was then sworn in by the clerk before he took his seat on the stand. The DA told him to state his full name and occupation for the record. The DA then quizzed him thoroughly about the special training that he had undergone in order to become a CSI officer. When he had finished, the DA congratulated him on behalf of his impressive list of accomplishments, which he had earned while working for the Boston Police Department for the last twelve years.

"Now, Mr. Gold, you've stated in court today that you are presently assigned to the downtown precinct of the Boston Police Department and more specifically to the detective bureau. Would you please inform the court what your duties would be when you are summoned out to a crime scene by the detectives?"

It's my duty to make sure that all of the evidence that is gathered at a crime scene is properly collected and accurately documented. It is also my responsibility to secure these items until they are needed for trial and/or future testing back at the lab. I also make sure that the crime scene is properly photographed and even videotaped sometimes for the detectives. It is also very important that I make sure that the crime scene is kept free of all unnecessary foot traffic until we have finished collecting all of the evidence. This includes the collecting of blood samples, weapons, ammunition casings, letters, fingerprints, and anything else that might aid the detectives in solving the crime. It is critically important that we prevent any of this evidence from becoming contaminated or lost in any way. Therefore, my men and I very carefully bag, seal, and log in everything at the scene before it is transported back to our lab. The chain of custody of all gathered evidence must be carefully documented and safeguarded."

"Now, Mr. Gold, were you involved directly with two of the crime scenes in this case? I'm referring to the Sanford Office Building and the two empty offices located directly across the street from it?"

"Yes, I was. I directly oversaw all of the evidence gathering that took place at both of these locations for Detectives Bates and Bolten."

"And did you also assist in the searching of the defendant's automobile for evidence after it had been impounded by the police out at the airport and transported back to your lab?"

"Yes, I did. Under orders from Detective Bolten, I had the defendant's car sealed and towed back to our secured police yard. Then later that day, I personally began a thorough search of the car for evidence. I noted in my field notes that the vehicle was still locked and sealed when I attempted to open it. I used a special tool to jimmy open the vehicle's door. I recovered from inside the defendant's vehicle several rounds of nine-millimeter ammunition and an empty shell casing from a .30-06 rifle. They were found lying between the two front seats."

"Now you said that these items were found lying inside the defendant's locked car, didn't you?"

"That's correct. The vehicle was both locked and sealed by us earlier. The driver of our police tow truck did not have to get into the vehicle. He simply impounded it and towed it back to our yard."

"Now if I recall correctly from the ME's autopsy report and statements, our victim was shot twice and by two different types of weapons."

"Your Honor, may I approach the witness?"

"You may, Mr. Parker."

"I have here a copy of the ballistic report that was compiled by your lab on the bullets that were recovered from our victim's body and from the wooden porch's support beam that was behind our victim's body. Would you please look over this report and tell us what types of bullets were recovered from Dr. Mathews's body and from the Newton crime scene?"

"The ballistic report states that the two bullets were fired from a nine-millimeter handgun and a rifle."

"Are these the same types of bullets and casings that you found inside the defendant's vehicle?"

"Yes, they are."

Another soft wave of conversations could be heard coming from among the spectators in the courtroom.

"The state wishes to place this ballistic report into evidence at this time, Your Honor."

The judge looked over at the defense table to see if Mr. Tucker had any objections to his request. Not hearing any, he so ordered the clerk to mark it up as another exhibit for the state's case.

"I have no further questions for this witness, Your Honor. Thank you, Mr. Gold."

"Do you wish to question this witness, Mr. Tucker?"

"Yes, I do, Your Honor," he answered as he slowly walked over to the podium again. "Now, Mr. Gold, you have testified to this court that the collecting of all evidence in a criminal investigation has to be handled very carefully. First, it has to be collected and documented accurately. Then a chain of custody has to be properly maintained. Am I correct in these statements?"

"You are, sir."

"Now the reason for this so-called chain-of-custody rule for evidence is to guarantee that it is not contaminated or tampered with in any way between the time of its collection and its eventual testing in the laboratory. Isn't that so?"

"Yes."

"Now the two arresting detectives out at the airport had testified earlier in this case that the defendant had said to them that he had gone out there to meet with someone. At least that's what the two detectives had written down in their reports now in evidence. They said that they thought he had said this to them as they were taking him away. Now how long was the defendant's motor vehicle parked out at the airport before it was sealed and then subsequently towed by the police back to the police impound yard?"

"Well, I would have to say approximately one and a half hours."

"Now that's quite a long gap in your so-called chain-of-custody rule. Isn't it, Mr. Gold?"

"No, not that long. We found the defendant's motor vehicle still locked and parked out in the open airport when we impounded it."

"Well, let's examine the official record a little bit more closely. You just testified to the court that the defendant's car was left unattended at the airport for about one and a half hours."

"I believe so."

"Would it surprise you to learn that the defendant's car was really parked unattended out at the airport for over two hours and ten minutes. This is the actual time difference between when the defendant was taken into custody at the airport and when the police tow truck driver recorded impounding his car. The two police reports show this quite clearly, don't you agree?"

"I'm not quite sure. I don't have those reports in front of me right now."

"Your Honor, may I approach the witness?" Paul asked the judge.

"You may, Mr. Tucker."

"Now from these three reports that I have here, can you more accurately ascertain for the court how long the defendant's car was left out at the airport unattended?" Paul handed a copy of the two detective statements and the police impound yard's report to him. He looked over the three reports very carefully. He observed the time statements clearly written on all of the three reports.

"I guess my previous statement was not accurate. Your statement of two hours and ten minutes was more accurate."

"Now, Mr. Gold, while this car was parked unattended out at the airport, wasn't there ample enough time and opportunity for someone to carefully open the defendant's vehicle, like you did back at your station later, and to plant evidence inside the car? Then they only had to lock it back up again?"

Mr. Gold hesitated slightly before answering Paul's hypothetical question. He carefully thought about the three police reports and the long time delay that existed before they took custody of the vehicle.

"Would you like me to repeat the question again, Mr. Gold?"

"No, I heard the question. I suppose someone could've done what you suggested, but it's highly unlikely."

"No, Mr. Gold, this is probably what happened that very day out at the airport, especially given the ploy used to get my client out there in the first place!"

"I object, Your Honor! Defense counsel is once again trying to offer unsubstantiated hearsay on his client's behalf without calling him to testify."

"Sustained," the judge responded back quickly. "Now, Mr. Tucker, I warned you earlier not to get into this particular area again. If you want your client to testify as to the reason why he was out at the airport, you may call him as a witness."

"But, Your Honor, the detectives out at the airport wrote in their reports that my client had told them that he had gone out there to meet with someone. I have only repeated what they had written in their official police reports and nothing more. These reports were placed into evidence earlier by the district attorney."

"The jury is to only consider what is written down in the detective statements concerning what the defendant might've said to them when he was being taken into custody," the judged clarified to the jury.

Mr. Tucker waited a few minutes to allow his point to sink into the jurors' minds more deeply before he resumed his questioning of the witness.

"Well, Mr. Gold, we can now see the importance of the chain-of-custody rule and how a source or piece of potential evidence can become suspect to tampering or contamination if it is not properly protected! I'm through with this witness, Your Honor."

"Mr. Parker?"

"I have no further questions, Your Honor."

"The witness may step down. You are excused," the judge said to him politely.

"The state now wishes to call Ms. Nina Kline to the stand."

Nina was a good-looking woman. She had just turned twenty-nine last month and had celebrated her birthday in the laboratory with her friends. By choice, Nina was still single. She didn't want to settle down too early in life like her mother had done. As Dr. Mathews's junior assistant, she was very happy in her job for the last three years. But now that her closest friend was dead, the entire research laboratory was filled with uncertainty.

John watched her closely as she walked up to the stand and was sworn in by the clerk. He and Nina had become very close friends over the years, and he knew how much Helen's death must've really hurt her.

"Now, Ms. Kline, how long have you known and worked with the deceased?" the DA asked her.

"I met Dr. Mathews about three years ago when I came to work with her and Dr. Stern. We seemed to hit it off very well from the very beginning. She made everyone around her feel important and special. Dr. Mathews, or Helen, as many of us got to know her, Carol, and I all became very close friends over the last three years."

"Did you happen to notice anything different about Dr. Mathews's demeanor or actions over the last couple of months?"

"Yes, I did. I don't know whether it was Carol or me who first noticed a definite change in her. You have to understand that Helen was always in a great mood every day, but about three months ago, she seemed to take on a genuine glow of happiness. It was something that she couldn't hide. She was always smiling and playing small tricks on us. The lab was like a second home to many of us, and she was like a big sister to me. I was the last person to leave the laboratory on the night that she was murdered. I checked in on her just before I went home for the evening. She appeared to be deeply involved in her work that night. She told me that she was planning on working a little later that night. She asked me to make sure that the outer door to the lab was locked when I left. I left her there all alone and . . ."

At that point in her testimony, she broke down emotionally on the witness stand. The fact that she had left her best friend there all alone that night still haunted her every day. She couldn't stop blaming herself for not having stayed with her longer that night.

"Your Honor, may I approach the witness?" the DA asked.

"You may, Mr. Parker."

"I'm sorry, Ms. Kline, for having to put you through this, but it is necessary. Here are some tissues. Can I get you a glass of water?" the DA politely asked her.

"No, thank you. I'll be okay now. It's just that I can't seem to get her out of my mind. I keep thinking that if I had stayed there with her that evening, she might still be alive right now!"

"That's something, Ms. Kline, that you should never blame yourself for. In your capacity as her assistant and friend, did she ever confide in you that she was afraid of someone or something?"

"No, never!"

"What about her work? Was she working on something very important? Something that someone might've wanted to steal from her?" he continued to probe her gently for clues.

"No, as far as I know, she never discussed what she was working on with any of us in the lab. She did her thing, and we did ours. However, whatever she was working on seemed to take up a lot of her free time."

"Now, Ms. Kline, as a researcher in Dr. Mathews's laboratory for the last three years, were you acquainted with the defendant, Mr. Haggerty?"

"Yes, I know John very well!"

"While you worked in the lab, did you ever happen to observe Dr. Mathews and the defendant together?" he continued to probe.

"Yes, I did. In fact, whenever I saw them together, they appeared to be quite cordial and very much at ease around each other. I didn't really observe her showing any special signs of affection toward him in the lab, but then again, that wasn't what Helen would do at work. She was very professional in the lab except when us girls got to clowning around together."

"Did you see the defendant and Dr. Mathews ever arguing?"

"No, I can't say that I ever did."

"Did you happen to notice anything strange or unusual about the defendant's actions in the lab on the day after Dr. Mathews was found murdered?"

"Well, most of the girls in the lab, including myself, were pretty much emotionally in shock that day. Some of the men weren't doing too well emotionally that day either. John, however, turned into a hermit. He just buried himself inside his cubicle and continued to work. David said that it was his way of handling Helen's sudden death. I guess he was trying to somehow deny that she was really gone."

"Did you or any of the other people in the lab know that they were romantically involved with each other before that day?"

"No, I don't believe any of us had the slightest idea that they were romantically involved."

"Thank you, Ms. Kline. I have no further questions."

"Mr. Tucker, do you wish to question this witness?"

"No, Your Honor. The defense has no questions for this witness at this time."

"Ms. Kline, you are excused. You may step down from the witness stand," the judge said to her politely.

The DA then called Carol Masterson to the stand. She was another coworker in Dr. Mathews's laboratory. Her testimony lasted a little bit longer than Ms. Kline's, but still there were no bombshells dropped by her testimony that the defense would have to deal with. It was just after twelve thirty when the DA finished questioning her, and so the judge halted the trial for their afternoon lunch break. He rescheduled the trial to resume again at two o'clock.

A short while before the judge reconvened the trial at 2:00 PM, the district attorney met privately with Detective Murphy for about ten minutes. Harold Parks watched the two men as they quickly discussed something that appeared to be very important. When they were through, the detective hurriedly exited the courtroom. Harold was tempted to trail him, but he felt that it wasn't necessary.

At 2:08 PM, the trial was finally called to order again by Judge Zimmer. The DA called his next witness, the security guard who worked at the Sanford Office Building. After he had been sworn in, he took his seat on the witness stand.

"Now, Mr. Tingos, could you please state your name and occupation to the court?"

"My name is Brad Tingos, and I am presently employed as a night security guard at the Sanford Office Building in Boston. I have been working there in that capacity for the last four years."

"Will you please summarize for the court all of the events as you recall them that occurred on the night of April 10 at your place of employment?"

"I had just completed making my evening rounds of the lower two floors of the Sanford Office Building, and I was returning to my security station in the main lobby. As I neared the front doors of the main lobby, I thought I saw what appeared to be a large pool of dark red liquid smeared across the marble floor just below the main escalator. I walked over to the area to investigate what it might be. Upon closer examination, I became convinced that the red substance was indeed blood. As I followed the smeared blood trail across the lobby floor, my heart began to pound away uncontrollably in my chest. I nervously followed the trail of blood into the garage elevator and then down into the now-empty garage. I then quickly returned to the lobby once again where I proceeded to take a better look around the place. I soon discovered that there was a substantial amount of additional blood splattered against the left side of the escalator and also on top of its railing.

"I ran back over to my security desk in the lobby to check the building's night log and to determine if anyone was still working inside the building. I quickly learned from the night log that Dr. Mathews was still working in her office. I attempted to contact her by telephone, but without any success. I shut down the escalators and then hurried up to her offices on the mezzanine floor. I knocked quite loudly on the outer door but received no response back. I then inserted my master key into the lab door's outer security lock and typed in my security override code into the security keypad located next to the door. I swung open the door and entered the laboratory. I looked around the darkened offices and found them all to be empty. I relocked the lab and reset the lab's alarm system before returning to my security station in the lobby. I reviewed the security tapes of the executive garage and saw Dr. Mathews on them. I observed her driving alone in her vehicle up to the garage's outer door control panel. I watched her enter her private code onto the keypad to raise up the closed security grid in front of the garage's exit. I was able to see on the film that she appeared to be in obvious pain and that her left hand appeared to be covered in blood. The security grid opened, and she quickly drove out of the garage. I then called the police and waited for them to arrive."

"Is this the tape made by the garage's security cameras that evening?" the DA asked him.

"Yes, it is. Detective Bates told me to turn it over to Mr. Gold that night, which I promptly did. I believe he was one of the CSIs on the scene that night."

"Your Honor, I will need a few minutes for my associates to set up a few monitors around the courtroom so that the jury and court can watch this short security tape."

"Mr. Tucker?" the judge inquired in his direction.

"The defense has no objection to this tape being shown to the jury," he responded back.

After a few minutes, all of the monitors had been carefully set up around the courtroom. One of the DA's assistants signaled his boss that they were ready to proceed.

"May we have the lights in the courtroom dimmed please?" Mr. Parker said to one of the officers in the courtroom.

John stared stoically at one of the monitors that was facing the defense table. On the monitor, he silently observed Helen slowly driving up toward the garage's exterior door. She pulled her car up alongside of the exit door's control panel. John's heart was overcome with a sudden wave of emotion when he saw Helen's blood-covered left hand reaching out her car window to type in her access code. From her facial expressions, he could plainly see that she was in a state of terrible pain and panic. Her once-beautiful smiling face reflected back the pain and fear that she was experiencing. On the tape, he could also hear the sound of her labored breathing and her faint groans of pain as she typed in her code. In anguish, he lowered his head down into his cupped hands as he watched the last few recorded moments of her precious life slowly slipping away. Paul reached over and patted him supportably on his back. He whispered to him to stay strong.

"Your Honor, the state wishes to place this tape into evidence at this time," the clerk took the tape from him and recorded it into the record as such.

"Without objection," Mr. Tucker responded.

"The state is through with this witness, Your Honor," the DA concluded.

"Your witness, Mr. Tucker."

"The defense has just a few questions for this witness, Your Honor. Now, Mr. Tingos, you have stated to this court that you have been working as a security guard at the Sanford Building for about four years."

"Yes, that's correct."

"Now during the brief period of time in which Dr. Mathews had moved her complete laboratory operations into your building, did you happen to form an opinion as to what kind of a relationship existed between the defendant and Dr. Mathews?"

"I object! The witness is no expert on relationships. His opinion has no bearing on this case. It's immaterial," the DA interrupted.

"Sustained. Mr. Tucker can you please restate your question differently?"

"I will, Your Honor. Now in your capacity as a professional security guard, Mr. Tingos, you have to continuously observe people all day long as they enter and exit your building. Some of these people you recognize, and some of them are strangers. Isn't that true?"

"Yes, it is. It's all part of my job's duties," he explained.

"Now when you first see a stranger entering your building, do you size them up or form a general opinion about them?"

"Well, the first thing that I have to determine is whether they even belong in the building. By this I mean, are they lost or merely looking for one of our residents? These people can be helped right away and are often very thankful for the assistance. Now when I see strangers entering the building who look very suspicious, either because of how they're dressed or by the way that they're acting, then I usually confront them right away. Over the years, I have become quite adept at reading most people's faces. I can usually determine quite accurately what emotional state they're in or what they're up to by just looking at and talking to them. People are always sending out signals. The trick is in learning how to recognize them."

"Now I want you to carefully think back over your memories of Dr. Mathews and the defendant. What did you observe about their body movements, their daily attitudes, and their general feelings, if any, that they may have displayed for each other when you saw them together in public?"

"Well, Dr. Mathews was a real charmer. She was always very friendly to me and to other people that I observed her sometimes talking to in the lobby. She was a real classy lady. I'm really going to miss her. Mr. Haggerty, on the other hand, was much more reserved. He appeared to be less confident or sure of himself when he was around other people. In the beginning, just after Dr. Mathews had first moved her operations into our building, she and the defendant appeared to be just polite associates who worked together. Gradually, I began to see a definite change occurring in the two of them whenever they were together. She liked being close to him. Late one night, while they were riding the escalator down from their office, I happened to observe their body language. It was the subtle but purposeful glances that they gave each other that especially caught my eye. I often witnessed them teasing each other by casually bumping or brushing into each other. There appeared to be something very special going on between them. I'd bet my job on that fact!"

"Now did you ever see the two of them arguing?"

"Yes, but just once. It was on the mezzanine floor next to the escalator one evening. I couldn't be sure what they were arguing about, but she was quite upset about something. From what I observed, he didn't hit or threaten her in any way. When they descended the escalator a few minutes later, they both appeared to be very calm and composed."

"Like they had reconciled or made up?"

"I guess you could describe it like that."

"Now do you remember when this argument took place?"

"I'm pretty sure that it took place a couple of days before she was murdered."

"Thank you, Mr. Tingos. I have no further questions for this witness at this time, but I reserve the right to recall him at a later time."

"Mr. Parker, do you wish to cross-examine this witness again?" the judge inquired.

"No, Your Honor," the DA responded back.

"The witness is hereby excused."

"The state wishes to call Ms. Emily Wicker to the stand."

Ms. Wicker was brought into the courtroom and escorted up to the witness stand by the bailiff. After she had been sworn in, she took her seat on the witness stand.

"Now, Ms. Wicker, can you please state your full name and occupation to the court?"

"My name is Ms. Emily E. Wicker. I am presently employed as a waitress at the Silent Wave Restaurant in Rockport," she said nervously into the microphone.

"Now, Ms. Wicker, have you ever met or seen either the defendant or the victim in this case before?"

"Well, I was never really introduced to either of them, but I have seen both of them before. I first happened to meet them a couple of days before the victim, that poor Dr. Mathews, was found murdered. They were having dinner together in the restaurant where I was working. I recognized her right away from a newspaper photo of her that was published a few days after she was found murdered. I called the police to tell them about what I had overheard and seen that evening. They were having a heated argument about something. I believe I heard him say loudly to her something like, "It's your stupid lab and all those long hours you spend in it that really bothers me the most!" I'm not really sure what else they were arguing about that night, but their argument did last for almost five full minutes. They eventually managed to calm down and order dinner from their waitress. I didn't really give the matter too much thought until after I had read about her murder in the newspapers a few days later."

"Are you sure you can't remember overhearing anything else about what they were arguing about that night?"

"No, but I do remember hearing her call him John a couple of times that evening."

Another less noticeable murmur of conversations seemed to float through the audience again when they heard John's name mentioned by the waitress. The judge hit his gavel a few times against the strike plate on his desk to restore order in the courtroom.

"And do you recognize anywhere in this courtroom today the person that you saw in the restaurant that evening who was arguing with Dr. Mathews?"

"Yes, I do. He's sitting right over there!" she said while pointing her finger at John.

"Let the record show that the witness has pointed to the defendant, Mr. Haggerty," the DA stated for the record that was being recorded by the court stenographer.

"Thank you, Ms. Wicker, I have no further questions," the DA added as he walked back to his seat.

"Your witness, Mr. Tucker," the judge responded.

"Now, Ms. Wicker, during this so-called heated argument that you happened to only briefly and faintly overhear, did you ever see the defendant raise his hand or act threateningly in any manner toward the victim in this case?" he calmly asked her.

"No, I never did."

"Thank you, Ms. Wicker. I have no further questions for this witness, Your Honor."

"You are excused, Ms. Wicker. You may step down from the stand," the judge said to her.

"Your next witness, Mr. Parker."

Detective Savanovitch entered the courtroom again and handed a folder over to one of the court officers standing guard next to the courtroom exit. He whispered something to him and then stepped back out into the hallway again. The court officer brought the folder up to the DA's table. The DA quickly glanced over its contents for a few seconds. He then stood up and placed a copy of the police report on the defense table in front of Mr. Tucker.

"The state wishes to call Detective Peter Savanovitch to the stand."

Detective Savanovitch was called back into the courtroom again and told to take the witness stand. He was sworn in and then questioned by the district attorney.

"Will you please state your full name and occupation to the court?"

"My name is Peter Savanovitch. I am presently employed as a detective on the Newton Police Department. I have been working closely with my partner, Detective Sean Murphy, on the Dr. Helen Mathews murder investigation."

"Now, Detective, I was just handed a copy of an old police report that was filed some seven years ago by the defendant. Where did this report come from?"

"Well, during the course of our investigation, my partner and I started to piece together a number of facts in this case. From the medical examiner's report, we learned about the type of weapons and bullets that were used to kill our victim. We then learned about the suspect's identity from a thorough FBI fingerprint search and that he once held a handgun permit. Then through a properly executed search warrant, we learned about the suspect's involvement with our victim in this case. Since we did not find a handgun in the defendant's house or on his person or in his vehicle, we decided to look at old police records to see if the defendant had ever filed a police report for a stolen or lost weapon in the past. We asked the Arlington police to search their old file records for any such reports since he has always resided in their town. They eventually came across this old police report filed by the defendant seven years ago for a stolen handgun."

"I strongly object, Your Honor! I don't see any relevance of this old report to this case!" Mr. Tucker strongly protested to the judge.

"Sustained! Mr. Parker, where are you going with this report?"

"I will show the relevance of this testimony very shortly, Your Honor."

"Mr. Parker, I will allow you just a little more leeway in this matter, but you had better show me the relevance of it very quickly!" he warned him

"I will, Your Honor. Now, Detective, can you look through this old police report and then tell us what the caliber of that stolen handgun was?" the DA asked him.

"It lists the handgun as a nine-millimeter pistol."

"And what was the final disposition of that case, Detective?"

"According to the Arlington Police, the case is still unsolved."

"Your Honor, the state would like to place this police report into evidence at . . ."

"I object, Your Honor! This report has no bearing whatsoever on this case!" Paul protested loudly to the judge.

The Judge motioned the two attorneys over to the side of his bench for a sidebar conference away from ears of the jury.

"Your Honor, my brother is attempting to poison the jurors' minds with this report. It's simply an old police report filed by a responsible citizen regarding a lost or stolen handgun. My client was required by law to file such a report when his weapon disappeared. Now after seven years of failed police work to find the weapon, we are now supposed to let the jury assume that my client never really lost the weapon in the first place. It's a setup by the state that's completely unfair and highly prejudicial to my client."

"Well, Mr. Parker, what have you to say about that?" the judge asked him.

"We feel, Your Honor, that the report may've been filed properly by the defendant at the time when the handgun had disappeared, but what if the defendant found that same gun later and never reported that information to the police? Then the existence of this gun could become very important to the outcome of this case. This scenario of a recovered handgun could be a very viable possibility. But even if it isn't true, then the jury can be told by Your Honor to treat this report as a simple filing of a police report. They can be told that they are not to infer anything out of the report except that the defendant once owned a nine-millimeter handgun."

The judge waived the two lawyers back to their respective tables. He sat quietly at his bench, thinking about his dilemma with the old police report. While he was thinking about their two arguments, some of the spectators in the courtroom began to get a little noisy. He used his gavel to quiet them down again. A few minutes later, he made his decision known to everyone.

"It is the decision of the court that the old police report will not be allowed into evidence. I'm sorry that you the members of the jury even heard about it, but you did, and that is my fault. The existence of this document is to be forgotten by all of you. Its relevance to this case is nonexistent. If you find that you cannot forget what you have just heard from this witness, then you may only infer from it that the defendant once owned a gun in his lifetime and that it was stolen or lost many years ago."

"You may continue with the questioning of your witness, Mr. Parker."

"I have no further questions for him at this time, Your Honor."

"Mr. Tucker?"

"The defense has no further questions for this witness either, Your Honor."

"The witness is excused. Due to the late hour, we shall adjourn the trial at this time and reconvene at ten o'clock tomorrow morning. As per my previous instructions, the jury is once again reminded not to discuss this case with anyone or each other until they are told to do so by me. You are again warned not to listen or watch any of the media's coverage of this trial also. Case adjourned!"

"All rise!" the bailiff shouted out loudly to the courtroom as Judge Zimmer stood up and quickly left the courtroom. The bailiff then escorted the jury out of the courtroom.

"Well, I would say that we did a pretty good job attacking the DA's case. My spirits are beginning to feel a little bit more confident about our chances of winning this case. I don't want you to think, however, that it's going to be easy! We still have a long way to go in successfully acquitting you of this murder," Paul said to his client with a newfound sense of confidence.

"So you really think that things went much better for us today?"

"Positively! And if I were you, I'd certainly sleep a lot sounder tonight."

* * * * *

"Well, Sam, what do you have to report to me about our present situation?"

"I feel that the district attorney's case is not going as well as we had hoped. Most of the DA's hard evidence is not hitting the jury as hard as we had intended it to. We may have to deal with our problem in a more personal and direct manner."

There was a few seconds of silence on the phone before the voice on the other end of the call began to speak again.

"I will clear my schedule and make all the necessary arrangements to see you in a couple of days at our regular meeting place at 11:00 PM."

"I look forward to seeing you, sir, in a couple of days," he said just before the line went dead.

All of the phone calls that he seemed to have with his boss were always short and right to the point. He knew all too well from the tone of his boss's voice that everything that was happening around him was about to become a lot more complicated in a few days.

CHAPTER 13

Harry sat in his car outside Karen's townhouse condo for almost fifteen minutes before he finally found the courage to knock on her front door. She had been patiently waiting for him to arrive for dinner for over thirty minutes. She had planned their special evening dinner together as a way in which they could catch up on old times. He hoped he wasn't making another foolish mistake in rekindling the flames of their one-time serious relationship again. In her office last Saturday, they had both experienced the same mutual attraction for each other that had existed between them in the past. He finally gave in to his desire to see her again and hesitantly exited his car.

"Well, there you are! I was beginning to think that I was going to be stood up again. How come you're so late this evening? No, on second thought, don't tell me until I make both of us a drink. Are you still drinking scotch?" she asked him as she walked sensuously into her kitchen to fix them both a drink.

"Yes, scotch will be just fine," he answered back quickly.

"Do you want it on the rocks or straight up?" she shouted out to him from the kitchen.

"On the rocks, please!"

Karen lived in a small but spacious two-bedroom townhouse condominium. Down near the Charles River. She had furnished and decorated it tastefully in her own unique style. Her subtle feminine touches could be seen everywhere throughout the unit. The room's interior lighting had been purposely dimmed down to give the entire place a softer, more intimate atmosphere. The entire townhouse smelled faintly of her intoxicating perfume and the scent candles that she had lit earlier in the day. In another room, he could hear some classical guitar music playing softly on her stereo. His nose could smell the delicious aroma of the dinner that she had prepared for them emanating from the kitchen. It awakened his forgotten appetite. The overall atmosphere of her entire place seemed to relax him completely. She returned to the living room carrying a glass of scotch and handed it to him. She sipped nervously on a glass of white wine that she had poured for herself.

"What shall we toast to, Harry?" she asked him as she tapped her glass gently against his.

"How about our renewed friendship?"

"Well, that sounds safe enough," she answered back with a smile showing on her sensual lips. "You would've toasted to a lot more a few years ago!" she echoed back at him.

"I know, but now I've grown to be a lot wiser and more careful in what I wish for." He smiled back at her teasingly.

He took another sip from his glass of scotch and allowed its strong taste to stimulate his tongue's senses before he swallowed it. She watched him carefully as he leaned back on the sofa and enjoyed his drink.

"Something smells really good in here. What is it?" he asked, trying to make small conversation with her.

"Well, it could be both the dinner that I've prepared for us tonight, or it could be me and the intoxicating perfume that I'm wearing."

"I think it's probably both," he answered back while looking up at her from the sofa. "Come over here and sit by me on the sofa for a few minutes. I want to ask you something."

She eagerly took up his offer and snuggled up close to his right side.

"How have you been really doing these past few years since we last saw each other?" he asked her with a sound of genuine concern hanging on his words.

She lowered her eyes and thought for a brief moment and then answered his disarming question. She answered him without looking up into his caring face.

"I've been really lonely, Harry," she said to him quietly. Her words showed him how vulnerable she was really feeling at that very moment.

Harry placed his arms around her and held her tightly. He wanted to take her in his arms at that very moment and carry her upstairs to her bedroom. He wanted to make love to her over and over throughout the night, but he knew that he would be taking advantage of her weakness. So instead, he held her close to him and kissed her tenderly on the lips. He could feel her responding to his every move. His hands stroked her soft hair and cheeks with a purpose. His nose breathed in her intoxicating fragrance, while his mouth tasted her sweetness.

"I know all too well what you're feeling right now, my love, because I've been very lonely myself. Since you and I parted ways, there has been no one else in my life. We owe it to each other to move much slower this time. I don't want to hurt or lose you a second time."

She looked up into his strong face with her inviting eyes and smiled sensually.

"Nor do I want to lose you again either."

Their eyes seemed to meet in a warm, mysterious embrace as they both looked longingly into each other's soul. It was as though their years apart didn't matter anymore to either of them. There was along sensual moment of silence between them before either of them spoke again.

"Well, I hope you're hungry at least!" she said to him teasingly.

"I could eat a horse!" he answered back with a smile. He then passionately kissed her once again on her waiting lips. When their lips finally separated, he looked into the warmth of her eyes and whispered, "And where is that horse anyway?"

They both seemed to break out into a laugh at the same time. "Well, I do declare! You're just like all the other men that I have ever known in my life, and as you know all too well, there has been very few of them. Food has always seemed to turn them on the most!"

"You greatly underestimate yourself, my dear."

"I sincerely hope so!" she said to him as she rose up from the sofa with him in tow. "Let's eat. I've prepared for you a feast for a king," she said to him as she led him out into the dining room.

The dining room was decorated beautifully with what he assumed was her best china and silverware. In the center of the table, she had a set of candles that softly illuminated the dinner table. He was quite impressed with what he saw.

"Sit here while I bring out our salads and another drink for us."

When she returned and joined him at the table, he began to regret the years that he had lost without her at his side.

Their dinner was everything that she had promised. She had expertly prepared for them a Caesar's salad, veal marsala, linguini in a light sauce, homemade Italian bread, and for dessert, a mound of fresh blueberries perched carefully upon some lightly whipped heavy cream. He couldn't remember having eaten so well in years.

When they were finished eating, she escorted him back out into the living room to enjoy a cup of hot coffee with some Sambuca, while she quickly cleared off the dining room table. As he sat there enjoying his coffee, he closed his eyes and listened to the soft background music. He felt completely at ease in her home; it was a feeling that he didn't want to ever lose again.

"Well! Am I a good cook or not?" he heard her ask as she curled up on the couch close to him again.

"I haven't eaten that well in years. I never really knew that you could cook so well. If I had, I think I would've come looking for you a lot sooner."

"Liar! Men like you are extremely rare and almost impossible to hang on to. When you lost your wife seven years ago, a part of you seemed to close up forever. It's as though you didn't want to disturb that fragile memory that you and Mary had built together. In a way, it was the same for me and Kyle. When we divorced each other, a part of me seemed to give up on life altogether. I didn't want to ever bring another man into my life again. When you and I became involved for a short time, you were like a lifesaver to me. When you suddenly broke off our relationship, I was really hurt. In time, I slowly got over it, but it wasn't easy."

"I'm sorry for what I did to you back then, but I had my reasons. I now know that I should've shared them with you. It was very selfish of me that I didn't."

"You should've!"

"I felt guilty that you and Kyle were having problems in your marriage. After the two of you separated, you became emotionally very vulnerable. When you and I suddenly became romantically involved, I kept feeling that I was responsible in some way for the two of you not getting back together again. It was tearing me apart inside. I had to leave to see if I was right."

"Well, you weren't, you dope! The problem was between Kyle and me."

"I know that now, and I'm deeply sorry for whatever hurt I may've caused you."

"Then I forgive you," she said to him softly as she moved her lips in close to his. Her sensual tongue moved teasingly against his lips.

"I haven't thought about anything else but you since I saw you in my office the other day. There must be something in the air that's making me want you more than ever before. I wonder what it is."

His heart started to pound away wildly in his chest as their lips met and hungrily embraced and tasted each other. Their tongues explored and teased each other. At that very moment, the years that they had spent apart were gone. She wanted and needed him as much as he desperately needed her. It was their destiny to be together forever . . .

When the first rays of the warm spring sun began to filter in through the sliding glass doors of the second floor bedroom, they fell upon the two sleeping bodies of Harry and Karen. Harry slowly opened his eyes and looked sleepily around the room until they came to rest upon Karen's partially covered sleeping body. He had forgotten how beautiful she really was. He continued to watch her as she slept peacefully beside him. How long he continued to look at her beautiful face, he did not know. Time did not seem to matter to him anymore as long as she was at his side. At that very moment, he knew that he still loved her and that his life would not be complete without her in it. He carefully reached his left hand over toward her face and gently brushed a long curl of her hair away from her sleeping eyes. He gently began to caress the soft skin of her thin shoulders. As he did so, he began to think about John Haggerty. He tried to imagine what he must've felt when he discovered his fiancée's body lying under the front porch. He couldn't imagine the emotional pain that John's heart must've felt at that terrible moment. He suddenly felt really sorry for him. It was a feeling that he couldn't seem to shake.

Karen shifted the position of her sleeping body so that she was now lying on her left side facing him. As he continued to caress her soft skin, she opened her eyes and looked lovingly at him.

"Hello, stranger," she said to him softly. "I feel wonderful this morning. How did you sleep last night?" she asked him.

"Better than I have for years! I forgot what it felt like to make love and to wake up beside such a beautiful woman."

"I'm glad. I've waited years to hear that from you again."

"Thank you for waiting for me! You know, while I was lying here beside you, allowing my eyes to bathe in your beauty, I couldn't help but feel sorry for John Haggerty. He's the guy that I told you about the other day that we're defending in the Dr. Mathews murder case. I couldn't help but think about what he must've felt when he found his murdered fiancée's body that night. We really have to get this poor guy off. He's already suffered much too much in having lost her. If something like that ever happened to me, I don't think I'd want to go on living."

"Don't worry, Harry! The truth has a way of eventually making itself known. One way or another, the people who murdered her will be brought to justice. The only problem that we are fighting right now is time."

"I know that, but we have so little of it in this case to spare," he echoed back at her. I have to get up and go to work. I'm going to take a shower. Do you want to join me?" he whispered in her ear teasingly.

"I wouldn't miss it for the world," she answered as she tossed back the bedspread and leaped from the bed. The bright sunlight illuminated her nakedness and stirred all of his senses again. He dragged his own naked body from the bed and followed her into the bathroom. Soon the morning quiet was replaced with the sounds of running water and muffled voices of lovers in play.

"Did you find out anything new from Karen last night?" Paul asked him while they stood together just outside the courtroom.

"I had breakfast with her early this morning, and she informed me that she has run into a block wall in almost every direction that she searched. Our governmental conspirators were very thorough in covering their tracks over there. Karen and I both agree that any further time that we spend over there is going to be a complete waste of effort."

"Then we have to start looking at this whole conspiracy theory from another perspective."

"What do you mean by that?" Harry asked him curiously.

"I mean, these people have covered their tracks much too well. They have made sure that if anyone tries to uncover anything about Helen's past from the school's computer files, they will ultimately fail. We have to look at this entire puzzle from another angle. Dr. Mathews was a scientist, and as a researcher scientist, she had to keep herself abreast with all of the new advances coming out of the scientific community. What type of publications or organizations do people like her subscribe to? She would have to keep herself up to date and current with all of the latest breakthroughs. As a member of one of these organizations, she may've submitted for publication some articles about her own work. And if she didn't, she still might've communicated with some of these other researchers from time to time. Try to get a lead on some of these professional organizations, Harry."

"I will right away! You may've stumbled upon a good idea. Nobody would ever expect us to look in that direction. I'll start looking into it today."

"In the meantime, I believe the DA is about to wrap up his case against our client by tomorrow. I still don't have very much to hang our defense on. An unsubstantiated conspiracy theory will not gain us any points with Judge Zimmer. He's fair and open-minded, but only hard facts will impress him in the long run."

"Then let me go and try to find for you some of those hard facts that you will need," Harry said to him as he turned and exited the lobby of the courthouse.

Paul watched his friend leave the building through the heavy exterior doors before he shrugged his shoulders and headed back into the main courtroom to do battle with the district attorney again.

CHAPTER 14

It was raining quite hard early Wednesday evening when the executive jet touched down smoothly at Logan International Airport. It carefully taxied off the main runway and came to a complete stop in front of a small private terminal located some distance away from the other major airlines. In the reverberating echoes of the rain's protest, it had delivered its lone passenger to Boston.

A tall stranger could be seen standing alone with a briefcase just inside the jet's open outer door. He snapped open an umbrella to protect himself against the cold rain as he hurried down the plane's steps. His long strides quickly traversed the open tarmac to the dimly lit passenger terminal beyond.

Once inside the small private terminal, he continued his brisk strides over toward the doors that connected his building to the adjoining passenger terminals beyond. A short while later, he arrived at the car rental booth. He handed the car rental agent his driver's license and a credit card. There was no way that she could have known that both of them were fake. She thanked him for his patience as she handed them back to him with his rental keys.

"I hope you have a pleasant stay in Boston, Mr. Jones," she said to him. "Your car is parked outside in space number 7."

"Thank you. I'm sure I will," he answered back politely.

The drive from the airport through the Callahan tunnel was slow due to the bad weather and the last of the city's commuters rushing to get home after work. It was almost seven o'clock, and he had plenty of time to spare before his meeting with Sam later that night.

He drove straight to his motel on Route 2 on the Belmont-Arlington line. It was an out-of-the-way place that he had stayed in before. After he had checked into his room, he quickly showered and changed out of his expensive dress suite. He changed into a casual set of clothes that would help him to blend in better that evening with the people of Cambridge. When he had finished dressing, he carefully placed one of his two bags under the bed. It was the bag that he had removed from one of the terminal's few remaining coin storage lockers after receiving his rental car keys. He looked around the room one last time before he switched off the room's interior lights.

He drove into Chelsea to a small out-of-the-way barroom that he felt served the best steak tips in the city. He ordered a bottle of domestic beer to enjoy with his meal. As he sipped on his cold beer, he looked around at the establishment's patrons. He wondered to himself how many of these so-called good citizens would've done what he had done to preserve their country's security. *Probably none of them*, he thought to himself . . . *A nation of hypocrites!* His dinner order of steak tips and salad soon arrived in front of him at the bar. He unconsciously kept a watchful eye on his surroundings for any signs of danger. It was something that he had grown accustomed to doing ever since the Cold War had ended with Russia. Now their enemy had simply become more independent and elusive. Now, even in his own country, he had to remain alert at all times. It was a price that he had willingly decided to pay in order to keep his country safe from foreign espionage and terrorism.

His return drive back into Boston was quite uneventful. When he arrived at their usual rendezvous, he found Sam already waiting for him at a corner table in the crowded lounge.

"Can I get you a drink?" Sam asked him.

"A beer would be good."

Sam caught the eye of his waitress and held up two fingers as he pointed at his beer. She nodded her head in understanding and went back to the bar to get their order.

When she returned with their drinks, Sam handed her a twenty-dollar bill and said, "Keep the change." She happily thanked him and left them alone.

"In our business, it helps to be generous. It eliminates a lot of loose ends, but in Mr. Haggerty's case, it certainly hasn't!" Sam said to his boss.

"Tell me, how did it go for us today in court?" Mr. Jones asked him.

"The DA called his last witness today. Then just before noon, he rested his case. Even with all of the hard irrefutable evidence handed to the jury by the prosecutor, I cannot be completely sure how the jury will vote on this one. The DA's case against Mr. Haggerty is rock solid, but their motive is still weak. Taking both of these things into consideration, I can't safely say that they will convict the bastard for her murder. What do you think we should do?' Sam quietly asked him.

"It's a mute question now that the district attorney has played out his case fully in court. We cannot allow the defense to break down the state's case. The evidence has to remain unchallenged so that the entire matter will simply disappear. How much time do we have before Mr. Tucker starts to present the defense's case?"

"He told the judge that he could be ready to start by Friday. Judge Zimmer, however, decided to give him the full weekend also to prepare. Court will reconvene on Monday at 10:00 AM. That gives us at least four full days to do something."

"That's perfect! I'll start the ball rolling in our favor tomorrow. I don't intend to allow this matter to get any further out of hand!"

"What are you planning on doing?" Sam asked him.

"Our Mr. Haggerty is about to get his freedom. After all, he really deserves it, doesn't he? An anonymous benefactor who believes in his innocence will put up his bail tomorrow. That will give us our window of opportunity to do what we have to do," Mr. Jones said to him, smiling.

"To the successful end of the poor man's nightmares!" Sam raised his glass in a mock toast to their successful plan.

"To success!" Mr. Jones tapped his glass against Sam's in support.

After a few more drinks, the two old friends left the barroom together and headed off in opposite directions in the cold damp night air. Sam was told to wait for his boss's phone call the next day. It was a call that he would be eagerly awaiting. He felt that he had spent enough time in Boston, and he wanted to return to Washington as soon as possible.

* * * * *

It was late Thursday afternoon and almost time for the bail bondsman to close up his office for the day. As he stared into the briefcase full of money, his eyes and words hungrily asked the stranger what he had to do to earn the money. He could see that the stranger standing in front of him was made up in disguise. He was also wearing a pair of gloves and a hat when the weather outside was much too warm for either of them.

"There is a murder trial going on in Cambridge, where a man has been accused of murdering a woman by the name of Dr. Helen Mathews. My people believe that he is completely innocent of her murder. He does not have enough assets to free himself on bail. Therefore, we want you to post his five hundred thousand dollar cash bail for us. We believe that he has already suffered much too long for a crime that he didn't do! If anyone asks you why you are putting up his bail, tell them that you believe he's innocent. Tell them that you have followed the case every day in the news. Remember this is your bail money and your idea and nobody else's!"

"Is that how much money is in the case?" the bondsman asked him.

"No, the case contains six hundred thousand dollars. For your satisfactory service in this matter, you will be paid one hundred thousand dollars of the case's contents. The fee is yours to keep no matter how the jury eventually decides on Mr. Haggerty's fate. If the court revokes Mr. Haggerty's bail, you may take your fee as earned. A messenger will be sent by to collect the balance of the money the next day. Is this arrangement satisfactory with you?"

"Yes, oh yes!" the bondsman answered back greedily.

"There's just one more thing. Bring the two security tapes out from the backroom that just recorded our discussion."

The bail bondsman was about to deny that he had any security cameras recording the interior of his shop, but he thought better of it. He returned to the counter a few seconds later, carrying the two videotapes for the stranger.

"Here they are!" he said as he handed them over to the stranger. He was about to ask the stranger if he wanted a receipt for the money, but he quickly reconsidered it.

"Now remember everything that we just discussed and forget everything that you remember about me! My friends and I are not to be taken lightly or crossed in any way. Life is much too short, if you know what I mean! Remember the money and the idea of posting his bail were yours alone. You did it as a sympathetic citizen concerned about the defendant's state of mind. You felt truly sorry for him and the terrible loss of his fiancée and nothing more. You will then have nothing to worry about from anyone except where to spend your newly earned money."

The stranger turned and left the shop with the two security tapes in his hand. He seemed to drag his left foot noticeably as if he had an old injury to his left leg. When he was gone, Roman hurried over to the front door and locked it securely. He pulled down the front shades and flipped over his Open sign to now read Closed.

As he sat in his back office counting through the contents of the briefcase, his conscience seemed to bother him for a brief moment. But as he continued to count the stacks of money in front of him, his guilt feelings soon gave in to his greed. After all, he thought to himself, Mr. Haggerty was probably an innocent man. He remembered reading in one of the newspapers that he had said that he had discovered her dead body under the porch. He had told them that he had fled the scene in panic. Over the years, he too had experienced his own unfavorable interactions with the police. He knew that Mr. Haggerty's story would never have been believed by the police if he had remained there. At that very moment, he made up his mind that Mr. Haggerty was innocent, and nobody in the entire world would ever convince him otherwise.

CHAPTER 15

"I'm getting tired Harry! Let's take a break and get something to eat. We've been at this for almost six straight hours. I don't think anyone out there in the scientific publishing world has ever heard of our Dr. Helen Mathews!" she complained to him.

"Maybe you're right. We both need a break from this place. Come on! I'll buy you dinner at a nice restaurant near Copley Square. You deserve it!" He smiled back at her.

"It feels great to be appreciated by someone for a change."

"And besides, we have to think about everything that we've learned so far from our efforts today."

"Learned! You've got to be kidding! We haven't learned a single thing about this woman's past. She certainly hasn't subscribed to any of the major or even minor scientific periodicals for that matter. In fact, for all we know, she may've never joined any of the professional organizations in her field of expertise. What the hell did she earn her degrees in anyways?" she complained.

"From what I was able to find in her apartment when I searched it, she was some sort of a brilliant chemical and/or electrical engineer. She was supposedly involved in something that dealt with neural impulses and data storage. She seems to have also been an expert in writing complex computer programs. At least, that's what I think I read about her on an old document that I found over there."

"What kind of a person would waste their life studying something like that? I've always believed that over three quarters of these geniuses who are going to school in this place are too smart for their own good. They waste their time doing research in areas that can't possibly benefit mankind in any way."

"You might be right, but we'll never really know for sure. Will we?" he added.

It was nearing five o'clock, and Boston was already heavily congested with traffic. Their relatively short drive across the city took them almost forty minutes, but Harry had promised her that it would be well worth the extra time. Harry's beeper went off on his belt, and he looked down at it to see who was trying to reach him. It was Paul calling from his office. He decided that he would call him back after they had reached the restaurant.

Harry and Karen sat down at a small cozy booth in the corner of the lounge next to the hotel's restaurant and ordered a round of drinks. As soon as they were brought over to the table by the waiter, Harry excused himself in order to call Paul.

"What's up, Paul?" Harry curiously asked him.

"We have gained a few extra days to prepare our defense. The district attorney wrapped up the state's case a short while ago. I told the judge that we could probably be ready to start by Friday, but he decided to give us the full weekend to prepare our end. So it looks as though we have gained a few more days to come up with something more tangible to help our end."

"That's great news!"

"Now if we can only put all of this extra time to good use. Did you happen to come across anything important today?" Paul asked him hopefully.

"No, we struck out completely today. Our Dr. Mathews is still a total mystery to both of us, but we haven't given up yet!"

"Well, keep in touch with me."

"I will, Paul."

He hesitated near the phone, thinking about their wasted efforts that day. Karen had been a lot of help to him that day. He felt that they made a good team together. It had been her day off from work, and she had spent the entire day trying to help him. He walked back over to where she was sitting alone in the corner booth. *God was she beautiful!* he thought to himself as he sat down beside her again.

"Anything important?" she asked him.

"No. Paul just wanted to tell me that we have until Monday to dig up something new on our mysterious Dr. Mathews. He said that Judge Zimmer moved the case up to Monday so that we would have some more time to get ready. Well, are you ready to eat?"

"I'm starving, but I need to visit the ladies' room first. I'll be right back."

He stood up to allow her to get out. He then sat back down and sipped on the last of his drink until she came back to their table.

"All ready!" she said to him when she returned. They walked into the dining room area where the maître d' showed them to an out of the way table next to the fountain.

Dinner was perfect, and Karen was completely impressed with Harry's choice of restaurants. The food was even better than she could've imagined. As she sat next to Harry holding his arm lightly in her small hand, she thanked him for dinner. He leaned in close to her and kissed her tenderly on her soft inviting lips. He thanked her for making him feel like the luckiest man in the whole world.

"Did you know that I've always had a secret fantasy about being seen around town with the most beautiful woman in the world, and tonight you just made that wish come true for me?"

"Now you're teasing me," she whispered to him a little embarrassed.

"No, I really meant what I said. I can't believe that I wasted these past three years of my life without you," he confessed to her.

"Well, we can always try to make up for those lost years, can't we?" she said to him romantically.

"We most assuredly can!" he repeated back to her with a devilish smile showing on his face. "Waiter, the check please!"

* * * * *

It was unusually quiet in the jail for a Thursday evening. John had just finished eating and had been returned to his cell for the night. He tried to concentrate on a new novel that Paul had bought for him to keep his mind occupied. He found his thoughts, however, constantly drifting away from the plot of the book. He knew that his mind was much too restless to read that night, and so he eventually threw the novel down onto the cell floor in frustration. The walls of his cell were beginning to close in on him, and he was starting to become seriously depressed. The DA had rested the state's case against him that morning, and now it was all up to Paul and Harry to convince everyone on the jury that he was indeed innocent.

Thursday had come and gone like Wednesday, and still, John was alone with his nightmares. The more he tried to relax, the more depressed he became. His captivity in the small prison cell was slowly beginning to tear him apart. He had to get out of there, before he went completely insane.

John stood up in his cell and began to nervously pace around the small area. The concept of time no longer seemed to be a constant in his mind as the minutes soon turned into hours and hours into days. His mind screamed in silence for rest, but there was none to be found within its own outer walls. Fatigue soon began to overpower his body's senses, and it demanded rest as its payment. He lay back down onto his thin mattress and tried to close his eyes again. Slowly, he drifted off into a deep plateau of unconsciousness, a place where his exhausted mind began to dream about his wonderful memories with Helen again.

* * * * *

The desk sergeant looked down at the bail bondsman's paperwork and called up to his lieutenant to come down and verify its authenticity. When he arrived at the front desk, the sergeant handed the stamped documents over to him to read. As far as the lieutenant could see, all of them appeared to be in order, and so he authorized the sergeant to process Mr. Haggerty's release. He asked for the bail bondsman's identification in order to make sure that he was who he had said he was. Since Mr. Haggerty's bond had been posted, he had no other choice but to release Mr. Haggerty from their jail.

"Who's responsible for posting this SOB's bail?" the lieutenant asked him.

"I did! The man's innocent, and if you had been following his case in court like I have, you would've also come to that conclusion yourself. Let's face it, Lieutenant, you guys blew this entire investigation, and Mr. Haggerty deserves to be released. I waited until I heard all of the evidence against him before I decided to post his bail. You guys, on the other hand, just reached for the most logical suspect and stopped looking for anyone else. Wake him up and bring him out here. I'm in a hurry. I haven't had my breakfast yet!" he demanded from them.

"Hold on to your horses! I've sent word upstairs for them to get him ready. He'll be down here as soon as he's ready," the sergeant echoed back at him just as loudly. "Take a seat and wait over there!"

The sound of the night guard tapping his night stick against his cell's bars woke John up from his shallow sleep. "Get up, John! You're out of here. Your bail has been posted."

"It has?" he said in surprise. "Who posted it?" he asked him sleepily.

"I don't know! Probably your attorney or a rich relative! They have been known to do stupid things like that in the past. So unless you want me to tell them that you want to stay in here, I'd suggest that you get yourself ready and as soon as possible. Call me when you're ready to go."

As John was led out into the central booking area by one of the guards, he looked around to see where Paul was sitting. He didn't see him anywhere in the waiting area. The officer behind the bench handed him an envelope that contained all of his personal possessions inside of it.

"Thank you," he said to the officer as he handed back the signed receipt to him.

"Don't thank me. If it was up to me, you'd never be leaving this place because of what you did to that poor woman!"

"But I'm innocent! I never killed my fiancée! I loved her!"

"That's what everyone says!" the officer threw back at him in disgust.

John walked out into the main lobby of the station and continued to look around for Paul. As he stood there, a short overweight man walked up to him

"Mr. Haggerty, I'm Roman Tschischewski, but my friends all call me Romy for short. I'm the one who just bailed you out of here. I need you to sign a few documents for me over there, and then you will be free to leave this place."

"Why did you post my bail?" John asked him.

"Because I believe you're innocent. Now according to the terms of your bail, you will have to report in every day to the court. If you fail to do this, the court can revoke your bail on the spot. Do you understand the importance of what I've just told you?"

"I do!" he answered a little bit bewildered.

"Good! Now I've prepared a document for you to date and sign that says that you are placing your house up for collateral to me in lieu of my posting your bail. If you fail to show up for court, you could lose your house to me since I will be holding it as collateral for you. I'm posting a lot more than what your house is worth, but what the heck, I believe in you. Now if all of this is clear and agreeable to you, please sign on the two lines that I have so indicated in the documents."

John signed the two documents where Roman had indicated. "Is that all?" he asked him excitedly.

"That's it! You are now free to go, but you cannot leave the jurisdiction of the court. Now please make sure that you show up for your trial every day. We don't want them to come looking for you, do we?" he impressed upon him strongly.

"Thank you, Mr. Romy. I didn't think that there were any people left out there who really cared. I just want you to know that I never hurt my fiancée. I really loved her with all my heart."

"I believe you, John, and I sincerely hope that you can prove your innocence."

Mr. Tschischewski turned and walked out of the police station. John stood alone in the waiting area for a few minutes longer before he eventually walked out the front door of the station also.

John took his wallet out of his pocket and counted his money once again. He had more than enough money to get home. He slowly made his way down the street to the entrance of the underground Park Street subway station. From there, he would be able to catch a subway train to the Alewife Station. Once there, he would be able to take a taxi to his home in Arlington. He couldn't wait to get home and sleep in his own bed again.

The lieutenant contacted the DA's office a short while after Mr. Haggerty had been released from their custody. He was under no obligation to do so, but he felt that the DA should be informed that their suspect had made bail and been released. The news shocked Mr. Parker and sent a wave of concern running through his mind.

"Call Detective Bates and make her aware of what just happened! Thank you, Lieutenant, for letting me know right away."

"No problem, sir. We just thought that you should know."

"Bailed out! You've got to be kidding! How the hell did he raise five hundred thousand dollars cash bail? From what we know about Mr. Haggerty, he just doesn't have that type of money or assets lying around!" she shouted over the telephone in disbelief. "How long ago did he leave the station?" she asked the sergeant.

"Around 6:30 AM, he was released. That's about an hour ago!" the sergeant answered.

"Well, that's just great! By now, he could be anywhere. I'll call my partner and tell him that we will have to set up surveillance on his house right away."

"Yes, ma'am!" the sergeant responded back.

* * * * *

"Our guy just got bailed out. He's making his way home right now by the subway system. Meet me at two o'clock this afternoon in Arlington at the Buttrick's Ice Cream Shop. It's located right behind the high school. The clock is now ticking."

"I'll be there," Sam answered back.

* * * * *

John arrived at his home about forty-five minutes after he had left the police station. He discovered his front door lock broken and the door clumsily nailed shut. He was forced to enter his house by the rear door. When he got inside, he soon discovered that the police had made a real mess of his house while searching it for evidence. *What a pack of animals!* he thought to himself. He reached for a phone book and called a local twenty-four-hour car rental company to come by and pick him up. Since his own vehicle was still impounded by the police, he knew that he needed to rent a car to get back and forth to the courthouse every day.

While he was waiting for the car rental company to come by and pick him up, he brought up some of his hand tools from the basement and began to repair the frame of his front door. He couldn't understand why the police had pushed in his front door when they knew that he wasn't even home. He ripped the crime scene tape off his front door. He completed the repairs on the door's frame just as his ride drove up to his house. He quickly checked his refrigerator for supplies and then hurried outside to the waiting courtesy van.

CHAPTER 16

"Did you know that your client was going to make bail early this morning?" the DA excitedly asked Paul over the telephone.

"No, I can assure you that I had absolutely no idea that he was about to make bail. But if anyone ever deserved to be out on bail during his trial, my client certainly does. You know that also, Tom. That stupid motive that you are trying to hang around his neck won't convince anyone that he murdered his fiancée, and you know it!"

"Come on, Paul! You and I both know perfectly well that the evidence in this case speaks loudly and clearly for itself. He's as guilty as sin!"

"I can't accept or believe that for even a second. Even my chief investigator in this case, Harold Parks, who's a retired career detective from the Boston police, agrees with me. He said that if something looks too good to be true, then it usually isn't! Even he agrees that the amount of hard evidence found in this case is just too overwhelming! Dr. Mathews's real murderer is somewhere out there and nobody's even looking for him. Don't worry about Mr. Haggerty. He's going nowhere until he clears his name of this murder. I'll bet my reputation on that. So I'll see you in court on Monday."

"Okay, but I'm going to make sure that my people keep a very close eye on your client until then!" he warned him.

"I wouldn't expect anything less from you, Tom."

* * * * *

Paul hung up the telephone and immediately paged his friend Harry to tell him about what he had just learned from the DA. Harry responded to his page a few minutes later with a phone call from Karen's place.

"What's up, Paul?" he asked him a little bit surprised at receiving such an early morning page from him.

"I just got off the telephone with Tom from the DA's office. He just informed me that our client made bail early this morning. Did you know anything about this earlier?"

"No, I knew nothing about it. That doesn't make any sense to me. I'll check into it right away and let you know what I find out about it."

Harry called his old precinct to talk to one of his old friends still on the force down there. He was told that someone had indeed posted Mr. Haggerty's bail early that morning. He asked for the name of the bail bondsman who had posted the five hundred thousand dollar cash bail. He learned that it was his old acquaintance Romy . . . Roman Tschischewski. He had always been a pain in his side when he was on the force, a real anathema. He was a man whom he had come to know would do anything for money. He thanked his old friend and told him that they should get together for a few drinks next week. His old friend laughed and told him to call him back when he was free. Harry promised him that he would and then hung up the telephone.

"Something doesn't seem right about this bail posting. We know that our Mr. Haggerty doesn't have any money to speak of, except for, say, the collateral that he has in his house in Arlington. So how does he raise the five hundred thousand dollars that he would need to post his bail? He doesn't! Someone else must've done it for him, but who? If he had that type of money or collateral lying around, he would've bailed himself out a long time ago! I think I'm going to pay my dear old friend Romy a visit to discuss who's really behind the financing of Mr. Haggerty's bail"

"Do you want me to come along? I could call into work and tell them that I'm not feeling very good today. They could get along just fine without me," she volunteered.

"No, this is something that I must do alone. I know this Mr. Tschischewski, and I know what to ask him in private."

"Okay, but promise me that you'll be careful," she pleaded with him.

"I will, my love. I promise," he answered as he finished dressing.

* * * * *

The news of Mr. Haggerty's release from police custody sent a wave of panic running wildly throughout the two detective divisions of Boston and Newton. There was an immediate scramble to place him back under police surveillance as quickly as possible. Detective Bolten was steadfastly convinced that their suspect would attempt to flee the state again at his first opportunity. Therefore, he wanted to set up the surveillance right away. The Newton police detectives agreed with him completely. They agreed to split the twenty-four-hour surveillance details with the Boston detectives, a plan that Detective Bates eagerly approved.

* * * * *

Harry peered into the bail bondsman's shop through his dirty front windows. He could see that Romy was all alone inside the place behind the high counter. He had dealt with this jerk on many occasions in the past. To Harry, Mr. Tschischewski was nothing more than a piranha, a bottom feeder, one who thrives on the misery of other people. He had waited patiently for several hours for him to be alone so that they would not be disturbed. He slowly opened the shop's front door and walked inside. Harry reached for the Open sign and turned it around so that it now displayed Closed. Romy looked up toward the door when he heard it open and recognized Harry when he entered his place of business.

"Now don't do that! I'm still open, and I have to make a living!" he shouted over to him.

"I know, but I don't want to be disturbed while we talk."

"We don't have anything to talk about, Detective Parks! I haven't seen you for so long that I thought you were dead. But now I can see that you are still around, bothering innocent people who are trying to make an honest living."

"Well, I have been around, but I officially retired from the police force a couple of years ago. Now I was thinking that you and I should have a private little chat."

"Chat? Chat about what?" Romy asked him indignantly.

"About a common acquaintance of ours, a Mr. John Haggerty. You know, the man whom you just bailed out of jail for five hundred thousand big ones. Now that's a lot of money in anyone's world, but especially in yours. Why did you do it?" he pressed his question loudly at him.

"I felt sorry for the guy! After very closely following his trial on the news every day, I was convinced that the poor bastard was innocent . . . so I posted his bail! There's no law that says I couldn't!"

"No, there isn't, as far as I know, but I don't think that you did it on your own. Leopards don't change their spots, and I know all too well that your heart is as black and hard as cold tar. So let's be honest with each other. Who really put you up to it and gave you the money to do it?"

"No one did! See, I even made him put up his house in Arlington as collateral to secure part of it just in case he skips town!"

Harry looked over the document carefully and saw that his client had indeed signed it. Still, his mind could not accept the idea that this piranha had acted alone. He threw the document back down onto his desk. *It just doesn't make any sense!* he thought to himself.

He thought for a second about what to do next. He then had a brainstorm of an idea. "I want to see your security tapes for this place for Wednesday and Thursday of this week!" he demanded.

"You don't have the power to demand them from me!" he responded back timidly to him.

"You're probably right about that, so maybe I should give my friends downtown a call to come by and make it an official investigation," he quietly threatened him with.

Roman thought about his threat and all of the problems that a search of his records might cause him. He decided not to risk it.

"Okay, okay! Let me see what I can do for you." He went into the back room of his shop and pulled a tape from the shelf dated for Wednesday of that week. "Here it is!" he shouted as he handed it over to him.

"Where's the security tape for Thursday?"

"There isn't one! I forgot to put one in that morning!" he explained to him.

"Do you expect me to believe a bullshit story like that from a guy like you?"

"But it's the truth. I swear it is!" he pleaded back. "Look back there yourself. The tapes are all arranged chronologically by their dates."

Harry went back into the back room of the small shop and looked at the shelves of security tapes. He could see that there were no tapes on the shelves dated for Thursday. He might be telling the truth, and then he might be lying. He thought to himself. He returned to the front room again to confront Romy.

"How convenient! If I find out that you've been lying to me, my friends downtown will hear about it and tear this place apart. I'll bring this tape back in a few days," he said as he turned and exited the small shop.

Roman knew that Harry's threats were not to be taken lightly. He carefully locked his front door and went into his back office to work on his books again. He knew that he had to finish transferring some of his bank funds around to back up his paperwork. By moving everything around electronically, he did not have to use his suitcase full of money. All of that cash had been secretly hidden at another secure location, safe from prying eyes and legal searches. He turned on his computer, entered some security codes, and went into his banking accounts. He quickly transferred the money that he needed in each of the accounts and exited the system. "Well,

Mr. Parks, that's the end of that loose end," he said to himself proudly. He thought about Mr. Parks's surprise visit to his shop and smiled. He had caught him completely off guard when he had showed him Mr. Haggerty's collateral agreement on his house. It was a work of art. It reinforced all of his arguments.

* * * * *

Sam sat in his vehicle in the Buttrick's parking lot, enjoying a cone of vanilla ice cream. The temptation had been too much even for him to resist. He looked out across the fields behind the high school and watched some of the kids running track. It was an experience that he had never been able to enjoy as a young child while growing up in Russia. As a young teenager, his constant concern was to find food and shelter each day. His entire youth was nothing more than a bad nightmare.

Mr. Jones pulled his car up alongside of his vehicle but facing in the opposite direction. They opened their driver-side windows so that they could talk undisturbed to each other.

"Enjoying your ice cream, Sam?" his boss asked him with a smile on his face.

"As a matter of fact, I really am! I like ice cream." He smiled back.

"Good! I picked up a few things today that I believe we might need later on this evening. We're going to be paying a surprise visit to our friend Mr. Haggerty's home tonight when he's not expecting us. I drove by his house a short while ago to make some visual notes of the surrounding area. I observed that his house has a gas service line feeding up to his house. It may prove to be very useful to us. I believe our Mr. Haggerty is going to have a very tragic accident this weekend."

"That will be so very unfortunate for him!" Sam added without even the slightest hint of compassion sounding in his words.

"I'll contact you when I decide when we can do it. When I contact you later on, be ready to meet with me right away. This problem has to be eliminated once and for all for both of us," he said as he shifted his car back into drive and slowly drove away from the area.

Chapter 17

Throughout the day, Paul Tucker became increasingly more frustrated with every failed attempt he made to reach his client by telephone. Every time he tried to reach him, he received a busy signal on the line, or his call would go unanswered. It wasn't until around eight o'clock on Friday night that he was finally able to reach John on the telephone.

"John, is that really you?" he asked into the telephone receiver. "I've been trying to reach you all day. You know, you surprised the hell out of Harry and me when your bail was posted early this morning! I tried to reach you earlier at the jail, but they told me that you had already been released," he said to him happily.

"I suppose my release must've caused quite a stir in the district attorney's office and the two police departments!" he said jokingly to Paul.

"Not to mention that a number of their hearts probably skipped quite a few beats in panic also. Now I hope your bail bondsman, Mr. Tschischewski, went over all of the terms and conditions of your bail with you?"

"He went over some of the conditions with me, but he said that the most important thing to remember was to show up for court every day. He also mentioned that I should not attempt to leave the area under any circumstances."

"Those two points are extremely important! Any violation of either one of those terms will provide instant grounds for the revocation of your bail. Now the DA's office and the police would like nothing better than to have you placed back in jail for the remainder of your trial. So whatever you do, don't give them a reason to do it. I can almost promise you that sometime this evening, if it hasn't already happened, you will find a police surveillance team parked somewhere on your street or outside your front door. Early this morning, the district attorney assured me that the police would be placing a twenty-four-hour surveillance team on your every movement from now on. Now I don't know how you were able to get that bail bondsman to post your high bail, but you did. So whatever you do this weekend and throughout the rest of the trial, try to lead a somewhat normal lifestyle every day. We're all pulling for you over here. I promise you again that we're going to beat this charge one way or another!"

"I sincerely hope so, Paul, because I couldn't spend a lifetime behind bars for a crime I didn't do. I'm sorry for not having answered the telephone earlier, but my phone hasn't stopped ringing all day long. All sorts of nuts keep calling me to say that I'm going to burn in hell forever for murdering Helen. I'm going to purchase an answering machine sometime tomorrow. If you need to reach me before I get it installed, ring the phone twice and then hang up. If I'm in, I'll call you back right away."

"Okay, John. That'll work out just fine for us until you get your answering machine hooked up. Now remember to call me every day at either my office or at my home to let me know how you're doing. In that way, you and I can talk away from all of their prying eyes and ears to plan out a strong defense strategy for your case."

The first unmarked police cruiser pulled down the street from John's residence a few minutes before ten o'clock that Friday night. The two detectives sitting inside the car made themselves comfortable for the long boring night of stakeout duty that lay ahead of them. Detective Ryan took the first half of their long eight-hour stakeout of Mr. Haggerty's home, while his partner, Ed, tried to catch a few hours of sleep. At 2:00 AM, Ed agreed to relieve his partner for the second half of their long stakeout. A second team of undercover detectives was scheduled to relieve them around six o'clock the following morning.

"Ed, do you still think he's inside the house?" Ryan asked him curiously.

"I'm sure he is. His car's still parked outside in the driveway, and the lights are still on inside his house," he answered back.

"I guess he must be in there at that."

"Now let me catch a few hours of sleep. Don't wake me up unless you see him trying to sneak out of the house in the middle of the night!"

"Okay, Ed, I'll wake you when it's time for you to take over."

The long boring hours of stakeout duty on Mr. Haggerty's house passed by very slowly for the two detectives. It was a night without incident. They were glad to see the two detectives from the Newton Police Department pulling up alongside their cruiser at 6:00 AM to relieve them.

"How did it go last night, guys?" one of the young Newton detectives asked them.

"Our pigeon never left his roost all night. So he's all yours for now. We're out of here," Ed answered as he started their car and slowly accelerated down the deserted street.

"Now I remember why I've always hated these late-night stakeouts. They knock the hell out of you the following day," Ed said to his partner.

The two Newton detectives got their first glimpse of Mr. Haggerty at approximately 9:00 AM, when he exited his house and jumped into his car. Their unmarked cruiser followed him from a safe distance all the way over to Watertown to a small diner. He took a seat at the counter and ordered breakfast.

"Hell, if we had known that he was going to do this, we could've had breakfast in there also," the slightly overweight detective said to his younger partner. "It looks like they have a takeout service in this place also. I think I'm going to go in and order a couple of fried egg sandwiches to go. Do you want anything?" he asked his partner.

"Yeah! Get me a large regular coffee and a fried egg sandwich also. Here's some money, and bring me some ketchup too."

"Okay, I'll be right back," he said as he left their cruiser, which was now parked inconspicuously down the street from the diner. From their new vantage point, they had a clear view of their suspect sitting inside the diner.

Their suspect left the diner about twenty five minutes later and then drove to a discount department store. The young detective followed him casually into the busy store to keep him under surveillance. After purchasing a few items in the store, they followed him over to a hardware store in Arlington and then back to his house again.

For the rest of the day, John kept himself busy performing various chores around his house. He decided that his first project had to be the installation of his new telephone answering machine. When he had finished installing it, he then set about cleaning up the mess that the police had made of his house when they had searched it earlier. He knew that there wasn't very much else that he could do but stay close to home every day until his trial resumed again on Monday morning. He had to laugh when he first caught sight of the two detectives trailing him around town in their unmarked cruiser. He couldn't help but wonder if they really believed that they had not been seen by him.

Later that evening, he drove down to one of the local video stores to rent a movie. It wasn't very long, however, before his exhausted body dozed off in front of his old television.

* * * * *

Sam looked down at the vibrating pager on his belt and observed the special code numbers from his boss being conspicuously displayed on it. He immediately placed a phone call to his boss's private cell phone.

"Sam, meet me in the main public parking lot across the street from the Regent Theatre in Arlington around midnight tonight. Be prepared and bring your tools," his boss told him over the telephone.

"I'll be there at midnight sharp!" he answered back.

The telephone call ended abruptly a few seconds later. Sam knew all too well what his boss meant by being prepared. It meant for him to wear dark-colored clothes and to bring along his special bag of tools. His bag of special tools contained everything that they might need from picking open a simple lock to opening a locked safe. It contained explosives and almost every tool needed to work on any type of an explosive device or a very complicated electrical circuit. Sam was an expert field operative, and he had been called on by his boss many times over the past ten years to solve many complicated problems for the agency. His many years of faithful service and unquestionable obedience had made him one of Mr. Jones' best field agents.

Just before midnight, the two men secretly rendezvoused in the main public parking lot behind Arlington center. Sam parked his vehicle in a darkened corner of the lot and quietly jumped into his boss's waiting vehicle. They quickly exited the parking lot and headed up toward the Morningside area of Arlington.

"Do you have everything with you?" Mr. Jones asked him.

"Absolutely!" he responded confidently.

"There's no moon out tonight, and so there will be plenty of cover for us to hide behind. By now, I believe the police will have most likely placed a surveillance team somewhere in the area to keep an eye on our Mr. Haggerty. We'll park behind his house on the next street over. It's late, and so no one will even notice our car parked in the area," he declared confidently.

"We have a number of options available for us to use tonight. Once we get inside his house and take a good look around, we can decide on what to do. If he discovers us inside his house, we will have no other choice but to take him out. We can then make it look like an accident. One way or another, he's a dead man tonight!" his boss emphasized strongly.

"I agree!"

"The first thing that we have to do is to locate the police surveillance team's present location. That way, we can keep a watchful eye on them. We can get into Mr. Haggerty's house through his basement's rear door. We will have to be very quiet because he's probably sleeping upstairs. We don't want to wake him up, but if we do, then our options will become very limited. I would prefer that his death be caused by an accident, but if we have to stage something more radical, then so be it. Let's go!"

The faint silhouettes of the two darkly dressed agents seemed to float without a sound across the darkened landscape of the neighborhood's backyards. The barking of a lone dog just a few houses down the street from them seemed to sense their unauthorized presence in the area. He sounded the alarm that there were strangers in the neighborhood, but his loud barking went unheeded by everyone. He soon tired and returned to his doghouse once again to sleep.

The two detectives sat quietly in their cruiser. Only one of them was awake, and he stared sleepily out into the darkness of the neighborhood. He was listening to a CD on a set of new headphones. The movements of the two silhouettes behind their suspect's house went unnoticed by the preoccupied detective. Sam picked away quietly at the basement door's locking mechanism until it opened a few seconds later. The two men slipped unnoticed into the darkened room and quietly closed the door behind them.

Sam stood guard at the top of the basement stairs as his boss loosened all of the bulbs in their ceiling sockets. Using a small flashlight, Mr. Jones walked around the room carefully studying the gas water heater, then the gas dryer, and finally the old oil-fired boiler. When he had finished, he knew exactly what he was going to do to each of them.

"This will take me only a few minutes. Keep your eyes and ears open for our Mr. Haggerty."

Sam nodded his head in understanding.

Mr. Jones quietly turned off the gas supply to the water heater at its gas cock. He then very carefully began to work on the appliance's gas valve. He carefully forced the unit's seal so that the valve's diaphragm could not shut off the water heater's main gas supply. He then carefully re-piped the gas valve and its related gas pipes back together again. He made sure that the main gas control valve was turned to its highest temperature setting and that the pilot was unlit. He then went over to the gas dryer and shut off its gas cock also. He then very carefully split apart one of the rings of the double-walled gas connector with the sharp point of his knife.

He then walked over to the hot water boiler and switched off its main power switch. He checked out the low water temperature control setting on the boiler's main operational control box. He adjusted it downward another fifteen degrees. It was cool outside, and so he assumed that Mr. Haggerty would have his windows closed for the night. He disconnected one of the two low-voltage thermostat wires attached to the TT terminals of the boiler so that the upstairs thermostat wouldn't work. He then carefully disconnected the circulator's relay so that it couldn't kick in the circulator. He reset the differential control setting to twelve degrees. Everything was now set for a massive gas explosion when the boiler's primary control relay closed on water temperature fall. The ignition of the oil burner would ignite the gas fumes that would've by then filled the entire basement from the split gas connector and the forced gas valve. It would be a fitting end to their troublesome Mr. Haggerty.

With his flashlight, he signaled Sam to make his way over to the basement's outer door. He then turned on the water heater's gas cock. He could smell the gas escaping quietly from the gas valve out into the room. He then went over to the gas dryer and turned on its gas cock also. Gas immediately began to rush rapidly out of the split gas connector and out into the room. He smiled at his deadly handiwork as he switched on the main power switch to the oil-fired boiler. They exited the basement through its lone rear door, making sure that it was closed tightly behind them. They silently scurried across the grass backyards toward their parked car again. In a few minutes, they found themselves safely inside their vehicle and driving away from the area.

"How long before it explodes?" Sam asked him.

"Not too long. The temperature of the water in the boiler has to drop down a few more degrees before its operational control relay kicks in the oil burner's ignition to reheat it. By the time the boiler's water temperature has dropped down to this lower activation setting, the entire basement should be filled with gas. The house will go up like a bomb, and our Mr. Haggerty will go up with it also! It's a completely undetectable accident, just another piece of bad luck in his sad pathetic life. No one will ever suspect it as being anything other than a gas leak at one of his appliances."

"By this time tomorrow night, everything about Dr. Mathews and her boyfriend will be no more than a distant bad memory for the two of us."

"I certainly hope so!" Sam said to him as they drove into the public parking lot near Arlington center.

As Sam exited the car, there was a massive flash and a loud explosion seen in the distance. The two men smiled at each other, knowing that their night's surreptitious efforts had paid off.

"I told you that we had nothing to worry about! Now go back to your place and get a good night's rest. We shall probably hear about the explosion on the early morning news."

The two friends departed company and headed back to their different motels for the evening.

* * * * *

The young detective took his headphones off his head and placed them on the car's dashboard. He quietly exited the cruiser in order to go to the bathroom. As he relieved himself in the darkness against a small hedge, he watched in shock as Mr. Haggerty's entire house exploded directly in front of him. The force of the explosion threw him backward against the cold asphalt. The heat from the explosion was so intense that he swore that his hair had caught fire. The massive fireball continued to roll upward into the night sky until it gradually dissipated into a dark rising cloud. In its wake, there remained only a hole in the ground and several piles of burning and charred boards. Windows were blown out everywhere, and alarms were screaming loudly into the cool night air. The force of the explosion rocked the cruiser violently and woke up his partner. As he looked through his car's windshield in horror, he instinctively reached for his vehicle's two-way radio.

"Unit 33 to the Arlington police dispatcher, please come in!" he shouted frantically over the radio's emergency frequency.

"This is the Arlington police dispatcher. Please identify yourself."

"This is Detective Frank Black from the Newton Police Department. My partner and I are on a stakeout up on Ridge Street in Arlington, and we just witnessed a massive explosion in one of the houses near us! It looks as though it may've been gas related! We need the fire department along with some ambulances and additional support units up here right away!" he shouted over his radio.

"I'm dispatching help out to your location as we speak!" the dispatcher informed him.

"Let's go over there to see if there's anything that we can do to help! I don't think anyone could've survived an explosion like that!" Detective Black yelled over to his partner.

The entire neighborhood had, in less than a split second, become a scene of complete mayhem and destruction. Their suspect's house had been completely destroyed, and several small fires could be seen burning uncontrollably in different locations around the property. What remained of the house's exterior walls, floors, and roof was no more than smashed piles of burning rubble. People were beginning to stagger out of their homes from every direction. The houses that were located closest to Mr. Haggerty's residence had all been severely damaged by the force of the explosion. Broken glass and windshields were everywhere. Some of the neighbors from further down the street were arriving on the scene to offer help to some of their friends. One man from one of the abutting houses appeared to be severely cut and dazed.

As the two detectives carefully combed through the debris with their flashlights, they thought they heard the faint sound of someone moaning from beneath a collapsed wall and a twisted charred pile of boards. They slowly began to remove the smoldering planks one by one. As they carefully lifted parts of the collapsed wall, they caught sight of John Haggerty's injured body in the rubble.

"I don't believe it! He's still alive!" Frank said to his partner in amazement. He appears to be severely burnt and in terrible pain. Help me clear some more of these boards off him."

"People, we need some help over here!" his partner shouted over to some of the younger men standing on the sidelines watching them. A couple of young men hurried over to help them lift the heavy planks off the man's blackened body. In a distance, the emergency sirens of the ambulances, fire trucks, and police cruisers could be heard racing to their location.

As they removed the last of the smoldering pieces of planking and plywood covering his body, they could see the true extent of his injuries. Most of his injuries appeared to be very serious. His entire body looked as though it had been severely burnt from the fiery explosion, and his left leg and arm were both badly twisted and shattered. Protruding pieces of shattered white bone could be seen poking through his hanging skin. He had to be in terrible pain. He was starting to bleed profusely from his left side, a positive sign that his body had additional internal injuries, which they couldn't see.

"Where the hell is that ambulance?" Frank shouted out toward the street.

A police cruiser arrived on the scene a few seconds later, and the officer ran over to where the two detectives were standing.

"Are you the two detectives that called this in?" he asked.

"Yeah!"

"Who do we have down here?"

"This man was in the house when it exploded. His injuries appear to be really serious. I think we may have to have him taken by med flight into Boston for treatment if he's going to have any chance at all of making it. He appears to be burnt over most of his body, and his left arm and leg appear to be shattered completely. He's now starting to bleed from his left side also!"

The young patrolman contacted his dispatcher to tell them that they had a critically injured victim at the scene and that his injuries appeared to warrant an immediate air transport to a trauma facility, or he probably wouldn't make it. The first ambulance to arrive on the scene was directed over to where Mr. Haggerty was sprawled out in agony on the twisted wooden flooring. The two EMTs first secured his neck with a brace and then carefully slid him onto a backboard in order to prevent any further damage to his spine. After he had been properly tied down, he was gently lifted up onto a stretcher and carried over to the ambulance. IV's were immediately hooked up to his body, and he was covered with blankets to keep him warm. A call came over the police radio telling them that a med flight chopper was en route to Kenny's field at the bottom of Overlook Road. They were told to have the medics stabilize their victim's condition as best they could and to transport him ASAP to the chopper's LZ for an airlift into Boston.

Because of all of the steep hills in the Morningside section of Arlington, the fast ambulance ride down to the chopper's location was a rough one for everyone. The EMTs knew that time was their patient's biggest enemy. John kept drifting in and out of consciousness while he was being transported. Finally, they arrived at the wide baseball field. The two EMTs transferred their patient into the waiting med flight chopper as quickly as possible. Within a few minutes, the chopper began to lift off into the night sky. It was now a race against time for the pilot and the onboard doctor to try to save their critically injured and almost-comatose patient.

As more and more help began to arrive in the neighborhood, the two detectives found some time to talk to the officer who was now in charge of the scene. They informed him how they had been looking directly at the house when it exploded. They described to him how they had observed a growing ball of fire rising up and outward from the disintegrating house. They described to him how one of them had been thrown backward to the ground from the shockwave of the explosion. They both described to him the intense heat that had accompanied the initial explosion. Neither of the two detectives had seen anyone else in the area just before the explosion had taken place.

"Well, from what you have both just described, it certainly sounds like a gas explosion to me! You're probably both very lucky that you weren't any closer to this guy's house when it exploded. If you were, you'd probably be on your way to the hospital right now!" he said to them as he went over to offer some assistance to an injured man being gently lowered down onto a stretcher to await medical treatment.

"He's right about that, Frank! We could've both been killed if we had been any closer to that house when it exploded!"

The doctors at the New England Medical Center worked feverishly on Mr. Haggerty for the next five hours, trying to stabilize his condition.

As one group of surgeons worked on his two shattered limbs, a second team of doctors worked to remove his severely damaged and bleeding left kidney. From what they could determine from the extent of his injuries, a piece of flying debris had slammed into the left side of his body during the explosion. The blood vessels near and around his bleeding left kidney had been so severely damaged that the surgeons were having a problem trying to stop the severe bleeding. The entire left side of his body was now showing some visible signs of the massive trauma that it had been subjected to. In addition to these injuries, the CAT scan showed that he had also received a severe concussion to the back of his head.

As soon as John's arm and leg injuries had been addressed by the first team of doctors, more and more of the staff members shifted their attention over to John's more critical burn injuries that covered most of his body. A team of doctors dressed his burns and changed his earlier bandages to make him more comfortable before he was transferred over to the Shriner's Burn Hospital for further treatment. The first two trauma teams had done their best to stabilize his most severe life-threatening injuries. Now it was time for them to send him on his way over to the next group of specialists waiting impatiently for him at the Shriner's Burn Hospital. It would be their expert skills that would attempt to treat his most severe burns, which covered over 80 percent of his body.

* * * * *

While sitting at the breakfast table with her husband, Paul's wife was the first to reach for the ringing telephone. It was still quite early that Sunday morning, and so she couldn't imagine who could be calling them at such an hour. She soon learned that it was a phone call from one of the local newspapers asking her husband for a comment about his client's recent accident. The expression of horror showing on her face made Paul quickly reach for the telephone.

"This is Atty. Paul Tucker. What can I do for you?"

As he listened to what the reporter had to say about the early morning explosion and the critical injuries that his client had sustained, his heart sank to a new low. The terrible news had caught him completely by surprise. He slowly sat down in his chair again.

"I'm sorry, but this is the first news that I have heard about this accident, and I have no comment to make at this time. Thank you for informing me about it," he politely added as he hung up the telephone.

"I don't believe this. I was just talking to him yesterday, and now he's in a burn ward in Boston, fighting for his very life again. What else can possibly happen to this poor guy?" he pleaded out loud to his wife.

"Are they sure that he will be okay, Paul?"

"The reporter said that the doctors don't know yet. He's listed as very critical at the Shriner's Burn Hospital. I . . . I have to go over there and talk to his doctors."

"I understand. You have to do what you think is necessary. I'll be here with the kids if you need anything," she said to him in support.

An hour later, Paul walked through the main entrance of the Shriner's Hospital and found out where John had been taken for treatment. As he exited one of the elevators just outside the hospital burn ward, a couple of reporters rushed over to him for a statement.

"Please . . . Please, ladies and gentlemen! I have only just learned about my poor client's terrible accident. I don't know what else to say to you except that my client has always maintained his complete innocence in the murder of his fiancée, Dr. Mathews. This accident is just another terrible tragedy in a long list of accidents that have devastated my client's life recently. First, he has the untimely fate of discovering his fiancée's body in Newton, and then he's arrested for it, almost killed in jail, and now on the eve of proving his innocence, he's been struck down in another terrible accident. Once again, he's fighting for his very life. Please, I have no further comments to make at this time. Let me pass by now!" he said to them as he pushed his way past them and through the outer doors of the guarded burn ward.

He walked over to the nurses' station and asked to see the doctor who was in charge of treating John's injuries. He identified himself to the head nurse as John's lawyer and closest friend. The nurse picked up a telephone and paged the doctor for him. Ten minutes later, a doctor came out of one of the patient's rooms to see him.

"Doctor, my name is Paul Tucker. I'm Mr. Haggerty's personal lawyer and closest friend. I just learned that he was brought in here for treatment early this morning. How's he doing?"

"At this moment, he's holding his own but just barely. Does Mr. Haggerty have any other relatives that you know of?" the doctor asked him.

"As far as I know, he's all alone. I guess, in a manner of speaking, I've become the closest person in his life ever since his fiancée was found murdered."

"Well then, as his attorney and closest friend, you may want to take on the role of his legal guardian when it comes to making critical medical decisions for him. To be honest, Mr. Tucker, we do not hold out a lot of

hope for him to survive his injuries. As it is right now, we are amazed that
he has even lasted this long. The trauma teams at NEMC did a lot of work
on him to stabilize his condition when he was first brought in to them. We
are treating his burn injuries right now, but they are quite extensive. He
has third-degree burns over 80 percent of his body. The risk of infection is
extremely high. He's being kept in complete isolation right now. He cannot
be seen by anyone but my medical staff at this time. You can look in on
him through an observation window."

"Thank you, Doctor. I'd really like to do that."

"Please put this mask on and follow me down the hall."

Paul looked through the small observation window and saw the
battered and burnt body of his client lying uncomfortably on the bed.
Even though he was unconscious, he still appeared to be in a state of severe
pain. Paul turned away from the door and walked back out to the nurse's
station with the doctor.

"Here are a couple of my business cards listing my personal home and
cell phone numbers. If you need me for anything at all, Doctor, please don't
hesitate to give me a call. This poor man has lost almost everything and
everyone who has ever been close to him. Please keep me informed if there
is any change in his condition. Spare no expense on his behalf. I'll take
care of everything. Thank you, Doctor, for being there for him right now."

"You're welcome, Mr. Tucker. My staff and I will take very good care
of him, and I'll keep you informed of his condition."

* * * * *

Harry found out about John's terrible accident while he and Karen were
watching the morning news on her television set. The news caught both
of them by surprise. In his mind, however, he couldn't help but think that
this terrible accident was no accident at all. *A gas explosion! Not very likely!*
he thought to himself.

"It's probably nothing more than another staged accident used to get
rid of our client and subsequently the whole Dr. Mathews murder trial for
good," he said to Helen as they silently continued to eat their breakfast
together in front of the television.

"I'm going to go over each and every aspect of this case again. We
must've missed something very critical along the way, but what? No setup
can be this perfect! Her murderers had to have made a mistake someplace
along the way! I just have to find out what that something is that they
overlooked!"

"Well, you can do what you want today, but I have made some personal plans to visit my friend's beauty parlor later today," she announced to him.

"What I have to do today is not going to be very exciting. The questioning of old witnesses never really is. So go and have a good time pampering yourself. You deserve it. I'll call you later this afternoon so that we can make plans for dinner tonight."

Harry's first order of business for the day was to make a stop at Paul's office to go back over all of the case files once again, including all of the reports from the detectives and the labs. There had to be something in them that everyone had missed, but what? He kept asking himself.

The next three hours passed by slowly for Harry as he flipped through each of the witnesses' sworn testimonies and all of the police lab reports. It wasn't until he came across the official transcript of Brad's testimony made at the trial and the initial crime scene report that he noticed that one of them was different. He had found something that none of the DA's staff or Paul had picked up on earlier. He decided to call Paul at his home and to tell him what he had just discovered from reading over the police reports again. He had no idea as to whether or not this new information might lead them to some new clues in the case. Still, it was something that they had to check out together.

Paul eagerly agreed to meet him at the Sanford Office Building in about an hour to check out the whereabouts of Dr. Mathews's missing briefcase.

"Let's hope that this doesn't turn out to be another wild-goose chase. We could certainly use a break in this case. Even a little one might help us quite a lot," Paul announced hopefully.

It was Sunday, and so most of the building was vacant for the day. They entered the building through the main lobby and made their way over to Brad's security station. He was sitting alone behind the desk. He looked up and recognized Paul immediately.

"How's it going counselor? Have you uncovered any new revelations in the Dr. Mathews case that I haven't heard about yet?"

"No, nothing yet. Did you hear the news about Mr. Haggerty's terrible accident? He was almost killed last night in a massive gas explosion at his house in Arlington. He's listed in very critical condition at the Shriner's Burn Hospital. His doctors don't know whether he's going to make it or not," Paul announced to him sadly.

"That's awful! I didn't hear anything about that! I heard about a gas explosion in Arlington, but I never would've guessed that John was involved in it. That's terrible news! I certainly hope he pulls through because I believe in my gut that he didn't hurt Dr. Mathews. As I testified in court, they were really in love. Now what can I do for you two gentlemen today?"

"This is my law firm's private investigator, Mr. Harold Parks. He has been working very closely with me on this case from the very beginning. He used to be a detective a couple of years ago on the Boston Police Department before he got smart and retired. Now earlier today, when we were reading over your testimony and that of all the other witnesses in court, we came across a very interesting fact that seems to have been overlooked by everyone in this case."

"And what was that?" Brad asked them curiously.

"Well, during your testimony in court, you stated that you first saw the pools of blood and then the subsequent blood trail on the lobby floor right after you had returned from making your security rounds in the building. Isn't that so?" Paul asked him.

"Yeah, that's right. I first noticed the blood on the marble floor as I rounded the corner near the escalator."

"In Detective Bates's police report, however, she wrote down that you had also told her that you had found a briefcase on the lobby floor not too far from the blood trail. Do you remember telling her about the briefcase that night?"

"I think so, but they never asked me about it again! Did I do something wrong in not making them aware that I was still holding on to it for them?" he asked them a little bit concerned.

"No, Brad, you did absolutely nothing wrong. In fact, during all of the testimony that was given in court by the detectives and their field investigators, nothing was ever mentioned about the briefcase again. It was completely overlooked by all of us! That's why we came by here today to retrieve it. We're hoping that it might contain some evidence that might point to the identity of her real killers. However, even if it doesn't help us in any way, as an officer of the court, I am bound to turn it over to the DA's office as soon as possible. Do you still have the briefcase in your possession?" Paul asked him.

"Of course I do! I have it locked up in our security office. Come with me while I get it for you."

As they entered the locked security room, everyone's eyes seemed to focus in on Dr. Mathews's blood-splattered briefcase sitting on a shelf across the room. It was much bigger than Harry or Paul had expected. Upon seeing it, their hearts began to race in anticipation and hope that it might contain some explosive new pieces of evidence or clues as to who wanted to harm her.

"Now I won't get into any trouble if I give this briefcase to you, will I?" Brad asked them a second time as he reluctantly handed the case over to them.

"Absolutely not! In fact, I want to give you a signed receipt for this briefcase. This is all that you would have to give to the detectives or the DA's office if they ever ask you about the briefcase. As I said to you earlier, a lawyer is a representative or officer of the court, and he or she is bound by law to turn over any new evidence that they may find at a crime scene. This briefcase is just such an item."

He carefully wrote out the receipt to Brad for Dr. Mathews's briefcase. He noted on the receipt that the black briefcase was still locked and splattered with what appeared to be heavy traces of dried blood. He then dated and signed the receipt. Harry then signed the receipt as a witness to the exchange.

"I certainly hope that this briefcase contains something that will bring Dr. Mathews's murderers to justice," Brad said to them.

"And so do we, Brad, especially for poor John's sake," Harry said to him as they all walked out of the security office. Harry held the briefcase tightly in his hand as they exited the building.

CHAPTER 18

As the two friends walked out of the Sanford Office Building together, their minds were preoccupied with thoughts about John Haggerty. Paul's mind kept seeing his client covered in oozing bandages, attached to multiple monitors, breathing machines, and several IV tubes. He was fighting the greatest battle of his life, a life so filled with tragedies that he may not even want to win this last battle.

Harry, however, excitedly jumped into his car for the short trip back to their law offices. He held the blood-stained briefcase of Dr. Mathews firmly in his right hand. His thoughts were focused clearly on the mysterious contents of her briefcase. Would the black case contain clues about her work, her employers, her friends, or maybe even some clues or information about her enemies? The possibilities were endless in Harry's mind. He hoped that the contents would at least prove that John Haggerty was innocent of her murder.

Paul and Harry arrived back at their law office at almost the same time. The usual traffic was missing on the side roads, and they easily made the short commute without any real delays. A short while later, the two friends were sitting across from each other on a pair of sofas in the waiting area of their law office.

"What do you think Judge Zimmer will do with our case on Monday?" Harry asked him.

"I really don't know! He could simply declare it a mistrial because of what just happened to John. On the other hand, he could decide to continue the entire case for a short while until we know more about what's happening with John's health. Still, there might be a third option available for him . . . to allow the trial to go forward! I don't really see this as a viable option for him, though. If he allows the case to continue, it would be very unfair to the defense not to be able to draw on Mr. Haggerty's personal knowledge of the facts as they were presented during the court's proceedings against him. His injury has taken away from the defense a very valuable tool, our ability to call on him to testify in his own defense. This fact alone is a major legal obstacle for the judge to overlook. It would be the grounds that we would use in our appeal to have the trial declared a mistrial. I believe that the judge's only real option might be to give us a short continuance for about a week. Then if our client's health hasn't improved drastically by then, he will have no other choice but to declare it a mistrial," he explained to Harry.

"Well, that certainly sucks."

"I know, but on the other hand, we still don't have a hell of a lot to offer against their very damaging evidence."

"Can I get you a drink, Paul?" Harry asked him as he walked over to the conference room's small bar.

"No, not right now. I'm just tired and a little bit too depressed to start drinking right now. After having seen John's badly burnt and shattered body lying in that burn ward today, I have started to see my entire life from a completely different perspective. It made me realize just how precious our lives really are and how much we take them and the people around us for granted every day. What kind of a world do we live in, where we are constantly being pitted against each other every minute? John Haggerty was just another poor fool like us out there, trying to get ahead, trying, in his own unique way, to grab a little piece of happiness along the way. Now look at him and everything that has happened to him lately. Today I was told by his doctor that he doesn't really think that he's going to make it. He said that his injuries are so serious that his state of mind may be the only thing that can help will his body back to life. It's his only chance to recover and a very slim one at best. Now you and I both know how depressed he has been these last two weeks. Without his fiancée around, he just seems to have lost his will to survive," Paul said to him sadly.

"Then everything that we do for him right now won't really matter very much, will it?" Harry asked him.

"Sure it will! We will be clearing the reputation of an innocent man. And we may even be able to bring those bastards who're responsible for Dr. Mathews's murder to justice. That reason alone makes it all the more worthwhile, doesn't it?"

"I suppose it does at that."

"Well, what do you think we might find inside our good doctor's briefcase?" Paul asked him now, having grown a lot more curious about its contents.

"There's only one way to find out and that's to open it!"

"Yes, but for our own legal protection, we should document everything that we see and find inside of it. I'm going to set up a video camcorder to record everything that we discover inside the briefcase," Paul said as he left the room to get his camcorder.

He soon returned carrying his camera already attached to a tripod. He carefully set it up on one side of the room so that it would record everything that they were about to do.

"All set!" he announced as he turned it on and returned to his seat next to Harry.

Harry reached into his jacket pocket and pulled out a small set of lock picks.

"This is something that every PI carries with him at all times. You never know when you might need them to get yourself back into your car or house after you've accidentally locked yourself out." He smiled over to the camera.

The speed at which he opened the two locks with his picks alarmed Paul. "I don't know why they even bother to put locks on cases like this when someone like you can open them up so easily without a key."

"Paul, you have to understand that locks are there to only keep out an honest person. Crooks will never be stopped by such a simple locking mechanism. Now let's see what surprises this briefcase holds for us."

Harry opened the top of the thick briefcase and swung it around immediately to face the camcorder. He gently tilted it upward so that the entire contents of the case could be seen more clearly on the video film. At the same time, Paul got up and adjusted some of the office lights so that they pointed directly into the case. Paul then returned to his seat so that they could both go through the contents of the briefcase together.

Inside the briefcase, they discovered a treasure chest of documents. Some of them were typed, while others looked like handwritten notes from Dr. Mathews. They found journals that contained the results of hundreds of research experiments. They also found a bundle of personal letters and pictures of her and John together. Among the contents of the briefcase, they discovered two specially labeled and numbered computer disks. It was a veritable gold mine of information.

"I think we've struck pay dirt, Harry! In here, we will probably find everything that we need to know about who our mysterious Dr. Mathews really was and what she may've been secretly working on."

"Wait a minute, what do we have over here?" he said as he picked up and began to flip through some of the pages of her personal phone directory. His fingers came to a stop under the name of their missing MIT scientist, Dr. Phillip Stevens. Under his name, she had written the address and phone number of a Mr. Thomas Michael of Phoenix, Arizona.

"I assume this means that one of us is going to have to fly out to Phoenix, Arizona, and to meet with this Mr. Michael in order to locate our elusive Dr. Stevens."

"I guess it does at that! And since I cannot leave here right now, I guess that someone will have to be you, Harry!" Paul smiled back at him teasingly.

"Okay, I can take a hint. When should I plan on leaving?"

"It might be best that you plan on going out there either Monday afternoon or early Tuesday morning. You should probably wait until we hear how Judge Zimmer rules on our trial on Monday morning."

"I suppose you're right."

"You never really know how a judge will rule in a case like this until he actually does it!" Paul volunteered.

For the next four hours, the two men carefully sifted through the thick folders and piles of loose documents inside Dr. Mathews's briefcase. Most of the journals and notes that they found were much too complex for them to understand. They found themselves becoming even more confused after they had read through just a few entries. Eventually, they turned their attention back to the bundle of saved personal letters and pictures, which she had received from John. After carefully reading through some of John's long and intimate love letters to Helen, the two men soon came to understand the deep love that he and Helen had finally found in each other. Paul knew all too well what these letters alone really meant. They would have a devastating effect on the DA's case against their client. The contents of the letters captured in print forever the hopes and dreams of the two lovers. Anyone reading them could easily see into the heart and soul of the writer. Paul's heart was deeply moved with the sincerity of John's words. As he looked at a picture of the two lovers posing on a beach somewhere down the Cape, he made a solemn promise to himself that he would not give up until he found the perpetrators who had been responsible for this terrible injustice.

"I think we've done enough for today, Harry. We have enough evidence in here to completely destroy the DA's flimsy motive in this case. When I get through reading some of these letters into the official court record, there won't be a person on that jury who would ever even remotely consider convicting John of murdering her," Paul boasted confidently.

"I think you're right! Every one of them is emotionally very powerful!"

"Harry, go home to Karen and try to relax. You've done a great job for us today. You've found the one piece of evidence that all of us lawyers and police officials had completely overlooked. So on Monday, no matter what the judge decides in court, our next job will be to find the real murderers behind this heinous crime. We owe that much, at least, to Dr. Mathews and John. Nobody should be allowed to walk away scot-free from something like this. Whoever was responsible for this crime has got to be brought to justice," Paul announced to him.

"A swift and merciless justice, like they showed Dr. Mathews that night!" Harry echoed back at him.

The nurses kept a close vigil over their new patient throughout the entire night. They made sure that his IVs were full and flowing and that his medications were administered exactly as the doctor had prescribed. Kelly had worked in the burn ward of the hospital for almost four years, and during that time, she had developed almost a sixth sense for determining whether a patient would survive his or her injuries. She carefully inspected all of John's dressings and expertly attended to a few of them that had to be changed. It was a procedure that she had performed thousands of times while on the ward. She often joked with the other nurses that she could probably do it in the dark. John was still in an induced coma to allow his body some time to heal from the severe injuries that he had sustained in the explosion. The emergency procedures that had been performed earlier at the other trauma hospital had repaired most of the severe damage, which had been done to his left arm and leg, and they appeared to be slowly improving. An emergency nephrectomy had also been performed on him over there in order to remove his shattered left kidney and to stop his internal hemorrhaging. But even with all of these emergency procedures behind him, he was still listed in very critical condition. Most of his doctors had given him less than a 30 percent chance of recovering from his injuries. Kelly looked down at her patient's bruised and bandaged face and gently pulled back his closed eyelids. John's pupils responded to the intrusion of light that her actions had caused. His pupils narrowed in an effort to keep out the bright light of the overhead lights. She began to softly speak to him in her pleasing Irish brogue.

"Well, Mr. Haggerty," she said to him as she gently blotted his forehead with a cool damp sterile cloth, "I can see that you're hurting quite a bit right now and that your body is putting up a real good fight. Now I've heard about all of your legal troubles and everything else that you've been through. Now nobody can promise you that everything will be all right in the future, but there's always a chance that it just might be. God is good, and He never seems to close all of the doors for us without first opening up a few new ones. So it's all up to you as to whether you want to come back to us or not. And I bet that if Dr. Mathews was standing right here in front of you now, she'd probably be telling you to fight with all your heart to live. So don't give up, John, life goes on, and it can be very beautiful for you once again. Only you have to give it a second chance. Your body's injuries are very serious. In time, they can heal, but only if you keep on fighting. You must find that inner strength and willpower to live from somewhere deep within yourself. God loves us all and only gives us those crosses that he knows we can carry. So I'll be praying for you to find that willpower to get well," she whispered softly into his right ear.

A few minutes later, she quietly left his room and returned to the nurses' station again. The other nurses on the floor could see from Kelly's concerned look that Mr. Haggerty's body was still fighting hard to overcome his life-threatening injuries. Inwardly, Kelly seemed to sense that her patient had given up all hope and, with it, his will to survive. She knew that it was only a matter of time before his body would soon become racked with infection. It was a condition that seemed to afflict all of their serious burn victims. To stave off these infections, his body would have to be strong, and it would have to possess the willpower to get better.

"Our Mr. Haggerty appears to be a man without much hope right now, but I won't give up on him quite yet! When he regains consciousness, we will have to convince him that his life is not over yet and that it is well worth fighting for. And besides that, all of us have seen quite a few miracles occur in this place before! Haven't we?" she said to the other two nurses working with her on the night shift.

"I guess we have at that!" Maureen and Jane answered back.

Kelly looked down at her watch and then recorded the time on Mr. Haggerty's chart. She then carefully recorded his vital signs and her observations about him onto his chart also. She then turned and walked down the corridor to check on one of her other patients.

* * * * *

"Gentlemen, I'm afraid that I have no other option in this case but to declare it a mistrial! The present circumstances in this matter have left me with no other options," Judge Zimmer declared to the group of lawyers sitting in his office.

"It just doesn't seem fair, Your Honor!" Mr. Tucker responded back to him, sounding a little bit disappointed. "My client is truly innocent of this crime, and I know that with a short continuance in these proceedings. I can prove it to the jury!"

"Now, Paul, how can you say that to us with a straight face. You've been sitting in this very same courtroom with the rest of us for the last two weeks, listening to all of the damning evidence being presented against your client. That evidence cannot possibly be refuted by you or anyone else. The sworn testimony given by my witnesses to this jury has also been irrefutable. The state's case against your client is a rock-solid one, and you know it. Your client is as guilty as sin!" the DA retorted loudly back at him in frustration.

"Guilty maybe in your eyes and those of your investigators, but none of your so-called evidence proves that my client murdered his fiancée! I haven't even begun to present our evidence and our defense against your case yet. The only thing that you and the police have presented to the jury has been purely circumstantial evidence. Evidence that says that my client visited the crime scene at some time after the crime had been committed. Evidence that smells so much like a setup that not even you can believe it! Admit it, Tom!" he shouted back at the district attorney.

"Admit to what? That the evidence by itself isn't damning! That your client wasn't at the crime scene when she was murdered! Circumstantial my foot! How could anyone have placed your client's bloody fingerprints at the murder scene, except your own client? The truth is that you are being blinded by your own client's refusal to face the fact that he lost his temper and killed his fiancée in cold blood. A crime, which I must say, happens every day across this country!" Mr. Parker argued back at him.

"Gentlemen! Gentlemen! This type of arguing is getting any of us nowhere! The facts of this matter still remain before this court. The defendant's rights are on the line here, and the court cannot sit back idly and allow those rights to be violated. By law, he is guaranteed to receive a fair and speedy trial, not one that has a long hiatus right in the middle of it. The defense has the right to have their client available for both consultation and testimony. This is something that they no longer have available to them. Up until now, I haven't seen any reason to sequester the jury in this trial, and it would serve no purpose to do so now. Therefore, my decision is that I will continue this case for one week and no more. I want to be kept up to date by the DA's office of any changes in the condition of the defendant's health. At the end of this short continuance, I will make a final ruling on this matter. If I don't receive some very positive news before that time, I will declare it a mistrial. Now do either of you have any other questions?"

"No, Your Honor." they both responded at the same time.

"Good! Then I'll see all of you in my chambers next Monday at 9:00 AM sharp!"

The judge's decision to declare a mistrial was something that both sides had been expecting. The fact that he had allowed a week's continuance in the trial's proceedings had caught both of them a little off guard.

"Well, Paul, I hope you can pull a rabbit out of your hat for your client's sake in the next seven days, or else we'll all be going through this nightmare all over again. That is if your client survives his injuries," Mr. Parker said to him as he walked out of the judge's private chambers.

"I'll do just that, Tom!" he snapped right back at him confidently.

The district attorney had originally begun the trial a little doubtful that that the defendant was really guilty of murdering Dr. Mathews. But now after having presented the state's entire case to the jury, he was sure that he had the right person on trial for her murder. Paul hurried back to his office to tell Harry about the judge's decision to continue the trial for one full week. In a way, the delay was just what he and Harry had needed to find the missing pieces of their case.

As he hurried into his office with the good news, Harry let the air out of his balloon by telling him that he had already heard the news from one of his friends down at the courthouse.

"Well, that just goes to show you that there are no secrets in this city and especially from the police!"

"Isn't that a bitch?" Harry said jokingly back at him.

"Well, at least we've gained a little extra time for you to do your thing out West. Do you think you can locate our missing Dr. Stevens in time?"

"It all depends on our Mr. Michael and what he knows. I may have to threaten him a little bit with obstruction in our investigation if he doesn't cooperate."

"Now you know very well that you don't have any legal powers in this investigation!"

"I know that, but he probably doesn't! I intend to draw upon my many years of gentle but firm powers of persuasion to get him to cooperate with me. I'll have him telling me everything about our mysterious Dr. Phillip Stevens in no time at all."

"Now that is something that I would like to see come true," Paul responded back.

"Now what else have you learned from the contents of our doctor's briefcase?"

"Well, early this morning, I started to look more closely at some of her files for something that you might be able to use out West in your investigation. That briefcase of hers is really a treasure chest of information. The CDs and the two computer disks that we found inside the case are all encrypted. I asked Carol, my secretary, to take a look at them. She said that she didn't have any ideas as to how to break through the complex encryption code. Maybe you might be able to find a way to crack them when you're out in Arizona. I feel that the fewer people who learn about our discovery, the better off all of us will be! Neither one of us knows for sure whether someone has been dogging our investigation. When are you planning on leaving?" Paul asked him.

"My flight leaves Logan at two this afternoon. In fact, I had better start getting ready for it right now."

"Call me when you touch down out there, and let us know where you'll be staying. If you find out anything new out there, let me know right away."

"Okay, Paul, I'll keep you in the loop. I'll see you when I get back."

"Have a safe flight, and remember to always watch your back at all times!"

* * * * *

Phoenix was a city that Harry hadn't been back to visit for almost thirty years. From the very first moment that he stepped off the plane, he knew that many things in the old city had changed quite drastically. It was much bigger than he had remembered. The airport gave him that first clue. The weather outside the terminal was much hotter than he had expected, even for that time of year. Since it was a drier heat, it was a lot more comfortable to walk around in. His first order of business was to pick up the rental car that he had reserved. Without some personal transportation at his disposal, he felt like a duck out of water. As he sped away from the airport, he kept his thoughts focused on what he was going to do that day. Harry decided to stop for a quick lunch before paying their Mr. Michael a surprise visit. He liked dropping in on people unannounced. It always seemed to make them feel a little bit uneasy and much more willing to talk unrehearsed. Most of the time, he was able to get them to talk with some gentle legal arm twisting. People generally liked to avoid getting involved with the law, and so they often tried to convince him that they had done nothing wrong. He hoped that Mr. Michael was one of those people too.

In preparation for his anticipated meeting with Mr. Michael, Harry had done some preliminary research work on the firm of Brickman and Price before he had boarded his flight to Phoenix, Arizona. He had learned that they were a professional medical research consulting firm. They made their money primarily in the financing and selling of new medical technologies to larger more aggressive corporations. As it was explained to him by a friend back in Boston, they took promising new medical inventions and helped their inventors procure all the necessary patents before marketing.

They then put these inventors in direct contact with the right marketing teams. Any deals that came out of these meetings brought a handsome profit back to their firm. Their real efforts, however, were concentrated in the development of new pharmaceutical drugs. It was this lucrative and always expanding market that had placed them at the forefront of many new medical technologies and innovations.

Harry found the receptionist at Brickman and Price to be very friendly and quite attractive. When he introduced himself to her, he had purposely avoided mentioning anything about what he really wanted to see Mr. Michael about. He felt that it was better to speak to him in private and undisturbed. He therefore just told her that he wanted to meet with him about a very important personal matter. He knew that if Mr. Michael was worth his weight in what he did at Brickman, then his curiosity would get the best of him and that he would have him brought into his office. It would be bad business to allow a possible new client to get away.

"Please follow me, Mr. Parks. Mr. Michael will see you right away."

The corridors of the modern office building were decorated with what appeared to be very expensive oil paintings, sculptures, and other unusual pieces of ornate wealth. It was an interior that had been expertly designed by someone to catch the hungry eye of a struggling scientist or inventor. It was a ploy that probably worked much more often than not, Harry thought to himself as he followed the receptionist down the winding corridor. They soon arrived at another private secretary's office. The first receptionist whispered a few brief words into her ear and then returned to her own station near the building's main entrance. The second woman asked him to follow her over to Mr. Michael's office. The young woman came to an abrupt stop just outside a huge closed oak door. She knocked on the solid door loudly and then pushed it open. She directed him through the open door. Once inside, she introduced him to Mr. Michael before she turned and left them both alone.

"Well, Mr. Parks, I usually don't meet with people unless they have made a specific appointment with me in advance. In your case, however, I've made an exception. You were quite mysterious with my receptionist concerning the purpose of your visit, but she did say that it was both very important and personal. So what is it that I can do for you today?"

"Thank you, Mr. Michael, for meeting with me without any advance notice. It seems as though the present circumstances have made it quite necessary for us to meet this way today."

"And what circumstances are you referring to, Mr. Parks?"

"I'm referring to a mutual acquaintance of ours, a Dr. Helen Mathews."

Harry observed how the simple mentioning of her name had made Mr. Michael's entire body suddenly stiffen in fear. His demeanor appeared to become a lot more agitated and nervous. He rose up from behind his desk and slowly crossed the room to a large rosewood cabinet. He opened it and took out a bottle of Jack Daniels and poured himself a drink. He politely offered Harry one also, but Harry thought it best to decline his offer.

"How can I help you, Mr. Parks?" he asked him curiously as he slowly sipped his drink.

"I have flown out here from Boston in order to meet with you. Dr. Mathews has informed me that you can put me in direct contact with Dr. Phillip Stevens. Is that not so?" Harry slyly inquired of him. He knew that he was taking a big chance in asking him to probably break a confidence that he and Dr. Mathews had obviously set up for some very good reasons in the past. He knew that he had to be very careful not to give away the fact that she had been brutally murdered. He knew all too well that if Mr. Michael became aware of this fact, he would probably not want to cooperate with him in any way. The entire matter would then have to become a legal one involving the courts. Harry was also hoping that Mr. Michael had not learned on his own about Dr. Mathews's recent murder. He knew that he was taking a big gamble, but he also knew that it was the fastest way to get to meet with Dr. Stevens. He held his breath as he waited for Mr. Michael's next response. It came after what felt like an eternity of waiting.

"Your information is correct, Mr. Parks. Helen and I did make an arrangement a number of years ago that made me her secret liaison between Dr. Stevens and herself. She explained to me that this special arrangement was necessary in order to hide Dr. Stevens from some rather dangerous people. She said that their future research was much too important to be compromised in any way. It was a technology that she hoped would prove extremely beneficial to mankind in the future and, I might add, potentially very profitable also. I won't try to hide the fact, Mr. Parks, that I'm in this game for the profits. I have no great ulterior motive to save mankind from itself. Money and the bottom line is what have made this place into what it has become today . . . a very successful business. Our unlimited financing of special projects such as theirs ensures that we get the first rights to all of their discoveries. In the long run, all of us get very rich. Some of us, however, a little more than others. We are the risk takers in these ventures because we advance all of the funding that they may ever require in their research. They, on the other hand, are the real dreamers. It's their long hours of sacrifice and work in the labs that could bring forth a discovery that could change the face of a nation or even the world."

"But what happens if their research doesn't pan out? Then you'd be out a lot of money, wouldn't you?" Harry inquired with curiosity.

"I guess you could say that we would be out a lot of money, Mr. Parks, but what if they do succeed in their efforts. Just think of the financial windfalls that could be made! More often than not, they do succeed. This building and the success of the people behind it are a true testament to this fact." He smiled back at him.

Harry could see from Mr. Michael's attitude that he was a pure capitalist. He was a man driven by one desire, and that desire was to make money. He knew that he would have to be very careful how he handled Mr. Michael in the next few minutes. If he wasn't careful, Mr. Michael might become suspicious and refuse to give up Dr. Stevens's location.

"Yes, I can see what you mean. This building and what I have been able to see inside of it so far does appear to be a true testament to the successful pursuit of wealth and what it can buy. When I first walked into this place, I thought I was entering a museum. Your collection of art and sculpture is really profound, a little overwhelming to behold."

Harry could see that his words were having a positive effect on Mr. Michael's demeanor. He observed Mr. Michael carefully as he walked back over to his desk again. He seemed to be pondering what he was going to do next with Harry.

"Now what is it exactly that Helen has said that I could do for you today, Mr. Parks?" he asked him again curiously.

"Please call me, Harry. It's a lot less formal and much friendlier. Dr. Mathews gave me your name and location in order to be put into direct contact with Dr. Stevens."

"And why are you trying to reach Dr. Stevens?" Mr. Michael probed a little deeper from his mysterious guest.

"I have been told to see him regarding some very critical matters in Dr. Mathews's research." The sheer mentioning of the idea that he might have some important knowledge about Dr. Mathews's work made Mr. Michael's interest skyrocket. When Harry reached into his jacket pocket and took out a couple of her computer disks, he knew that he had won Mr. Michael over.

"What is on those disks that you are showing me, Mr. Parks, I mean, Harry?" he eagerly inquired of him.

"As you can clearly see by her personal labels attached to them, they are copies of her latest research experiments. I can only discuss them with Dr. Stevens and no one else. So you can now see my present dilemma. If I am unable to meet with him directly, then I must return to Boston immediately. I was instructed by Dr. Mathews to say to you only that what was put on these disks is extremely important and of a time-sensitive nature." Harry voluntarily added the last part of his statement to bait the hook even more effectively.

"I see. Well, I will need at least a couple of hours to look into this matter more closely. Where can I reach you later on today?"

"Well, because of my extremely tight time schedule down here, I haven't made any definite plans to stay in your city. I can, however, be reached directly on my personal cell phone while I'm in your area." Harry handed him a business card with only his name and personal cell phone number printed on it.

"Then I will give you a call on your cell phone within the next two to three hours."

"Thank you again, Mr. Michael, for seeing me. I'm looking forward to hearing from you later." Harry rose up from his chair and extended his right hand out to Mr. Michael. They shook hands politely. Harry then turned and walked out of his office. He hurriedly made his way out of the building and over to his car. Once inside his vehicle, he quickly placed a long distance phone call to Paul's office. He knew that it was imperative that he reach him without delay. He needed Paul to back up his cover story. He had to get him quickly over to Dr. Mathews's apartment in order to intercept any phone calls that Mr. Michael might attempt to make to her apartment concerning his inquiries about Dr. Phillip Stevens out in Phoenix, Arizona.

The switchboard operator in Paul's office recognized Harry's voice and immediately transferred his call over to Paul's private line.

"Harry! I was wondering how you were doing out there in sunny Arizona?"

"Not too bad. I think I may have convinced our Mr. Michael into cooperating with us. I suspect that he may still try to contact Dr. Mathews at either her lab or her apartment to confirm that I'm out here at her request to meet with Dr. Stevens. Now since her lab is still closed, he'll probably try to reach her at her residence. Do you still have the key to her apartment?"

"I think so! It should still be on John's original set of keys. With all that has happened to him, I never got a chance to return them to him yet. What exactly do you want me to do over there?" he asked him, sounding a little bit confused.

"I want you to go over to her place and wait there for his call. If I'm right, he'll try to contact her within the next two hours. If he asks for Dr. Mathews, stall him by telling him that Dr. Mathews is out of town for the next few days and that she cannot be reached. If he asks who you are, tell him that you're one of her research assistants. If he asks about me, tell him that she did send me out West suddenly to meet with someone. Our Mr.

Michael is definitely no fool, and I know that he will keep trying to contact her or someone at her place by telephone before he arranges any meeting between me and Dr. Stevens. I also believe that he will not leave a message on her answering machine if she's not at home. So whatever you do, please sound convincing! I flashed Dr. Mathews's computer disks at him and told him that there was something on them that is extremely time sensitive. I also told him that the material is for Dr. Stevens's eyes only. He's so intent upon making a future buck on their research that he'll do anything to not let me get away with her disks. He said that he'd contact me within a few hours once he has arranged the meeting. So if I was you, I'd hurry over there and try to allay any of his suspicions if he indeed attempts to contact her by telephone!"

"Okay, I'll try to be convincing! Call me back as soon as you hear from him again. I'm not very good at waiting, you know!"

"You don't have to remind me about that, Paul. I've known you long enough to have become familiar with most of your idiosyncrasies by now. I'll give you a call back as soon as I hear from him," he quickly promised before he ended their phone conversation.

Paul jumped into his car and drove quickly over to Dr. Mathews's apartment. Even though her place wasn't located too far from his office, Paul sensed that the short drive was taking him much too long to make. After twenty minutes of frantic driving in and around the congested commuter traffic of Cambridge, he finally arrived at her building. Paul hesitated for a brief moment just outside Dr. Mathews's front door. He had not been inside her apartment since he had first taken on Mr. Haggerty's defense. He carefully cut and pealed back the police tape that had been carefully placed across her front door. A strange sudden feeling of uneasiness came over him as he slowly pushed John's key into her front door lock. He all too clearly remembered how he had never liked visiting a dead person's apartment in the past because he had always felt as though the victim's restless spirit was in some strange way still trapped inside of it. As he slowly opened her front door, he could see that the interior of her apartment was very dark. All of the drapes surrounding her windows had been tightly drawn. The air inside the apartment was stale and heavy with an odor of spoiled garbage. It seemed to be crying out to him to open a window. The added smell of the stale air made his stomach feel even more nauseous than it had on his previous visit to her place. At the direction of the DA's office, the police had sealed her apartment right after the police and Paul had finished searching it for evidence.

He made his way out into her kitchen and found the source of the strong odors emanating from her trash container. He carefully lifted out the partially filled plastic trash bag and twisted it closed. He walked back out into the hallway again and closed her apartment door tightly behind him. He silently made his way down the hall toward the elevator. He rode the elevator down to the basement where he suspected the rubbish was disposed of daily by each of the building's tenants. He came across an alcove at the back of the building where he saw a large pile of trash bags being stored. He lazily tossed the bag up onto the pile and hurried back upstairs to Helen's apartment.

Inside Dr. Mathews's apartment, Paul tried in vain to make himself feel more comfortable on her living room sofa while he waited impatiently for Mr. Michael's phone call. After only ten minutes of waiting, the telephone on her coffee table began to ring loudly. Paul nervously jumped toward the phone. A brief smile seemed to form on his lips as he hesitated for a few seconds to regain his composure. Harry had been quite right in his suspicions that their Mr. Michael would first attempt to check out his story personally with Dr. Mathews. Paul played out his role on her private line to perfection. When he was through, he carefully hung up the telephone and smiled in satisfaction at his small part in their plan of joint deception. He hoped that Harry would call him back soon with the good news.

He decided to remain in Dr. Mathews's apartment for another half hour just in case Mr. Michael attempted to contact Dr. Mathews again by telephone. Without receiving any other phone calls from Mr. Michael, Paul happily exited her apartment thirty minutes later. As a young boy, he had often dreaded death and everything that was even remotely associated with it in any way. Now here he was, a lawyer who was sometimes called upon to defend people who were charged with violent unspeakable crimes such as murder. The irony of his career wasn't lost on him.

CHAPTER 19

As Harry slowly drove his car out of Brickman and Price's parking lot, he knew that he had done all that he could possibly do to set their gambit into motion. He knew all too well that their Mr. Michael was a highly experienced player in the high-stakes game of moneymaking and that he would not be easily fooled. He had expertly dangled Dr. Mathews's computer disks in front of him in an effort to entice him even more so. Now he could only hope that Paul would be able to play a convincing role in their joint plan of deception.

As he accelerated his small rental car toward the outskirts of Phoenix, he knew that the next few hours would be nothing more than a long waiting game for him. If Paul was able to convince Mr. Michael that Dr. Mathews had indeed sent him out there, then it would be up to Mr. Michael to make all the necessary arrangements for him to meet with their mysterious Dr. Phillip Stevens.

He looked down at his watch and observed the time. Some of the afternoon had already slipped away, and so he decided to spend the next few hours in an old restaurant that he and his wife used to frequent when they lived in Phoenix. The warmth of the Arizona sun was something that he and his wife had missed the most when they had moved back East to Boston many years ago. It was a choice that they had both mutually agreed upon so that he could become a law enforcement officer in Massachusetts. It had been the high pay scale that had convinced them both that it was the right thing to do. Now after having been away from Phoenix for so many years, he began to miss the brightness and cleanliness of the city. He also missed the many wonderful times that he and Mary had shared down there when they were first married. It was a place where the memories of his now-deceased wife seemed to be the strongest.

When he made the sharp turn into the old parking lot, he discovered that the old tavern had been torn down and that a new 99 Restaurant had been erected in its place. Harry took a seat at the far end of the bar and ordered a tall cold glass of draft beer. As the minutes slowly ticked away, Harry sipped on his beer and lost himself in the memories of his past. Soon the passing minutes had turned into an hour, and that hour had gradually evolved into two hours. An expression of disappointment seemed to form on Harry's face as he looked down at the face of his wristwatch.

"Two hours and still no call from him!" he whispered quietly to himself.

Harry soon began to experience a growing feeling of doubts as to whether he had successfully convinced Mr. Michael that Dr. Mathews had indeed sent him out to Phoenix. Harry began to ponder in his mind what their future options would be if Mr. Michael did not call him back within the next fifty minutes. He knew all too well that a meeting with Dr. Stevens was critical to their understanding of what was behind Dr. Mathews's secret research. Both Paul and Harry were hoping that the knowledge that Dr. Stevens possessed might provide them with at least one of the missing pieces that they needed to solve Dr. Mathews's murder. They knew all too well that Mr. Haggerty's entire legal fate rested on the outcome of this one meeting. There were just too many unanswered questions out there regarding Dr. Mathews's past and her mysterious research. Harry was convinced now more than ever before that Dr. Mathews was murdered to prevent her research from becoming known . . . research that neither of them had even the slightest clue about.

Harry slowly raised his beer glass up to his lips and took another long drink from it again. He then carefully placed the empty glass back onto the bar in front of him. It was his fourth beer, and he was starting to feel the effects of the alcohol. He preferred to drink scotch, but being in Phoenix had brought back the pleasant memories of his beer-drinking days. He unconsciously brushed the back of his left hand across his lips to wipe away the excess foam. The unexpected sound of his cell phone ringing in his pocked had a sudden sobering effect upon him.

"Harry Parks's line, can I help you?" he announced clearly into the telephone.

"Yes, Mr. Parks. This is Mr. Michael over at Brickman and Price. I have made those arrangements for you that we discussed earlier. Can you please come by my office again and pick up an envelope that I've left for you in our receptionist area?" he asked him.

"Yes, I can, Mr. Michael. I'll be there in fifteen minutes."

"Excellent! Your plans will involve your leaving the area tonight to meet with your party. You said that you didn't have too much time available, and so I took it upon myself to schedule a private meeting with him at nine thirty tomorrow morning. I hope that you will find everything in the envelope to be satisfactory. Please make sure that you are not being followed. Give me a call after you are through with your meeting with Dr. Stevens. If I can be of any further assistance to you in this matter, please do not hesitate to give me a call," he added with an air of professionalism.

"Thank you, Mr. Michael. You have been very helpful in this matter as Dr. Mathews had said you would be."

"Please give her my best and tell her to give me a call when she has the time."

"I will and thank you very much again," he added politely. Harry sincerely wished that he could've relayed Mr. Michael's wishes on to Dr. Mathews. Maybe, he thought to himself, his helping to solve her terrible murder or at least trying to prove her fiancé's innocence would be good enough to help her spirit rest in peace.

The receptionist area at Brickman and Price was almost completely deserted when he arrived to pick up Mr. Michael's envelope.

"I believe you are holding an envelope for me from Mr. Michael?" he inquired at the front desk.

"And your name is . . . ?" she politely inquired.

"Mr. Harold Parks."

"Oh yes! Mr. Michael's secretary just left it here for you a few minutes ago. May I see some identification please?"

Harry reached into his pocket and took out his driver's license and business card. She glanced at the two documents and then politely handed them back to him along with the envelope that she had been holding there for him.

"Thank you. You have been most helpful." Harry added with a smile.

Harry turned and exited the building. He drove out of the parking lot and continued to drive west on the main boulevard for a few miles. When he was absolutely sure that no one had followed him, he pulled off to the side of the road to look over the contents of the envelope. Inside the envelope, he found a short letter from Mr. Michael. In the letter, he was told drive out to a small airfield where he was to catch a 5:15 PM flight on a small private airplane to New Mexico. Looking down at his watch, he saw that he had plenty of time to reach the airport and make his flight. He put the rest of the papers back into the envelope and drove directly out to the airport. He decided that after he had reached the airport, he would then have time to look over the additional papers that Mr. Michael had sent along for him to read.

The private airport was very small and quite out of the way. As he sat in his car preparing to go over the additional papers in the envelope, a man standing inside the small terminal began to walk slowly over toward his vehicle.

"Are you, Mr. Parks?" he asked him

"Yes, that's me. What can I do for you?"

"I'm your pilot. Mr. Michael has made arrangements with me to fly you out to a place in New Mexico. Our flight will be a relatively short one, lasting about fifty minutes. So if it's okay with you, we can leave right away. There will be a vehicle waiting for you at the other end of your flight," he cheerfully informed him.

"Well, I guess I'm ready to go right now. I'll meet you in the terminal as soon as I get my bags."

"Let me give you a hand with them," he happily volunteered.

"Thank you! That would be very helpful."

The young pilot picked up Harry's two bags and headed over toward the small terminal. Harry made a quick phone call to Paul back in Boston. He explained to him what had happened and where he was about to fly out to. He then hurried over to the plane where his pilot was already loading his two bags into. It probably wasn't the smallest plane in the world, but it certainly wasn't too far off from being it either. Harry thought to himself. After a five-minute delay, the small plane got its clearance from the tower to take off. Harry soon felt the small aircraft leaving the relative security of the ground behind them as it rose steeply up into the clear bright sky.

"Is this your first flight in a small airplane?" the young pilot asked him.

"Yes, it is!" Harry shouted back loudly in order to be heard over the sound of the loud engine.

"Put these headphones on. We can then talk a lot easier."

"Thanks. Have you been flying very long?" Harry asked him.

"Ever since I was eight years old! My father taught me to fly a plane before I could even ride a bicycle. I fell completely in love with it. It's like nothing else on Earth. When you're up here you seem to develop a special closeness with God. You don't appear to be from around this area, Mr. Parks?"

"Many years ago, when I first got married, I used to live in Phoenix. I moved East to Massachusetts some thirty years ago. I lost my wife a few years ago to a sudden illness, and now everything in life doesn't seem to be quite the same to me anymore."

"I'm sorry to hear that. If I had known, I wouldn't have asked."

"No, don't worry. I don't mind talking about her now. She was the best thing in my life, and talking about her helps me to keep my memories of her alive in me."

"My name is Roberto Shuka, but everyone around here just calls me Bob for short. If you need a cold drink, there are some cold sodas in the cooler next to your seat."

"No, I'm fine for now."

"Well then, just sit back and enjoy the flight. We're going to be flying over some very beautiful mountains in a short while."

Their flight into New Mexico was a pleasant one without any incidents. The sky was clear, and the sun was slowly moving lower in the sky. Its rays accented the beautiful contours of the terrain passing beneath them. After a short while, Harry observed that the rocky terrain below them seemed to flatten out. Roberto made a slight correction in their easterly course. About five minutes later, Roberto informed his passenger that they would be landing soon. The plane made a slow gradual descent toward the ground. Harry looked out across the terrain below them and observed what appeared to be a short dirt runway constructed among the dry brush and rolling hills.

"Is that where we are going to land?" Harry asked him uneasily.

"It sure is! Now don't worry, I've landed here dozens of times in the past with no problems"

"Oh, I wasn't worried so much about your landing of us safely out here, as I was about knowing where the hell we are! From what I've been able to see so far, we are right smack in the middle of nowhere!" Harry proclaimed uneasily to the young pilot.

Bob glanced over at him and smiled. "To be perfectly honest with you, we really are quite far away from everything that you'd call civilization. But I can promise you that you will like being out here. I took Dr. Mathews out here a couple of times in the past, and she told me that she fell completely in love with this place."

"Well, I think I'm going to reserve my opinions until I see a lot more of it," Harry added jokingly.

Strong crosswinds kept pushing the body of the plane sideways as they made their final approach to the dirt runway. As soon as the plane's wheels had touched down firmly on the dirt runway, Harry breathed a sigh of relief. Bob taxied the plane over to a small roof-covered structure without any walls. Harry could see a wooden table and some simple wooden benches tucked in tightly underneath it. He surmised that the simple structure had been built there to protect visitors like him from the searing hot rays of the sun and the area's infrequent sudden downpours.

"That wasn't such a bad landing, was it, Harry?"

"No, I guess it really wasn't. But it does bring to my mind an old saying that my father used to tell me about flying . . . Any landing that you can walk away from is a good landing."

"I'd have to agree with your father completely." He grinned back at him.

"Now what do we do?" Harry asked him.

"Well, we arrived a little bit earlier than scheduled. Someone will be here for you very shortly. I'll get your bags out of the plane while we're waiting," he volunteered as they exited the plane.

Even though it was quite late in the afternoon, the air temperature outside was still quite oppressive. Bob carried his two bags over to the covered area and set them down on the table. Harry shielded his eyes from the bright sun as he looked out across the flat landscape for any signs of activity. He didn't see or hear anything in the area.

"Are you sure that this is the right place?"

"Positive! As I told you before, I've landed here many times in the past."

Roberto reached into the cooler and took out two cold sodas. He handed one of them to Harry who now eagerly accepted it. The two men slowly drank their cold sodas and allowed their eyes to take in the unique beauty of the surrounding terrain.

Harry thought about how he was going to have to play all of his cards close to his chest from now on. He knew that for his gambit to pay off, he couldn't tell Dr. Stevens or anyone else out there about Dr. Mathews's murder until he absolutely had to. His first priority was to learn as much as he could about Dr. Mathews's research. More than anything else, he needed to learn what role, if any, the Federal Government had played in her research.

Roberto was the first to catch sight of the distant dust cloud being kicked up by the fast-moving tires of the SUV racing toward them. Since the vehicle was still quite far away, the two men continued to sit and enjoy their drinks under the protection of the wooden canopy.

"See, I told you that someone would be meeting us out here after we landed!" Roberto shouted to him confidently.

"What do you think the chances are that Dr. Stevens will be in the vehicle that's heading toward us?" Harry asked him.

"Well, if I was a betting man, I'd bet that he's not in it. I only saw your Dr. Stevens once before when I flew out here to pick up Dr. Mathews. On that occasion, I think they rode out here together while they were discussing something very important. If I remember correctly, he never met any of my flights out here in the past. Now as I said to you earlier, I have never been formally introduced to Dr. Stevens. I just naturally assumed that he was the stranger that she was talking to that day. I could've been wrong."

"Then you also feel that there is something quite strange or secretive about this place and Dr. Stevens?"

"Maybe, but I'm only a pilot," Roberto answered hesitantly.

The white Ford Expedition with dark-stained windows made its way slowly down the unpaved access road that ran parallel to the dirt runway. As the SUV approached the two men, it seemed to make a wide turn away from them in order to allow most of the trailing dust cloud to pass by them unobtrusively. The vehicle slowed down and came to a full stop a few yards away from them. When the dust cloud had completely dissipated, the driver's door opened, and a young man stepped out of the vehicle. He walked over to them.

"Are you Mr. Parks?" he asked him politely.

"Yes, I am. Didn't Dr. Stevens drive out here to meet me?" Harry asked him, sounding a little bit annoyed.

"No, he didn't, but he will be meeting with you in a short while back at the ranch. Are these your bags, Mr. Parks?" he asked, pointing at them.

"Yes, they are."

The tall athletically built chauffeur picked them both up in one hand and walked over to the back of the vehicle. He opened the rear door and carefully placed them both behind the rear seat. He then walked over and opened the car's rear door for Harry to enter. Harry followed his lead and stepped up into the vehicle. The door closed tightly behind him. Harry looked on curiously as the chauffeur walked over to Roberto and handed him an envelope, which he promptly placed in his back pocket. A few minutes later, Harry waived a polite good-bye to Roberto as the luxury sports utility vehicle sped out across the arid landscape to points unknown. Harry assumed that it wasn't going to be a very long drive by any means. Still, he carefully studied the terrain in the event that he might need to leave in a hurry.

The powerful engine of the large SUV easily propelled the wide tires over the soft gravel-like terrain. The chauffeur made no attempt to strike up a polite conversation with his new passenger. The drive out to Dr. Stevens's isolated ranch took them only twenty minutes to make.

"Mr. Parks, Dr. Stevens's ranch facility is located just over the next rise. We should be able to see it quite clearly after we clear the top of the next bluff," the chauffeur announced to him.

The SUV continued to make its way up the soft terrain of the bluff until it finally reached the top of the rise. From the top of the bluff,

Harry could easily see a beautiful desert ranch home nestled up against an elevated rock outcropping just a few miles ahead of them. Located just to the left of the main ranch house, he observed what appeared to be a barn and another small building. The large ranch house appeared to be surrounded by a garden of rich vegetation and a small pond. It offered a striking contrast to the dry terrain of the surrounding hills. The barn appeared to be attached to a large fenced-in paddock area. A number of horses could be seen walking around the enclosed corral. Even from such a distance, the ranch and its surroundings gardens appeared to be something out of a picture catalogue. It was like a secret oasis in the middle of nowhere. Harry couldn't help but wonder why such an elaborate ranch had been built so far away from everything and in such a desolate part of New Mexico. What was even more disquieting to him was the question of who had borne the enormous cost for the construction of such an elaborate and isolated retreat?

After a bumpy ten-minute drive, the SUV came to a full stop directly in front of the door of the main house. A young man came out of the building and politely opened Harry's rear door. As Harry exited the vehicle, the chauffeur walked around to the back of the vehicle and pulled out his two bags. The young man with a Spanish accent politely asked Harry to follow him into the ranch house to a room that had been specially prepared for him earlier. The chauffeur, carrying Harry's two heavy pieces of luggage, quietly followed a few steps behind them as they made their way into the main house. The interior of the building had been tastefully decorated with a Western motif in mind. Various Indian artifacts and displays of pottery lined its numerous walls and tables. The interior of the structure was constructed predominately of exposed wooden beams and tiled floors. From what he could see as they walked through the house, most of the rooms contained exterior glass patio doors that opened out onto private terraces and the plush gardens beyond. The structural joists of the roof had been designed in such a way so as to purposely overhang the ranch's exterior walls. Harry surmised that the design probably offered its occupants a lot more protection from the day's hot sun. This unique framing detail seemed to create a pleasant draft or circulation of cooler air moving gently throughout the interior of the house. Decorative flowering plants and vines could be seen hanging from just about every beam in the house. The entire floor plan was so open and cheerful that it reminded Harry of a tropical resort.

The guest room that had been prepared for him earlier by Dr. Stevens's household staff was even more beautiful than he could have ever imagined. As he stood next to the large queen-sized bed in his room, he looked out at the private garden that lay beyond his open patio doors. He could hear the sounds of running water splashing against some rocks somewhere out in the garden. His eyes quickly searched the garden for the source of the sounds of the running water. Eventually, they came to rest upon a tall man-made waterfall and a wide pond beneath it. The warm air blowing gently through the open patio doors of his room filled his senses with the rich smell of aromatic flowers. Looking around his room, he observed a small desk for writing and a lounge chair for reading. The overall feel of the entire ranch had a very soothing effect upon Harry's nerves. He couldn't help but wonder if Dr. Mathews had stayed in this very same guest room in the past. He felt a slight pang of guilt in the knowledge that he was there on false pretenses. He knew that what he was about to do was both necessary and right and that Dr. Mathews would probably approve of his actions. After all, he thought to himself, it was for John Haggerty's very freedom and life that he was out there at all.

"Dr. Stevens has asked me to apologize to you for his not being here to personally welcome you to his ranch. He has asked me to explain to you that pressing matters in his laboratory have required his immediate attention. He hopes that you will join him for dinner at eight thirty this evening. In your private bathroom, you should find everything that you might need in the way of personal items. If you should need anything else, please give me a call. My name is Carlos. Dr. Stevens hopes that you will try to make yourself feel right at home while you're here. Please feel free to walk around and explore the ranch house and all of its beautiful gardens," he cheerfully said to him.

With those words, he excused himself and silently followed the chauffeur out of the guest room. Harry sat down on the edge of the bed and thought about what he would say to his host later that evening at dinner. After a momentary reflection, he stood up from the bed and went into the bathroom to take a shower and to change into something more comfortable for dinner. When he had finished dressing, he stepped out into the garden and began to marvel at its numerous varieties of flowering plants and trees. He soon found himself sitting on a small bench next to the waterfall. He stared intently at the flowing water as it fell from the rocks some ten feet above him. It landed noisily onto the half-submerged rocks in the pond directly below it. For some time, the sight and sounds of the falling water continued to mesmerize him. How long he continued to stare at the falling water, he didn't know. It was the faint sound of footsteps slowly approaching his location from somewhere behind him that seemed to bring him back to his senses. He turned his head to catch sight of a man in his late thirties walking toward his location. He was holding a drink in his left hand.

"I see that the sounds of my waterfall have drawn you magically to this location also, Mr. Parks. It has the same effect on everyone who comes out here. I've found this spot in the garden to be my most favorite place to visit," he said to him proudly. "Oh! Let me introduce myself to you. I'm your host, Dr. Phillip Stevens."

"I'm terribly sorry, Doctor. I wasn't informed that you had returned from your laboratory yet! I've been thoroughly enjoying your magnificent garden and its spectacular waterfall. They seem to have had quite an amazing effect upon me! Your unique selections and arrangements of exotic flowering plants and trees are quite breathtaking to behold! The sheer beauty and therapeutic sounds of this place seem to have brought me back to a time in my past that I had long ago forgotten about. You're quite a lucky man to own such a beautiful place as this, Dr. Stevens," he said proudly to his host.

"Please, Mr. Parks! All of my friends call me Phil. I think we will both get along much better if we dispense with worldly formalities and just call each other by our first names. Don't you agree?" he asked him.

"I couldn't agree more with you. All of my friends call me Harry."

Harry couldn't help but notice that Dr. Stevens appeared to be quite young, much too young to have accumulated all of the necessary capital needed to have built such a grand retreat in the middle of nowhere. To Harry, a ranch retreat like this would have required two lifetimes of hard work to even begin to accumulate enough money to build it.

"Okay Harry, can I get you a drink?"

"Right about now, I could really go for a scotch on the rocks," Harry eagerly responded.

"An excellent choice, Harry! Follow me into the main house where I keep a well-stocked bar for all of my guests and staff to enjoy. Around here, all of my friends affectionately refer to the ranch's central entertainment room as the watering hole. About this same time every evening, I usually settle down into a routine of slowly sipping on an Old Fashioned while sitting out in the garden by the waterfall. It helps me to somehow unwind from the daily rigors of my research. The sounds of the cascading waters seem to have quite a therapeutic effect upon my strained nerves every day. That's probably why you too were magically drawn to it earlier. I don't think I could ever live in another place that didn't have some sort of a fountain or cascading waterfall nearby for me to enjoy!"

"In the few short minutes that I spent alone in your garden by the pond, I can attest to its strange magical powers. Maybe you've stumbled upon a real cure for mankind's depression and frayed nerves. Should that cure become better known, you may be guilty of forcing a lot of psychiatrists out of business for good!" Harry teasingly joked back at him.

"No, I don't think the psychiatrists out there will have too much to worry about if my private discovery becomes too well-known. There will always be enough sick minds out in the world to keep them all in the lap of luxury!" he echoed back at him cheerfully.

"I do hope that you're hungry tonight? Carlos's wife, Maria, has prepared a wonderful dinner for all of us this evening. The two of them manage to take care of just about everything around this place. If the day-to-day chores of running this place were left up to me, this place would've fallen into a tragic state of disrepair a long time ago! My research takes up far too much of my free time every day. People like me tend to have no balance in their lives. We're either working ourselves into our graves at a very young age or else we're engaged in some crazy out of control lifestyle. Sometimes I wish that my lifestyle was the latter of the two," he confessed to Harry as he handed him his drink.

"Thank you! I'm sure that everything that she prepares for us tonight will be just fine, like everything else that I've seen around here so far," Harry added confidently.

Dr. Stevens quickly glanced down at his watch as he slowly lowered himself down into one of the six wicker chairs in the room. The chairs were placed around a beautifully carved wooden table on the left side of the room. The table looked like it had been constructed out of a cross section of a very wide old tree. Its surface had been expertly sanded and finished with many thick coats of lacquer. It seemed to match the décor of the room perfectly.

"Have a seat, Harry. Some of my other guests and associates should be arriving here any minute now. Every night, around this time, we gather in here for a few drinks before dinner. They're a lively group of friends of mine. I know you'll come to like them once you get to know them a little better."

"I'm sure I will."

The watering hole, as Phil had affectionately referred to the main room of his ranch, was indeed a party room. It contained a well-stocked bar built in the right-hand corner of the room against an exterior wall. Placed around it strategically were six comfortable high stools. Located in the very center of the room, there was a magnificent fireplace. It was open on all sides to allow the fireplace to be seen from every vantage point in the room. It was vented straight up through the roof of the house by means of a wide piece of black duct pipe. A U-shaped sectional sofa encircled the central fireplace and faced the two exterior patio glass sliders. An old upright piano occupied a prestigious location in the room near the bar. It faced sideways to the room's many sofas. Harry could just imagine a group of friends standing around it, all playfully trying to sing along to an old tune. As the two men relaxed in their chairs facing the open patio doors, they listened to the numerous sounds emanating from the private garden and the darkening desert landscape beyond. Soon, additional people began to slowly filter into the room. One by one, they gradually made their way over to the bar to fix themselves a drink before dinner. Dr. Stevens introduced to Harry the three men and two women as members of his research team. About ten minutes after everyone had entered the room, Carlos entered the room to announce that dinner was being served.

Throughout the course of their evening meal, the conversations at the table seemed to drift back and forth onto many different topics. Sometimes the topic of conversation focused on the weather, other times it shifted over to politics, but in time, it always seemed to find its way back to everyone's personal relationships. When the conversation eventually shifted to Harry, he casually discussed his long-term relationship with his now-deceased wife and how he had just recently become involved with a wonderful woman named Karen. When one of Dr. Stevens's aids shifted the topic of conversation to a question about Dr. Mathews's work, Dr. Stevens politely interrupted him. He reminded him about their house rule that work was never discussed at the dinner table. The subject matter was immediately dropped, and a new topic of conversation was quickly brought up for discussion.

Harry felt quite relieved when he heard Dr. Stevens's objection to questions about their work. When everyone had finished eating dinner, they returned to the watering hole for some coffee and a little fun at cards and playing on the piano.

When eleven o'clock finally rolled around, everyone appeared to be quite exhausted. Harry thanked all of them for being such great dinner companions and for making him feel so welcome. He then excused himself and retired to his private room down the hall. Sleeping in such a quiet location so far out in the flatlands of New Mexico had a very relaxing effect on him. He soon found himself drifting off into a very deep and restful sleep.

* * * * *

It was probably a combination of the gentle sounds emanating from out in the garden and the sounds of someone's footsteps quietly passing by his door that suddenly awakened Harry around five-thirty the next morning. As he lay in bed listening, he couldn't help but wonder what could be so important to make someone get up so early in the morning. It was the ranch's isolated location so far out in the barren hills of New Mexico that made the quiet footsteps catch his attention. For some strange reason, his body felt completely awake and refreshed at the early hour. He knew that it would almost futile for him to try to fall back to sleep again. So in a determined effort, he pulled his now-wide-awake body up out of bed and into the shower. When he had finished showering and dressing, he opened his bedroom door and quietly walked down the darkened hallway toward the kitchen. To his surprise, he came across Dr. Stevens sitting alone in the main room of the house. He appeared to be intensely reviewing a pile of important papers lying on the table in front of him. Harry curiously observed him for a few seconds before the doctor finally caught sight of him standing in the hallway.

"Good morning! I hope I didn't wake you, Harry?" he asked him apologetically.

"No, not at all! In fact, I slept like a baby last night. For some strange unexplainable reason, I just found myself totally awake and fully rested a short while ago."

Dr. Stevens took another long sip from the mug of hot coffee sitting on the table in front of him. "Harry, have you ever gone horseback riding before?" he asked him.

"Only once, I remember, when I was just a young boy. I don't really remember very much about the experience, but I do believe I thoroughly enjoyed it!"

"Well then, fix yourself a cup of hot coffee, and we'll take a short ride together before breakfast. The experience will make you feel like a new man. The terrain in this area is quite beautiful to observe at such an early hour. I'll go out to the barn and saddle up another mustang for you to ride. And don't worry. I'll make sure that I pick out a real nice horse for you. That way, you won't get too overwhelmed with the experience," he happily announced to him as he stood up and went out to the barn.

When Harry had finished gulping down some of his morning coffee, he made his way down the hall toward the front door of the house. Once outside, he found Dr. Stevens already waiting for him with two saddled horses. He slowly walked over to the two horses and gently began to rub one of them on the side of its long head. The animal seemed to respond favorably to his soft caresses. Phil gave him a quick lesson on the fundamentals of horseback riding and then helped him up into his saddle. When Phil felt that Harry had learned enough about how to control a horse, he slowly turned his horse around and headed out toward the open range. Harry's horse seemed to instinctively follow after Phil's horse. After a short while, Harry began to feel a lot more confident up in the saddle. As the two men rode off together in a northerly direction toward the hills, Dr. Stevens glanced back over his shoulder at Harry.

"See, I knew you'd get the hang of it real quick! I try to go riding every morning to keep myself in shape. It's a great exercise for the body. Without your even knowing it, you're using just about every muscle in your body to control the horse's movements. Whenever Helen came out here to go over something very important with me, she insisted upon us going horseback riding every morning. You know, she really loves this place. It was her efforts that helped build this research facility in the first place. I think she had secretly planned on settling out here a long time ago, but something very important must've changed her mind. A few years ago, she just suddenly deeded the whole place over to me. I don't know if she ever mentioned me to you before or not, but we have been very close friends for many years. I have been collaborating with her on her research for quite a few years ever since we first started working together in Cambridge."

"You must be referring to the research work that you and her worked on together at MIT, aren't you?" Harry casually interjected into their conversation. "Didn't you both work directly under Dr. Tinkoi over there?"

"That's right! I see that Helen has taken you into her confidence, Harry!"

"Whatever made you and her stop working together at MIT?" Harry probed him ever so gently for additional information, making sure that his questions didn't alarm him in any way.

"I don't know whether you've come to know this or not, but Helen is really quite a brilliant scientist! Some of her research ideas and theories about nerves and nerve impulses are quite fascinating. Her efforts into understanding the storage and interpretation of the nerve impulses of the human brain were so far out there that none of us could even begin to keep up with her . . . let alone help her whenever her research ran into a brick wall. I do know, however, that someone in our government was spending an enormous amount of time and money on her research ideas back then. It made all of us suspect that these same people had some very definite plans in mind for using her research."

"Did she ever give you any sort of a clue as to who those people in our government were that she was working for?"

"No, I don't think she ever did!" he responded back. "Why, is their identity important?"

"I think so. Did she ever refer to them as the CIA or the agency or some other names like these?"

"Now that you've mentioned it, I once heard her say that the agency was driving her crazy in its relentless pursuit of her research! She said that they did not want to accept failure as a viable excuse after having spent so much time and money on her research," he boldly announced as he recalled some of his old conversations with Helen.

"Then one day, out of the blue, she told me that she was getting a hell of a lot of pressure from someone high up in the government to come up with some positive results very soon. I remember her telling me back then that she was becoming a little frightened of them. She advised me to start looking for some inconspicuous way to extricate myself from her research team before I became too deeply involved in it also. Her warning came to me about the time that I took sick with a burst appendix. I was forced to leave MIT for a year to fully recover. It was the perfect excuse for me to leave her team. I returned to MIT about a year later to complete my doctoral studies. During that time, I learned that her research grant had been suddenly cancelled six months earlier. During the time that I was finishing up my studies, I received another alarming phone call from Helen. During that conversation, she warned me that my life might be in danger and that I should try to leave MIT as soon as possible. As a result of her dire warning, I decided to take my doctorate degree and simply drop out of sight. With Mr. Michael's financial help, she helped me to secretly set up this research facility out here. From this location in New Mexico, Helen and I have been able to secretly continue to work independently on some of her original research ideas. The ranch's isolated location is well out of sight of the government's many prying eyes.

"Helen told me that, for many years, she had been secretly siphoning off some of the government's grant money that had been specifically allocated for her research work in their budget. She informed me that she had secretly purchased this large tract of land out here in New Mexico with some of those funds. With Mr. Michael's help, she made all the necessary arrangements for the construction of this ranch and its state-of-the-art laboratory facilities. The two of them then carefully put in place an elaborate security scheme to keep Helen and myself from ever dealing directly with each other. It's the perfect arrangement. For someone to find me, they first had to know about Mr. Michael. Nobody in Helen's office had any idea that Mr. Michael even existed. In exchange for his help, his investment group was to get the exclusive first marketing rights to anything that came out of our research. Helen and I never lost touch with each other for all these years. She's like that. She was always looking out for the welfare of the people that she worked with. I always felt that all her cloak-and-dagger secrecy was just a little bit too much on her part!" he announced to him somewhat skeptically.

"After years of intense research and millions of dollars, in special funding, she told me that her contacts in the government had eventually decided to abandon her research project altogether. Helen, however, was never one to walk away from something so important. So against their explicit orders, she continued to secretly work on the problems that had apparently stopped her original research dead in its tracks. Both of us continued to collaborate on the progress of our research. Neither one of us, however, ever discussed our work with outsiders," he said to Harry.

There was a brief but noticeable hiatus in their conversation. Dr. Stevens picked up on Harry's obvious hesitation to respond to what he had just told him.

"Phil, what reason did Mr. Michael give you about my wanting to meet with you right away?"

"He just said to me that you were sent out here by Helen to go over something that she felt was very important. He said that you had some vital information that she wanted me to look at right away. I believe that he mentioned to me that the material in question was very time-sensitive," he explained to Harry, now sounding a little more worried.

"Well, in a roundabout sort of way, that's true. You see, I came out here to meet with you because I found it necessary to learn more about what Dr. Mathews had been secretly working on. I don't know any other way to tell you this except by being very direct! What I am about to tell you will probably tear your guts out! You see, Dr. Mathews was savagely murdered by someone a few weeks ago!"

The shock of his words caused Dr. Stevens to suddenly pull his horse up to a full stop. His entire face suddenly appeared to turn pale white in front of him. An expression of cold fear seemed to form suddenly upon his previously smiling tanned face.

For the next few minutes, Harry slowly related to him the heinous details of Helen's savage murder. He explained to him how she had first been shot in the leg by a high-caliber rifle while leaving her office. He then told him how she had somehow found the strength to escape her would-be attackers. He listened intently to how she had desperately but futilely eluded her assassins after the initial attack. When Harry began to describe to him how her assailants had eventually tracked her down and executed her in cold blood, Dr. Stevens suddenly began to feel sick to his stomach. The news was so shocking to him that his mind couldn't believe that it was really true.

He suddenly jumped off his horse and began to nervously pace around the area. He then just as suddenly squatted down on the parched dry grass and began to vomit. After a few minutes, he managed to regain some of his composure. He got up and slowly walked back over to where Harry was patiently holding on to the reigns of his horse.

"I know that what I just told you has come as a real shock! Neither one of us will ever really know the utter terror and loneliness that she must've felt during those last few minutes of her life. Her assailants not only appear to have gotten away with her murder, but they have also managed to maliciously implicate her fiancé in their crime. He discovered her body under her porch a short while after she had been murdered."

"How do I know that what you have just told me is really true and not just another lie?" he asked him.

"When we get back to the ranch, I'll show you a picture of the crime scene and a copy of Dr. Mathews's death certificate."

"Then it's really true! Helen is really gone! And to think that she was out here smiling and having a wonderful time with all of us less than a month ago," he emotionally announced to him.

In his mind, all the parameters of time suddenly seemed to no longer exist for him as he tried to come to grip with Helen's death. Her existence had been the one underlining constant in his life since he had become a successful researcher. She had been his one and only true mentor. He could feel his mind becoming overwhelmed with a rush of images and cherished memories that they had shared together. He tried in vain to focus his thought on something else, but his mind kept telling him that she had been responsible for everything that he now owned. The very fibers of his heart began to cry out to him for some sort of revenge against her murderers. But the more that his mind tried to focus on revenge, the more his heart gave in emotionally to the pain of his loss. After some time, he managed to find the strength necessary to speak to Harry again. Harry had remained silent throughout the ordeal in order to allow Dr. Stevens the time he needed to accept the terrible news.

"Harry, what can we do to bring these animals to justice?" Dr. Stevens asked with a newfound strength of purpose.

"Now, Phil, this entire situation is still extremely volatile. It has to be handled very carefully. The police haven't even learned the true identity of her murderers yet! If we are dealing with the CIA or some other rogue branch in our government, then we will all have to be extremely careful! If they were behind Dr. Mathews's murder, they will have no problem with murdering anyone else who attempts to uncover their sinister role in this. I suggest that we return to the ranch and discuss this matter again after you've had some time to recover emotionally. I've brought with me a number of things that we found relating to her research, but they're all encrypted. Maybe you can help us to decipher them. Like you, my partner and I want nothing more than to bring these people to justice!" he stated with authority.

"Now, Phil, I have to warn you once again that no matter what we may do in the future, our actions will involve high risks and consequences! These people will resort to whatever it takes to stop us!" Harry reiterated strongly.

"I understand!" Dr. Stevens echoed back. "I think we have both had enough riding for one day!"

Dr. Stevens turned his horse around. They rode back to the ranch in silence. When they came within sight of the ranch house, Dr. Stevens stopped again to ask Harry for a special favor.

"Whatever you do, please don't tell the others about Helen's death. I'll inform them all later on, but in my own way. After we get back to the ranch, please act as if nothing has happened. We'll meet in a couple of hours to discuss what you think has to be done. I'll send Carlos out to find you. In the meantime, I think I need to spend some time alone right now!"

"I understand completely! I didn't know that you and Helen were so very close. I'm truly sorry for having been the bearer of such terrible news," Harry added.

"All of us out here loved her very much, especially me! She was a brilliant scientist and a very dear and close friend. We are all going to miss her an awful lot!"

"Did you know that she was engaged?" Harry asked him curiously.

"No, I didn't! He must be completely devastated by her death!"

"Whoever was responsible for murdering Dr. Mathews framed him almost perfectly for her murder. My boss and I believe that they may've also been behind a suspicious gas explosion that occurred in his house the other night. He almost died in the gas explosion. If he had died in the explosion, the entire murder investigation would've just simply been closed. That's why we have to be very careful in whatever we decide to do next," Harry explained in warning.

"Is he going to be okay?"

"When I last saw him, he wasn't doing too well. He was just barely hanging on in a burn ward back in Boston. They don't seem to know whether he's going to make it!"

"What a bunch of cowards! Helen was really right when she warned me to get out of the project when I did several years ago!"

"Her advice to you back then probably saved your life! Everyone else that was associated with her old research back then has either mysteriously disappeared without a trace or met with some sort of a deadly accident!" Harry informed him.

When the two men finally arrived back at the ranch, they dismounted their horses next to the paddock area. Carlos came out of the barn and took hold of the reigns of their two horses. He led them away into the barn. Dr. Stevens went directly back to his room to reflect upon the terrible news of Helen's death. Harry made his way out to the kitchen to get himself some breakfast. His horseback riding experience had made him extremely hungry. When he had finished eating breakfast, he too returned to his room to get washed up and to rest for a while.

After a few hours of restless sleep, Harry was awakened by the sound of loud knocking at his door. It was soon followed by the sound of Dr. Stevens's voice.

"Harry, are you awake? We have to talk!" he asked him through the closed door.

"Yeah, just a second!" Harry answered as he swung open the bedroom door.

"I have to see what you brought with you regarding Helen's research."

"I'll get them for you. They're in my suitcase," he said as he lifted his bag up onto the bed. He unlatched its two locks and quickly threw open the suitcase.

Dr. Stevens's eyes meticulously glanced over the contents of the old suitcase. At first glance, he didn't appear to be too impressed with what he saw inside the bag. When his eyes caught sight of the two specially labeled computer disks and the two thick research journals partially hidden under a shirt in the suitcase, he smiled excitedly.

"Harry, I believe we are looking at Helen's heart and soul!" He smiled back at him. His eyes began to water as he held the two worn journals tightly in his hands. He began to flip through some of the ruffled pages. It was a painful act for him to endure because his mind began to envision her sitting alone at her desk late at night, carefully recording her secret theories and observations on those very pages.

"Do you think that you can decipher her notes?" Harry asked him hopefully.

"Decipher them? My dear friend, I'm very well-acquainted with Helen's secret encryption system. She took great pains to teach me it when we were working together back in Cambridge. She had insisted that I become thoroughly familiar with it in the event that I might need to translate her notes some day when she wasn't around to help me. Her secret system of encryption is actually a combination of two very unique systems. I haven't seen it for quite some time, but I can assure you, Harry, that I will be able to decipher all of her notes and disks completely. It will take me at least a few hours alone in my lab to familiarize myself with it once again before I can begin translating them accurately.

"I'll send Carlos out to get you when and if I learn anything important. In the meantime, try to be patient because this whole process is going to take me quite some time to accomplish. I only hope that Helen has managed to overcome some of the dead ends that her research had run into. She told me about some of them on her last visit out here. She was very confident that she was on the right track!" he happily informed Harry.

Dr. Stevens's newfound sense of confidence seemed to greatly elevate Harry's spirits. Dr. Stevens picked up Helen's two computer disks and her journals from inside the suitcase and hurriedly exited his room. He headed straight for his laboratory. Harry's excitement was so great that he could hardly contain himself. He reached for his cellular telephone to call Paul back in Boston with the good news. The news greatly lifted Paul's spirits also.

Since there was nothing else for him to do except wait, he decided to spend the time hiking up the rocky slopes of the hill that rose up sharply behind the ranch house. Everything was solely in Dr. Stevens's hands. The climb up the hill's steep rock face was much more difficult than Harry had anticipated. When he had finally reached the top of the rocky hill, he exhaustedly dragged himself up against a flat boulder to rest. As his eyes looked out dreamily across the arid landscape, his thoughts shifted to Karen back in Boston. He was missing her quite a lot, much more than even he had thought he would. He decided to call her later that evening to see how she was doing. After an hour of restful daydreaming, he began to carefully descend the steep slopes of the rocky hill once again. When he finally arrived back at the ranch, he found Maria waiting for him near the front door. She informed him that she had prepared a nice lunch for him to eat out in the dining room. His solo hike up the hill had given him quite an appetite. He washed up and eagerly headed for the dining room for lunch.

After he had finished eating, he returned to his room where he found Carlos waiting patiently for him outside his room.

"Señor Parks, Dr. Stevens has asked me to escort you out to his laboratory right away!" he politely announced to him. The two men hurried off together toward Dr. Stevens's laboratory. After a short walk down a brick path that wound its way through the gardens, they soon arrived at a second building located about fifty meters behind the main house. When they entered the building, they observed Dr. Stevens nervously pacing around the room while holding one of the two journals tightly in his hands.

"Thank you, Carlos. That will be all for now," Dr. Stevens said to him. Harry, please take a seat next to me at my desk. We have a lot of things to talk about!"

"Did you learn anything important from reading Dr. Mathews's research notes?" Harry eagerly asked him.

"Much more than even I had originally hoped to learn! So far, I have learned that Helen's research has been much more extensive and successful than even I had ever imagined possible. In fact, she has discovered one of nature's most elusive master keys, a key that unlocks one of our body's most secretive mechanisms. She has been able to decipher the very nature of the sensory nerve impulses or signals that travel throughout our bodies to the various parts of our brains. I can't really grasp the idea that she has been so successful in accomplishing this feat. But in her journals, she has reported that she has really done it! It's utterly fantastic! A truly brilliant leap in scientific research . . . something that only her mind could've envisioned possible! In one brilliant sweep, she may have unlocked the doors to blindness, hearing loss, and all of the other sensory organs of our body. In fact, if what she has written is true, then her scientific breakthrough is both priceless and its commercial applications unlimited!

"Now I must remind you that so far I've only just touched on the outer fringes of her notes. I will have to stick with this for several more hours to discover what she was actually working on when she was murdered. Someone wanted to control this new technology and to keep its existence a secret. Her advanced research on the body's neurons and their special chemical and electrical properties combined with some new computer programs that she had designed have unmasked the secret of our brain's ability to hold thoughts and images. According to her notes, she has somehow devised a method or system of breaking down these electrical impulses chemically. Then through some miraculous leap of brilliance, she has stumbled upon a way to interpret them. I didn't think that it would ever be possible to discover this mechanism so completely in my lifetime. In one of her journals, I read a footnote that states that she has actually accomplished just that!"

"Now I don't want you to jump to any conclusions quite yet, Harry! Give me and my people a few more hours to dig even deeper into her journals and files and to find some more answers!" he excitedly announced to him.

"The ball is in your corner, Phil! Do whatever you have to do. I just want to get to the truth of who was behind her murder! If her notes and files can finger the bastards that killed her, then go for it! I'm going nowhere until you're satisfied!" Harry shouted to him supportably. "I'll be back in the main house whenever you have something more to tell me. Keep up the good work, Phil!"

Harry got up from his seat and left Phil and his colleagues alone in the laboratory. With his mind now filled with endless possibilities, he walked back to the ranch house in silence. His mind tried to focus in on their newly discovered motive probably behind her murder. For some reason, he couldn't see monetary gain to be the real reason behind why she had been murdered. There had to be something else that he was missing. In any event, the potential use of her research would be overwhelming to society in the future, to say the least! He tried to think about what her research could mean to thousands or even millions of people who were handicapped. He had to learn more about her work!

Dr. Stevens and his coworkers continued to work in the lab throughout most of the night. They made arrangements to have their dinners brought in to them so that they could continue their work undisturbed on Dr. Mathews's research files. In the meantime, Harry spent the next few hours alone. While sipping on several drinks at the bar, he tried in vain to become interested in a novel that he had found in the ranch's small library. In time, he eventually gave in to the fact that his mind was much too distracted to concentrate on it. He put it down and returned to his room to sleep.

It was not until around 5:00 AM the following day that he was awakened by the sound of Dr. Stevens's footsteps and those of his colleagues returning to their rooms to sleep. He knew that all of them had to be quite exhausted, and so he decided not to bother them. In a few hours, he knew that Dr. Stevens would eventually inform him about what they had been able to so far decipher from her journals.

Harry closed his eyes and once again excitedly drifted off to sleep. A few hours later, Harry lazily awoke and made another phone call back to Paul. He learned that John's condition was still listed as very critical and that he had not showed any further signs of improvement.

"Harry, when do you think you'll be flying back here? We're running out of time! The judge will need to hear something much more substantial to keep this case alive."

"I hope to be able to wrap up my work out here within the next twenty-four hours."

"That'll be great, Harry! I wish we could've found out much sooner about what she had been working on. We might've been able to use that information to help John when it would've mattered more to him."

"I agree! Dr. Stevens and his colleagues have been working around the clock to decipher her journals and disks. I'll give you another call after I talk to them again later today. How's John doing? Has his condition improved at all?"

"No, not really. He's still listed in very critical condition, and he's starting to show some signs of infection and pneumonia."

"That's terrible news!"

"I know. I just hope that whatever you find out there can clear up his innocence before it's too late!" Paul added as they ended their phone call.

CHAPTER 20

The weapon looked clean enough to pass an inspection at the academy, but he nervously continued to polish its dark metal surface. There was something bothering him that he couldn't quite put his finger on. Something, he thought, just wasn't right. He and his boss had done everything to kill Mr. Haggerty and to make it look like an accident . . . and still, he was alive!

"Boy, Mr. Haggerty, you're such a persistent bastard. Why don't you just give up and die? Your life's just not worth living anymore. Your fiancée is dead, and your body's burnt from head to toe. All of this pain is not worth putting up with! Why not just give up and move on? Your girlfriend's spirit is probably waiting for you somewhere out there," he said to himself in frustration inside his motel room. It was a wishful thought that he hoped would telepathically connect with John's mind lying trapped inside his burnt shell of a body at the Shriner's Hospital.

As he continued to polish his nine-millimeter handgun, he found his mind searching back over the events of the last few days. There was still something out there that he was overlooking. *But what?* he kept asking himself over and over in his mind.

Like a bolt of lightning, the answer to his question came to him a few minutes later. "The private eye! He hasn't been around! Where the hell is he, and what has he been up to?" he asked himself.

Sam picked up his coat and quickly ran out of his motel room. He drove over to Paul Tucker's office building and arrived there a few minutes before midnight. Sneaking into a locked building after hours and getting past its rent-a-cop security personnel would not be a problem for him. Using his highly trained skills, he quickly bypassed the building's rather simple electronic security system and then opened its locked outer doors with his well-used set of lock picks. Most buildings in a city were protected by very simple security systems. Owners, for the most part, had a tendency to rely much too heavily on their security personnel's ability to intercept an intruder inside their building's lobby. However, once an intruder had managed to get safely into a building's lobby and past its easily distracted night security guards, they were usually able to freely wander throughout the building without any fear of being discovered.

Sam quietly made his way up an emergency stairwell to the tenth floor, which housed the offices of Paul Tucker and Associates. The law office was protected by a simple keypad with a coded entry system. Sam carefully opened the keypad device and exposed its wire leads. Using insulated alligator clips, he attached a small gray box to the pad's three-wire leads. Satisfied that his computerized descrambler was attached correctly, he switched on its power supply. Within a few seconds, the red alarm light on the keypad went dark, and the green safe light lit up. Sam carefully disconnected his descrambler and reattached the keypad to its base plate, which was still mounted on the wall. He took out his set of lock picks and quickly proceeded to unlock the outer door of the office.

Once he was inside the main office, Sam moved quickly from room to room until he found Mr. Tucker's private office. He carefully took the telephone on his desk apart and inserted a small plastic transmitter microphone inside the phone's headset. He then placed a few more hidden listening devices around his office. When he was satisfied with his handiwork, he quietly exited the office and secured the main door tightly behind him. His footsteps echoed lightly against the concrete walls of the deserted stairwell as he made his way down them to the basement of the building. When he reached the basement, he carefully made his way over to the building's main utility room. Once inside it, he looked around it for the building's main telephone circuit panel. He opened it and carefully installed a small transceiver just inside the metal casing of the panel box. The transceiver's only remaining requirement was to be hooked up to an outside energy source, which Sam found readily available next to the panel box.

Once he had the device safely wired into the power source, he checked it for signal strength and pickup. The purpose of the small but very powerful electronic device was to receive the various electronic signals that were being transmitted by the electronic bugs hidden upstairs in Paul's law offices. The main transceiver would then both amplify and transmit those signals back to a secondary receiver already set up in Sam's motel room. Having made sure that the transceiver was working properly, Sam picked up his bag of tools and hurried over to one of the basement's unarmed exit doors. He quietly pushed it open and disappeared undetected out into the cool night air.

From the relative security of his motel room, Sam was now able to eavesdrop undisturbed on most of the conversations that went on inside Paul's law offices. For two long days, he tirelessly listened in on Paul's many private conversations for information about Mr. Haggerty's deteriorating condition and what the court was planning on doing with the case. With each passing hour, he became more and more bored and frustrated with his fruitless efforts. He had grown tired of listening to the boring conversations between the firm's many lawyers and their stupid clients. As he slowly paced around the narrow confines of his room, he frustratingly complained about what he was doing. For over twenty years, he had been involved in the planning and execution of many covert operations for the agency all around the world. Now he felt as though he was just wasting away his skills in a cheap motel room just outside of Boston.

He soon began to believe that his earlier suspicions about the law firm's missing private investigator were simply unfounded. He had grown tired of his assignment in Boston, and he wished that he was back in DC with his friends and colleagues. With each new passing hour, he became more and more convinced that Harry Parks had simply taken some time off and was out of their lives forever. It was time for him to return to Washington.

By the next day, however, he had once again begun to suspect that his initial concerns about Harry's whereabouts were indeed justified. The microphone in Paul's office had picked up and recorded a short cell phone conversation between Paul Tucker and a man whose voice he immediately recognized to be that of Harold Parks, the firm's missing private investigator. Sam's microphones had missed most of the details of their conversation, but to Sam, it had sounded as though Harry was still working on Mr. Haggerty's case. As Paul was exiting his office, Sam faintly overheard him telling his PI to keep him apprised of any new leads that he might turn up in his ongoing investigation.

The words "keep me informed" were still echoing in Sam's ears when he turned off his listening device. "So our Mr. Parks is still poking his nose into places where it doesn't belong!" he said to himself. "An action I fear that will cause him some very serious consequences!"

Sam leaned back against the headboard of his bed to think about what those consequences should be. Without knowing Mr. Parks's present location, he knew that it would be virtually impossible for them to stop him. It was a situation that he knew his boss would want to be informed about right away.

* * * * *

Harry neatly packed up the last of his personal belongings back into his two suitcases and then sat down again on the edge of his bed. He allowed his eyes to gaze transfixed for one last time at the lush gardens of vegetation growing outside his patio door. These images and the sounds of the cascading waterfall suddenly made him feel sad at the prospect of leaving such a beautiful place for good. He had thoroughly enjoyed his brief three-day visit to the desert and the new friends that he had made. Even though the purpose behind his trip had been initially business, he couldn't help but feel that he had been on a brief vacation. His only regret was that that he didn't have Karen along with him to fill the empty periods of waiting. *She would've really liked this place*, he thought to himself as he stood up.

He hoped that his memories of the beautiful ranch and his many hours of laughter and conversation with his newfound friends would stay with him for a very long time. He wished that his brief stay out there could've been longer, but the pressing problems back in Boston had to be addressed first. The friendships that he had formed with Dr. Stevens and his associates would be hard to forget.

As he made his way down the hall to the central room of the ranch house, he was surprised to see that everyone had gathered in the watering hole to see him off. Each of them personally wished him the very best of luck in his quest to find Helen's murderer.

"Well, Harry, you came here as a stranger, but you will be leaving here as a new friend to all of us. We're going to miss your smiling face at the dinner table every night. I know that I speak for all of us out here when I say that we all loved Helen very much. This place, in a way, is a living memorial to her and what she was trying to accomplish. I only hope that what we have given you so far will be enough to help you track down her murderers and to put them behind bars forever!" Dr. Stevens said to him.

"What you have discovered so far will help Paul and me to move our investigation in the right direction," he announced confidently to all of them.

"We will continue working on her last CD to see if we can break through the last of her security code lockouts. In the meantime, I know that you and Mr. Tucker have a lot of work to do in order to just keep her case alive. I'll let you know the minute we find out anything important," Dr. Stevens promised him.

"Well, it seems as though my chauffeur has arrived, and I still have two planes to catch," he answered back sadly.

"Have a nice flight back East, Harry!" everyone yelled over to him as he turned and exited the ranch house.

"Come back and visit us again real soon, Harry, when this entire tragedy is all over . . . and bring Karen along next time! All of us would love to meet her!" Dr. Roberts shouted at him as Harry waved good-bye and closed the front door firmly behind him.

His flight back to Boston left Phoenix at 2:15 PM. It was a long flight, and so he decided to take the opportunity to carefully read over one of the deciphered copies of Dr. Mathews's journals. Most of the material that he read about was well out of his range of cognitive understanding, but he endeavored to absorb as much of it as he could. After glancing through most of the journal's pages, he began to get a real understanding of what Dr. Mathews was trying to discover with her research.

When he flipped through some of the pages of her second journal, he kept seeing small notations referencing some footnotes that he couldn't find. He was a little curious as to what they all meant, but he soon shrugged them all off as being nothing important. When his flight finally touched down in Boston, he made a quick phone call to Paul's cell phone and reached him driving in his vehicle.

"Paul, I've just landed in Boston. Can you pick me up in a short while at the United Airlines baggage claim area? We have a lot of things to talk about tonight!"

"No problem. I've just wrapped up my last appointment for the day and . . . I can be there in about thirty minutes. At dinner, you can bring me up to date on everything that you learned out West."

"That sounds great! I'll see you in a short while."

Paul caught sight of Harry standing next to one of the security guards in the baggage claim area of the terminal. Paul hurriedly approached him because he had parked his vehicle in a restricted zone in front of the terminal. To most visitors to New England, Logan International Airport had earned an unsavory reputation for its often harsh and indiscriminate ticketing and towing policies employed around its terminals. When Harry caught sight of Paul rushing toward him, he picked up his suitcases and started walking toward him.

"Where did you park?" Harry asked him.

"Right in front of the terminal . . . in one of those restricted parking zones. So we'd better hurry or else we may both be looking for a ride away from this place!" Paul teasingly added.

A short while later, the two friends could be seen sitting across from each other in a quiet out-of-the-way restaurant just west of Boston.

"Well, Harry, did you enjoy your vacation out there in Arizona and Mexico?" Paul smiled back at him.

"Yeah, some vacation! The next time you send me someplace, make sure that there's some water in the area to swim in. But to be really honest with you, Paul, I had a pretty good time out there after all. Dr. Stevens and his associates were really a great bunch of people to be around. Their research facility is more like a plush resort hotel built out in the middle of a secluded oasis. It's a fantastic ranch, not like some dusty old dude ranch out in the desert. It was really quite relaxing staying out there."

"From what you've been telling me about the place, it certainly seems to lend credence to the idea that a number of different groups must've spent a hell of a lot of money trying to prove Dr. Mathews's research theories. After all, someone had to provide a lot of money to build that place out there in the middle of nowhere!"

"A couple of days ago, Dr. Stevens informed me that for several years, Dr. Mathews had been secretly skimming off thousands of dollars from some of the government's special research grants that were being given to her. He told me that she used some of those proceeds to help purchase that huge parcel of undeveloped ranch land out in the middle of New Mexico. She then enlisted the added financial support of our Mr. Michael and his partners at Brickman and Price. Together they managed to build the present-day state-of-the-art research facility in the middle of nowhere," Harry explained to him.

"Why would anyone want to loan her so much money?" Paul asked him.

"Well, first you have to look at the enormous economic potential for profits that could be realized if any of her research ideas ever panned out. Combining that fact with the fact that Dr. Mathews gave them the exclusive first rights to market all of their research discoveries, they couldn't begin to help her enough. So far, I have been told they've made out quite well financially on some of the lab's earlier discoveries. I got the distinct feeling from talking to Mr. Michael that everyone was eagerly waiting for some new breakthrough that she had been working on!"

"So what exactly did your new friends in New Mexico learn from deciphering some of Dr. Mathews's journals?" Paul asked him.

"Well, as I told you the other day, I was quite surprised to learn that Dr. Stevens was already quite familiar with Dr. Mathews's secret encryption codes. It took him no time at all to re-familiarize himself with them again. When he was ready, he deciphered most of her research notes rather quickly. With Dr. Stevens's help, I tried to briefly summarize her journals in this three-page report that I prepared for you to read. I've added footnotes and specific journal page numbers in the report for easy referencing to the transcribed text. I think you'll find my notes quite illuminating to say the least!" he announced with some degree of satisfaction to Paul.

With a keen eye for details, Paul began to carefully read through Harry's report. It was something that he had been eagerly waiting to do for several days.

"From what I've just read in this report, you believe that the real motive behind Dr. Mathews's murder had to have been her research. You've speculated in here that you think that someone wanted to either steal or exploit her new discoveries economically for themselves or else they desperately wanted to prevent them from ever going public. Now in regards to your second hypothesis, we both know that our government has never been in the market of disseminating new sources of technology to anyone. It's also quite possible that some people in our military might've seen this new source of technology as a possible threat to our national security!"

"In what way do you see it as a possible security threat to the country?" Harry asked him curiously.

"Well, let's imagine for a moment that you're a spy and that you've just stolen or looked at some top-secret documents. You are now able to scan these documents into a receiver buried inside your head, or more simply, you've imprinted them onto the memory cells of your brain. If you were then mentally able to turn these neurons or memory cells off in order to keep these files intact, then you have, in effect, become the perfect spy. When he eventually escapes, he later downloads them from the device or directly from his memory. Even if he is killed during the mission, the files are still stored in his brain to be later removed when his body is claimed."

"That's kind of stretching her research quite a bit, Paul, don't you think?"

"Maybe, but remember . . . the technology is relatively quite new right now! Who knows where it will eventually go in the long run!" Paul explained to him.

"So where do we go from here? When are we supposed to go back before our judge again?" Harry asked him.

"The case is still scheduled to be heard again before Judge Zimmer on Monday. I still have a lot of motions and supporting paperwork to get ready for this hearing. I don't think I can convince the judge from declaring it a mistrial. Our only hope is to try to convince him to keep the case open unofficially a little longer."

"Dr. Stevens and his team are still trying to decipher Dr. Mathews's last CD for us. So far, they've been unsuccessful in cracking her new security lockouts. I know they won't give up. Phil said that he'd contact me as soon as they make any sort of a breakthrough!"

The two friends settled down to enjoy their late-night dinners, which the waitress had just brought over to their table. While they ate, Harry kept thinking about the deciphered journals and the numerous notes that Dr. Mathews had scribbled on the sides of some of the journal pages. His mind kept on seeing these undeciphered notes or references as though they held the key to everything that they were seeking.

* * * * *

On the following day, Harry drove over to Karen's office to see her again. When she caught sight of him, she boldly ushered him into her office and closed the door behind them. She passionately began to kiss him and to tell him how much she had missed him. The feel of her body pressed tightly up against him and the taste of her sweet lips against his own began to excite his passions for her again. Every day that he had spent away from her out in New Mexico had felt like an eternity to him. After a few minutes of unbridled kissing and exploration, the two of them managed to regain some control over their passions again.

"Well, I guess we both missed each other these last few days!" Harry happily admitted.

"There hasn't been a moment since you left that I haven't been thinking about you!" she confessed to him seductively.

"I wish you had been out there with me also. The ranch that I stayed at was like an intimate resort hotel built in the middle of a beautiful oasis. It was almost perfect except for the fact that I missed you terribly," he conceded to her also.

"Then I'm glad. It made your true feelings finally break through. We'll have to get together at my place tonight to explore them more fully!" she smiled back at him teasingly. "So what else did you learn about our mysterious Dr. Mathews while you were out there?"

"Well, it looks as though the key to her murder is tied in directly with her research. We believe that whatever she was working on was so important to someone, that they killed her to either steal her new technology or to prevent it from ever becoming known. Now if our first theory or motive is correct, then they failed completely because we found her briefcase at the original crime scene. It was filled with all of her journals, CDs, and research papers. I believe, however, that our second motive is the real one. From what we have learned about her research so far, she may've been about to announce a major breakthrough in her neural research. Her successful research could've advanced the field of medical neurology years ahead of where we are currently at."

"How did you find out so much information about her research in such a short time?"

"Do you remember a man by the name of Phillip Stevens? You told me about him when you checked out some of the university's records for me. He worked with Dr. Mathews in Dr. Tinkoi's laboratory back then. For personal health reasons, a ruptured appendicitis, he was forced to take a leave of absence from his doctoral studies at MIT. He returned to MIT about a year later and completed his doctoral work. He then just mysteriously dropped out of sight completely. Well, I found him out West, and he was able to help us to decipher Dr. Mathews's journals," he explained to her.

Harry's ringing cell phone suddenly interrupted their conversation. He answered it and listened intently to someone on the other end of the call. Karen watched in curiosity as his facial expressions changed from one of concern to one of total elation.

"That's fantastic, Phil! I'll let Paul know right away! When should we expect to see you? In one or two days? Okay, I'll pick you up at the airport when your flight arrives. Give me a call back when you find out which flight you'll be coming in on. I'll make all the necessary arrangements for your stay in the city. I'll see you soon!" he answered as he snapped his cell phone closed.

"Well, I'll be damned!" he whispered to himself quietly.

"Damn it, Harry! Who was that?" she asked excitedly.

"That, my love, was Dr. Philip Stevens formally of MIT. They just succeeded in breaking Dr. Mathews's final security codes that were preventing them from reading her last CD. He said that he wants us to exhume Dr. Mathews's body. He said that there's something in it that the ME must've missed during his autopsy. Now if he's right about that, then this whole matter has to be handled very discreetly. We don't want to alert her murderers that we might be on to them. I'm sorry, Karen, but I have to go!" he said as he kissed her quickly on the lips.

"I understand, but be careful. Whoever is behind this conspiracy could have eyes and ears everywhere. Don't trust anyone, and especially the telephones," she worriedly warned him.

"I will!"

Once inside his car, he wanted to call Paul and tell him the good news, but he remembered Karen's warning about the phone lines and how someone could be listening in on them. He decided to meet with him in person rather than risk telling him over the telephone. He called Paul's secretary and learned that Paul was over at the courthouse meeting with one of the assistant DAs regarding another case. He turned his car around and headed downtown.

The young receptionist outside the DA's office asked him who he was looking for. He explained to her that he had some very urgent business with his boss who was meeting with one of the DAs. She picked up the telephone and called around until she eventually reached the correct office.

Harry hurried down the hall to room number 413. The secretary sitting outside the office asked him if she could be of any assistance. He explained to her that he had some urgent business with his boss, Atty. Paul Tucker. She nodded her head in understanding and knocked on the outer door of the DA's office.

"I'm sorry to disturb you, Mr. Flarrerty, but there's a Mr. Parks out here who says that it's very important that he speak to Mr. Tucker right away. What shall I tell him?" she asked.

"Tell him that we will be through in here in a couple of minutes."

"Please have a seat, Mr. Parks. They're almost finished with their meeting. It'll be just a few minutes."

"Thank you."

The door to the DA's office opened a few minutes later, and Paul exited the office with a curious expression showing on his face.

"Now what's so important, Harry, that it couldn't wait until we got back to the office?" he asked him.

"I'm sorry to bother you again, Miss, but is there an empty office around here that we can use for a few minutes to talk privately in?" Harry asked her.

"Yes, there's a conference room down the hall on the left that's not being used right now. Please follow me."

They followed her down the hall to the small conference room. Once inside the room, she closed the door quietly behind them and then returned to her desk.

"Well, Harry, what's so important?"

"I just received a telephone call from Dr. Stevens. He said that they just succeeded in cracking Dr. Mathews's security code lockouts on her last CD! He also said that we have to exhume Dr. Mathews's body right away. He believes that the ME may've missed something that might've been surgically implanted inside her body. He said that the device may hold the key to identifying her assailants!" he excitedly announced to him.

"You've got to be kidding. He told you all of this just a short while ago?"

"Yes, and he emphasized to me that time may be very critical in preventing any further degradation of the information that may be stored in the device."

"If that's true, then we have to go over and see the DA right away. I can promise you one thing, and that is that he won't be too receptive to your idea about exhuming Dr. Mathews's body. He's already quite disappointed with the fact that his entire case may have to be legally thrown out by the judge. On the other hand, this news may be the one thing that might help us both bring this case to some sort of a satisfactory closure. Let's go over to Mr. Parker's office right now. He might still be around. And if he goes along with us on this idea, we can try to meet with Judge Zimmer later on today to request an order for the exhumation of Dr. Mathews's body. Did Dr. Stevens say anything else to you?"

"Yes, he did. He told me that he's planning on flying into Boston on either Friday or Saturday. He's bringing along with him some very specialized pieces of equipment as well as Dr. Mathew's two data CDs to help him interpret the data."

"Excellent! That, in itself, may be the one thing that might convince the DA and the judge that we are really convinced about what we've just discovered."

They found the DA still in his office, and from what they heard him discussing with one of his subordinates, he wasn't in the best of moods that morning.

"Well, if it isn't our famous defense attorney Mr. Paul Tucker and his loyal private investigator, Mr. Harold Parks. And what may I ask brings you two gentlemen by my humble little office this fine morning, as if I didn't already know?" He politely gestured them over to some chairs in front of his cluttered desk.

"It's about the Helen Mathews case, Tom," Paul smilingly volunteered.

"I'd never have guessed that!" he teasingly shot back at them.

"We know that this case has become a real pain in the ass to you. You were really hoping to get a conviction in this one until my client got severely injured in the recent gas explosion. Now both of us know that the judge is probably going to declare it a mistrial on Monday morning for that reason."

"Most likely!" he answered back with disgust.

"Well, Harry and I may have found a way out of this entire mess for all of us. We have always maintained that our client is innocent and that he was framed for Dr. Mathews's murder. What would you say if we can show you a way to get your hands on some solid new evidence that will both help you to identify and convict the real murderers in this case and also prove that our client is innocent? Do you want to hear more?" Paul asked him.

"Go on, I'm still listening!"

Harry explained to the DA what they had already learned from reading Dr. Mathews's files and what Dr. Stevens had been able to decipher from her computer disks. When he explained that the proof was buried inside Dr. Mathews's body, the DA threw his hands up in the air in disgust.

"I knew that there had to be a catch to this! You mean that all that I have to do is go along with you in asking Judge Zimmer for an order to get her body exhumed? You've got to be kidding, Paul! It's bad enough that this case has already cost the taxpayers of Massachusetts tens of thousands of dollars and all for nothing in the end!"

"I know that what I've just told you may seem quite tenuous at best for you to go along with, but it may hand you a conviction of a much bigger fish in the long run. We now believe that someone in our own government is behind this whole murder conspiracy. Just think about what a conviction like this could do for your career, Tom!"

The very idea of getting a conviction of someone much more important than Mr. Haggerty seemed to convince him that their proposal had some strong merits to it. After all, he thought to himself, he was already facing a hearing in a few days with nothing left to argue before the judge.

"All right, I'll go along with you on this, but it had better pan out. This entire thing could make me look like a complete fool in the eyes of the media. You're going to owe me big-time on this one if it ends up making me look real bad!" the DA threw back at him.

"I promise you, Tom, that what Harry and I have learned about Dr. Mathews's research will most likely bring this whole case to a favorable conclusion for everyone involved . . . and at the same time put another big feather in your political cap!"

"It had better, or else come next election time, I'll be out looking for another job."

Later that afternoon, their meeting in Judge Zimmer's chambers went smoothly enough. The judge did not like the idea of declaring the trial a mistrial in a few days, but he was going to have to do it. The idea of ordering Dr. Mathew's body exhumed for a second autopsy also did not sit too well with him either. However, the DA's insistence that justice demanded that the truth be uncovered seemed to convince him to go along. He issued an immediate order for the exhumation of Dr. Mathews's body by the ME's office.

On his way back to his office, Paul decided to make an unscheduled stop at the hospital to check on John's medical condition. The nurse taking care of him said that he appeared to be holding his own with some minimal signs of improvement. She told him that John was also showing some faint signs that he was slowly trying to awaken from his coma. His doctors, however, were still not too optimistic, and so they continued to list his condition as very critical. Paul put on a surgical mask and robe and followed the nurse into John's room. Paul whispered quietly into John's ear that he may've found out a way to learn who was really responsible for murdering Helen. He told him to stay strong and to fight to get well. He promised to return in a day or two with more news about what they had learned so far.

As Paul left John's bedside, he had no idea as to whether his words had been heard by John. In his heart, he truly hoped that John had heard him and that his words would encourage him to get better.

Over the next four hours, special arrangements had been made by the coroner's office for the exhumation of Dr. Mathews's body. The dirt-covered mahogany casket was carefully lifted from her grave and transported back to the morgue for another reexamination by the medical examiner. The telephone on Paul's desk rang a short while later. It was a call from one of the morgue's security guards informing him that Dr. Mathews's body had been safely delivered to the morgue a half hour earlier. He informed Paul that the ME had scheduled the second autopsy for nine o'clock the next morning. Paul thanked him for the information and left his office for the night.

Without his knowledge, the entire phone conversation had been secretly overheard and transmitted by Sam's eavesdropping equipment back to his motel room. The voice activated recorder in his room switched on automatically and recorded their conversation. Later that evening, around nine o'clock, Sam returned to his room to listen to the recordings that his equipment had recorded earlier in the day when he was out. As he listened to the recordings, a cold sweat seemed to form over all of his body. It was a feeling that he had experienced only a few times before, when things had suddenly gone wrong on a covert operation. He listened to the recording a second time to be sure of what he had just heard. He then made an urgent phone call to his boss in Washington DC for instructions about what to do next.

Thirty minutes later, Sam received a call back from his boss, telling him to expect some help from two additional agents that were already en route to his location. He was told that it was imperative for them to intercept anything that the ME might discover in or on Dr. Mathews's body. He was told that the ME was to be eliminated at all cost and that his report was to be destroyed. He was to expect agents Ned and Frank to be arriving around twelve thirty that morning. When their assignment was completed, everyone was to leave the area immediately.

It was an order that Sam had been eagerly waiting to hear for quite some time. He had grown tired of his long stay in Boston. He missed the familiar sights and sounds of the nation's capital. Sam had never met special agent Ned before, but he had met Frank once before on another mission in Europe. He was a cold-blooded killer. He enjoyed the act of killing more than anyone else that he had ever known. When their mission was over, he wanted nothing else to do with the man. He didn't trust him. It made no difference to Frank whether their target was a man, a woman, or even a child. He just enjoyed the act of killing too much.

* * * * *

The ME arrived at his office the next morning forty minutes earlier than usual in order to catch up on some of his unfinished paperwork. At approximately 9:00 AM, his assistant arrived to help him remove the cold stiff body of Dr. Mathews from one of the morgue's many coolers. They carefully transferred it onto one of the examination tables and prepared to begin their second autopsy of the body. His assistant placed a labeled cassette into the recording machine so that Dr. Witherspoon could begin the second autopsy.

"This Dr. James Witherspoon, I am the chief medical examiner for the coroner's office in and around the city of Boston. The following is the official audio record of this the second autopsy being performed by me on the body of Dr. Helen Mathews. The body before me is that of a young woman, aged approximately in her midthirties. The body is currently showing some general signs of decomposition from its five-week internment in the ground. It appears to have been put through the standard embalming procedures before it was placed in a casket for burial. From a gross examination of the body, I can clearly see two areas of severe trauma. The most prominent area of trauma encompasses both the neck and the lower right jaw. It appears to have been inflicted by a large caliber handgun. There appears to be a lot of powder burns both in and around the wound itself. This suggests that the weapon responsible for this damage was fired from extremely close range. The massive loss of blood, bone, and soft tissue in these areas was caused primarily by the weapon's large caliber bullet and the close proximity of the weapon's discharge to the body.

"A second area of noticeable trauma on the body can be seen clearly on the victims left leg. It too appears to have been caused by a single gunshot. From my examination of the wound, it suggests that the bullet was more powerful and that the bullet blew through the leg's soft tissue and then partially shattered and lodged itself in the underlying bone matter. I would guess that the weapon used on the leg area was a high-powered rifle as confirmed in the ballistic report done on the recovered slug. After carefully reviewing all of my field notes and those of the investigating detectives present at the initial crime scene, the crime scene pictures, and my notes and pictures taken at the first autopsy, I again conclude that the victim had been bleeding profusely for some time prior to be shot in the neck area of her body. The victim has . . ."

The medical examiner went on further to record his observations about the pressure lines that were now clearly visible on her body's upper left leg just above the wound. He concluded that it had been caused by a quickly applied tourniquet to the area. When he had finished addressing the exterior conditions of Dr. Mathews's body, he prepared to turn his attention to the interior examination of her body.

"It has been suggested by the state that there may be some foreign bodies implanted somewhere inside our victim's body. To determine whether this is indeed a possibility, we shall take a full series of X-rays of our victim's entire body. In the event that the films do confirm the presence of such a foreign object or objects inside of her, I shall then be able to better locate and extract them more carefully from the underlying soft tissues for further study."

The ME and his assistant completed the last of the X-rays of Dr. Mathews' body and then waited patiently for their films to develop. When they were ready, the two men placed each of the films up on the illuminated viewers for a closer examination.

"Well, I'll be damned! Look at this, Bruce. It looks like some sort of a metallic cylinder has been implanted inside her head. It appears to also have a few leads leading outward away from it. I wonder what it is. Do you see any other similar objects in the other films that we just took of her body?" he asked his assistant.

Bruce snapped the other X-rays films up on the viewers one by one to see if there were any other similar foreign bodies visible in any other areas of her body.

"No, all of the other films are clear. Only the X-ray taken of her head shows this unknown foreign body inside her head. I wonder what it is."

"I don't know, but we'll soon find out," Dr. Witherspoon declared as he continued with the autopsy.

"In examining our victim's head for visible scarring, I have discovered the presence of an old scar line hidden just under our victim's hairline. It appears to have been made from a surgical operation that was performed on her years earlier. I am able to conclude this because of the color and texture of the old scar tissue. In addition to these clues, there is also our victim's hair growth in and around the vicinity of the old incision. I will now cut back the scalp and remove some of the cranial bone in order to expose the brain below. This will also allow us a better opportunity in which to locate, observe, and remove the foreign body implanted inside her skull . . ."

The MEs completed their autopsy of Dr. Mathews's body around eleven forty that morning. Dr. Witherspoon washed up and sat down in front of his computer to type up a detailed autopsy report on what they had just discovered. When it was almost completed, he made a quick telephone call over to the DA's office where Mr. Parker was impatiently waiting.

"I don't know how you guys knew that there was something inside of her, but I think we found what you are looking for. We found it implanted inside her head, a strange-looking cylindrically shaped capsule. It has a couple of shielded leads attached to it. One of the leads terminated up against the optic nerve and the other one terminated in the vicinity of the cochlear nerve. I have absolutely no idea what this strange-looking capsule with its two leads was doing inside her skull. I've never seen anything like this before in my entire life. I can say one thing, though. Whoever put this thing inside there was one hell of a skilled surgeon! The capsule or device had to have been placed precisely where we found it for some specific purpose. Tom, I would really like to know what this capsule is and what it's supposed to do! My official report should be completed within a half hour."

"Thanks, Doc, I really owe you one. I'll send someone over there right away to pick up the capsule and your report. In the meantime, don't tell anyone else about what you found . . . and for God's sake, don't let anyone near it until we get there! We strongly suspect that Dr. Mathews was murdered to prevent the knowledge of this device from ever becoming known! Do you understand what I'm saying?" he explained to him in order to make him more aware that his discovery could also be putting his own life in real danger too.

"I understand, Tom! Just make sure that you get someone over here right away! I've never been too keen on being the target of a murderer," he worriedly confessed to him.

"We'll be there as soon as we can. Don't go anywhere until we get there."

"Don't worry, I won't!"

Tom placed a second phone call over to Paul Tucker's office to tell him about what the ME had found inside Dr. Mathews's head. It was the good news that Paul had been eagerly waiting to hear.

"Are you sending someone over to the ME's office right away to pick up the capsule?" Paul asked him a little apprehensively. "In this case, too many things have already mysteriously disappeared in the past, and we can't afford to let this critical piece of evidence get away from us now!"

"Believe me, it won't! I've already asked my secretary to put a call in to Detective Bates's office to have the capsule picked up along with the ME's autopsy report. I'll let you know as soon as we have them in our possession."

"Harry, did you hear that? They actually found something, some sort of a cylindrically shaped capsule implanted inside her brain. I can't believe it! I wonder what the hell it is or does."

"I don't know, Paul, but I don't like the idea of that device not being already under guard. I think I'll take a ride over to the morgue to make sure that nothing happens to it in the meantime."

"That might be a good idea, but be careful! Call me as soon as you get there."

"I will!" he shouted back as he rushed out of Paul's office.

When the three agents overheard the DA's telephone call to Paul's office, a wave of anxiety seemed to hit all of them at the same time. Sam tore his headphones off and threw them up against the wall of his motel room. It was the worst possible news that they could've heard. The cheap plastic headphones shattered against the wall and fell to the floor in a tangled mess. All of the agents seemed to spring into motion toward the outer door at the same time. The rest of the DA's phone call didn't matter to any of them as they slammed the door tightly closed behind them. The recovery of the capsule, along with the elimination of the ME and his report, were all vitally critical to the success of their mission.

Dr. Witherspoon placed the strange-looking capsule in a small glass test tube and packed tissue paper all around it for protection. He then placed it inside his inner shirt pocket for safekeeping. He then thought about what Tom had said to him about the importance of the device. He reached into his desk and pulled out a small box that contained some loose parts from his shattered old pocket watch. He pulled out a solid brass dowel that looked like a cylindrically shaped capsule and placed it inside another test tube. He sealed it with some tape and then carefully placed it on the upper shelf above his desk.

He then exhaustedly settled down in front of his computer to type up the final draft of Dr. Mathews's second autopsy report. He knew that it would be one of the strangest reports that he had ever written. When he had finished typing up his report, he instructed his computer to print out three copies of the report: one for himself, one for the DA's office, and one for the police. For some strange reason, the printer connected online to his computer wouldn't print the final draft of his autopsy report. He carefully checked out all of the computer's cable connections and tapped on the printer's sides. It still wouldn't accept his print commands. In disgust, he made a hard copy of the report and file on a CD and walked upstairs with it in hand to one of the other department offices to print out three copies of the report.

Since it was Saturday, most of the municipal building's outer doors were locked except for its two front doors. The three undercover agents quietly entered the building and made their way down the hallway toward the morgue that was located in the basement. The lower level of the building contained only the MEs' offices, the morgue, and some storage rooms. The men had no trouble finding their way downstairs to the morgue. Sam peered in through one of the opaque glass windows and saw a lone man dressed in a white lab coat and apron leaning over the body of a woman. Sam immediately recognized the partially dissected body to be that of Dr. Helen Mathews. The man had his back to the door, and so the two agents quietly slipped into the room and looked around to make sure they were alone. Seeing no one else in the lab, Frank quietly sneaked up behind Dr. Witherspoon's assistant and took aim at the ME's back and shot him two times. He fell to the floor like a rock. He then leaned over his motionless body and added a third bullet to the back of his head to make sure that he was really dead. A pool of dark red blood began to form around his head on the floor.

"Is he dead?" Sam asked him.

"Oh yeah! This man will never rise again," he joked back at them coldly.

"Ned, look around the office for the medical examiner's autopsy report while I keep my eyes on the hallway!" Sam motioned him over toward the desk area of the ME's office.

"He hasn't printed it out yet! It's still showing on the monitor's screen. It looks as though he was just about to print it when we surprised him."

"Even better! Erase the file completely from the computer's hard drive and then shut it down. Make sure that there are no similarly referenced files attached to it. If you see any, erase them also."

"Frank, look around the lab for the audio tapes of the autopsy. They always make them for their records."

"Finished!" Ned announced proudly a few minutes later as he fired several rounds from his weapon into the hard drive of the computer. "Should I help Frank look for the capsule?"

"Yes, but be quick about it! The police could be here any minute!"

The two men searched through all of the draws of the old desk and found nothing. They then turned their attention toward the office's many filing cabinets. Once again, their efforts turned up nothing. Nowhere did they see anything that even faintly resembled the small capsule-shaped device that they had heard described over the telephone. Time was rapidly running out for the three agents, and they knew that they would be discovered by the police unless they got out of there right away.

"We found the audio tape of the autopsy, but we can't seem to find that damn metallic capsule anywhere, Sam!" Frank shouted over to him.

"Check his pockets! He may've put it inside one of them."

"Nothing! What are we going to do? We have to find that capsule. Everything depends on it!" Frank again shouted over to him from across the room.

Sam walked over to the ME's desk and looked around. His eyes came to rest upon a plastic container sitting conspicuously on the top shelf above the ME's desk. "What's up there in that container?" he asked them pointing at the bookcase.

Frank reached up and carefully pulled the container down from the shelf. He reached into the box and pulled out a sealed test tube that contained a brass metallic-looking capsule. He held it up for Sam to see.

"This has to be what they found implanted inside her head! Now let's get the hell out of here before the police arrive!" Frank shouted back to his two partners.

With Sam at the point, the three agents retraced their steps down the hallway and up the back stairs toward the rear exit of the building. As they were making their way up these stairs, Dr. Witherspoon, accompanied by Detectives Bates and Bolten, were making their way down the other hallway toward the front stairs and the morgue in the basement. As they walked into the autopsy area of the morgue, they discovered the dead body of the assistant medical examiner lying in an expanding pool of dark red blood next to the autopsy table.

"Damn it, he's dead! This must've just happened! Come on, they might still be in the area!" Carol shouted over to her partner. She drew her handgun and ran down the hallway toward the rear exit of the building. The two detectives raced side by side up the stairway and burst through the rear exit and out into the parking lot area behind the building. They caught sight of the three men in a dark-colored sedan slowly starting to drive out of the parking lot. While flashing their badges at them and shouting at them to stop, they ran toward their suspect's vehicle. Sam caught sight of the approaching detectives and quickly accelerated their vehicle out of the parking lot.

"Now that we've been seen, we have to ditch this car and the capsule right away!" Sam yelled to his associates.

His words had hardly cleared his throat when he caught sight of the unmarked police cruiser rapidly closing in on them. He took a sharp left turn onto a side street and pushed the accelerator to the floor as hard as he could. The new sedan took up the challenge and rapidly began to pick up speed. When he had accelerated just a few blocks, he once again took another sharp turn. This time, he swung the car's steering wheel to the right at full speed. The wheels of the sedan broke loose from the rough pavement and skidded violently through the sharp turn. Sam held on to the steering wheel and expertly maneuvered his car through the high-speed turn. As he looked back through his rearview mirror, he could see that he had gained some distance on the pursuing cruiser.

"We have to get rid of that capsule right away! When I take a turn onto Atlantic Avenue ahead, I want you to throw it out the window and into the ocean. Wipe down the gun that you used to shoot the ME and throw it into the ocean also. Keep your registered handguns on you!" Sam shouted back to Frank, who was sitting in the rear seat of the car.

As they sped down Atlantic Avenue toward the bridge, Sam could see the flashing blue lights of the cruiser closing in on them. As they made their way up onto the new bridge, Frank tossed the capsule out the rear window and watched it disappear into the ocean below. Detective Bates smashed her vehicle into the rear bumper of Sam's car just as Frank was about to toss his unregistered handgun into the ocean also. The weapon fell onto the roadway and skidded to a stop up against the curb.

"Shit!" Frank shouted out in anger as he watched his gun skid to a stop against the curb. "My gun never made it to the water, Sam. It's still on the road!"

"Then we have a real problem. We have to get rid of these two guys now and ditch this car fast!"

When Detectives Bates and Bolten had first begun their hot pursuit of their suspects, they had radioed their dispatcher for additional police units as backup. Jim had radioed in a general description of their suspect's car and a general description of its three male occupants. As their high-speed pursuit continued through the narrow streets of the waterfront area, Detective Bolten kept their dispatcher apprised of their location at all times. A police helicopter was ordered into the air by their captain to aid in the apprehension of their fleeing suspects. The dispatcher was informed that the three male suspects were armed and should be considered extremely dangerous. She was told that the three men were the primary suspects in the brutal murder of Dr. Bruce Baxter of the coroner's office. The dispatcher was also informed to send a unit out to the Atlantic Avenue Bridge to retrieve a discarded handgun that had been thrown out of their suspects' vehicle. Carol told her to make sure that whoever retrieved the weapon took precautions in handling it for possible fingerprints.

"Where the hell is our backup?" Carol yelled over to Jim.

"Don't worry. I think I see them coming right now!" he shouted back as their vehicle became airborne a few feet as it shot up over a sharp rise in the road. "Now that's a first for me!" He smiled back at her while still pressing his open hands against the roof of their car.

A second and third police car took up positions behind them in the high-speed chase. The cars were now reaching speeds in excess of over seventy miles an hour whenever the roadway straightened out. Their three suspects tried in vain to lose their pursuers by bouncing off other vehicles, but Carol was not about to let them get away that easily.

"They're trying to lose us in the congestion of the Big Dig!" Carol shouted over to Jim.

"A large pay loader carrying huge concrete drainage pipes was moving slowly across the intersection in front of them. Sam steered his car recklessly around the huge piece of construction equipment. The heavy equipment operator hit his breaks in panic to keep from hitting him. Detective Bates did not break off her pursuit and stayed on Sam's speeding bumper. The sudden stopping of the huge pay loader caused the three huge concrete pipes in its bucket to slide forward up against the heavy steel links in the safety chains that secured them. The inertial forces were so great that they easily snapped the thick chains. The huge concrete pipes came crashing down out of the bucket and fell onto the roadway. They partially shattered directly in front of the other two pursuing police cruisers. The drivers of these cars spun their steering wheels sharply to the right to avoid crashing into the heavy equipment or its smashed cargo of concrete pipes.

"Push that crap out of our way so that we can get by!" the driver of the first cruiser screamed up at the operator of the big rig.

The operator shifted his machine into reverse and dropped his bucket down onto the asphalt roadway so that he could push the pile of broken concrete pipes out of their way. As soon as they saw a clear opening, they accelerated around his rig. They sped down the now-empty streets toward South Boston.

Detective Bolten got on the radio to inform their dispatcher that they had lost their backup. They gave their present location to their dispatcher and waited for her response.

"Understood, 86, two additional units are converging on your location from two directions. You should be seeing them any second now," the dispatcher answered back.

"We can see them!" Jim shouted back to her.

Sam caught sight of the approaching police cruiser coming directly toward them. He made a sudden left-hand turn directly in front of an oncoming vehicle and headed back down toward the waterfront area once again. His sudden move caused the driver to slam his breaks on hard and to skid sideways into the intersection, thus blocking the side road. Detective Bates was forced to jam her brakes on also in order to avoid crashing into the side of his car. The shaken driver of the car slowly moved his vehicle out of her way. She slowly swung her vehicle around him and down the side road after their suspects.

"We're running out of options, guys! I think we're going to have to take our chances back in the city."

Sam accelerated his car recklessly down a narrow side street toward the Southeast Expressway. As he worked his car in and out of the traffic, he kept a watchful eye on Detective Bates's car that was still pursuing them. As he steered his car up the new on-ramp of the expressway, his progress was impeded by two slower-moving vehicles that were making their way up onto the highway also. He nudged the nose of his vehicle up against the rear bumper of the car in the right lane. The driver instinctively pulled his car further to the right side of his lane in order to avoid further contact with Sam's car. It was the opportunity that Sam had anticipated. He quickly accelerated his car into the narrow space now created between the two vehicles. His vehicle scrapped its way between the two cars, forcing them into the two side barriers of the ramp. The drivers of the two heavily damaged vehicles slammed on their brakes as he slipped by. Detective Bates was forced to once again slam on her own brakes to avoid the stopping traffic. She watched in frustration as their suspects' car moved out into the northbound flow of traffic heading back into the city.

"I can't believe that this is happening! Move one of those cars so that we can get by!" she yelled at the two stopped drivers arguing on the ramp about their damaged vehicles.

"But what about our cars?" one of them shouted over to her.

"File a MV accident report at the Downtown Boston police station and contact your insurance companies. Now move those cars immediately!" she yelled back at them again angrily.

One of the cars moved quickly out of her way to allow her to get by. She could just barely see their suspect's sedan in front of them as it disappeared into the expressway tunnel under the city. She radioed in their suspects' last location. As her car entered the tunnel a few minutes later, the traffic in front of them suddenly came to a full stop. Jim looked up the expressway and caught sight of their suspects' abandoned vehicle left halfway up and across the exit ramp. He could just barely see their suspect's running up the ramp toward the South Station Terminal. He notified their dispatcher and jumped out of their car and began a footrace up the roadway. He worked his way through the tunnel and around its many stopped vehicles toward the blocked exit ramp.

When Jim ran past their suspects' abandoned vehicle, his eyes caught site of a set of keys lying on the ramp about a hundred feet in front of the abandoned car. He exhaustedly picked them up and looked back at the empty car. He guessed that the keys had to belong to their suspects' car blocking the main exit ramp. He ran back to the car with the keys and exhaustedly jumped into the driver's seat. He inserted the key into the ignition and tried to start it.

"Come on, baby, you can do it!"

The car's engine started. He shifted the transmission into drive and accelerated up the long ramp. As his vehicle exited the tunnel, he caught sight of their three suspects running into the South Station Terminal. He pulled his vehicle up against the sidewalk; its wheels bounced hard off the curb. He quickly jumped out of the car and raced into the terminal building in pursuit of their suspects. Detective Bates arrived at the terminal a few seconds later. She drew her handgun and raced into the terminal after her partner.

Sam and his associates raced down a set of stairs that would eventually lead them to the subway trains on the lower level. Looking back over his shoulder, Frank caught sight of Detective Bolten chasing after him with his gun drawn. Frank stopped and fired a single shot in his direction. The bullet bounced harmlessly off the tile-covered walls, just narrowly missing his head. The loud sound emitted by Frank's powerful handgun seemed to echo everywhere at once. The massive terminal building with its high ceilings and polished tiled walls and floors became a willing host to the reverberating sound wave. A sudden wave of panic seemed to take hold of the commuters walking in the subway areas. Some of the people fell to the floor in fear, trying to shield their heads from the sudden source of terror. The majority of commuters waiting in the subway area took a more active response; they panicked and ran. An ocean of bodies suddenly began to push its way back up the subway stairs to flee from the madman's weapon.

Jim was unable to return fire for fear of hitting some of the innocent people rushing past him. A couple of patrolmen walking inside the terminal heard the echo of the loud gunshot and ran toward the subway entrance, but they too were forced backward by the fleeing mob. In the melee, Detective Bates somehow managed to catch up to her partner, Jim, who had only managed to reach the first landing of the stairs. They informed the two patrolmen that they were pursuing three white males who were wanted as suspects in a recent murder at the coroner's office. Together, the four officers slowly inched their way down the stairway while trying to stay as close as possible to the far wall for protection.

"For God's sake! How many more people can there be downstairs on that subway platform?" Jim complained to the two patrolmen.

"Quite a lot more, I'm afraid, especially at this time of day," the older of the two officers responded back.

Terrified crowds of commuters continued to rush up the stairs past them in an attempt to escape the gunman on the train platform below. As the rushing wave of terrified commuters slowly began to thin out, Jim saw an opportunity for them to move further down the stairway.

At the same time, Sam and his two associates had managed to make their way three quarters of the way across the train platform through the many remaining and screaming commuters. Most of them were either pressed up tightly in fear against the concrete walls or crouched down almost flat against the concrete floor of the subway platform. Sam and his men had also shrewdly crouched down among the prostrate bodies of the people around them in order to shield themselves from their pursuers. Sam yelled out to the terrified commuters to remain where they were so that they wouldn't get hit by any flying bullets. His words only brought on a new chorus of moans and cries from the terrified people around them.

Sam and his men kept their guns aimed at the stairway at the far end of the platform while they waited for the next subway train to arrive. The air in the subway station smelled stale as it always did. It was a thick heavy mixture of odors. Sam was able to identify some of the smells as those coming from the numerous food shops that lined the system's many underground stations. The majority of the odors, however, came from the damp underground tunnels themselves. Today, however, the air seemed to carry the added smell of fear from its many terrified commuters. The system's many subway trains acted as a mixer in spreading the odors evenly back and forth throughout all of the underground stations.

The air in the station slowly began to move against Sam's face, a sign that a train was fast approaching them through the tunnels. Sam shouted out to all of the people lying on the ground to stand up before the train arrived. Slowly, the people around them began to stand up as he had ordered. He didn't want the chief engineer on the train to see the problems in the station and to pass it by without stopping.

"Now when the train gets in the station and stops, I don't want any of you moving until I give the word. Otherwise, my men and I will fire at those people who start to move. If you all do as I say, no one else will get hurt! When I shout that it's okay, you can all run out of the station as fast as you can!" Sam shouted to the people standing on the platform around them.

As the subway train moved into the station, Sam and his men prepared to jump into the nearest car for cover. The train stopped, and its outer doors opened, allowing its riders to exit the cars. Sam and his men waited a few seconds longer and then gave the word for the people on the platform to move.

"Run! Run as fast as you can!" Sam shouted at them as loud as he could while he and his men ran toward the first car. Frank fired a few rounds at the ceiling of the station in order to get them to move even faster. It was all the encouragement that any of them needed.

The terrified mob of commuters pushed their way up the wide stairway in an undisciplined frenzy. Detectives Bates and Bolten had guessed what their suspects might be planning and so all of the officers had quietly inched their way almost all the way down to the bottom of the stairwell before the train had even opened its doors fully. They had just managed to get themselves off to the right side of the exit stairway when the sounds of gunfire sent the entire crowd running toward them in a panic. The four police officers carefully inched their way along the side of the now-opened doors of the subway train's cars in an attempt to get even closer to their suspects.

When they had reached the fifth car, one of their suspects stuck his head out of the first car's open door and caught sight of the detectives quietly sneaking up on them.

"We've got company, guys!" he shouted over his shoulder to his comrades. "Get this train moving while I slow these guys down!"

Sam and Frank walked up to the engineer sitting in his locked command compartment. They pointed their guns at him through the safety glass that enclosed his compartment. He looked at the large nozzles of their guns and swallowed hard. In his training, he had been told that the safety glass around him was bulletproof, but he didn't want them to prove that it wasn't.

"What do you want?" he timidly asked them.

"Close the doors and get this train moving!" Frank shouted at him with his raspy-sounding voice while tapping firmly on the glass with his gun.

"Okay! Okay! Just as you say! I have to first reengage the master door override control to lock out the other engineers," he told them as he nervously inserted his key into the master control panel.

Ned caught sight again of the four officers still sneaking up on their location. He reached out of the open door and fired a hail of bullets in their direction. Just as he did, a group of passengers ran out of the third car directly in front of the officers. The bullets from his gun slammed into the sides and legs of a number of them, sending them crashing forward in a twisted pile against the hard concrete platform. A terrifying chorus of screams and moans of pain filled the air.

Ned once again leaned out through the train's open door to fire off another volley of bullets at the approaching officers. As he did, Detective Bolten took aim and carefully fired two shots from his weapon at his head. The first bullet struck Ned against the side of his head, cutting a clear path across his scalp. The second bullet penetrated his neck and tore deeply into his arteries and throat. His weapon wildly discharged several more rounds down the platform toward some of the prostrated bodies of the commuters before he fell backward into the car, grasping tightly at his neck. For a few long seconds, his body began to convulse violently before his eyes slowly closed and his labored breathing stopped.

The muffled quiet of the subway train's interior was suddenly interrupted by the loud sound of chimes signaling a warning that the doors of the subway cars were about to close. Detective Bates and her partner leaped in through the open doorway next to them just before the train's doors closed. The two officers crouching behind them were not as fortunate because they were not next to one of the car's open doors. The train began to slowly accelerate out of the station, leaving the two patrolmen on the platform facing a scene of carnage and cries for help.

The two officers began to immediately offer assistance to some of the more seriously injured people lying on the subway platform. Some of the shooting victims had already died from their wounds, while others were beginning to slowly slip into shock from their loss of blood. One of the patrolmen got on his radio to contact his dispatcher for ambulances and EMTs to be rushed out to their location. A number of shooting victims were moaning in agony on the platform as volunteers attempted to stop the bleeding from their wounds. The officer also let his dispatcher know that Detective Bates and her partner had managed to board the subway train just before it pulled out of the station. He informed his supervisor that the detectives were in the fourth car and that one of the suspects may've been shot by one of the detectives when he returned fire.

Sam and Frank looked down at Ned as he fell backward into the car while grabbing frantically at his neck in panic. Massive amounts of red blood shot out through the fingers of his hands as he clenched them tightly around his neck. The bullet had torn through some of the major blood vessels in his neck. They both knew that it would be only a matter of seconds before he would be dead. Soon, the violent shaking of his body slowed down and his tightly clenched fingers and hands slowly fell away from his neck. Blood continued to flow from his neck wound until his heart eventually stopped beating. The pool of blood on the floor of the train moved down his body to the rear of the moving subway train.

"Now you know what will happen to us if we are caught! So do whatever you have to do to escape. And remember, never admit to knowing me or anyone else in the agency!" Sam warned him.

"I know the drill! I don't plan on being taken alive if it comes down to that! So just take care of yourself, Sam."

Sam looked up the tracks and saw the lights from the next station beginning to illuminate the tunnel ahead of them.

"Don't slow down! Keep this train going until it gets to Central Square. Do you understand? If you don't do anything stupid, all of this will just be a bad memory that you lived through!" Sam proclaimed to him loudly through the glass.

The empty train sped through the underground station without slowing down. Sam caught sight of a number of police officers running down the platform toward the train as it sped past them.

"I knew they'd be waiting for us at the next station. They must really think that we are stupid! Now they'll have to cover all of the stops at the same time," he boasted to Frank.

"The entire scenario repeated itself again and again at each station as the train sped by. Sam could see that the number of policemen waiting in ambush for them at each succeeding station was becoming smaller and smaller. As they entered the Central Square subway station, Sam did not see any policemen waiting for them on the platform. He ordered the engineer to only open the doors of the first car after they came to a stop. The train came to an emergency stop near the end of the platform where Sam and Frank bolted out of the train's only open door.

As the two men carefully made their way up the stairs toward the street, they heard the sounds of policemen running into the station above them. Sam and Frank put their guns away and quietly pretended to be riders exiting the station. The officers pushed their way past them. Sam smiled and allowed them to pass. Sam felt relieved as he caught sight of the light from the street shinning down the stairs toward them.

"Police! Stop right there!" came a shout from far below them.

The words brought an instant reaction from Frank as he drew his weapon and spun around to face them. He fired off at least six rounds toward the officers before he was hit several times by a volley of bullets from the police below. The force of the bullets hitting him in the chest and head sent his body reeling backward up against the stairs. He fired off one more round as he fell.

Sam was able to safely exit the station when Frank had turned to return fire against their pursuers. Sam made his way through the crowds of people walking by on the sidewalk. People began to crowd around the subway exit to see what all the commotion was about. Seeing the blood gushing out from Frank's wounds sent cries of horror through the gathering crowds of curious onlookers. In the confusion, Sam was able to make his way unobserved across the street. He attempted to flag down a taxi when Detectives Bates and Bolten exited the underground station. Detective Bolten pushed his way through the afternoon crowds to the next corner. He was hoping to catch a glimpse of their third suspect whom he hoped was still in the area. Not seeing him anywhere, he ran back over to where Carol was still standing.

"Did you see him or anyone that might've fit his general description?" she asked him.

"No, but he still has to be somewhere in the area. He didn't have that much time to get away from here. Let's keep looking around for him. We might get lucky if we can seal off the area quickly."

Detective Bates and her partner kept a watchful eye out for anyone who looked as though he was trying to leave the area in a hurry. As they looked up and down the two sides of Massachusetts Avenue for anyone who might fit their suspect's general description, their eyes caught sight of a man trying to flag down a taxi cab a few hundred feet down the street. He looked across the street and saw the two detectives looking in his direction. A taxi pulled up next to him, but as Sam bent over to open its rear door, the driver caught sight of the gun in his holster. The cab driver wanted no part of him and quickly sped away. Cursing him, Sam turned and casually walked down the street, looking for another means to escape. He found it a short distance away. A man had just exited his pickup truck when Sam walked up behind him with his gun partially exposed.

"Give me your keys, and I will let you live!" he demanded from the terrified man.

"Here they are! Just don't shoot me!" he shrieked back at him in terror.

While Sam quickly opened the truck's door and slid the key into the truck's ignition, the two detectives had been quickly closing in on his location. As he got the engine started, the two detectives ran up to the side of the stolen truck. Sam smiled back at them politely, causing them to believe that maybe he wasn't their suspect. Sam very slowly shifted the transmission into drive. He then very slowly leaned his body slightly down to the right and raised his gun in their direction. At the same time, he pushed the accelerator down to the floor. Sam's gun blasted two rounds at the detectives through the steel door of the truck as it started to speed away.

Detectives Bates and Bolten reacted automatically to the sound of the discharging firearm. They moved back and fired their guns directly at him through the door of the truck. One of their bullets struck the truck's window, causing the glass to explode into a thousand small pieces onto Sam's crouching body. Three other bullets managed to cut their way through the thin steel door panel and into Sam's body. One bullet lodged itself deep into Sam's upper left arm, while the other two entered his prostrate body and penetrated deep into Sam's chest cavity. Blood began to flow out of his wounds and onto the seat of the truck. The pickup continued to accelerate down the street away from them.

"Shit, we didn't even hit him! We have to get a car!" Detective Bates shouted as she looked around the area.

Jim clutched his left shoulder as a pool of red blood began to soak his shirt. Carol looked over at him and saw that he had been hit by one of their suspect's rounds.

"You've been hit!" she worriedly shouted.

"Yeah, but not too seriously. He just nicked me slightly in the shoulder."

As they turned their attention back to their fleeing suspect, they observed his vehicle slowly drifting off to the right and crashing into a row of parked cars. The two detectives and a group of other officers converged on the truck a couple of hundred feet down the road. The two detectives reached the stalled truck first, and with their guns still pointing at him, they carefully opened the driver's door.

As Sam felt the energy of his life rapidly slipping away from him, he tried to focus his eyes on the sky above him. He couldn't help but think about his village back in Russia and the cold Siberian winters. His mind kept seeing the living fog just floating in the cold Arctic air around his village. The image of the fog somehow made him feel at peace. He began to wonder if something of his life, like the living fog, would be left behind to remind the people that he had passed by that way. A few seconds later, he closed his eyes for the last time and stopped breathing.

Detective Bates reached into the truck to recover his weapon and to check his body for a pulse.

"He's gone!" she announced to Jim. "I wonder who he is?" she asked as she reached into his pockets for a wallet or some other identifying items. She found one and opened it.

"Look at this, nothing! It contains some cash and a single credit card with a name. It says that his name is Samuel Rubin. It's probably an alias! We can run it when we get back to the station," she said to him.

She turned to the two people from the coroner's office who had just walked over to their location. "I want all of these guys fingerprinted and run through all of the systems as soon as they're brought over to the ME's office."

Central Square had been closed off by dozens of policemen and special investigators. All road traffic was quickly rerouted around it. Police cruisers, ambulances, and several vans from the coroner's office were parked in the area also. Patrolmen were stationed around the two crime scenes to keep the crowds of curious spectators away. The bodies of the two dead suspects were bagged and carried out of the subway station to the waiting vans. The third suspect's body was removed from the stolen pickup truck, bagged, and then placed in a second van for transport.

A couple of wounded police officers who were hit by some ricocheting bullets fired from Frank's gun were treated briefly at the scene and then rushed to Mass General Hospital for further treatment. The police did not find any other forms of identification on the other two suspect's bodies recovered from the subway station.

* * * * *

While all of this had been going on in and around the city, Harry had arrived at the morgue a few minutes after the two detectives had stormed out of the building in hot pursuit of the three suspected murderers. He sat down in a chair next to Dr. Witherspoon to offer him some support over the loss of his close friend, Dr. Bruce Baxter.

"I'm sorry, Doc, that we weren't here to help Dr. Baxter. How well did you know him?" he asked his old friend.

"I've known Bruce for over twelve years, but he's been only working in this office for the last eighteen months. We've been close friends ever since medical school. Why in the world would anyone want to kill him? As far as I know, he didn't have an enemy in the whole world. How am I going to tell his wife and two kids that he was murdered?" he emotionally broke down in front of Harry for a few minutes.

Harry tried his best to console his old friend. He had worked with Jim on many cases when he was on the force. "I really don't know why they killed him, Doc. But I'd bet my last dollar that his death is related in some way to Dr. Helen Mathews's murder and that strange-looking capsule that you found inside her head. You still have it, don't you?" he asked him with a little bit of concern reflecting in his words.

"Yes, I still have it. I thought it would be a lot safer if I kept it in my shirt pocket! I put a cylindrically shaped brass dowel in a test tube just in case someone came looking for it before the detectives arrived to pick it up. I put it in a plastic container on the top shelf above my desk. I figured that it would trick anyone who came in here trying to force me to give it to them! I looked around my office a while ago and learned that they must've taken it with them. They killed poor Bruce when I went upstairs to print out my autopsy report. They probably thought that he was me standing over Dr. Mathews's body. They then shot my hard drive to pieces with a couple of bullets.

"I suppose they figured that with me dead and all of my records of the last autopsy missing, there would be no information about what I found inside her head."

"You're probably right! Have you formulated any opinions about what the capsule was doing inside her brain?" Harry asked him.

"To be honest with you, Harry, I don't have the slightest idea! What I can say, however, is that whoever implanted that device in her was no fool. The placing of the two leads next to the optic and cochlear nerves was deliberate. It'll take a hell of a lot more sophisticated equipment to figure out what this device is and does than I have around here," Dr. Witherspoon declared with authority.

Harry left the ME's office and went back out to his car to place a phone call out to Dr. Stevens's lab in New Mexico. It was a phone call that he knew Phil would want to get as soon as possible. It took only a few minutes for Carlos to bring him to the telephone.

"Harry, it's good to hear from you and so soon! Does this mean what I think it does?" he hopefully inquired.

"It sure does, Phil. The ME found a cylindrically shaped capsule implanted inside her head. He said that the capsule had two leads attached to it. One lead terminated next to the optic nerve and the other one next to the cochlear nerve in her brain. At least that's what the ME told me today. Is that what you expected them to find?"

"I really didn't know what they'd find inside her head. We just found a number of references inside her journals and on the CDs that seemed to suggest the existence of just such a device. We should have a lot more answers for you within the next twenty-four hours. I'll let you know what else we find when I arrive in Boston on Sunday at 2:20 PM on American Airlines flight 222," he said to him.

"Okay, Phil, I'll meet you at the baggage claim area of American Airlines on Sunday afternoon. I hope you have a smooth, safe flight into Boston, my friend."

"Thanks, Harry. I know I will. Give Karen a kiss for me," he jokingly said to him.

"I certainly will, Phil."

CHAPTER 21

The afternoon traffic and crowds at Logan International Airport had become almost unbearable for the last four years due to the confusion and detours created by the Big Dig transportation fiasco and the recent terrorist attack of September 11 in New York City. Harry looked down at his watch to see if he was going to be late for the arrival of Dr. Stevens's flight.

Damn it! I can't believe it's already ten after two. I hope his flight is running late today, he thought to himself as he inched his way through the harbor tunnel traffic toward the airport.

As he pulled up to the arrival area of the American Airlines terminal, he caught sight of Phil already waiting patiently for him just outside the revolving doors. He was surrounded by what appeared to be a mountain of large suitcases and boxes.

"I thought you said that you were only going to be staying in Boston for about two or three days!" Harry yelled over to him as he walked around his car to where he was standing.

"I did. Most of this equipment we found listed inside Dr. Mathews's last journal and on her two CDs. She emphatically referred to all of it as being absolutely necessary for accessing the data files of the neuroencapsulator. I certainly wouldn't have brought along all of this stuff unless I thought we might really need it!" he said to him.

"Then I'm glad that you brought all of it with you. What the hell does all of this stuff do anyways? And where the hell did you come up with the term 'neuroencapsulator'?" Harry asked him as they began to carefully load the heavy boxes and suitcases into the trunk of his car.

"I found the term listed several times in the pages of Helen's first journal. She said that it was a data storage device that she had designed to specifically record human nerve impulses. I'm not really sure how this device and most of her equipment is even supposed to work yet. I do know, however, that it's going to take me quite some time to figure out the correct wiring sequence and filter arrangements before all of this equipment can be made to even begin to function correctly. Dr. Mathews's journals were quite remiss in describing how to set up all of this stuff. We don't even know the strength or frequency of the initial signal that our amplifier has to generate and send out to the capsule. She made a number of incomplete and confusing entries in her journals right after she had scribbled in this equipment list. She probably didn't get a chance to go over them again before she was murdered," Dr. Stevens speculated.

"Then there's a distinct possibility that all of this equipment could even do harm to the data storage device or neuroencapsulator?" Harry uneasily asked him.

"Yes, but what else can we do! The data has to be retrieved before it degenerates any further. I'm going to need a quiet place alone to set up and tinker with all of the equipment. I'll try my best to be ready for your courtroom hearing tomorrow morning," Phil promised him.

"Phil, we're really counting on your expertise at this hearing. So do whatever you can to help us retrieve that data. We have to at least try to learn what's inside it. I also fear in my heart that there's a distinct possibility that the device may not even work at all."

"You could be right about that, but either way, I'll do my very best for you and Helen!"

"I know that goes without saying. Did they feed you on the plane, or could I tempt you with a good meal tonight?"

"I'm famished! I always try to avoid eating airline food unless it's absolutely necessary."

"Great! Let's first get you checked into your hotel suite so that you can relax and get cleaned up for dinner. Then I'll come by and get you around 6:30 PM and take you out for a first-class dinner in Boston. We have a lot more to talk about."

At dinner that evening, Harry informed Dr. Stevens about the tragic events that had taken place in the coroner's office the day before. Upon hearing the news that the three assailants had been killed in a fierce gun battle with the police in the city's subway system, Phil seemed to become more at ease. Dr. Stevens was totally convinced that the entire incident in the coroner's office was all part of the conspiracy centered around Dr. Mathews's murder. At first, Phil couldn't understand why the police had purposely downplayed the entire incident in the press. They had even gone so far as to put out a false cover story to the media. The official police press release reported that three deranged mental patients had escaped from a high-security facility, stolen some weapons, and had gone on a wild shooting spree. Harry told him that the police had released the false cover story at the request of the DA's office, a request that would help keep the true facts surrounding Dr. Mathews's murder and the three shooters of the ME quiet. The DA didn't want any news about the three unknown murderers leaking out into the national media until the police were able to identify who they had been working for.

Dr. Stevens was glad that he hadn't heard anything about the recent murder in the coroner's office because the news might've made him feel more reluctant about coming to Boston for the hearing. It felt good to know now that all of the assailants who had been involved in the ME's murder had been justly dealt with. Phil was now free to concentrate completely on the complex work that lay ahead of him. He felt a little disappointed that Dr. Mathews had not finished sketching out or even briefly describing in her journals her ideas on how to connect all of the listed pieces of electronic equipment to the neuroencapsulator. Now he would be faced with solving the unique challenge alone, a challenge that would require all of his knowledge and skills as a scientist to solve. In a relatively short span of time, he would have to try to design a procedure that would cause the data capsule to begin generating a feedback signal with all of its stored data imprinted on it. That new feedback signal would then have to be recorded, scanned, and filtered and, lastly, analyzed by the programs on Dr. Mathews's two CDs. The exact signal strength of the amplifiers and in what sequence each piece of monitoring equipment had to be connected was still a mystery to him. If he was successful, he would be responsible for unlocking the mysteries of her neuroencapsulator. In the back of Dr. Stevens's mind, he had just one major concern, and that was that he did not want to damage the small data capsule forever.

Dr. Stevens's red eyes stared at the stack of rejected schematic diagrams lying in front of him. A heavy feeling of uncertainty seemed to hang over him as he finally closed up her notebooks and files at two o'clock that morning. As he finally closed his tired eyes to sleep, he imagined Dr. Mathews's face smiling back at him from a shared moment in their past.

"Helen, I can only hope that I've made no mistakes in what I've just designed. I've never really had the imagination and the knowledge that made you so brilliant. I pray to God that I don't screw this whole thing up for you," he whispered to her in the darkness of his hotel suite. It was a prayer that he sincerely hoped she had heard.

Early the next morning, Harry and Dr. Stevens enjoyed a quick breakfast together in the hotel's only dining room. When they had finished eating, they loaded up all of Dr. Stevens's equipment into his car and then drove over to the courthouse together. Harry couldn't help but notice how nervous Phil appeared to be as he began to connect all of the different pieces of electrical equipment together inside the small courtroom. The last two items that he set up were the two notebook computers and a VCR to record any and all of the data that the neuroencapsulator might generate onto the monitor's screen. Harry politely introduced Dr. Stevens to the DA and Atty. Paul Tucker before Judge Zimmer entered the small courtroom to preside over the special hearing. The clerk had made arrangements for a stenographer to be present at the hearing to record a formal and final transcript of the proceedings. The clerk called the special closed hearing to order as soon as Judge Zimmer had taken his seat behind the bench.

"Well, Mr. Parker, does the state wish to place any additional motions before me before the court makes its final ruling on the disposition of the Dr. Helen Mathews murder case?" he asked him.

"No, Your Honor, the state has presented all of its concerns and arguments against ending this trial today in its motions submitted to the court earlier. We do ask, however, that the defense be allowed to present some new evidence to Your Honor before the court makes its final ruling in this matter. The evidence and testimony deals with our victim's secretive research," he announced to the judge.

"Since the jury is not present at this informal hearing, I will allow the defense some extra leeway in this matter. Now, gentlemen, the rules of this closed hearing are a little bit more relaxed than what I would insist upon in front of the jury. We are here today to find a way to protect the defendant's rights in this trial. Any new evidence that may be presented here today is being provided for my benefit only. It may or may not be used by me in my decision to declare a mistrial. As both counsels know, the defendant is entitled to a fair and speedy trial. In the matter before this court, the defendant, through no fault of his own, has been prevented in participating in his own defense. Now, Mr. Tucker, I understand that you wish to make a brief statement to the court before you present your new evidence. Am I right, Mr. Tucker?"

"That's correct, Your Honor. We believe that the murder and robbery that took place at the coroner's office yesterday were directly related to the secretive research that Dr. Mathews was engaged in for many years for some very powerful people in our government. So far, we have been able to learn from our ongoing investigation that Dr. Mathews continued to work on this special project well after she had been ordered by her financial backers to stop. We contend that she was not murdered by Mr. John Haggerty, her fiancé, but by other assailants as yet unknown. To better explain this new type of technology to the court, I wish to have Dr. Stevens sworn in to testify. The defense considers his expertise in this matter critical to the court's understanding of this complex subject material."

"Does the state have any objections to this witness and what he may offer in the way of testimony before this special hearing?" he asked the DA.

"Not at this time, Your Honor, but we do reserve the right to raise an objection if we feel that the defense is merely taking us all on a fishing expedition. At this time, we will rely on Your Honor's judgment as to whether the testimony of this witness has any direct bearing on the case before us."

Dr. Stevens was sworn in by the clerk and told to take the witness stand.

"Now, Doctor, can you please tell the court your full name and your educational achievements that would qualify you as an expert in the testimony that you are about to give before this court today?" Mr. Tucker asked him.

Dr. Stevens proceeded to give his full name and a long list of his educational credentials to the court. He informed the court that he had worked very closely with Dr. Mathews when they had both been employed in Dr. Tinkoi's laboratory at MIT many years earlier. He explained how he had been stricken with a very serious medical condition around that time and that it had forced him to interrupt his doctoral studies at MIT. He explained how he had been forced to drop out of MIT for about a year in order to fully recover from this medical condition. He then testified that when he eventually returned to MIT to complete his doctoral studies, he learned that Dr. Tinkoi and all of his research team's personnel had left the institution some six months earlier. He testified how he had received a strange phone call from Dr. Mathews one day, just before he had completed his final doctoral work at MIT. During the course of that telephone call, he said that Dr. Mathews had advised him to leave the school as soon as possible and to drop out of sight."

"And did you follow her advice?" Paul asked him.

"Yes, I did!"

"Now, Doctor, can you please tell the court what convinced you to follow Dr. Mathews's advice about leaving MIT right after you had just earned your doctorate degree?"

"Well, during our phone conversation, she told me that she was becoming more and more frightened of her employers. She explained to me that some people in our government who had been financially backing her secret research for many years were starting to put a great deal of pressure on her and some of the other people in her lab. They wanted to see some definite results from their long financial support of her research. She suspected that my life might also be placed in real danger if they learned that I was back. She told me where to go and who to contact out West after I left MIT. She promised me that she would keep in touch with me on a regular basis through a Mr. Michael in Arizona. For the next six years, we kept in close personal contact regularly and remained very close friends. During that time, we collaborated on and shared some of our research results on a regular basis every other month. She was a brilliant scientist."

"Now, Dr. Stevens, are you trying to tell us that she was in fear for her life?" Paul asked him in order to clarify her state of mind to the court more accurately.

"Your Honor, I really must object to this witness's conversations with the deceased in this case. As we all know, they cannot be substantiated! The defense is attempting to present to this court a foundation for its earlier theory that someone else had threatened our victim's life. We cannot allow this testimony to be entered into the official record without a challenge or exception," the DA complained.

"Sustained. Well, Mr. Tucker, the DA is correct. Now just where are you going with this witness's testimony? The court has been very patient in allowing your witness to bring us up to date on some of his alleged involvements with the victim in this case. But I warn you, my patience in this matter is not without limit. I said that I would be lax in allowing you some time to present some solid new evidence in this matter, but I haven't seen or heard any yet! I'm going to give you just a few more minutes to show me where you are going with all of this," Judge Zimmer impatiently said to him.

"I will, Your Honor, shortly. You may answer the question, Doctor."

"Well, I really didn't think that she was afraid that they were going to kill her, if that's what you mean! However, I did feel that she strongly believed that they might physically harm her. Dr. Mathews was always looking out for the well-being of everyone around her. I believe in my heart that she called me that day to send me as far away as possible from these people because she now saw them as being very dangerous. About a year later, after she had set me up in a new research facility out West, she called me again to tell me that she had been ordered by these same people in our government to cease all work on the project altogether. She said that they had demanded all of her notes and files on the project. She said that they then warned her to never again attempt to continue with the research without their permission. Dr. Mathews, however, told me that she was going to secretly continue working on the project without their financial backing or knowledge."

"Dr. Stevens, I want you to jump ahead now to last week when you and my chief investigator met out West at your research facility. Can you tell the court what you and Mr. Parks discussed and subsequently learned from Dr. Mathews's research notes?"

"Well, Mr. Michael contacted me by phone last week to tell me that a man wanted to meet with me. He said that the man had been sent out to his office by Dr. Mathews so that he could arrange a meeting between the two of us. Mr. Michael informed me that the man appeared to have in his possession some very important papers that he said Dr. Mathews had given to him for me to look at. Under this pretense, I agreed to meet with him early the next day at my research ranch. During our meeting the next day, he informed me that Dr. Mathews had not really sent him out there to see me. He informed me that she had been savagely murdered by someone back in Boston. It was the worst news that I had ever heard. After I had recovered from the news and shock of Helen's death, he showed me a few of her personal research journals and some CDs that she had with her on the night that she had been murdered."

"Mr. Parker, I didn't see any of these items mentioned earlier in the state's case. Why weren't these items placed into evidence at the trial?" the judge asked the DA for an explanation.

"Because, Your Honor, we didn't even know of their existence until just now!" he sheepishly explained to the judge.

"If you didn't know of their existence, then when and how did the defense get its hands on this kind of evidence? Mr. Tucker! Where and when did you find these items and why weren't they turned over to the DA's office right away?" he suspiciously asked Mr. Tucker. His voice was now raised a little louder, showing his anger with the way that the defense may have purposely withheld some very critical evidence in his murder trial.

"Your Honor, Dr. Mathews's briefcase had been left at the first crime scene. The defense only became aware of its existence a short while after our client had been involved in the gas explosion at his home last week. When we learned that it had been completely overlooked by everyone involved, we went to the Sanford Office Building and took possession of it from one of the security guards. He had placed it inside a secured locker on the night of the murder. We gave the guard a signed and dated receipt that night for the briefcase. Later on that evening in my office, we opened the briefcase on camera to record all of contents inside of it for the court. We found inside the briefcase an address book that eventually led us to discover the whereabouts of Dr. Stevens. We have the briefcase and all of its contents in the courtroom today. We would've turned it over to the DA's office a few days sooner, but the trial case had been put in limbo due to the unfortunate accident involving my client," he shrewdly explained to the judge, knowing that he may've just dodged a legal scolding.

"Extraordinary! I can't believe that such a major piece of evidence from a high-profile murder trial such as this could have been left in a security locker all this time. That, Mr. Parker, is very sloppy investigating work by both the police and your office! Make sure you let them know about my displeasure in this matter! And you, Mr. Tucker, I'm sure that you know quite well the rules about turning over all evidence found at a crime scene to the police right away! I will let it go this time because of the confusion surrounding the disposition of this case, but don't ever let it happen again!"

The DA looked over at Mr. Tucker and frowned. He did not appreciate the fact that Paul had not shared his knowledge of the existence of the briefcase with his office much sooner. It had made all of his staff and the police look like fools in front of the judge.

"You may continue, Mr. Tucker, and remember my previous warning about not wasting this court's time with irrelevant or unsubstantiated facts," the judge warned him.

"Thank you, Your Honor. Now, Dr. Stevens, you said that Mr. Parks showed you some journals and CDs that he said were taken from Dr. Mathews's briefcase."

"That's correct. I recognized her handwriting almost immediately on the CD labels and inside the journals. The real test as to their authenticity was that they were all encrypted. She always wrote her journals in a unique encryption code. She had insisted that I learn it thoroughly during the first years that we had worked together at MIT. It took me a few hours to re-familiarize myself with it again. It eventually all came back to me quite fast."

"Can you please tell the court what you learned about Dr. Mathews's research when you were deciphering and transcribing her journals and CDs for Mr. Parks and me?"

"Certainly! Well, I was quite surprised to learn that Dr. Mathews's research had been a lot more successful than even I had ever imagined possible. According to her journals, she had succeeded in discovering one of nature's most elusive master keys: a key that unlocked one of our body's most secretive mechanisms. In her research journals, she wrote that she had managed to decipher the very nature of the sensory nerve impulses that travel throughout our bodies and up to the various parts of our brains. Do you know what that means? It means that in one brilliant sweep, she has been able to unlock the doors to some forms of blindness, hearing loss, and some of the other sensory systems of our bodies. If what she wrote was true, then her discovery is both priceless and its applications to the good of our society almost unlimited!"

"Were you able to uncover any other hard evidence in her papers that could help you prove to the court that the assertions that she made in her journals were indeed accurate?" the judge asked him hopefully.

"I think so, Your Honor. But I haven't been able to test out my theory until this very moment. You see, in her first and last journals, Dr. Mathews mentioned the existence of a certain device that she had created. She referred to it as her neuroencapsulator. In several parts of her journals, she said something about it having already been implanted inside a test subject's body. Nowhere in her records did I come across the identity of her test subject or the name of the surgeon who had performed this unusual medical procedure. So I tried to guess who she would've used as a test subject. It finally came to me the other night who she would've used . . . herself! You see, Dr. Mathews was a person of very high ethical standards, and I know that she would never have put anyone else at risk without an absolute certainty that her research wouldn't have caused them some irreparable harm," Dr. Stevens stated with admiration in his words.

"So the order that I signed the other day to exhume her body was for the sole purpose of looking for that device inside her body!" the judge asked him.

"That's right, Your Honor. After Mr. Parks talked to Dr. Stevens the other day, we went over to the DA's office and convinced him that Dr. Mathews had to have been the most likely candidate for that medical procedure," Paul announced to the judge confidently.

"Now, gentlemen, where do we go from here?" the judge asked them curiously.

The DA stood up and walked over to the defense table and handed a copy of the ME's latest autopsy report to Mr. Tucker. He then approached the clerk and handed him a copy of the same report for the judge to read. "Your Honor, the tragic murder of the medical examiner over at the coroner's office yesterday was a direct attempt by someone to destroy this report and any new evidence that might've been discovered during the second autopsy that was performed on Dr. Mathews's body."

"So the media reports about three deranged mental patients who escaped from the state hospital and going on a wild shooting spree was only a cover story?" Judge Zimmer asked him.

"That's right, Your Honor. The real story is to be found in the ME's second autopsy report that I've just handed over to Mr. Tucker and the clerk. In this document, Dr. Witherspoon clearly summarized his investigative findings. He reported that he found a strange-looking cylindrically shaped capsule implanted inside the head of Dr. Helen Mathews. After documenting its exact location, he then very carefully removed the small capsule from her brain. He especially noted in his report that the device had to have been implanted by a highly skilled neurosurgeon. He explained that the precise placement of the capsule's two leads in close proximity to the optic and auditory nerves was by no means an accident. The device had to have been placed there for some specific purpose," Mr. Parker explained to the court.

"The three assailants who were killed in the subsequent police chase and shootouts have not yet been identified. I'm still waiting for the official police report to be delivered to me any minute now by Detective Bates. In my opinion, Dr. Baxter was murdered by these men to prevent this information from ever becoming known. The capsule that was removed from Dr. Mathews's brain is in a sealed test tube inside my briefcase." Mr. Parker reached into his briefcase and took out the test tube for the judge to see.

"Your Honor, may I see the capsule?" Dr. Stevens excitedly asked the judge.

"Mr. Parker, you may hand the capsule over to Dr. Stevens to look at."

For several long minutes, Dr. Stevens studied the small capsule very carefully. As he was doing this, there was a light knock on the back door of the courtroom. One of the guards walked over and opened it. He recognized Detectives Bates and her partner and let them in. Detective Bates walked over to the DA and handed him a few copies of their official police report. The two detectives then sat down in the courtroom a few rows behind the district attorney. The DA quickly glanced over the report and then suddenly looked up in surprise after reading it. He then handed a copy of the report over to Mr. Tucker and the clerk for the judge to also read.

"Your Honor, what I just handed over to Mr. Tucker and to the court is a copy of the official police report that was compiled on our three dead assailants from yesterday's deadly subway shootout. When the police ran their fingerprints through all of the data bases, including the military and FBI's, they discovered that all three of these men were listed as killed in action in Vietnam. They were all part of an elite army ranger unit that was supposedly wiped out on a secret mission into Laos over thirty years ago. Since that last report, the police were unable to find any record of their existence. So it seems, Your Honor, as though we're being faced with yet another unexplained mystery. This entire case is beginning to smell more like a giant governmental conspiracy," He proclaimed strongly to the judge and Mr. Tucker while they were still looking over their copies of the police report.

"Mr. Tucker, have you finished questioning this witness, or is there something else that you want to ask him?" the judge inquired.

"Your Honor, Dr. Stevens has brought along with him today a number of pieces of highly sensitive electrical equipment. He has informed me that this equipment was listed on page 287 of Dr. Mathews's latest research journal. I have a couple of copies of Dr. Mathews's deciphered and transcribed research journals here for the DA's office and the court. Along with this list of electrical testing equipment, there was a footnote written in the journal that referred to this list of equipment as being absolutely necessary for accessing the information stored on the device's core. It is our hope that the court will allow Dr. Stevens the opportunity to attempt to access the device's data storage core right now," Mr. Tucker explained to the judge.

"Do you think you can do that, Dr. Stevens?" the judge asked him curiously.

"I honestly don't know, but I would like to at least give it a try, Your Honor."

"I will allow Dr. Stevens to go forward with his demonstration. Does the prosecution have any objections to this, Mr. Parker?"

"We do not, Your Honor."

"May I get up and connect the capsule or neuroencapsulator, as it was called in Dr. Mathews's journals, to my test equipment?" Dr. Stevens politely asked the judge.

"You may, Doctor," Judge Zimmer answered back.

"Your Honor, I must also point out to the court and to both sides of this case that what I am about to do in here is highly speculative on my part. My team of scientists and I were unable to find even a single schematic layout or diagram in any of Dr. Mathews's journals that would've showed us how to connect all of this equipment. We believe that she was tragically murdered just before she was able to record that information in her journals.

"As a result, I have been forced to spend many long hours carefully studying every piece of equipment that was listed in her journals. I have managed to put together what I believe is a good working hypothesis as to how all of the equipment might interface properly. I can now only hope and pray that my efforts will allow us to safely unlock the mysteries of her neuroencapsulator. I've set up a camera in the courtroom to record any and all of the information that we might observe coming from the capsule. I only hope that my methodology doesn't cause any harm to the neuroencapsulator itself!" Dr. Stevens humbly announced to the court as he carefully checked out the last few connections and setting on his equipment.

Feeling satisfied that everything had been properly connected, he nervously began his demonstration. At first glance, the low-level electrical signal that the amplifier sent through the capsule seemed to have no apparent effect on it at all. He did not want to increase the intensity of the amplifier's signal too fast until he was absolutely sure that he had induced a feedback signal from the neuroencapsulator. Once he had generated one, he began to send the signal through all of the various filters and analyzers. He kept adjusting the range of the filters and analyzers until he was sure that the feedback signal was strong and clear. He then directed the signal into the first computer where Dr. Mathews's first CD had already been preloaded onto. He activated the program and waited for something to happen on the monitor screen.

"Nothing's happening!" he quietly whispered to himself.

He then sent the signal from the first computer over to the second computer's input terminal. Phil had already preloaded Dr. Mathews's other CD into it earlier. He pressed the enter key. It took the program a few seconds to boot up. The monitor screen began to fill up with a series of broken images and sounds. Dr. Stevens moved back over to the amplifier and slowly increased the intensity of the signal being sent over to the capsule. The feedback signal increased dramatically.

"I think something's happening! Can you clean up the signal a little bit more?" the DA excitedly asked him.

Detective Bates and her partner moved up closer to one of the monitors for a better view. The judge and the clerk had also moved in a little closer to the other monitor for a better view of the small fractured images showing up on the screen.

"I want to make a small change in the layout of my equipment. He quickly reversed the order of the two computers and increased the amplifier's signal even more. When he increased the signal this time, the monitor screens all filled up with a faint image of what appeared to be a highway. Everyone tried to figure out what they were looking at. Dr. Stevens tinkered with one of the analyzers and two of the filters until he managed to separate out a sound wave from the data stream. From the speakers came the clear sounds of a car's engine running and cars driving by. He then hurriedly went over to the other analyzer and its two filters and made additional adjustments to each of them. The images on the monitors came into a sharp focus.

"I think you've got it, Doctor!" Mr. Tucker shouted over to him.

Everyone in the small courtroom looked on in amazement as the images and sounds of Dr. Mathews's last moments of life played out on the monitor screens in front of them. On the screens were the clear visual images that she was seeing through her own eyes. The speakers were broadcasting all of the sounds that her ears were hearing at the same time. They watched in horror as she pulled herself in agony out of her car. She then crawled along the ground over to the front porch of her house. As she agonizingly dragged and pulled her bleeding body through the small opening in the latticework of the front porch, her sobs and cries of pain as well as the sounds of her labored breathing filled the stillness of the courtroom.

Under the front porch, she exhaustedly worked on the tourniquet tied around her left leg in an effort to stop the bleeding. She cried out loud in pain again. The sounds of her agony pierced the heartstrings of all of the observers sitting in the courtroom. She exhaustedly raised her eyes up from her leg wound and leaned her head back against the foundation wall of her house. Her eyes seemed to focus on the eerie images of the wooden latticework beside her. The light from the streetlight in front of her house illuminated some of the darkness around her.

The sound of a car driving up to her house made her turn her head to the right to see who was coming. The courtroom was filled with the soft cries of her terrified words escaping from her lips: "Oh please, God! Don't let them find me under here!"

The unknown vehicle came to a stop a few feet behind her car. It was hard to make out the exact type or make of vehicle being seen on the screen. Everyone could hear the muffled sounds of two men talking and walking around her car. She could hear one of the men making his way to the back of her house, while the other one walked up the steps to her front door. From the speakers came the sound of glass being broken somewhere. Everyone speculated that they had just broken into her house. Soon her front door opened and the second man entered her house.

The images on the monitor moved around slightly as if she was shaking. Frozen in fear, she fixed her eyes to the right under the porch. Her breathing was becoming much more labored as she started to whisper some words to her fiancé. "John, I don't know if I'm going to survive this or not, and if I don't, I just want you to know how much I really love you!"

The words had hardly left her lips when the speakers picked up the sounds of the two men descending the front steps of her house. They walked over to her car again and then slowly made their way back over to the side of the porch. One of the men peered in at her and then pulled the latticework away from the side of the front porch. She tried to focus her eyes in on his face, but the light from their bright headlights was blinding her. In terror, she tried to scream, but her loss of blood had made her throat too dry to cry out. The silhouette of the man bent down and moved in closer toward her. She looked into his cold dark eyes and instantly recognized him.

"It's you!" she struggled to say to him.

"Yes, it's me! I told you what would happen if you continued with your research, but you wouldn't listen to me. Now you will pay the ultimate price!" he slowly raised his gun up to her neck to fire.

She let out a faint last cry. "Oh, John, what have I done to us?"

The force of the bullet threw her head backward hard up against the concrete foundation wall. The partially muffled sound of the loud weapon discharging its deadly projectile made everyone in the courtroom jump. As her body slowly slipped into a coma, her killers disappeared into the night and could be heard driving away. The images on the screen appeared to freeze for a minute or two. Everyone then saw the face of John Haggerty hurrying over to her dying body and crying out in anguish to her. From the emotional images, they saw the true depth of his despair. The images on the monitor screen slowly darkened as her eyes stopped sending images back to her brain.

Everyone in the courtroom remained completely silent and frozen in a state of shock. The court stenographer was holding a handkerchief up to her eyes in sorrow at what she had just witnessed on the monitor screen. The two detectives behind the district attorney were also both deeply moved by what they had just witnessed. The very emotional images were not lost on Judge Zimmer either. He sat back in his chair, contemplating his next move. The DA's voice was the first to break the long silence in the small courtroom.

"Your Honor, I think that the evidence that we have all just witnessed in here speaks for itself. The defendant, John Haggerty, has been shown to be completely innocent of all of the charges brought against him by the state. Therefore, I make a motion to the court that all charges against him be dismissed at this time," he said to the judge emotionally.

"To that end, I would have to agree with you wholeheartedly. Therefore, it is the judgment of this court that all charges against the defendant John Haggerty are hereby dismissed. I only hope that he survives his present injuries and knows that the court apologizes to him for its terrible mistake."

While everyone in the courtroom was trying to get a handle on their emotions again, Detective Bates and her partner asked the judge and the DA whether they had recognized on the monitor that one of Dr. Mathews's two assailants was one of their dead suspects from the ME's murder the day before.

The DA looked down at the photographs of their three dead suspects included in the police report handed to him earlier. "I believe I saw this man on the screen standing behind our shooter under the front porch!" he announced to them.

"I think you're right! We recognized him almost immediately because we had seen his picture earlier. He was definitely at Dr. Mathews's house that night! Now there remains only one thing left for us to do, and that's to identify our shooter in this nightmare before he finds out that we are on to him!"

The clerk and the DA discussed quietly off to one side of the bench what the DA needed to get a warrant for their new suspect's arrest. The judge slammed his gavel against the strike plate on his desk to declare the proceedings closed. The mood in the courtroom was very somber as the DA and Paul Tucker turned to face each other.

"Paul, I don't know what else to say to you except that I'm very sorry for what I put your client through. None of us will ever really know the true depth of the horror and pain that he must've felt when he discovered her body that night. From what we just saw and heard on the monitors, she really loved him and wanted him to know it before she died. If there's anything else that I can do to help him right now, please let me know. Tell him that our actions were based solely on the evidence that was being expertly manipulated by her killers to make us all believe that he was guilty. I can only pray that he will recover from his terrible injuries," he said to Paul with a sad heart.

After the hearing was over, Paul and Harry drove straight over to the hospital to check on John's condition. When they arrived at the nurses' station on the eleventh floor burn ward, they found the area alive with a flurry of activity. From their location on the floor, they could see a team of doctors and nurses anxiously standing around John's hospital bed. One of John's doctors caught sight of Paul and hurriedly exited the room to talk to him. From his facial expressions, Paul assumed that something terrible had just happened to John.

"Well, Mr. Tucker, it appears as though your client is not quite ready to throw in the towel after all. Just a few minutes ago, Mr. Haggerty suddenly awakened from his deep coma. He's still a little bit groggy and confused right now, but we hope that he will continue to improve over the next few hours," his doctor excitedly informed them.

The news of John's sudden improvement caught the two men almost completely by surprise. It was not the news that Paul and Harry were expecting to hear from the doctors at the hospital that day. For the past several days Paul had grown accustomed to hearing every day nothing but negative reports from the doctors about John's deteriorating condition.

"I can't believe it!" Paul shouted in joy to John's doctor. "It was only yesterday that you were telling me to expect the worst in the days ahead. It's like John had suddenly found a reason to live. He won't have a relapse or anything like that, will he? I really want to tell him some really great news," Paul said to the young doctor.

"I think your friend is going to be all right, but in burn patients, there is no real guarantee. One minute they can appear to be doing just fine, and then they can take a sudden turn for the worse. We'll continue to keep a very close eye on him, but for now, I think its best that he is left alone to rest. He still has a very long road of recovery ahead of him. What happened at the hearing today?" Dr. Maguire asked Paul.

"John was proven innocent today! In the courtroom, we presented some new evidence that proved beyond a shadow of doubt that he didn't murder his fiancée. The state now knows who murdered her, and they're looking for him right now. The court will be issuing an arrest warrant for him very soon."

"Now that's what I call fantastic news! I'll let all of the nurses know right away. They have all been convinced that he was innocent all along. Now if he can only pull off another miracle and get better. His temperature is up a little bit right now because he's still fighting off an infection. If we can keep it under control and his lungs stay clear, then his chances of a full recovery get better with each passing day. He's still not out of the woods by a long shot, but at least he's heading in the right direction."

"Okay, Doctor, but please give me a call if his condition changes in any way. This poor guy really deserves some good luck for a change," Paul said to him as they headed toward the elevators.

"I certainly will, Mr. Tucker."

After the hearing, the two detectives drove back to their station in relative silence. Both of them were filled with a deep sense of remorse in what they had put Mr. Haggerty through. Detective Bolten felt even worse because he had been absolutely convinced that John had been guilty. Now after having seen the proof for themselves, there was no doubt of his innocence. They had made a terrible mistake, a mistake that they intended to rectify very soon.

"So how do you suggest we go about tracking down our mystery man's identity?" Jim asked Carol as he gently tugged at the bandages wrapped tightly around his injured shoulder.

"I think we have only one avenue open for us to pursue at this time. We have to call George over at the FBI headquarters in Boston," she responded back. "They have that new face recognition technology over there that they can use to try to put a name to our suspect's face a lot sooner. I think it would be a total waste of time to put out a John Doe APB through NCIC to all of the nation's law enforcement bureaus. The only thing that we might be accomplishing with that move is to alert our suspect that we're on to him. And if he has the assets and contacts that we suspect he has, he'd probably just disappear out of the country for good."

"I agree. Going to the FBI is probably our best and only move at this time. We have to put a name on this guy's face as soon as possible. Why don't you give your friend George a call as soon as we get back to the station? If he can meet with us today, he might be able to get the ball rolling for us right away," he added in support.

"Okay. Neither of us wants this bastard to get away with this crime any longer than what is absolutely necessary. I want him arrested and caged like an animal behind bars for the rest of his life," she emotionally added.

While sitting at her desk in the station, Carol telephoned Special agent George Anastas at the Boston offices of the FBI to set up a special meeting with him. From across the room, Jim listened impatiently to Carol as she flirted with George over the telephone. She always seemed to get much better results with George and the other agents at the Federal Bureau than he did. Jim knew that he had a terrible tendency of rubbing people the wrong way every time with his in-their-face attitude. It was an annoying habit that he was trying very hard to break. Carol was smiling as she hung up the telephone. She leaned back in her chair and stretched out her tight back muscles. It had been another stressful day for her, and her sore muscles were crying out for attention. Jim looked over at her admiringly. She was still quite a catch by any man's standards. She seemed to be thinking about something that George had just said to her. Her brief delay in calling him over to her desk seemed to bother him for some reason. He assumed that it was because his shoulder wound was starting to hurt again.

"Well, how did you make out with George?" he impatiently asked her.

"Good! He said that he'd be available to meet with us in about an hour. Why don't we leave now and stop someplace on the way for a quick sandwich? Taking the traffic into consideration, we should be there right on time," she eagerly suggested.

"I know a small place about a block away from their building that serves a great corned beef sandwich. It'll be my treat. I still owe you a lunch from the other day. You know, Carol, I was just thinking that this whole case still has me on edge. I can't seem to shake the feeling that I'm somewhat responsible for what happened to Mr. Haggerty! The only thing that I seem to think about is that cold indifferent look that our suspect had on his face when he shot that poor defenseless woman! We can't let him get away!" he confessed to her.

"Well, with a little bit of luck for a change, we'll get him, I hope."

The two detectives left the precinct station and drove across town to the small restaurant that Jim had suggested they eat lunch in. After they had finished eating their lunch, they walked the short distance over to the Federal Office Building to meet with Agent Anastas.

"Come in, Detectives, and have a seat. Can I get either one of you something to drink?" he politely asked them.

"No, thanks, George, we're fine. We just had lunch a short while ago," Carol informed him.

"Then what, may I ask, is so important that you had to get together with me right away to discuss?" he asked them curiously.

"Do you remember reading in the newspapers about a month ago about a young female scientist who was murdered in Newton? She was the one that was found shot to death under her mother's front porch with bullet wounds in the neck and leg."

"Yes, I did read about that murder in the newspapers. It was quite a hot story for a while, but then you guys charged someone for the crime, and it somewhat disappeared."

"That's right. We arrested her fiancé at Logan International Airport a few days later. While he was under surveillance, some of our detectives apprehended him out there with a one-way ticket to California in his possession. We thought he was about to leave the state to avoid prosecution," she quickly summarized some of the facts of the case to him.

"Well, what does all of this have to do with the bureau? You seem to have your suspect in custody and the case pretty much wrapped up." He smiled back at them.

"Well, that's not exactly true right now. You see, our suspect was injured in a recent gas explosion in his home about a week ago. He may not even survive his injuries. Since that so-called accident, some new facts have been discovered that have proven him completely innocent. We now suspect that the gas explosion may not have been an accident either. It may've been part of an overall plan to kill him and to bring a quick closure to our investigation. We now need a favor from you, George!" She smiled over at him using her feminine good looks to win him over.

"What kind of a favor?" He inquisitively smiled back at her.

"We need you to quietly try to find out the identity of someone from a photograph. The only thing that we think we know about him is that he may have something to do with our government. Now this is only a guess on our part, but we believe that it may be a very good one. We don't have any other information about him. Do you think you can help us with this problem?" she asked him as she handed him a couple of copies of their suspect's photograph.

George picked up the photographs and carefully studied the man's face. "Why are you looking for this guy?" he asked her.

"We have irrefutable proof that he was the actual shooter in the murder case that we just discussed."

"Ouch, that must've really hurt! Nobody likes to find out something like that especially after they've thrown just about everything at the wrong guy," he said to them.

"It does, and now we are trying to make it right for the poor guy if he ever manages to survive his injuries. George, do you think you can help us out on this one? It has to be a low-key investigation. This guy could be a big wheel in some part of our government. If he is, then we don't want him to become aware that we're on to him quite yet," Jim emphasized strongly.

"Has the court issued an arrest warrant for him yet?"

"The DA is working on getting us one right away," Carol informed him.

"Well, let me see what I can do for you right away. I'll show these photographs to a few of my people around here to see if any of them recognize him. You know, I can almost swear I've seen this guy someplace before, but I can't remember where. Maybe it'll come to me later. I'll let you know what we come up with in a few days. Now, Carol, you're going to owe me big-time on this one if I come through for you! Maybe I can collect on that dinner date that you promised me last year!" He smiled back at her teasingly.

"We'll see, George!" She winked back at him encouragingly.

George exchanged handshakes with Carol and Jim before they left his office. As he sat back down in his chair, looking at the photographs of their mysterious suspect, his mind kept thinking about collecting on the favor that Carol would owe him.

CHAPTER 22

For the next two days, the Dr. Mathews murder case went cold on Detective Bates's desk. She knew that it wasn't going to be a quick slam dunk revelation from the FBI, but she had been secretly hoping that it might be. Atty. Paul Tucker and the secretary from the DA's office had left numerous messages on her voice mail for constant updates. She called each of them back every day, informing them that the FBI was still attempting to identify their suspect. She kept telling them all to be patient. She also made a courtesy call over to Newton to Detective Sean Murphy to let him know what had happened in court and to keep him informed about the FBI's progress in identifying their new suspect from the photographs produced from the videotape's footage.

Three days after their initial meeting, Special Agent George Anastas and his partner, Kenneth Ward, walked unannounced into Detective Bates's office at three o'clock in the afternoon. He gestured over to Detective Bolten to join them. As everyone sat around her desk, he placed a file folder down on the desk in front of her. Jim moved around the desk to get a better look at the file with her. As the two detectives looked through it, their facial expressions noticeably changed. Carol looked up at George's face in shock.

"So this is our man?" she timidly asked him.

"Without a doubt! At first, I couldn't quite remember who the hell he was, but then last night, I had a brainstorm of an idea. I decided to check out a few of my old Washington DC case files, the ones that I couldn't solve. I remembered how someone was always placing roadblocks in my way every time that I tried to follow up on a lead on some suspicious governmental employees. It was not too much different from what happened in your case. First, there was a murder, and then the evidence seemed to grow exponentially against one of our suspects. Then that suspect would meet with an untimely deadly accident, and the case would be officially closed. I refused, however, to close any of these case files in the hope that one day I might be able to solve them. It took me quite a while to locate my old files, but as soon as I opened a few of them, I found your suspect's face staring up at me. We've always been interested in his domestic activities, but we've never been able to tie him to anything criminal. Since I left Washington, our friend has made a rapid climb up the ladder. As you can see from his file, he's now the assistant deputy director of the CIA, Mr. Frank Jones. I never thought that we'd get anything on him, but now with your help, he's going down for this one!" he boasted to them.

"Your DA's office and some of our Federal attorneys have obtained all of the necessary arrest warrants that we'll need to pick him up in DC. We're flying down to Washington in two hours to get him. Since it's your case, I thought you would like to come along for the arrest. I've reserved the bureau's jet for our trip. In Washington, we've put together a task force of Federal marshals and some of the local police to assist us in the arrest. We will be meeting up with some of them at the DC airport. What do you say?" he asked them.

"We wouldn't miss this show for the world!" they both answered back at the same time.

"Great! I've cleared everything with your captain and the DA's office already. I'll meet you both back here in an hour. That should give you both enough time to collect a few things for the trip," he said to them as he exited their office.

"Well, let's get out of here. We don't want to miss this show!" she announced with satisfaction as they hurried down the stairs to their cars.

* * * * *

The warehouse down the street from the main CIA Headquarters was a perfect staging area for the Federal marshals and the rest of the task force's members to go over their plan once again.

"Now is everyone clear on what we are going to do?" Agent Anastas asked his squad of Federal marshals and FBI agents.

"Yes, sir!" his men and women officers all responded back confidently.

"Now I expect this entire operation to go off without a hitch. No gunfire is authorized except when you have to defend yourself. There are a lot of civilians working in there that could get hurt if there's any unnecessary gunfire. So I want everyone to keep their cool, and this entire operation will go off without a single shot being fired. We're only after one man in there. He is to be considered armed and very dangerous. We don't know if he'll try to resist our efforts to take him into custody or if he might be helped by any of his other operatives to escape. Make sure you identify yourselves clearly. It's better that we take him alive, if at all possible. Now remember, everyone, these are our people in there. All of you have a copy of his photo. Take a good look at it again and be positive. Then if nobody has any other questions, we're ready to go!"

The caravan of police cars and unmarked vans drove out of the warehouse in an orderly procession and headed toward the CIA Building downtown. It was a nervous time for Detective Bates and Bolten as they tagged along behind the heavily armed agents and marshals in front of them. It was a moment that neither of them wanted to miss. They owed this moment to Dr. Mathews and her fiancé. Once inside the lobby of the great building, the task force of Federal marshals and agents made their way over to the security area located in the front of the lobby. The building was quite a testimony to the men and women who protected the nation from attacks from around the world. Carol couldn't help but feel a little bit hurt in knowing that the agency and its important work had become tarnished by the evil actions of a man who had gone bad.

Once the agents had identified themselves and what their business was in the building to the security supervisor, they were allowed to enter the building with their weapons. They were told that the offices of the CIA directors were on the seventh floor of the building. The task force of agents and marshals split up into several groups to cover all of the stairways and the elevators, thus effectively blocking all avenues of escape for their suspect.

As the agents made their way into the elevators and up the emergency stairwells, the building's security cameras recorded their every move. A security officer working alone in the backup security office on the upper floors caught sight of the armed agents when they first moved into the main lobby. He listened in on the conversation between the head FBI agent and his supervisor. He learned that they were after his boss, Deputy Director Jones. He quickly contacted the director on his private line to inform him of what was about to happen.

When he learned that there were armed FBI agents and marshals coming upstairs to arrest him, he contacted his pilot and gathered his files on the Mathews case into his briefcase. He then hurried out of his office and ran upstairs to the roof. On the roof, his pilot was already untying the helicopter from its safety tie-downs. Mr. Jones and his pilot jumped into the helicopter and closed the doors tightly behind them. The helicopter's engine slowly started to turn its rotors. Frank reached into his jacket and took out his automatic pistol. He pulled out its clip to make sure that it was fully loaded. He opened his briefcase and looked at the picture of his family that he had just taken from his desk a few minutes earlier. He shook his head in disgust at what he knew he had to do. Images of his wife and daughter flooded into his mind. He wondered if they would fully understand why he had done what he did in the past. He wished that he could see his wife and daughter one more time, but he knew that it was impossible. His close friends in the agency would make sure that his wishes were carried out completely. They would make sure that his wife knew the real reasons behind his actions.

Outside the helicopter, the access door to the roof flew open, and an army of heavily armed agents and marshals surrounded the aircraft. His pilot raised his hands in surrender against the overwhelming show of force encircling the helicopter.

"I'm sorry, Frank, but what else can I do? We don't stand a chance at getting off the ground now!" he shouted back to his boss.

"I know it, Sean, so don't worry about it. You're a good man, and you've served me and the agency loyally for many years. Everything will be okay. Give my love to my wife and daughter. Tell them that I was thinking of them and that I'm sorry," he said to him to ease his mind.

Frank knew that it was only a matter of time before they would try to force their way into the aircraft to arrest him. He cocked his gun to put a bullet into the gun's chamber. With his right hand wrapped tightly around the stock of his gun, he let his hand rest in his lap. He then leaned back in his seat to await the inevitable.

FBI Agent George Anastas walked up to the locked rear door of the helicopter. He yelled at him that they were there to place him under arrest for the first-degree murder of Dr. Helen Mathews. The charge seemed to ring hollow in his ears as he thought back to the night that he had killed her. He couldn't understand why they would be charging him with her murder. Had Sam squealed on him, or had they found some other evidence that they had forgotten to eliminate? He couldn't take a chance. The secrecy of the agency could not be compromised.

He knew that he had to kill her to prevent their new technology from ever becoming a threat to the security of the nation. Without the proper security safeguards having been put in place, the technology could have been used to copy and steal America's secrets. In time, undercover spies would only have to look at a classified top-secret document but once. Then they would be able to simply cross our borders with our secrets safely stored in the implanted neuroencapsulators in their heads. It would be a perfect crime, a completely foolproof method of espionage. There would be no basis for a prosecution of these people without the documents being physically in their possession. It would be a perfect recipe for disaster. Dr. Mathews had talked about using this new technology for the good of society. He could not allow that to happen. It was their technology, and he had warned her several times to stop working on it, but she had purposely ignored his warnings.

"I know why you are here, Agent, and I will not harm any of you. But what I did was for the good of our country, and I would do it again. When I first started working for the agency, I took an oath to serve and protect the security of this nation. To that end, I have always stood strong and steadfast. What I did was tragic but necessary. That is why I have to do what I am about to do."

The director slowly raised his right hand up from his lap and pointed his weapon toward the back of his head. He then aimed the nozzle downward at the stem of his brain. Amid the cries of the armed agents around him all shouting for him to drop his weapon, he turned his head sideways to look out the window at the Capital Building in the distance. A brief smile seemed to form on his lips as he squeezed the trigger of his gun. The force of the hollow point bullet slamming into the base of his skull sent his body reeling sideways. No other agent or marshal fired their weapon at him. They could see that he was one of them who had lost his way in the evil of their nation's silent war.

Detective Bates and her partner were among those who had witnessed the director's suicide. For some unexplainable reason, the entire incident did not bring a sense of closure to their case. Agent Anastas forced open the rear door of the aircraft and leaned in over the prostrate body of their suspect to check for a pulse, but there was none. He had blown away the base of his brain, and death had come instantly to him. As he stood up again, he focused his eyes out over the city's skyline. It was a beautiful city filled with the history and sacrifices of a great nation. He shook his head in disgust at what he had just witnessed.

In time, he looked back inside the helicopter and caught sight of the blood-covered picture of the director's family lying on the seat beside him. He picked up the picture and studied it for a few seconds. In disgust, he turned away and faced his men.

"Today there were three victims on this roof: a patriot who had lost his way and the lives of his poor wife and daughter. He abandoned them both without even an explanation or a sad good-bye. The poor misguided fool," he whispered as he walked away in disgust.

The flight back to Boston was a quiet one for all of the agents and the two Boston police detectives. For obvious reasons, there was no joy in the plane for having apprehended Dr. Mathews's murderer. They had dealt with all of her assailants conclusively, and still, their victory felt hollow. Detective Bates made a call over to the DA's office to inform him about the events that had unfolded in the CIA Building in Washington DC. He also felt that the entire case had turned out to be a totally unnecessary tragedy.

After he had finished talking to Detective Bates, he made a call over to Paul Tucker's home. "Hello, Mrs. Tucker, is your husband, Paul, in? This is Tom Parker from the DA's office. I have to speak to him."

"Yes, he is, Tom. I'll get him for you," she said to him.

"Thank you."

"Tom! So what's the good news from Washington DC? Have they arrested our guy down there yet?" Paul asked him.

"Yes and no. During the apprehension of our suspect, he managed to make his way up to a helicopter waiting for him on the roof of the CIA Building. Before our agents and marshals could safely disarm him, he committed suicide inside the aircraft. With his death, I guess this case is finally over for all of us now. You can tell your client that all of his fiancée's murderers have been identified and dealt with justly. I only hope that in time he too can put the memory of Dr. Mathews's tragic murder to rest for good. It will probably take him a very long time to do it, but time has a strange way of healing all wounds," the DA concluded sadly.

"I hope it does, Tom. Thanks for letting me know right away."

At eleven o'clock the next morning, Paul and Harry once again drove over to the hospital to check on John's condition. They once again put on masks and white robes before they were allowed to walk into John's room. John was drifting in and out of a restless sleep as they leaned in close to talk to him.

"Well, John, they've dismissed all of the charges against you. We even managed to find and eliminate all of Helen's real killers. Some of them were killed in a shootout in the subways in Boston. The actual shooter of your fiancée took his own life rather than face justice in the courts. I only hope that this news makes you feel a little better," he whispered into his right ear.

John made an effort to speak, but the breathing tube in his throat prevented him from speaking. He slowly reached up with his bandaged right hand and patted Paul's arm in gratitude. The effort was very painful for John to make, but he knew that he had to do it.

"Everyone now knows how much the two of you really loved each other. Years ago, Helen had a small capsule implanted inside her head. It recorded all of the last ten minutes of sounds and images that she saw and heard on the night that she was murdered. When this small device was removed from her body and activated, it showed us everything that she saw and heard when she was murdered that dreadful night. On the device, she made sure that she told you that she loved you with all of her heart. When you get better, you can view a copy of the tape if you wish. For now I just want you to rest and get better. Harry and I will check back with you tomorrow."

Tears began to form at the corners of John's eyes as Paul told him what Helen had said to him that night. He would never be able to forget the sight of her bloodied body lying in a pool of blood under the porch. It was an image that seemed to call out to him every night as he closed his eyes to sleep.

When Harry and Paul returned to their office, Dr. Stevens was anxiously waiting inside for them to arrive.

"Well, Doc, what seems to be on your mind this morning? Harry called you last night to tell you about what happened down in Washington DC, didn't he?"

"Yes, he did, but what I have to tell you now is even more important than anything else. I can't get the neuroencapsulator to work again! I've tried everything to activate it again. Since we have no plans or diagrams about how it was constructed or even works, I fear that all of Helen's new technology may be lost forever. Without knowing the interior construction of the capsule, all of her programs and journals are almost useless. What are we going to do?" he pleaded to them.

"I don't know, Phil, but maybe you can try to disassemble the capsule under one of your microscopes. You and your group are probably the best-suited people to try to reverse engineer her capsule. Dr. Mathews's research proved to all of us once that there is a viable solution to her quest of finding a way to interpret and store our brain's neural impulses. Now it's up to you and your team to rediscover those solutions all over again. In time, I know that you can do it!" Harry said to him confidently.

"Well, I guess we can at least try! After all, what's the worst thing that can happen?" he admitted to them with a newfound sense of confidence and hope in the future.

As the three friends stood in the waiting area of Paul's office, his secretary came out of her office to get him. "There's an important telephone call for you on line 2. It's Dr. Maguire at the hospital! He said that it's very important that he talk to you."

"I'll take it out here!"

The telephone on the table next to them rang. Paul picked it up and identified himself. He listened to the doctor on the other end of the line for a few minutes before he quietly thanked him and hung up the telephone.

"What did the doctor have to say?" Harry asked him curiously.

"He told me that John went into seizures about ten minutes ago. He pulled out his breathing tube and started calling out to his fiancée. His heart stopped beating a few minutes ago. They tried in vain to revive it but without any success. He's gone."

"Was there anything in this case that turned out well? I could've sworn that he was getting better when we saw him a short while ago. Now we learn that he too is gone! I honestly thought that when we told him that all of his charges had been dismissed and that all of Helen's killers had been brought to justice that he'd feel much better. Now I think it was the one thing in his sad life that kept him stubbornly fighting to stay alive! He must've just simply lost his will to go on. I'm really going to miss him," Harry sadly announced to all of his friends.

"We're all going to miss him! Without Helen in his life to love and to care for, it was only a matter of time before he was going to throw in the towel. His injuries were so severe that even his doctors were surprised that he had lasted as long as he did. I pray and hope that their spirits are now together for all eternity in God's kingdom!" Paul added emotionally.

The End

Printed in the United States
By Bookmasters